BLIND TRUST

Red Széll

First published in Great Britain by IndePenPress

All paper used in the printing of this book has been made from
wood grown in managed, sustainable forests.

ISBN13: 978-1-78003-160-6

Printed and bound in the UK
Indepenpress Publishing Limited
25 Eastern Place
Brighton
BN2 1GJ

A catalogue record of this book is available from
the British Library

Cover design by Omri Stephenson

About the author

Red Széll is a 41 year-old househusband living in London with the degenerative eye condition Retinitis Pigmentosa - the second most common cause of blindness in the UK.

After graduating into a recession with a degree in English from Cambridge, he spent the first part of his working life in a hospital mortuary. Having cleared his overdraft, he moved to London to follow his dream of journalistic greatness. Within three years he had scaled the dizzying foothills to achieve the post of Debutantes' Correspondent for *The Evening Standard*.

However, the need for sleep and regular income led him to change career and enter the 9-to-5 world of engineering recruitment. A few years of sending oil and tunnelling men to dodgy parts of the globe was enough to convince him that engineering is mostly boring. So with the arrival of his first child, he leapt at the chance to 'give up work' and stay at home with the baby. Ten years and another daughter later, he's still there and busier than ever.

Blind Trust is his first novel.

Just 4% of the blind and partially sighted population had no light perception; the majority (91%) could see the shapes of furniture in a room (or better); only 10% could see well enough to recognise a friend across a road.

Findings of *The Network 1000 Project* (University of Birmingham, 2007)

This book is dedicated to all those who stop to help.

Chapter 1

Picture yourself in front of a mirror. The mirror is misted by steam from a bath. Most of your bulbs have blown so the bathroom is gloomy. You have a dull headache caused by arcs of white light bursting before your eyes at the rate of about two a second; differently in each eye. To cope with the interference, your brain tries to compensate by producing random polychromatic flecks of light to fill the gaps. Consequently, all you see of your reflection is a dim, flickering outline, like the image given by an un-tuned TV.

Welcome to my vision of the world through kaleidoscope eyes.

Retinitis Pigmentosa (or RP) is a degenerative disease of the eye. Gradually the photoreceptive rods and cones on the retina die off. The less I see, the more my brain attempts to correct the visual information it receives. In time it all but gives up on the peripheral vision, hence the constant flares of white light. In anything less than bright daylight it's all a bit hit and miss; but, at the tail end of my thirties, I still have enough useful sight to get around with a white stick and without a guide dog.

On a good, bright and clear-headed day it is as if I'm looking through a periscope in choppy seas. The field is restricted but the view defined enough to establish what's going on around me. I've learned to ignore the film of salt on the lens and the occasional wash of a wave breaking over the image.

On a bad, gloomy day, and when I'm run-down or dull-headed after a late night, my vision is as limited as at twilight or dawn. I inhabit a world of shadows of things half

1

seen. Then, more than ever, it's my hearing that provides the focus. The different echoes produced by the tip of my white stick as it sweeps the way ahead of me, are my sonar.

The hail came horizontally and between bus shelters. With half the uphill mile from school ahead of us, we could only hope that it would be a brief if chilly dousing. A clamour of horns drowned out the grumbles of our fellow pedestrians as drivers, visually impaired by ice chips bouncing off their windscreens, vented their frustration at being further slowed down. Deprived in turn of much of my primary sense, I tapped the acrylic knob at the end of my white stick harder on the pavement, as much to hear and feel its reassuring beat as to check the path ahead.

Beside me, six year-old Nell squeezed my hand and I became aware of her small voice. "We did volcanoes today. Miss Davies showed us pictures of her holiday in Sicily where there's one called Etna."

"Yes its always erupting isn't it?" I was shouting slightly to make myself heard, but the greater part of my mind was occupied with getting us home safely.

"Horrid Phoebe Finch teased me all break-time shouting 'Nellie's mum's a volcano'."

The suppressed tears in her voice made me indignant on her behalf. Within a few years the same jibes would acquire a sexual slant—'does your daddy go to mount Etna on holiday?' Playground taunts, like nursery rhymes, get passed down through the ages.

"Yes little one, but Eithne's spelt differently."

"I told her that and she said her mummy says the Irish can't spell cos they're stupid!"

The idea of that scrawny perma-tanned clotheshorse, seventies-style sunglasses welded to her rhinoplasty, calling

2

anyone stupid left me struggling to find anything soothing to say to my younger child. But her older sister, Jenny's outrage came to my rescue.

"She's the stupid one, and selfish too. She doesn't need to drive that stupid big car to school when they live so close. She's destroying the environment for future generations!" Jenny is a chip off the old block to make her mother proud! Still I couldn't help thinking that it was a good day to be going home by car.

Vibrations pulsed at my thigh, but already holding my stick, Nell's hand, her violin, two gym bags and a very soggy papier-mâché globe, I didn't answer. Behind me, nine year-old Jenny was now muttering darkly and falling further back. With hail gusting into our faces, I realised we'd reached the stretch where the pavement narrows and called over my shoulder for Jenny to keep up. My pocket buzzed twice to let me know that whoever had rung had left a voicemail.

Momentarily distracted, I had forgotten about the broken paving slab. The tip of my tubular aluminium stick wedged in the crack, driving the rubber-covered handle up hard into my ribs and winding me. With crimson flashes of pain erupting through my squirming hundreds-and-thousands vision, I cursed Camden Council and then, as the buzzing started anew, my mobile.

My stick was stuck. I set about wrenching it free only to hear a sudden shriek from Jenny. Whipping round, I tried to focus my dim eyes on her but was completely blinded by two enormous searchlights bearing down on us. A horn blared and I made an instinctive lunge to gather both girls to me, only to be halted by something cold and hard.

The Milky Way burst in front of me, I heard a thud and Jenny shrieked again.

What little remains of my retinas had been bleached by the headlights, but all my other senses were tracking the large vehicle as it thundered along the pavement, so close that I felt the push and suck of the air displaced by its bulk. Diesel fumes filled my nose and mouth as I screamed Jenny's name again and again, but heard no reply over the roar of its engine.

Another thud followed by a chorus of klaxons, then the roar faded round the corner and I could hear crying—two lots of crying. My legs buckled under the weight of relief and I hugged the two girls close to me, heedless of everything but the life within them.

"Daddy, you're bleeding all over my parka." Ever practical, Jenny pushed me away, glanced at the dripping cut above my right eyebrow and said "Ouch!" With the adrenalin of shock ebbing away, I struggled against pain and giddiness to unhook my rucksack. My vision was beginning to clear to its normal level of opacity, but my wet hands were shaking and the zipper eluded me. I choked back on the rising fury I felt at my inadequacy, at the driver of the queue-jumping car who had endangered my family and at the shitty weather.

My phone resumed its insistent demand for attention, making me flinch. I prodded furiously through sodden denim until I hit the call divert button. Suddenly I felt faint. Nimbler, smaller fingers took over at the zip and with practiced efficiency Jenny plucked out the baby wipes and arnica cream and handed them to Nell. Less squeamish than her older sister, she dabbed the cut clean then gently applied ointment around it to counter the rapid swelling. Yet again the buzzing started at my thigh; whoever it was would not be put off. In no mood for talking, I slid my fingers into my pocket, found the on/off button, and stabbed it. The muffled theme to *The Prisoner* died abruptly.

4

"I'm sorry daddy, I tried to warn you, but it all happened too quick." Jenny was distressed, blaming herself because she was the older child. "And I tried to get the car's number, it started LM06 and it was enormous and silver, but I didn't get the rest. We could still call the police. He should go to prison—pavements are for people!"

Nell was hugging my shoulder, upset and worried, "Are you going to be alright daddy? Does it hurt lots?"

I forced a smile and pulled them both close. My silent, impotent rage had subsided and I felt only pain dulled by mild concussion and huge relief that it was only me who was hurt. "I'm fine girls, don't worry. Now is this a lamppost that's got me before, or is it a new one?" I hugged them again and, still unsteady, rose to my feet. I needed to get home and sit down with a mug of sugary tea.

The hail downgraded to steady, freezing drizzle as we crested the hill and dropped down into Hampstead. I tried to reassure myself that what had just occurred could have happened to anyone, but somehow, with my disability, these things always feel more personal. Nell and Jenny walked hand in hand behind me, increasing my sense of isolation. Experience has taught us all that it's better to let me extinguish the embers of my ire alone.

No amount of weather can halt the Friday afternoon procession of teenage chic on the High Street. I met it with a scowl. Just then my own carefree teenage existence felt two lifetimes distant. The area around Waterstone's was thick with soggy Marlboro Light smoke and the constant bleep of text messages. I strode ahead drumming an angry warning tattoo on the wet paving slabs with my stick. Occasional sniffling from behind reminded me that I wasn't the only one in need of cheering up after a shock, so I stopped outside the mini-market and gave the girls a two pound coin to buy a small bar of dark chocolate for me and whatever they wanted.

5

Off duty for a moment, I slumped against a pillar and listened to their excited chatter. My aching eyes were too weak to see them at this distance and the constant arcs of light I see had thickened and were strobing. I willed the girls to hurry up, then felt instantly guilty for allowing my needs to impinge further on their pleasure. Eventually they trotted out and Jenny gave me my chocolate and change. The rain had abated and we walked briskly, in happier silence towards Fawkes Close and home.

As we rounded the corner a waft of expensive perfume told me that my neighbour Lucia was, or had just been, there. The clack of her heels on the cobbles confirmed this moments before I was enveloped in a bosomy hug.

"Poor darlings you look like drowned sailors. You must come in for tea."

Her daughter, Natania, had already led the girls in, so, too weary to argue, I followed. Lucia was regaling me with a description of her day and my mind had drifted to thoughts of violence against dangerous drivers, when I heard her catch her breath. "Joe, is that blood on your face?!"

"Oh, yeah, probably. Another lamppost. Is it bad?" I lifted my wet fringe to expose my swollen and bloody eyebrow. I didn't have to see to know that she blenched, her exclamation and the way she began to fan herself were enough.

I felt awkward, "Er, would you mind if I went home and cleaned myself up?"

It was only a short split along an old scar and easily stuck together with medical glue. I checked for sticky patches on my raincoat and washed them away, then changed into dry clothes, had a cigarette and a very sugary tea, and felt much better. I was about to go back across to Lucia's when I remembered the string of phone calls.

6

Eithne was due back in a couple of days; it was probably her ringing to tell me that the conference had ended early, or, more likely, was going to overrun. Whatever, it would amuse her to hear what Jenny had said about Phoebe's mum. I took the phone off the radiator where I had left it to dry and switched it back on.

Six missed calls and four voicemails, all from Ted. I pressed 'listen':

Joe, this is Ted. I need to speak to you, pronto! Call me as soon as you pick this up.

He sounded stressed; far from his normal Baloo the Bear self. I guessed his marital problems had flared up again and played the second message:

Screw you Joe. Don't put me straight to voicemail. We gotta talk. I can't believe you're doin' this. Call me!

Even after its long journey down an imperfect line from the United States, the indignation and hurt in his voice rang through loud and clear. It found an echo within me. Close friend as I was, I could hardly be expected to be at his beck and call every minute of the day. I played the third message:

Asshole!

The fourth was just the sound of him hanging up. Like family, friends have a licence to be troublesome and be forgiven; it's just tiresome when they remind you of it. Ted Hansford had greater licence with me than most.

7

As if RP were not affliction enough, it makes erratic progress as it extinguishes the photoreceptors. The sufferer can remain on a plateau for years, as I did throughout my twenties, before inexplicably plunging downwards—in my case into a deep depression. Ted had been there to tend to my broken spirit, when I lay on the rocks at the bottom, unable to raise myself for fear of falling further.

His phone rang and rang and rang. I was about to hang up when it was finally answered. A young man's voice that I didn't recognise; "Yo! Hansford House. Is that the cops?"

I was taken aback and wondered whether Ted's older son's voice had broken.

"No, it's Joe. Is that Fisher?"

"Nah man, it's Karl, the dude that works here. Who'dya say y'are?"

"Joe, Joe Wynde. Look is Ted there please?"

"Yeah, well kind of man, but he's like…er…dead. Tha's why I thought you was the cops. They're s'posed to be here like twenty minutes ago."

My first reaction was to laugh, "Oh come on, he just rang me. Tell him it's Joe calling him back." But even as I uttered the words my racing brain had registered Karl's awkwardness and the lack of mirth in his voice.

"So maybe you know why he just blew his head off with a shotgun, huh?"

The room about me pitched violently, contracted and squeezed the air from my chest. Blood thudded in my ears and spasmed through my body as a gore-spattered vision of my friend's headless corpse jammed all other thought. Above the roar I heard Karl tut his impatience then mutter, "I gotta go." The line clicked and I was left clutching the work-surface for anchorage.

8

Chapter 2

Six hefty silhouettes manoeuvred the necessarily large coffin into position. To my English sensibilities it had seemed disrespectful to wear sunglasses to a funeral, so the merciless Texas sun that mocked my uncovered scalp was also scorching what remained of my retinas. Perhaps my godson would mistake the steady globular stream of sweat streaking down my cheeks for the tears that refused to come.

Seventy hours earlier, under the Tupperware skies of late summer London, this had not been part of my travel plan. Then my attendance here had possessed a nobility of purpose, been a pilgrimage to friendship. Lucia's insistence that she mind the girls while I went to give succour to the grieving family; the comparative ease with which I had prised the details of the funeral directors from Gail's secretarial firewall; Eithne's ability to convert a fraction of her amassed Airmiles into a return ticket for me; the smoothness with which I had been passed from hand to hand to arrive here; all had fed a shimmering fancy that my presence was somehow required—predetermined even.

But as the first clods rattled on the lid of the coffin, leaden reality left me feeling only a faint broiling resentment born of a disturbed night's sleep in a strange bed in a foreign time zone. I tightened my grip on the four metal rods of my folded white stick, and continued to worry the ridges of coarse elastic linking their joints against a stalk of chewed thumbnail.

There was to be no wake; no half-hearted attempt to celebrate a life well lived. The dozen or so mourners filed away through the incongruously green cemetery and back to air-conditioned SUVs. I imagined them heading to their pools to enjoy the remainder of this unexpected day off work, content that they had done their duty and seen closure performed.

Only Gail and her two sons lingered. Head bowed, I stood to one side to allow them privacy.

Gail Hansford, as she never tired of telling the world, headed up "the sexy part" of Texan Montanian Bank's European operation—Mergers & Acquisitions. On her appointment in 2002 she had become TMB's most senior woman, which, as Eithne observed tartly, also put her next in the firing line.

Relocated to London, Gail had a clear remit: double profits with half the staff. She had set about her task with gusto. Ted, however, was on a spouse's visa that denied him the chance to continue his career as a chef. I had met him in the playground, the focal point and refuge of any parent looking after toddlers. It was so rare to meet another stay-at-home dad, and such a relief, that I think we would have become friends even had we not shared a taste for good beer and 70s rock.

It had taken the best part of three months, but Ted and I had eventually identified a weekend when both Gail and Eithne were in London. Keen to try out the new grill he had purchased, Ted had invited a few of us over for an afternoon of Beaujolais and big steaks while the children wore themselves out on the bouncy castle he had hired.

The suspicion that Eithne and Gail might have differing views had not escaped me; Texan Montanian had after all grown out of money made from oil and GM crop production, whereas what had attracted Eithne to the environmental lobby-group where she is the senior legal advisor was more principle than salary. However, the frisson of mutual mistrust that had crackled between the two women when they shook hands was palpable.

"What's she like, wearing a power suit to her own barbeque?" Eithne had demanded, as we'd wound our way home, laden with protein and exhausted girls. The wine had t'ickened her Dublin brogue and made her lisp slightly; the way she had the night I fell in love with her. "She should wear somet'ing less tight if she wants to keep t'at bump a secret!"

"Eh? Nah, she can't be, she was knocking back the plonk quicker than me! It must just be an overhang from when she was pregnant with Fisher."

Eithne shrugged, "You, mark my words, Joe, t'ere'll be an announcement soon."

Within a fortnight she had been proved right. Flushed with excitement, Ted had nabbed me for a frothy coffee after drop-off and confided that Gail had just told him she was pregnant. His radiating happiness had obscured my lack of surprise.

The day before her due date Gail had reluctantly relinquished the reins of power to her deputy—a man. The Portland duly unzipped her and extracted Kelvin. As soon as the C-section scars allowed, Gail was back at her desk and her deputy 'reassigned' to the Far East.

Ted and I had assumed we'd be going to the mother and baby groups together. Nell was still only a year old and I was looking forward to no longer being the only one with a deep voice and two left feet at the "Bumpsadaisies Sing-along Club". Gail had had different ideas. First came the maternity nurse, then, when Kelvin was sleeping through the night, her replacement, Kristina, the nanny.

"Honestly, the woman has the maternal instincts of a rattlesnake!" Eithne was gathering her auburn hair into a bun and preparing to attack the washing-up, after a clearly disgruntled Gail and Fisher had accompanied Ted and three-month-old Kelvin to Sunday lunch at our house. "She didn't

11

touch that poor baby all afternoon. And just when I was thinking she couldn't look more pissed off if she tried, Ted asked you to be Kelvin's godfather! The poor man'll pay dearly for his insubordination. What a harridan! You don't know how lucky you are, buster!"

"Oh yes I do!" I'd been nuzzling the back of Eithne's neck and sank my teeth gently into her shoulder for emphasis. She gave me a faceful of suds in return.

I too had sensed Gail's annoyance and had given Ted the option of retracting his request, reminding him of my atheism. But he was not to be dissuaded; he believed that a modern child needed a variety of role models. Beside me I had heard Gail distractedly rolling the base of her empty wine glass round and round on the coaster, waiting for the next bottle to be uncorked. Partly out of sympathy and partly to escape the discomfort, I had disappeared downstairs in search of champagne, while Eithne went to the kitchen for clean glasses.

We had returned to raised voices and a bawling baby. Handing the bottle to Eithne, I had scooped Kelvin up to comfort him.

"The reason you don't qualify to choose the goddamn nanny is because you would have been looking at all the wrong attributes."

"Yeah right, Gail." Ted was embarrassed, all too used to her public outbursts.

"You woulda chosen the first cute bit of ass that walked in wearing a tight T-shirt, don't even try to deny it. That's why it was clearly a job for me and me alone." Gail sat back and drummed her fingers on the table while Eithne fiddled with the foil round the neck of the bottle. "Anyhow, you've got nuthin' to complain about. I chose you a nice bit of eye candy didn't I? I coulda gone for the French grandma with bad breath."

12

"All I'm saying is that I've gotta share the house with her and I think I shoulda had some say in who looks after our sons." What little fight was left in him petered out.

"Yeah and who earns the money that pays her wages and keeps you in beer and beef jerky? Answer me that, Mr Sit-On-My-Ass-All-Day-Stay-At-Home-Dad?" she spat back.

Eithne was twisting the cork in a threatening way and when she spoke, her voice had that naive ring to it that always makes me consider my next words very carefully.

"Surely then, having Ted look after the baby would have been the best solution all round?"

Gail snorted in derision, "You may have house-trained your man honey, but this useless bum wouldn't know which end to put the diaper on. Besides I can afford expert help."

The room had gone silent. Kelvin was dozing in my arms but Ted was picking at his fingernails and no doubt cringing. The cork popped and Gail thrust her glass at Eithne who poured the froth into it, watched Gail gulp it down and then set the bottle on the table.

"Well trust and loyalty bought off the shelf often comes with hidden costs. I prefer to grow my own; that way you can be sure of the provenance." She picked the bottle up again and filled the other three glasses before returning to Gail's. "Now," she had said pointedly. "I think we should drink a toast to Kelvin."

"But Mom, I wanna go talk with Uncle Joe." I looked up, Kelvin sounded close to tears.

"Oh go on if you must," she snapped at him, "but two minutes and that's all. I'll be waiting in the car."

I took a step towards them but Gail turned her back and marched away. My own progress was checked by Kelvin

13

hurtling into me. "Wow, Uncle Joe, you came! Mom never said. Are you stayin' with us? How're Nell and Jenny?"

"You brought us any presents?" this came from Fisher, who, though only eleven, was already somewhat surly. He was standing far away enough from us for me to catch his whole neatly combed head and tubby torso in my limited field of vision.

I reached into my jacket pocket and pulled out the cards that the girls had made. Fisher ripped his open but Kelvin, who was still holding onto me, mumbled his thanks before burying his face into my chest. I felt his warm tears through the cotton of my shirt and hugged him closer. He began to shake and I heard a muffled snotty sniff as he fought to control himself.

Clearly unimpressed by the contents of his envelope, Fisher began hurling clods of earth onto his father's grave. I called his name in a disapproving voice and he spun round to challenge me. "Why shouldn't I? It's like Mom says. He quit on us."

My heart skipped a beat and I felt the un-pumped blood drain from my face. Kelvin had frozen against me, my shirt gripped in his balled fists. I put a protective arm across his back and glared at the defiant Fisher.

"Why'd he do it Uncle Joe? Didn't he love us anymore?" mumbled Kelvin.

"Yeah, how come he blew his brains out, *Uncle Joe*?" sneered Fisher. "Mom said to be sure and ask you."

With his taunt a cold sliver of fear lodged itself in my chest. If Gail was in *that* frame of mind there was no telling what rubbish she was spouting.

"Guys, your Dad loved you more than anything in the world. But sometimes, when grown-ups get very upset they feel trapped and they can forget how much they mean to other people. When that happens, the world seems like a

14

horrid lonely place. But he never stopped loving you and, if you look for it, that love lives on inside you both."

After a couple more strangled sobs Kelvin drew away from my chest and looked up at me. I struggled to focus on his face. Finding his wide, frightened eyes I finally felt tears pressing behind my own.

"Yeah, right," jeered Fisher. The car horn blared out Gail's impatience and he was off through the gleaming white headstones. I stood up, meaning to follow hand-in-hand with Kelvin, but the little boy held his arms aloft, as he used to when he was a toddler, and I lifted him onto my shoulders.

Five year olds are seldom good with their lefts and rights and so our navigation towards the car park was halting and awkward.

He had grown heavier in the six months since I had last seen him; a rounded tummy suggested he had developed a Texan appetite. I looped an arm across his knees, needing the other to sweep the ground ahead with my white stick. Still he didn't feel properly balanced across the saddle of my back and, in seeking to shift him a little more onto my right shoulder, I must have missed the low stone cross by millimetres. My shin didn't and the jarring agony made my teeth ache. A stream of profanities filled my tightly clenched mouth as Kelvin giggled with embarrassment and a hint of fear at having failed in a task set for him. I forced myself to laugh and said, "Let's hope we didn't wake him up, eh?"

Immediately I regretted my joke, in case it gave the child false hope of seeing his dad again. I limped on, sweat trickling from every pore and painfully aware of the swelling bruise on my shin. Through increasingly short breaths I tried to reassure my godson. "Kelvin, look if you ever want to talk about your dad with someone, you know

15

you can always give me a call and we can chat about all the good times all of us had together, okay?"

He joggled up and down but remained silent; I hoped he was nodding. Reaching the edge of the too springy grass, I lowered him down and tried again. "Your dad will always be alive, in here and in here"; I tapped Kelvin on the heart and the head.

"I guess," he nodded and the bright sunlight caught the twinkle of tears in his black-rimmed eyes. The horn blared its summons again, although we were only a few feet away, and I heard the click and sigh of a door being opened.

I hugged him and tousled his hair, "Remember, you can call, whenever you want."

Unable to see Gail through the tinted glass, I leant into the car and pretended to help strap Kelvin in, although he was always going to make a better job of it than me. The move from bright light to the shaded interior rendered my embattled retinas absolutely useless. Not that I needed visual confirmation of Gail's brooding presence in the passenger seat. Beside her, the driver smelt too strongly of cheap aftershave, but neither it nor the peppermints could mask her alcohol breath.

"Hi, Gail, can I have a word please?" Bent double and craning my neck to look in her direction, my voice sounded reedy.

There was a long pause and then a noise as if she were trying to suck lemon juice from her lips without tasting it. Bitterness laced her tone when she finally replied. "Isn't seeing him buried enough? I hope you're proud of your handiwork."

She must have had a skinful the night before. Her breath was sour and hung in the air-conditioned space between us. I wondered how long it had been since her last sober day and whether it preceded Ted's suicide or not. Back in

16

London neighbours on both sides of their rented house and the proprietors of several pubs and restaurants could attest to the destructiveness of her alcohol-fuelled rages.

I had always tried to get on with Gail, not simply out of loyalty to Ted and Kelvin, but because I also saw that she and I fought some of the same demons. Both of us found ourselves virtually the sole representative of our respective sex in occupations jealously guarded by a conservative clique who viewed their supremacy as their birthright. In our bids for acceptance, we both subjected ourselves to constant scrutiny on uneven playing fields.

Moreover, while for now it was mostly under control, just like Gail my default setting for dealing with stress had for many years been found halfway down a bottle of spirits. Had she not dragged the children into her attack on me, I would have let it go unanswered. But now I needed to know what was festering in her mind. "Gail, we need to talk." I insisted.

"Can we go home now?" whined Fisher.

"Can Uncle Joe come with us?" pleaded Kelvin.

"No!" snapped Gail. "Joe is going back to England, where he is wanted. He should never have come here at all."

I caught a flicker of movement from her direction and the driver started the engine. As the car rolled forward I was forced to withdraw and only just had time to slam the door shut before its wheels kicked up gravel and it swept out between the gleaming white cemetery gates.

Dumbfounded and alone, I rolled up my trouser leg to expose my throbbing shin. The rising bruise was grazed but not bleeding. Too long under the midday sun, my head was thumping in time with the swelling; I needed to find shade and a taxi. With the wisdom of hindsight, I should have asked the cabbie who had brought me to the service to wait, but I had assumed that I'd be able to cadge a lift to the reception afterwards – it had always worked at weddings.

My resentment began to boil over; what the hell did Gail mean my "handiwork"? If anyone had pushed Ted into a corner it was she. His final email to me, sent ten days before he took his life, had made that pretty clear.

Hey Joe,

Thx for saying you forwarded the mail, I hope you included loads of funnies again, I need a good laugh...and some real ale too, gallons of it!

Home life has turned to shit. Gail wants a divorce. Last nite she told me she only agreed to get back together soes we could move back to the US. She says now we have been resident 6 months she can file for divorce on grounds of infidelity and be assured of getting custody of the boys. She actually told me she took the job in Houston cos Texan law favors the mom.

I am sick of being everyone's bitch. The kids spend all the time moaning that it's too hot and we're too far outta town and Gail is always on my case for wrecking our marriage. And there's nothing to do here. Still can't find any work and roasting by the pool or swapping recipes for pumpkin pie with the other moms is boring as hell.

What a crock of shit.

Even my goddamn iPod's screwed—1 week after the warranty expired—man, it's the pits.

Have a pint of Pride in the Duke for me.

Ted

Even the androgynous metallic voice with which my Mac had read these words to me could not disguise the despair they contained. But at the time I'd thought it merely another product of Gail's half-cut vindictiveness; the way she released, or at least transferred, some of the stress of her job onto those around her. More than most I knew how much damage a drunk's diatribe can cause. So I'd written it off as just another spat in their honey and vinegar marriage. Now it read like a suicide note.

Gail must have read it too and was now hedging her position. She had challenged me to reveal what I knew to Kelvin and Fisher, but had already undermined my credibility with them by implying that it was I who had something to hide. Anything I said about the email would look like I was trying to shift the blame away from myself. Like Eithne said, Gail always, always had to be in control. But surely Gail knew me well enough to see that I hadn't come here to bandy recriminations but to offer support. A godless godfather I may be, but my moral duties mattered none the less for it.

The sun was still blindingly bright and reflecting off every available surface. My vision was reduced to incoherent blocks of glare and shadow punctured by bright flashes of iridescence that hurt and made me wonder whether they were the final flickers of my few remaining photoreceptors being overloaded and burning out. I limped on towards where I thought I could hear the whirr of air-conditioning units.

It's claimed that sight provides 98% of people's sensory perception. Though I only have about a tenth of the vision of a 'normal' person, I still like to see myself as a functioning member of the human race. My other senses simply have to work harder to fill the gap.

19

The bulk of that burden falls to my hearing and never more so than when I'm in unfamiliar surroundings. Sound builds mental pictures for me, drawing from an archive of visual memory. Those images taken from the far past are clear and sharp; those from more recent years show a degeneration in quality, as will all those from the future.

A waft of cigarette smoke triggered a pang and told me someone was close by. When she spoke her laconic, seductive voice conjured an old image of Daisy from *The Dukes of Hazzard*.

"Well, howdy stranger, you look like you could use some help."

I smiled in the direction of the voice and forced my aching eyes to search her out. Eventually, they fixed upon a squat figure propping up a white wall. Well, perhaps, back in the early 80s, she'd borne a passing resemblance to Daisy; she may even have worn cut-off denim shorts and tied her shirt at the waist. But now, even my soft-focus eyes could make out a woman nearing retirement and sporting shapeless slacks and a baggy top over a body that had long since surrendered to the love of food. Still, when she saw that I had found her eyes, her smile had a reserved radiance from which the Texas sun could have taken a lesson.

Life as a V.I.P. (Visually Impaired Person, as the newspeak of political correctness likes to label my special need) does offer a few compensations. The most life affirming is the kindness of strangers. So it was without surprise, but with genuine gratitude that I accepted first the cigarette and, having explained my predicament, then the lift that she offered.

For once the putrid-green half-light of my hotel room soothed rather than confounded my aching eyeballs. A quick rummage in my wash bag produced a tube of arnica,

20

which I applied liberally to my swollen shin. A bruise the size and colours of a Creme Egg had risen and was painful to the touch. I glugged down a litre bottle of water, at what cost to my room bill I dreaded to think, and waited for the relief of the ointment to sink in.

While the truth hurts, false accusations chafe. Any hope I'd had of catching up on the parent's perennial dearth of sleep evaporated within a minute of flopping down onto the squishy bed. Did Gail really intend to use this to drive a wedge between Kelvin and me? Did I have a duty or a right to try and prevent her? How could I persuade her that I didn't hold her responsible for...for...Ted 'blowing his brains out'? My restless thoughts spiralled round and down.

How long Gail had known about Ted's infidelity is impossible to say, but long enough to have taken a short lease on a studio flat in Belsize Park where she could send him to eat humble pie while she decided their future. However, contrary to what she believed, I'd known nothing about it until the night Ted appeared on my doorstep and told me that she'd thrown him out.

Over a takeaway curry and a lot of beer, Eithne and I had heard how Gail's recent mammoth tour of her European dominions and fortnight in Houston presenting her findings had put a strain on their marriage. On her rare nights at home, Gail had preferred to use the spare room, so in all Ted reckoned it had been four months since he had shared a bed, or any intimate contact, with his wife.

All the while, what had started as a ribald joke between them about paying Kristina, the nanny, to fulfil that function too, was degenerating into threat and taunt. Gail even implied that she had deliberately chosen the bubbly Polish girl as a test of Ted's self-restraint. Until one night after a couple of pints with me at The Duke of Wellington, when his eyes had met Kristina's frank blue gaze and he'd

21

thought, "hell, I'm gettin' beat like I've been stealing from the cookie jar, so I might as well have a taste."

On her return Gail could apparently read his guilt and had banished him to Belsize Park.

"You can't dangle fresh meat in front of a hungry dog and be surprised when he bites", Eithne observed after Ted had wended his way down the hill to his new doghouse.

"Oh come on, you can't seriously believe that Gail set him up just to have an excuse to get rid of him? That's a bit far-fetched isn't it? Anyway she'll lose half her assets if they get divorced and she loves her money too much to let that happen."

"It's more to do with domination."

An unwholesome image of Gail with a whip strutted through my mind and I pulled a face.

"No you perv!" she giggled, "Look, from now on Gail will always occupy the moral high ground in their marriage. Ted's effectively enslaved himself. She'll let him crawl back when she deems he's done his penance and he'll be eternally grateful for her clemency." Eithne had been swilling out the takeaway tins and was now folding them flat and placing them in the aluminium section of our huge recycling bin.

"You're such a cynic, Eithne," I scolded, slapping her on the bottom, "or are all you high-powered women masters of machination?"

"Wouldn't you like to know? But I'd have to remove certain parts of your body before telling and that would be a shame." She lowered her hand and squeezed me, before skipping back to the sink.

As she ran the tap she continued. "The woman's a control freak. It's hard-wired into her to have everyone dancing to her tune, and it doesn't stop at work. She brings it home, along with the Blackberry and all those spreadsheets she leaves lying round the house to remind us how important she is. Sure, she'd be rid of Ted like scuffed shoes if it suited her but she never planned for him to jump in the sack with Kristina. But once she'd identified the risk, she couldn't leave it alone. She needed to check her position constantly. And now Ted's broken their deal, she's ensuring that the settlement is solely on her terms."

"Office politics on the home front. Talk about screwing up the work/life balance."

"Ted played his part too, Joe. He had a choice. You don't become a successful woman in business without developing some hard edges. He knew that when he married her."

"But you're successful and you're still lovely" I said winsomely.

"Just try shagging someone else and you'll see how lovely I am. Sure you won't find yerself in a cozy flat. And you'd be wearing yer bollocks for earrings."

"Ooh, I love it when you talk Belfast."

We left the remaining washing-up till the morning.

Eithne's mobile went straight to voicemail. Lucky her! She was probably on a flight home. Suddenly I felt terribly alone. Bloody Gail! She was my only point of reference out here and because of her stupid games I was laying on this lumpy bed, the incessant drone of the air-conditioning grating at my ears. It was no good, I couldn't let it go; I had to sort things out. I swung my legs off the bed, groped round the gloomy room for my jeans and sweatshirt and before I could change my mind, grabbed my stick and headed out.

The chime of the electronic doorbell was so horribly kitsch I couldn't bring myself to ring it a third time; instead I followed the noise of jet sprinklers round the side of the house and into a large garden that smelt too richly of sodden compost. Lengthening shadows had adjusted the contrast from the intense brightness of earlier and so, though heavily pixelated, the picture I received of the manicured half-acre was as clear as my tired eyes could have hoped.

For a woman in the wake of her husband's funeral, Gail Hansford cut an unusual figure. Her Rubenesque form reclined on a sun lounger by a glittering pool. On her lap was a glossy magazine and pressed to her ear, a Blackberry. I could feel her glowering at me as I approached. A tanned young man clad only in a pair of budgie smugglers was netting the pool. With her free hand she waved him away.

She finished her call and sat forward. Her ample sun-kissed cleavage was only partially restrained by a low-cut swimsuit and brought to mind a pair of gammon joints in a butcher's window. The jet-black Raybans remained glued to her face shielding me from her glare.

She called over her shoulder, "Hey, Karl, don't go too far, okay. I may require those muscles of yours when Mr. Wynde needs to leave." Turning back to me she hissed, "I thought I made myself clear, you're not welcome here. Go home!" The edge to her voice was dulled by the contents of the half-empty glass on the table beside her.

"Hi Gail, working late?" I was deliberately light and cheerful. "I'm sorry, I didn't really choose the best time to talk after the funeral did I? So I thought I'd come over and ask whether there's anything I can do to help."

She remained silent, her pugilistically set jaw illuminated by the light reflecting off the pool. I continued, "Where are the boys?"

"Bereavement counselling, not that it's any of your business."

I shuddered and forced myself to believe that, with Gail in this mood and state, help for the boys with bereavement was better coming from a stranger. Her hard stare was still on me, making me uncomfortable, so I pulled up a lounger and sat down facing her.

"Look, Gail, I guess you've seen the last email Ted sent me, but please understand, I don't hold you responsible for what's happened, that's not why I'm here..."

The sound she made reminded me of the whip-crack of a wet towel in the school showers and it took me a few moments to recognise it as a laugh. "Christ, Joe. I gotta hand it to you, you've got a fuckin' nerve! Or can't you handle the guilt of destroying a man who was proud to call himself your friend?"

Determined not to rise to the bait I held my tongue, wondering instead which medication she was on to make her so delusional.

The curl in her lip was audible. "Well, Ted always was a loser and now he's quit the game for good."

This time the anger that flared in me burst through the firebreak. "How dare you say that, especially to your children! Ted made a mistake and you hounded him to death for it. You made him lose, Gail!" Bile stung my throat. "Ted came back here believing you were going to make a new start, but oh no, you had no intention of working at it, you just had to hammer home your victory, didn't you!"

Having no peripheral vision, I got no warning of the slap until the heel of her hand connected with my nose. I knew that it was going to hurt, not only from the crunch the cartilage made as it crumpled under the force of her clumsy

25

blow, but from the amount of time it took for the pain to start.

As the multitude of small scars dotted across my head and body bear witness, sudden impact with hard objects is a fact of my daily life. If I felt any shock it was that Gail would stoop so low. Blood began to spatter heavily onto the white linen of the lounger cushion in front of me.

I felt strangely calm as I rose and scooped a handful of water from the pool. Washing my face and taking a few deep breaths gave me time to think.

Turning back to face Gail I caught a sudden movement down by her feet and flinched expecting another blow. Something soft landed in the crook of my arm and I gingerly wiped the sticky contents of my nostrils onto the perfumed towel.

Tiredness and pain was causing yellow and purple arcs to flicker across my watery vision and I was struggling to focus.

"Sorry Gail, I shouldn't have…" I mumbled.

Agitated, she was muttering, "Where the hell is Karl?" Her sunglasses were pushed up and even I could see that she looked exhausted and maybe a little scared. After a long swig from the glass beside her she replaced it rather too heavily on the table. I caught a whiff of Southern Comfort.

The blood had stopped now, but the pain had intensified. I dipped the towel into the pool and held its soothing coolness to my nose. After a long silence I laid the towel to one side and adopted the calm voice I usually reserve for angry toddlers. "Okay Gail, if we're going to get anywhere can you just tell me what the hell you think I've done?"

"How about you just tell me how much you want and then get the fuck out of my life." Her fury made me rock back on my lounger.

26

"I beg your pardon?" I felt as if I had started playing Whist only to discover that the game had changed, unannounced, to Poker.

"Don't come the innocent with me, Joe—it won't wash. I know Ted paid you to keep quiet. I've checked the statements; I've seen the copy of the Beckett Data Systems document you stole. Or did you get Kristina to do that for you too?"

When you don't know the rules but can't leave the table, the best thing to do is keep quiet, watch, learn and hope you're not rumbled. "Go on," I said.

"Texan Montanian doesn't do scandal. Ted knew that. Ha! He even tried to tell me that was why he paid you off in London; he said he did it for us! Well, I told him, if he had ever stopped to think about us, he would never have screwed that slut Kristina in the first place. As for insider trading, God help anyone even suspected of it; they're out – period. The whole industry will treat them like a pariah for the rest of time. Go figure how much you'll get if that happens to me, Joe." A hint of panic undercut her defiance.

"Wait, Gail, I need to get this straight. You're saying Kristina passed me inside information on one of your deals and I used it to blackmail Ted?"

She tossed her streaky blonde hair and snorted, "Oh spare me the act, Joe!"

"He told you I blackmailed him?!" I was having trouble staying seated, I felt hyper and fidgety and confused.

"Why are you doing this?" her screech was going to bring the pool boy back. "Do you enjoy watching me suffer?" Part of me did, but I also knew she doled the misery out to her family in return and I was concerned for Kelvin. "Do you hate me so much?" She flopped back in her seat and continued to breathe heavily. I had to get some answers before she had me thrown out.

27

"Look, Gail, did he actually tell you it was me who was blackmailing him?" My heart and brain were going at full tilt; I stared longingly at her drink.

"He didn't need to. I read your letter, you dumb asshole; the one you packed so neatly among the beer mats and the goddamn aniseed balls. He thought you were his friend and you stabbed him in the back. All that crap you fed him about making our marriage work for the boys' sake! He told me he really believed you cared. My God, even I felt grateful to you! But it was all bullshit to maintain access to the cash cow, wasn't it Joe?"

Bursts of purple and yellow wheeled around Gail's face, steadily encroaching on my field of vision as I stared at her in disbelief. Tiredness, the intensity of the light and the twin efforts of concentration and self-control were all taking their toll on me.

"Must've been a blow to your plan when Ted mailed you about the divorce," she continued. "Still you could use him one last time, couldn't you? So you sent your little package with its copy of the outline agreement I drafted for the acquisition of Beckett. And enclosed details of how to pay the hundred grand to stop you telling TMB that I'd deliberately passed restricted information to you for our mutual financial gains. Oh and not forgetting your pièce de résistance, 'P.S. sorry mate, but needs must.' Am I jogging your memory some, Joe? 'Cause that's what made Ted blow his fuckin' brains out."

The force of her contempt left me unable to speak or breathe sufficiently regularly to gain control of my thoughts. I could only shake my head in disbelief. It sounded like the packet I'd sent. From time to time I would pick up the Hansfords' un-forwarded post and pop it into one of the self-addressed Postpaks Ted had left behind for the purpose. Over the following few days or weeks I'd add things I knew he'd like; a compilation CD I'd made, the

28

new menu from the local Indian restaurant, beer mats from The Duke of Wellington or occasionally some of the English sweets he missed. Eventually, the envelope either achieved critical mass or I'd get sick of it cluttering the kitchen work-surface and I'd take it to the post office.

Someone could have slipped an extra envelope into the unsealed package, I supposed, but who? I didn't think I knew any blackmailers, or anyone who had that much of a grudge against Ted—or me.

"Look Gail, have you still got that letter, or the envelope?" Maybe I could prove it wasn't written by me.

She paused, then in a low voice that had me leaning forward to catch her words, confided, "Aw I'm sorry Joe, but they got destroyed, just like my husband's trust in you. That's the problem with trust—it's weak. It's the crutch of the ignorant. You trust Eithne not to screw around when she's outta town but you can't know what she really does all those long lonely nights."

It was calculated to hurt and I recoiled from her, biting back on the urge to refute the jibe.

"Gail, I give you my word…"

"Your word means squat!" she spat. "Now, get the hell out of my sight and if you contact me again I'll call the cops. Karl!"

Chapter 3

The first flight home was overnight and delayed. Unable to sleep and with neither the reading light nor the entertainment screen bright enough to allow me distraction, my mind was free to worry itself ragged.

Assuming it was true and not some addled fantasy to salve her conscience, Gail's accusation made sense of Ted's voicemails, but who had sent the letter and why implicate me?

I framed everyone who knew Ted, Gail and me and could have had access to the Postpak during the three or so weeks it had been lying around. None seemed capable of blackmail. I even considered the family who had moved into the Hansfords' vacated house. They had only arrived in London after Ted and Gail had returned to the States and I couldn't imagine them trying to extort money from people they'd never even met.

The more I turned it over the more likely it appeared that Gail had made it all up; her way of dealing with the trauma and getting me out of her hair. That she appeared to believe her story was simply a sign of how addled she was. However, that didn't explain Ted's voicemails. My thoughts banked and circled again and again, too late to make a difference.

Had the battery on my mobile not packed up in the departure lounge, I might have asked Eithne for her view. In our brief conversation we had worked out that, even with the delay, we should be able to snatch an hour at home together before she had to catch the midday flight to Madrid.

But further hold-ups had consumed those precious minutes and as I crawled into the back of a taxi at Heathrow, I knew that haste was futile. I just couldn't face the Tube or, it turned out, the prospect of asking the driver to stop shouting into his phone and use both hands to steer as he slewed across two lanes of traffic and onto the M40. Instead, I tried to slip my mind into neutral and wondered which of the passing blurs of colour contained my wife.

A faint whiff of her Impulse deodorant lingered in the hall as I propped my stick up in its usual corner by the front door. After days of using the white cane as explanation and comforter, I was glad to move about hands-free and in surroundings I knew well. I left my bag where it had fallen and hauled myself up the stairs. Our bathroom was still fragrant with a waft of Eithne's scented soap. Stripping off my sweaty clothes I climbed into her side of our unmade bed and sought out the contours she had left in the sheets and pillow.

My woozy mind fancied itself on a travelator gliding smoothly towards a first class cabin where my wife was to be my stewardess and would tend to my every need. The warm glow of needing to do nothing but relax and allow sleep to transport me to a higher, happier plane enveloped me.

At the point of embarkation the shrill of the doorbell dragged me back to groggy consciousness. As my eyes swam over the Technicolor tapestry of the ceiling I heard a key in the lock and knew that even hiding under the duvet would be no escape.

Pulling my clammy clothes back on, I wobbled downstairs to greet Lucia as she swept into the house with a rustle of supermarket bags and her pashmina billowing clouds of sickly sweet Parisian perfume. Still recovering from the assault mounted on it by non-specific airline glop my stomach lurched.

"Just a few essentials for the fridge, and a couple of little treats for you all!" she trilled, before catching her breath.

"Oh my goodness, you poor darling, what on earth happened to you?"

Exhaustion was causing flickering purple commas to dance with my usual white arcs, but in the bright light of the hallway I could just make out her dark olive face, framed by incongruously blonde ringlets. It registered shock and concern at my discoloured, swollen nose and puffy panda eyes.

"American lamp-post," I said simply, hoping that would satisfy her curiosity.

"Well, I hope you darn well put a dent in it," she quipped in a passable Texan accent. I shrugged and always observant of others' feelings, she changed the subject. "And the funeral, was it dreadfully upsetting?" she cooed with mingled sympathy and eagerness.

"Pretty awful," I sighed, leading the way into the kitchen. "So how are the girls, did they behave themselves? It was so kind of you to take them at such short notice. You truly are an angel."

She beamed, "Oh, they're wonderful, no trouble at all, you know that. They were a pleasure to have with us. I only wish their lovely manners would rub off on Natania, she's becoming such a madam!"

"And how are things round here?" my interest was waning and I longed for my bed.

"Oh, everyone's chasing their tails as usual, with no time to spare for the wider community."

Lucia's generosity seemed limitless. All the energy that had made her such a successful barrister before motherhood, she now channelled into helping the vast majority of people less fortunate than her. Robina, her ancient maroon Morris Traveller spent the days chuntering around the narrow streets or wheezing up the hill from Sainsbury's, laden with people's shopping, gifts to put a

32

smile on their faces and kindness that should have been lavished on the other children she'd never had.

"Oh and of course this blasted business with the playground on the Heath." I feared she was about to mount her current hobbyhorse, but she caught herself. "But I want to know all about your little trip to the US, that's far more exciting.

It was a small price to pay; so, over a pot of coffee and the packet of ginger thins she had thoughtfully brought, I gave her a sanitised account in which I was blameless and Gail coping. As I finished, Lucia burst into floods of tears and enfolded me in her ample bosom. Her body began to tremble and hot tears tickled my neck as she hugged me to her for comfort.

Unmoved, I found myself wondering at her ability to weep on cue. Did drastic fluctuations of emotion make her feel more alive? What a contrast to the feeling of hollowness between my stiff back and unyielding chest. Was I in shock or had the slow torture of degenerative disability left me deadened to the pain of others?

Lucia finally removed her blotchy face from my shoulder and went upstairs to fix her make-up. I turned on the radio to fill the vacuum and distract me, but the anger that Lucia could be upset and I couldn't and that it was she, and not Eithne, offering me support, persisted. Suddenly I felt very ungrateful, very tired and very unlovable.

As tears at last pricked my eyes, I heard the toilet flush and caught the whiff of freshly applied perfume at twenty yards. I blinked the tears away quickly and stood up, a little unsteadily. Face now perfectly intact, Lucia flowed down the stairs to stand at my side.

"Oh darling, you really do look terribly peaky. Why don't you go to bed and let me pick the girls up from school? Your lovely wife treated Natania and me to a pizza

33

last night so it's the least I can do. The girls have missed you sooo much and I can whiz them up the hill to you in no time."

I smiled feebly and a solitary tear streaked down my nose. "That's the best offer I've had for a week," I croaked and this time I did yield to her hug. Letting me go, she pecked me on the cheek before shooing me away. My leaden feet struggled with each stair.

Maybe it was the caffeine or Lucia's presence underscoring Eithne's absence, but I couldn't retrace my path to sleep. Lucia's perfume filled my nose, exacerbating the dull thud at my temples that had accompanied me over the Atlantic, so that now it beat a tattoo on my mind, 'where's Eithne? where's Eithne?' over and over. I twisted and turned under a duvet that now seemed too heavy; felt jarred by the sound of Lucia washing the coffee cups then jolted by her closing the front door behind her. My hands and feet seemed too big and every tiny movement I made felt alarmingly precipitous.

After an eternal half hour, the grinding of gears as Lucia set off on another mercy mission, made my irritation unbearable. I jerked myself upright and stomped back downstairs.

The hope that I would be able to lose myself in the monotony of housework was to prove just as elusive. There was plenty to keep me busy; Eithne had not had the time, or maybe the inclination to tidy up after her few hours at home. The overflowing laundry basket, unmade beds and toys scattered to the four corners of the house all demanded attention, as did the perennial stack of school uniform needing nametags (it is easier for a camel to pass through the eye of a needle than for a blind man to thread one).

Anger and resentment grew as I went from chore to chore. Surely Eithne could have got someone to go to

34

Madrid in her place; I really needed her right now. She would have a view on what had happened to Ted. She'd approach it like one of those fiendish Sudoku of which she's so fond; a man-made puzzle with a solution to be teased out. Each time I considered it, my brain gave up a step earlier.

More coffee and a couple of cigarettes just put me more on edge and had me grinding my teeth and wondering whether a shot of whisky would help subdue my dissatisfaction. Fortunately, I no longer kept spirits in the house—they make me even thirstier than wine and beer and so disappear too rapidly.

A sharp pain in the sole of my foot and an ominous crack had me cursing. Even before I picked up the shattered and limbless body I had my suspicions as to the identity of the deceased. One squinted look was enough to tell me that Nelly's favourite Polly Pocket doll was beyond saving.

A flash of fury at being denied the right to be normal, even in my own home, ignited the tinder dry bundle of bramble emotions I'd accumulated during the past few days. For the briefest moment, there was only yawning blackness before a firestorm of rage and self-loathing swept through me. I hurled the broken body across the room, sank to my knees and howled.

There's no catharsis in an outburst prompted by your own physical degeneration; it's more like having the valve on a pressure cooker lifted for a few seconds every now and then to prevent a catastrophic explosion.

Under the shower, shivering uncontrollably, I let the scalding water cascade over my shoulders. An image of Eithne's hair lodged in my mind's eye. Soon my shoulders were the same colour but inside I still felt frozen, numb. A shroud of memory enveloped me suddenly; a freezing winter's day a lifetime ago; my mother blowing hot potatoes onto my neck and shoulders to warm me up and my angry frustration as each of her hot breaths served only to leave the rest of me feeling colder and colder.

Clean but not refreshed, I felt fidgety and increasingly oppressed by my empty house. Knowing that sooner or later I was bound to need carrots, I headed up to the mini-market.

The brisk walk cleared my head a little, but it took a couple of seconds for me to realise that when Hashem, the shop's owner, said "nasty one" he was referring to my bruised face and not the £10 note I had just handed him.

Besides carrots and tobacco, I bought a can of cream soda to cheer myself up. It's a taste of my childhood that reminds me of clearer-sighted days. Unwilling to go back home so soon, I found a bench that would have been in the sun had there been any, opened the can and sat down to listen to the world going by.

The sound of rubber-soled feet pounding down the hill to my right made me look up, though more from old habit than hope of identifying who was approaching.

"Christ mate, you should get someone else to do your make-up!"

Glenn, an Australian stay-at-home dad, whose wife worked at the High Commission, was jogging on the spot in front of me. The heat of his exertions was radiating from him but he wasn't even out of breath. A love of beer verging on fanatical could not erase the fitness level acquired during a dozen years in the Aussie Marines and maintained by the self-defence classes he now ran in Camden. All of a sudden my cream soda didn't taste so sweet.

"Fancy a pint Glenn?" I needed company, even if it meant having to talk about my nose.

"Ah, sorry mate, I'd love to but I'm due down at the gym," he was side-bending now. "I've got a whole class of yummy mummies waiting to slam me on the crash mats. Tough job, but someone's gotta do it. How about tomorrow? Me and the other guys are meeting for lunch down at The Star, if you're up for showing your face."

I ignored the reference and told him I'd think about it, then listened to the receding sound of his trainers as I finished my fizzy drink. A little way from the bench a girl was trying to persuade a toddler to wear his hat. The way she struggled with her English vowels caused a grainy image of Kristina to flit across my mind.

Of course, Kristina! If Ted really had had a problem he was unable to discuss with me, then he may well have confided in her. My friend Miranda's nanny should know where she'd gone after Gail had sacked her and, even if she didn't, at least I would have tried, which was better than doing nothing.

By the time I heard Robina creak round the corner and into the Close, I had located all but one of Polly's body parts and buried them deep in the bin, where they would never be found. I felt lousy for doing so and could only hope that Nell wouldn't miss her before I made it to a toyshop.

Lucia parked in front of No.7, where she lives with her architect husband Freddie. It was he who designed the Fawkes Close development, his property-rich family having bought the site cheaply from the NHS in the 1980s. Balding and in his late fifties, he is the least tactile person I have ever met. I once asked a mutual friend how on earth Freddie had managed to impregnate Lucia when I've never seen him so much as hold her hand, only to be told that Natania is the result of many attempts at IVF. My girls idolise Natania, who with her mother's striking looks, her father's tall, slim

37

frame and her own large trust fund, will break a lot of hearts. More important in my kids' eyes though, she is a prefect at school and has a pony at livery on the outskirts of town.

Nell and Jenny came careening into the house with screams of "Daddy, Daddy, you're home!" Amidst a flurry of hugs I mouthed my boundless thanks to a dewy-eyed Lucia and blew her a kiss before she left us.

Children are no respecters of self-pity. Within seconds the trauma of the last few days had been shoved to the outer regions of my mind and I was immersed in the tribulations of Key Stage One and the vicissitudes of the playground. They didn't even comment on my battered face, so either Lucia had briefed them about it or seeing me bruised has become routine.

As the three of us peeled and chopped vegetables and shared our usual debate on the rights and wrongs of pricking sausages, I realised how much I had missed the normalities of life and just how lucky I was to be able to share these formative years with my children. The happiest days of my own childhood had certainly not been at any of the educational establishments that had sought to sculpt me. My blissful memories consisted of eating pastry off-cuts from blackberry and apple pies made with the wild fruit we picked on the common; of feeding spaghetti into macaroni tube missile launchers which I aimed at my sisters; and best of all running my fingers round the insides of mixing bowls to prepare them for the sink.

Nell, Jenny and I shared the chocolaty treat that Lucia had bought for us and then did the washing-up together. On another evening I may well have 'rewarded' the girls by letting them go and watch a DVD or play with their Nintendos, but tonight I wanted to be close to them. I needed to be reminded of the innocent enjoyment children can find in the simplest of things, so I suggested we play

Yahtzee, a game of chance I always seem to lose. The girls whooped with surprised delight.

Settled in the sitting room with a full stomach, a cup of tea and the girls throwing good die after good die, the glow at being part of something un-fractured and stable was transfusing back into me. Then Nell looked up from her second Yahtzee on the trot, fixed me with her round green eyes and demanded to know, "Why do daddies sometimes have to die?"

It was as if I'd bitten on metal with sensitive teeth. The child's worst nightmare, one I remembered so vividly every time my own father went away for work, what if he never came home again? Poor Nell must have been worrying ever since I had so hurriedly deposited her with Lucia. Her friends had lost their daddy and I hadn't been there to answer her questions. Good god, and we assume that kids lead such uncomplicated lives. They just can't express themselves as eloquently as us—if we're listening at all.

Getting the girls ready for bed that night took much longer than usual. I was asked to recite the whole of *The Lion and Albert* and Jenny read out three chapters from their favourite Enid Blyton book. Eventually, after many hugs and kisses goodnight I turned down their lights. Twice later on, Nell called me upstairs in tears that were soothed only by repeated assurances that I was still there and would not be going away again. Finally, she fell asleep in my arms.

The phone had rung periodically throughout the evening but not wanting to interrupt our family time, I had let it go to answer phone. Now, as I flopped down on the sofa with my laptop and a can of beer, it rang again. Whoever had used it last had forgotten to put the handset back on its cradle and in fumbling around the coffee table for it I upset a half-drunk glass of wine. The answer-phone cut in as I put the dripping receiver to my ear.

"Oh, so you are in then. I was about to leave you a message." It was Eithne, sounding perky against a muffled backdrop of honking traffic and exotic nightlife.

"Yeah, the girls didn't fancy going out and painting the town red tonight," I replied sourly, as Chardonnay dribbled over the magazines and onto the wooden floor.

"Well I should imagine you've had enough excitement for one week. How was your flight home? I checked the website, you were circling Heathrow for ages so I decided to take a view, cut my carbon footprint and catch a lift in with J-P."

Despite the obvious sense in her decision I still felt angry and let down that she hadn't waited on the off-chance that I made it, but I said nothing as I trudged into the kitchen to grab a J-Cloth.

"That shite was it? Pity Gail doesn't control the air traffic too, eh. It sounds like she couldn't be rid of you quick enough."

For once the invitation to poke fun at Gail seemed tasteless. I'd only had time to tell Eithne that Gail hadn't been expecting me and that there was nothing I could usefully do in Texas, before my battery had packed up. I really didn't fancy going into it now, bounced off some remote satellite. I wanted her physical presence; to be held by her as I revealed how shaken-up I felt. So I changed the subject and asked what the weather was like in Madrid.

She took the hint and we chatted for a couple of minutes while I mopped up and listened to her rummaging around her room for something.

"Anyway, Joe, you sound knackered. I'll let you get off to bed. I'll try and call Sunday lunchtime, so I can have a natter with the girls, okay?"

40

I heard a sharp 'knock, knock' and automatically turned to the door, knocking the now empty wineglass off the coffee table. I swore and in my ear a smooth French voice called "Aetna it ees time for us to go to dinnair."

"Are you okay, Joe?" Eithne sounded surprised rather than concerned. Then her tone became more girlish and she called, "One moment Jean-Pierre, I just need to finish this call."

On damp knees, groping under the coffee table for shards of glass I could only identify by touch, I bristled at just being a call that needed to be finished off. The hint of intimacy between my wife and her colleague twisted the barb that Gail had planted. I wanted to snap back, "That's alright dear, you go and enjoy yourself while I get on with cleaning up the mess caused by your inability to tidy up after yourself." The only word that escaped my clenched teeth was "Fine."

Eithne was fiddling with her keys. "Anyway, I've got a boring but important dinner to go to now. Send my love to the girls, and save some for yourself, heh?"

"Yeah, sure. They're missing you."

"And you'll be in Sunday lunchtime?" she sounded distracted.

"Yup. Eithne?"

"Mmm. Where is that shawl? Yes Joe, what is it?"

"I love you."

"Ah, there you are, at last."

'Knock, knock'

"Just coming, Jean-Pierre. Er, yes, Joe, me too. Till Sunday, okay? Byee!"

Our connection was severed and I felt instantly miserable. The past few days had shown me just how much of my independence I'd lost and had left me questioning my own judgement. With the addition of Gail's well-aimed vitriol, that vulnerability was curdling into peevishness.

I was too keyed-up to go to bed so set about the one hundred and forty-odd emails that had accumulated in my absence. Most were adverts for Viagra or offers to get rich quick from fraudsters purporting to be Nigerian businessmen keen to have my bank details. As I trashed everything containing the words 'Dear beloved in God', inspiration at last struck and I went to fish Polly's head from the depths of the bin.

Within minutes I had bid on, and won, her twin from an eBay seller in Wigan and returned to deleting my emails with renewed vigour. On this occasion at least, the repercussions of my disability should not upset my little daughter.

Only as I was plugging the laptop in to recharge did I notice the answer-phone light flashing and remember the other calls. The window cleaner to arrange a visit; Eithne's mum; and Miranda asking me to meet her for coffee the next morning. It was too late to ring back, but the prospect of unburdening myself to her made my tired body seem lighter as I climbed the stairs.

Chapter 4

The degree to which Retinitis Pigmentosa affects me each day is largely dependent on the weather. Under low leaden skies it's like wearing blinkers in a cave, where the only source of daylight is located somewhere far above. On such days the people I pass are mere shadows, and street furniture (often painted grey to be less intrusive) is painfully hazardous.

That next morning however, I was tapping my way back from dropping the girls at school under a cobalt blue sky. The early October day was crisp with a light wind that rustled the flame-hued leaves still clinging to the trees and sent their fallen fellows skittering across the pavements.

It's my favourite time of year; the sun is weaker than in summer and doesn't dazzle me, but there's enough daylight for both ends of the school run. The bright reds, yellows and oranges are so vivid that, for the odd few seconds, I can almost forget how damaged my vision is.

Well-rested and clear-headed, I was on my way to meet my oldest friend for a leisurely coffee in my favourite café. My face was healing as rapidly as you can expect in your late thirties and Texas seemed a long way away. Not even being forced off the pavement to skirt the huge pile of bricks and cement bags dumped there by the ubiquitous fug of Eastern European builders could cloud my good mood.

The Café Noir is aptly named. Inside it is so dark that the sunglasses-clad Hampsteadites eschew it for fear of having to remove their shades and reveal their medication-dulled eyes. It is a relic of a bygone age, only surviving because, being a windowless basement, it is not an attractive prospect for the estate agents and chain stores that have colonised the

43

High Street like grey squirrels dispatching the indigenous reds.

I like to feel that its sombre interior tips the odds slightly back in my favour, since everyone finds themselves groping their way around its muddle of tables and chairs. Most importantly though it serves proper coffee, rather than a baby beaker of skinny caffeine flavoured froth.

Mingled with the rich aroma of fine Javan grounds that wafted over me as I entered, the subtle musk of Miranda's lightly applied perfume simultaneously announced her presence and conjured the scene of our first meeting two decades earlier.

Then she had been Miranda Blewitt, rather than Lethbridge. Exams were over and the university was drunk on garden parties. Though not actually invited to this one, as a member of the college that was hosting it, I was free to attend, so I had pinched a bottle of Cava from a kitchenette suitably far away from my own and presented it like a ticket at the gate. In return, a bespectacled second year medic had given me a beaker of urine-coloured drink that he assured me was "lethal".

I had yet to be diagnosed with RP and put my poor eyesight and lack of coordination down to the myopia for which I had recently acquired contact lenses. My vision was still good enough to clock Miranda almost immediately though.

Like most of the young, straight women there, she was in a floaty white dress that showed off her perfectly proportioned petite figure. But it was her imperfections that caught my eye.

Even after three terms of 'being up' at Cambridge I was still far from at ease with its pervasive aura of superiority. Amidst the crowd of gilded youth, of tomorrow's MPs, landowners and captains of industry (most of whom are

44

now accountants, actuaries and solicitors), I felt conspicuously dull. Miranda's flawed beauty, her crooked mouth and unruly blonde hair, appeared to me as at odds with our perfect surroundings, as I felt. Her accent was still more Bognor than Brideshead and the floaty white number looked well worn and possibly second-hand.

I fiddled nervously with my cigarettes and matches waiting for her to stop chatting to another girl who I vaguely recognised from somewhere; if only I could remember her name maybe she could introduce us. Fern? Fennella? No something Irish, Ffion? No, Fionnoula that was it! I stepped forward more confident now that some part of my intellect had proved it was up to the job.

"Hi Fionnoula, it's Joe Wynde, isn't it a lovely afternoon for a garden party?"

She frowned, no doubt trying to place me; pretty girls are far more memorable than scruffy first year English undergraduates on the pull. Good manners, however, dictated that she should not admit to this. So while she tried to remember quite what she, a minor member of the Irish aristocracy, had in common with a grammar school boy from Sussex who sported a mullet, she bought time by introducing me to her friend.

"Oh, er hi...Joe...this is Miranda, she's at Newnham." We shook hands and I tried to think what I knew about Newnham, apart from that it was full of girls. I was fumbling to light yet another cigarette, but it was proving impossible to hold the packet, my glass and to strike a match at the same time and I felt a dribble of urine drink spatter my suede cowboy boot.

"Allow me." With a wisp of musky perfume Miranda plucked the matchbox lightly from my fingers and deftly struck and cupped a flame before raising it to my cigarette. Her low rich voice, and the elegance with which she

45

performed this small personal service made me catch my breath and I started to cough.

"Social smoker are you?"

Her voice was mischievous and she'd cocked the eyebrow on the left side of her face, where her mouth sloped down, giving her a doubly lopsided look. I was enchanted. Still lost for words and now slightly breathless, I could sense Fionnoula suppress a giggle as I performed an impression of a dying fish. Finally, for the sake of saying something, I blurted, "Oh, please excuse my Falstaffian manners. Do you want a cigarette, er, either of you?" Fionnoula glanced at the packet with suspicion then took one, but Miranda smiled and said she didn't smoke.

"Oh," I was surprised, "I assumed you did, you lit my one so, um, elegantly."

"Why thank you kind sir," she rejoined in a cod West Country accent. "No, my dad smokes, but since his stroke he finds it difficult to 'spark up', as he calls it."

"Oh, I'm sorry," and I was. I wanted her to be happy and stress free, I wanted to protect and cherish her.

"Don't be," she said airily, "he had enough people tell him he should give up beforehand." She said this perfectly matter-of-factly, a slight smile playing at the upside edge of her pretty mouth. If there was an implied criticism of me I didn't feel it.

Fionnoula glanced at Miranda, no doubt to check that she was happy for me to carry on boring her, then made her excuses and sashayed off into the crowd. Miranda and I were alone.

Years before, my sisters' many friends had kiss-chased out of me any boyish embarrassment I may have felt around the opposite sex, but in the presence of someone I really wanted to get to know better, my tongue seemed suddenly knotted and my thoughts to have gone through a liquidizer.

I was twirling the dregs of the sour vodka cocktail around the bottom of the plastic beaker, wondering which of the well-trodden paths of conversation to try and lead her down when she broke the awkward silence by declaring,

"First year, English."

Taken aback, I spluttered, "Okay Sherlock, I'm admitting nothing but if you're correct, what led you to your brilliant deduction?" I was both impressed and flattered that she had taken that much notice of me. "Oh and please don't say that it's only because I can't be an Engineer because I've had a bath this year."

She wrinkled her nose, pretended to sniff the air then looked serious. "Well, leaving aside that obvious point, it's a combination of clues. You are naturally pale skinned but have a bit of a tan. Therefore, I deduce that you can study outside with just one or two books; so it's almost certainly a literature-based subject. Modern languages and classics exams only finished this week and you have the air and the skin tone of someone who escaped the clasp of academe at least a fortnight ago. But, like me, you're ill at ease, not used to garden parties, so it's probably your first summer here. Of course the dead giveaway was describing yourself as having 'Falstaffian manners'; only an English undergraduate would say that. Your turn."

I put my hands up in mock submission. "Elementary my dear, you've got me bang to rights." I ran an appraising eye over her, but all I could see were tantalising clues to what she would look like undressed and I think she sensed me lingering too long on her pert breasts.

"Um, well, you're a first year too – you said 'like me you're not used to garden parties.'" She nodded in encouragement, "And, er, when you're not studying people your subject is, erm…Economics", I'd picked at random, desperate not to appear completely dense.

47

"And you arrived at that startling conclusion how precisely?" She was lightly mocking and I knew I was way off the mark. Time to make the best of a bad guess and be flattering without being obsequious.

"Because you demonstrate clear sighted logic and a wish to categorise things, which is indicative of studying a scientific subject such as maths, but you also have empathy and I guess an interest in others so you probably enjoy a bit of abstract thinking about the way in which humanity interacts—so Economics it is." I felt triumphant even though I knew I was wrong.

"Wrong." She echoed my very thoughts, but she was smiling at me; maybe she did feel flattered.

Raising what I hoped was a quizzical eyebrow, I waited for her to set me straight.

"Go on, have another guess? She cocked her head to one side and her hazel eyes caught some of the blue of the sky. I felt my own head move involuntarily towards hers as my heart commanded me to kiss her. I shook my head to clear my thoughts and deny my impulse.

"Um, er," where was my logic, "er, Classics?"

She clapped her hands in delight like a small girl winning a parlour game and made the noise of a cash register, "Kchung! See it wasn't so difficult. And you were nearly right; I did do Economics 'A' Level and thought about applying to study it here, but reckoned I'd stand a better chance getting in to do Classics."

Such self-deprecating honesty was a rarity in Cambridge and the next twenty minutes passed in a haze of unpretentious chat about home, siblings (lack of in her case) and music; of not being able to afford clothes or exotic travel over the summer vacation and of our hopes for the future.

I was just about to ask whether she fancied seeing the new Luc Besson film at the Arts Cinema when a tall, chunky young man in a loud and tatty blazer that matched his florid complexion pushed between us and, turning his back to me, boomed "Miranda, my sweet, where have you been? Lance is complaining that the twins are bored and so we're off for cocktails at Browns." With that he draped a proprietary arm across her upper back and started to steer her towards the gate.

I looked at my hands, partly to check that I was not invisible and partly in despair. Toff boyfriend, I should have known; the Establishment incarnate.

"Just a moment Hugo," I heard Miranda say firmly and removing his arm from her she wheeled him round to face me. "Hugo, this is Joe Wynde, Joe, Hugo Lethbridge."

I automatically held out my hand to shake his. The look of distaste slid slowly down his long equine nose and dripped past flared nostrils to sour the corners of his already down-turned mouth. A laconic hand barely even touched mine. Neither of us said anything. I glanced at Miranda, wondering how much of my disappointment this lovely, empathetic, young woman could sense. I had to see her again.

The whole university knew that there was a big drinks party planned at Granchester Meadow the next day and I tried not to sound beseeching as I asked her whether she planned to go.

"Oh, more than likely," she looked to Hugo for confirmation. He was puffing out his blotchy cheeks with impatience and looking anywhere but at me. Clearly my suburban ways lay beneath his contempt. "Well, till the next time then." She smiled at me and turned to leave.

On impulse, I did something that I have never done before or since. Gently catching her hand and raising it to

49

my lips, I kissed it—as if, in so doing, I could transmit my fervid desire for her to stay.

Nearly twenty years later she sat opposite me in the Café Noir, slowly stirring the froth on her cappuccino. As usual, she had thoughtfully asked for a tall candle to be brought to the table so that I might see a little in the gloom. Tresses of her still unruly hair that had escaped the clutches of the large clip she wore to keep them under control, glittered in the flickering light, gilt-framing her sleep-deprived face.

A week ago, when we had last sat here, it had been me railing against the vicissitudes of life; my shock at Ted's sudden death, my dislike of flying. Today she had done all the talking, bemoaning the school trip to the Natural History Museum that had left her five-year old daughter, Hope, having nightmares about death. Worse still, this very morning, nine-year old Christian, who is dyslexic (and thus a great disappointment to perfectionist Hugo) had told Miranda that he hated her, then turned to their nanny Marta and declared, "I wish Daddy had married you instead."

At last, an opportunity; "Actually Miranda, I wanted to ask you something about Marta. Do you know whether she…"

"Don't even mention her name! You'd have thought she'd have been embarrassed or at least corrected Christian, that's her job after all. But oh no, my so-called help chose that moment to inform me that she needs time off next week to visit her sick grandmother in Poland; as if! The little tart just wants a dirty weekend away with her new boyfriend!" she crescendoed with an angry thump of the heavy wooden table.

"Well, say no if it's not convenient," I sighed in frustration.

50

"I did," came her despondent reply. She adopted a heavy Eastern European accent, "This is my right, Mrs Lethbridge and Mr Lethbridge has told me if I need to I must go to Warsaw." I heard Miranda blow her cheeks out angrily.

"Well then Hugo should buy extra stock to cover your short position. That's his speciality isn't it?" It was a bit of a low, sarcastic shot but I could seldom resist the temptation.

Miranda ignored me. The past two decades had wrought less havoc upon her than me. Her hair was still thick and healthy. Her face, for the most part, remained uncreased by stress or smoking. Her figure was still firm and trim, aided somewhat by the rigours of the 'Body Doctor', a specialist in post-natal body toning, hours of whose costly time had become one of Hugo's annual Christmas gifts to his wife. Money can buy you the external appearance of happiness, I reflected, but underneath, the truth is seldom so straightforward.

I had knocked back my small coffee too quickly and was now feeling clammy and a little shaky. The urge to unburden myself kept pushing me to force a change of subject but, trivial as Miranda's woes sounded to me today, she had always heard me out and I knew only too well the importance of a sympathetic ear to a harassed parent.

"So you're giving Marta Poppins a wide berth then?"

"Mmn. What?" she was miles away.

"Your nanny. Keeping out of her way are you. That's why we are having this tryst, together, alone…"

I sensed her look sharply up at me, "No, no, it's the damned builders. Hugo's decided we need a home cinema, so he's having the basement extended next to the garage."

"Ah, that would explain the skip lorry that woke us all up at six-thirty this morning. Honestly, does Hugo ever consider the lives of others?"

"Hmmm, sorry." Slightly abashed she continued, "Believe you me, I'm far from happy either. He knows I can't stand all the noise and dust and constantly bumping into workmen round the house."

"I thought you'd put your foot down after Mission Control was installed." This was Hugo's home office, an armoured glass box built at the top of their house and over the roof terrace. It had taken the whole of the previous summer to construct and had culminated in an eight-wheeled crane blocking Fawkes Close for two days as the glass plates were lifted the three storeys into place. The other neighbours, including Lucia, had sent Miranda to Coventry for a month afterwards. In part to pacify them but also to preserve her mental health, which she confided had taken a severe battering, she had vowed never to allow major works to be performed on the house again.

Miranda sighed in exasperation, "Oh, you know Hugo, ever onwards and upwards, well downwards this time. It's what makes him so exciting, and infuriating, to be with. I suppose he meant it as a nice surprise, a present for the whole family, but when he told me on Sunday night my heart just sank. He says he's finalised all the details in advance so I won't have to deal with the builders, but they'll be excavating right opposite my office. How on earth I'm meant to do any work, I don't know. Hugo's given me a set of noise-reducing headphones, but they're hardly going to stop all the dust and vibration from the bloody drilling."

"Can't you move up into Mission Control for the duration? Leave the navvies in the bowels of the house." I was trying to make light of it and failing dismally. I had noticed the distinctive liveried vans in the driveway and seen the woolly-hatted workmen traipsing in and out of her house, gabbling in Polish and smoking endless cheap high-tar cigarettes, but I'd assumed they were merely there to

52

redecorate. The prospect of yet more months of living opposite a building site filled me with despondence too.

She had her hands on her temples, splaying her long hair, which looked burnished in the candlelight. The coppery tresses gleamed as she shook her head, "No one enters the inner sanctum apart from Hugo. Besides, he's fitted an iris recognition security system." She ignored my snort of derision. "But it's having the builders there at all; I don't think I can stand it all over again, not so soon. It's the way they look at me, and everything in the house, like they're pricing up."

I laughed, a little perplexed, "Oh I don't know Miranda. If they're the same lot as last time they seemed decent enough. Anyway that firm works for loads of people round here. They're not going to blot their copybook by pinching the family silver or your bottom, shapely though it is."

She wasn't rising to any of my stale bait today. With a click of her tongue she pushed her fringe back out of her eyes. It was the sad gesture of an embattled woman.

I blundered on. My stomach was aching dully as the airline food made trotting progress through my digestive system. "Still I am flattered that you sought to call me to be your knight in shining armour. My Lady, I will defend your honour against the rapine tendencies of the Polack hordes. Let me at 'em! As you can probably divine from my bruised physiognomy I am battle-hardened from my tour of duty in the Wild West."

This time she did laugh, "Oh I'm sorry Joe, here I am droning on and you must be dying to tell me what happened." Then looking up from her now lukewarm cappuccino and peering through the gloom, she paused and leaned closer. "Good grief, what *did* happen to you?"

I told her everything, pausing only to order warm water in an attempt to ease my cramping stomach. Miranda

53

listened attentively, tutting occasionally in surprise. When I had finished she let out a long sigh. "Poor woman, she must feel that every aspect of her life is under attack."

"Oh great, so that gives her licence to bad mouth me to my godson, accuse me of blackmail and slap me about, does it? Thanks for your support, Miranda!" I sat back huffily and the ancient chair squeaked in protest.

"No of course not!" she retorted. "And I'm sure you'll find that she'll realise how unfairly she's treated you when the shock has worn off a little. But come on Joe, you have to see it from her point of view. You said it yourself; she's confused right now, the pain, the guilt, the worry about her family's future and a whole lot of anger at her powerlessness in the face of it all. Then you come galloping in like the tardy cavalry and provide her with a focus on which to vent some of her frustration. Think how the poor woman must have felt when she saw you empathising with Kelvin. She's his mother and has to use the medium of a counsellor to do that. It's classic transference of guilt," she concluded.

"Why thank you for your lecture, Dr Freud. As if I hadn't been feeling guilty enough already."

She harrumphed and then, transferring the focus from herself asked, "Well, what does Eithne have to say?" My hesitation told its own story and Miranda pounced. "Oh! So you haven't told her. Why's that, Joe? You have told me everything haven't you? Perhaps that girl who 'picked you up' left you a little guilt-*ridden*?"

It was old raillery, born of my more rampant twenties and probably meant to cheer me up, but today it tasted sour and I winced my disgust. "Christ, Miranda, you're obsessed! In the unlikely event that I was even to think of sleeping with someone else, you would be the first to know."

I let the implication sink in before changing tack to illustrate how a truly supportive friend should behave, "Anyway, Lucia has been a real star throughout. You know, she looked after the girls." Again, I paused and, taking her silence for contrition, felt slightly mollified. "Sorry to be tetchy, but it's pretty shit being accused of making your friend top himself. And I feel crap knowing he was trying to talk to me before he...he did it...and I...I turned the phone off on him...Maybe I could have stopped him...convinced him...oh...I don't know!"

My earlier good mood had evaporated. Maybe, like Miranda's glossy hair and trim waist, it had only ever been window-dressing hiding a jumble of half-opened boxes behind it.

Miranda gently cupped my chin in her cool hand and I tried to find her eyes; impossible in the café's gloom. "You mustn't blame yourself, Joe. You were always there for him; here and when he went back to the States. But as you well know, sometimes it all gets too much and we close everyone out, don't we? Then, there's nothing more a friend can do apart from wait and hope."

She brushed my cheek with her long fingers and I smiled weakly, "Thanks, oldest friend."

"I'm still younger than you," she quipped back; this time the old banter worked its comfort.

Elsewhere, however, all efforts had finally failed and I was forced to admit defeat. My bowels were on the move so I made my excuses, stood up and retrieved my stick.

I had just slotted the second of the three joints into place when Ildiko, the ever-attentive Hungarian waitress appeared at my elbow. With one hand on her shoulder and the other proffering the unfolded stick in excuse and explanation to any new patrons of the café, I followed her across the room. There was a practised ease in the way she worked in tandem

55

with the café's owner removing chairs from my path and discreetly warning fellow customers of my approach.

The poor girl then waited outside the door of the thunder box until I emerged five minutes later, bathed in relief and sweat. The mortification brought on by this necessary performance whenever I am out and need to go to the loo only really hurt on the first two-dozen occasions; the embarrassment I suspect it causes others is harder to inure myself to.

A scrape of chair legs followed by familiar footfalls on the tiled floor told me that Miranda had already paid. She took my arm from Ildiko and led me upstairs into the dazzling sunshine. Once outside she asked whether I wanted to wait until my eyes adjusted to the light; she remains the only person who's ever done so.

As we wended our way back down the hill to Fawkes Close, the splendour of the bright autumn day was only marred by the persistent whine of drills, the percussion of jack hammers and the crash of Victoriana being relocated to a fleet of skips. No road was untouched in this affluent part of North West London. We passed a house that we both recognised as undergoing its third refurb in as many years. A smashed marble work surface poked out of the top of a jolly pink skip and next to it lay a Neff cooker with its original polystyrene packaging still inside. The reality TV contestant-turned-personality who had bought the house from developers had not, apparently, liked the kitchen. Neither had he appreciated the colour scheme of the bathroom suites judging by the glinting porcelain mosaic they now formed beneath the kitchen.

Miranda followed my squinted stare and we watched a pair of bickering Eastern European workmen emerge from the house and lob a gleaming extractor hood into the

56

jumbled skip. She had her arm looped through mine and squeezed it closer to her to break my reverie. "Joe, what do you imagine they think of us? I mean, twenty years ago these men were living under the rigours of Soviet control, they are still citizens of poor countries. They make do and mend and yet, here they are chucking perfectly good and very expensive consumer goods into landfill."

"I'm just amazed they don't stick all this stuff in the back of their vans and drive it back to Poland, or flog it on eBay," I replied, incredulous. "Tell you what, let's go skip diving, I could do with a nice new cooker."

She smiled at me and shook her head, "C'mon Joe, seriously, put yourself where they are for a moment. Would you be jealous of us? Would you want to live like us? Or think us recklessly squanderous and trivial?" There was a brittle anger in her voice.

"Christ, how much is this home Odeon of Hugo's costing you, Miranda?"

"Oh, it's not the money," she sighed irritably, "it's…it's…argh it doesn't matter. Forget it."

We walked wordlessly along the High Street to the beat of my stick and the orchestra of urban sounds. While we waited at the zebra crossing for someone to have the courtesy to stop, I turned to her and apologised. "Look Miranda, I'm sorry. Erm if you'd like to decamp to my place while the builders are in yours, you'd be welcome. You can have the spare room to work in."

But the moment for chivalry had passed and she shook her head gloomily. "It's okay Joe, I've got my noise cancelling headphones remember. I'll just lock myself in my office, grin and try to bear it."

As we entered Fawkes Close a high-pitched whirring sound began to echo round the square amphitheatre formed by its three storey houses. In my absence the turning circle had become a builder's yard, cluttered with white transit vans displaying the red and white chequered logo of "Polish & Check – Home Refurbishment and Home Help" as well as stacks of materials and a large yellow motorbike with foreign plates.

"Extending your house over the communal areas too, are you?"

Miranda caught the chiding undertone to my comment and sighed, "I'm sure it's only temporary, Joe. Anyway, you and Eithne don't even own a car." She had to shout to be heard above the teeth-grating whine of a builder cutting rebar grids with a circular saw. He added a stream of orange sparks to my multi-flecked vision.

I stared hard at him and could make out that he wore neither gloves nor goggles. My ears were ringing at fifteen feet, but he had his white ear-defenders casually looped over the back of his neck; I shook my head in disbelief. Nearby, in the shadow of one of the vans, a tall, well-built silhouette was yelling into a mobile. Noticing us the figure waved and snapped the phone shut, then signalled to the builder with the saw. To my immense relief the painful noise stopped. As I drew closer the second man became more defined. He looked to be in his mid to late twenties, with high Slavic cheekbones and a neatly trimmed goatee that accentuated his pointed chin. A thick dark ponytail flowed down between his broad shoulders.

"Joe, this is Zarek. He is the, erm, Project Manager. Should you have any problems with the noise or the mess, come and talk to him. Also, I believe he is Marta's boyfriend, at least I caught them kissing outside my office this morning." The scolding tone in her voice was unmistakable, but my eyes were too slow to catch the young man's reaction.

"Zarek, this is Joe Wynde. He and his family live at Number 4. We are old friends and now our children are friends too."

His macho handshake and cheerful grin communicated self-confidence and reliability, making me even more jealous of his youth and chiselled good looks. He turned to Miranda and in a sonorous voice that sounded more designed to seduce than inform her, ran through the progress made that morning and his intention to begin excavating. I decided that I would go to the supermarket a day early; I feel excessive noise and vibration like a physical assault.

I wondered whether Miranda had paid any attention to what he had said; certainly her "Fine, fine" was vague and uninterested. She walked me to my front door, skirting vans and negotiating pallets of bricks and bags of cement. As I fitted the key into the lock, the pounding of a pneumatic drill reverberated around Fawkes Close, shattering the tranquillity so often vaunted by local estate agents.

With the granite setts beneath my trainers vibrating, I stared after Miranda as she returned to the building site that had been her home. Her slim back looked small and slightly hunched.

Chapter 5

Looking back on it, I went into house-husbandry without having my eyes fully open. Whereas the daily routine is the same as a housewife's, it was clear from the outset that many mothers considered I was missing a visceral link with my daughter and so, I was given only limited access to the mutual emotional support network provided by my co-workers. These women had borne their charges. They had played the title role. I was merely front-of-house at the theatre of pain; uninitiated in the performance of internal post-natal stitching.

Other men, their men, had for the most part scurried back to work, glad of the excuse to avoid dirty nappies. In a few cases they had baled out altogether. As the sole male representative, I inevitably became the reluctant sounding board for female frustration at male lack of understanding and general inadequacy.

Thank goodness for Miranda. Pregnant at the same time as my wife, she was my passport into this new world after Eithne went back to work and I took over childcare duties. As a pre-parenthood friend she could vouch for my not being a child-molester or stalker of lonely mums. Nevertheless, I was still an outsider—a man in a woman's world. Rolled together with my disability, I presented a challenge to my fellow homemakers. Some wanted to mother me, others to take solace in me. A very few preferred to ignore me altogether. But for the most part they accepted me, though on their own terms.

However, I couldn't ride on Miranda's coat-tails indefinitely. As she undertook more freelance work and employed a succession of au pairs to take Christian out of the house, I became a familiar fixture at the local playgrounds, where the timid female could easily affect an

60

escape should the male become over-familiar. Later, in the singsong groups, inhibitions began to be set aside as we all made fools of ourselves dancing in our socks and chanting 'The Grand Old Duke of York' while lifting and lowering our bawling bundles of joy.

Still, the invitations to join in coffee mornings were rare, maybe because of their association with 'Gold Blend' styled seduction. And, when they did come, I felt it incumbent on me to check that my hostess and I were not to be alone, to signal my lack of intent.

Meeting Ted was, therefore, like discovering a long lost twin; a big, fat, jolly one who had been brought up to cook and eat the bovine population of Oregon and wash it down with lashings of whatever fizzy drink lay at hand. Nell was a few months old and in the two and a half years since I had started, I had resigned myself to being the only dad in the area looking after his children full-time.

As usual we were at the playground on the Heath. Nell was asleep in her buggy and Jenny was playing in the sandpit, next to which I was stretched out on a bench, eyes closed, basking in the sun's hot rays. Jenny's sharp shriek of pain broke my reverie and I heard a gruff American voice snap, "Fisher, I told you if you did that again I'd tan yer hide, now come over here and drop yer pants. Now!"

I sat up blinking, astonished as much by the fact that someone was actually threatening corporal punishment out loud in these P.C. sanitised times, as by hearing another male voice. Locating Jenny by her sobs I saw her stumbling towards me, rubbing tears and grit into her eyes. As I scooped her up and set to work with a bottle of mineral water and a relatively snot-free tissue, I could make out a huge, silhouetted figure bending over a smaller one and I heard a single, open-handed 'smack', silence, then a wail of protest.

The large figure then loomed over me. "Sorry 'bout that, but justice has now been dispensed." He bent down to come level with Jenny's little head and spoke softly, "Hey little girl, ain't you just dolly? If I give yer daddy some candy for ya, would it help make things better?" Jenny stopped crying and nodded vigorously.

"Chocolate, never fails with the girls," he laughed as Jenny trotted back to the sandpit and sat down next to Fisher, "Well, that and being hung like a ruttin' bull." His guffaw woke Nell and he swore and apologised, then asked what he could do to help.

We introduced ourselves, then I passed Nell over to him as I sorted out her bottle. By the time I had it out of its thermal container and loosened the lid he had her gurgling happily on his knee. I was impressed and asked him how long he'd been doing the childcare.

"Nearly a year now, ever since we relocated here." He explained that he had been a chef and had met Gail when called in to cater for an exclusive weekend in Oregon for TMB's top executives. "Man, she just couldn't get enough of my saddle of beef!" He had followed her to New York and then London. Like almost all expat spouses coming to Britain, he had only been able to obtain a visa that allowed him to live but not work here. "And, man, that sucks. Especially when yer holed up in some nowhere place like Chelsea. I mean do I look like a lady who shops?"

That Whitsun Ted had taken Fisher to the funfair on the Heath and fallen in love with the place. Once Gail had discovered how many successful expat families lived in Hampstead, she had adopted the project as her own and quickly located a house in the middle of the Village. They had moved in three weeks ago.

"But man what really sucks now is that there's like dozens of women's groups here for all the moms. I mean like book clubs, and London walks, and cookery classes run by those crap TV chefs, and frikkin' crochet and all that shit. But like they don't want the guys to join so there's nuthin' to do unless I wanna join some exclusive gym and man, I just don't suit Lycra!"

Tears of mirth were rolling down my cheeks; mums didn't tend to do earthy conversation with me, unless they were trying for a bit of extra-marital action.

"Well it's time to strike back. I'm gonna take a stand for sexual equality and set up a men's group. We're gonna show the girls that we can have a good time and be good parents too. I've met this other guy, a Canadian but I don't hold that against him and we're havin' our first meeting tomorrow, at The Duke of Wellington pub, if ya wanna come along."

So 'MeNW3' was established. Within six months a dozen or so dads had joined, mostly Americans, but a couple of Aussies, a Kiwi and a Russian as well. Amongst expat City workers it's de rigueur to employ a nanny to look after the children, whether or not one parent is at home, and this allowed most members of the group to take Olympian lunches and go on golfing trips. Wary of being too wasted at pick-up time and with no one to send in my stead, I tended to pop in for just a pint or two. Besides I loathe golf, which cut down on my conversational input. But it didn't matter, I had a network of other dads and we did go round to each other's houses for a casual cup of coffee, or to eat beef jerky and talk about boy's stuff. Among them I was the native, not, as I had always felt amidst the mums, the immigrant.

Through Ted I had met Brad, a jovial product of the factories of Seattle, with a wardrobe full of lumberjack shirts and loose-fit Levis. Fifteen years on the aircraft production lines had given him an intolerance of human error and a limited way of expressing himself. His tiny blonde wife, Kelly, had been his high-school sweetheart and was now a high-flying corporate accountant who somehow always managed to be home in time to bath their son and daughter before bedtime.

Brad was, as usual, bemoaning the state of Britain's telecommunications network. "Eighteen months I've been in that goddamned house and BT still can't get me a ten meg internet connection. It's a joke!"

Beside him, Dino Cazale was egging him on with regular "Uh huhs" and "You don't says". Proud Brooklyn-Italians, he and his wife, Maria, had met on a Wall Street trading floor when he had been groping around her shapely legs trying to fix a faulty PSU on her computer. After a swift, pasta-fuelled courtship they had married and been reproducing regularly every two years. Their four children had each been born in a different world financial centre, tracking Maria's relentless progress through the upper echelons of international investment banking. Yet again I sensed his eyes rest on my nose.

Unpaid bills and week-old bedclothes should have been claiming my attention that afternoon. The day had started well enough when a parcel containing Polly Mk.2 had plopped through my letterbox. With immense relief I placed her in the dolls' house and set about stripping the beds. Then it started again. Even through the double-glazing the percussive crunch of drilling set my teeth on edge. I bundled the sheets into the machine, grabbed the library books Eithne had forgotten to return and fled the house.

An enormous cement mixer had doubled the din by the time I returned. In despair, I switched the radio on full blast, only to hear 'Werewolves of London' being played. A serrated pang ran through me as I recalled Ted's incredulity at finding that I had never heard of Warren Zevon, and my joy on first listening to the greatest hits album that he made for me.

Remembering what Glenn had said about lunch at The Star, I lingered only long enough to put out the recycling before escaping the house, the noise, and my thoughts.

It was unseasonably warm and we were sitting outside, round the corner from the neighbouring schools that our kids attended. There were about twenty minutes to go before the floodgates opened to release torrents of babbling children. I was nursing the dregs of my second pint and resisting the temptation to have another.

"How can you qualify for First World status if you ain't got a First World telecommunications network?" Brad's surprisingly high-pitched drawl was amplified by beer.

Dino and I had heard it all before; BT's refusal to authorise a new connection without previous UK bills proving residence. "How the hell am I meant to provide any of that shit when I've lived my whole life in Seattle?" The broken appointments and unreturned calls, "You have no frikkin' idea of customer service in this country!" and finally the inevitably botched job performed by "some asshole who couldn't speak or read English for christssakes. So I told their so-called Customer Liaison woman that her dumbass fitter was lucky that I only rent the place because if he'da made that kinda mess in a house I actually owned, I'd've taken the goddamned sonofabitch outside and kicked his sorry ass."

I was not about to defend the indefensible and sure that Dino was limbering up to stoke the fires by extolling the speed and ease with which his own link to cyberspace worked, decided that another trip to the bar was in order after all.

When I returned with the three halves, Brad was speaking sternly into his iPhone. "MILF wrestling is no excuse for missin' a beer with the guys...No, man, you gotta sort out your priorities...Yeah, yeah, well I hope your balls burst, you louse. See ya round."

"Glenn gotta work, huh?" The slight menace in Dino's New York accent never failed to put me in mind of Scorcese films.

"Yeah, something like that," sighed Brad. "Says he's gotta cover a kick-boxing class for some dude who's bust his wrist."

"Yeah right, more like he's gotta bit of private tooition to do in the locker room," scoffed Dino. "Whaddaya reckon Joe?" It was only banter, but I was sick of considering the infidelity of others and found myself patting my pockets for Rizla and tobacco.

"I reckon maybe Joe could do with a few lessons offa Glenn hisself. Teach you how to duck next time, huh, buddy?"

"Ah, it's nothing, another bloody lamp-post that's all."

None of us was fooled by my half-hearted evasiveness. Brad began sniffing loudly, "Mmhunh, it ain't horse, it ain't cow...I know, it's bullshit."

Through their chortling, I licked my Rizla, twisted the tip and lit up. "Okay, okay, so Gail took exception to something I said. It's nothing."

Brad continued chortling. After a working life on the factory floor he had seen his fair share of bruising and now applied his expert knowledge. "Man, she musta been pretty pissed to have bust your honker that bad."

"Oh yeah, she was pissed all right. But it was just a minor misunderstanding between two cultures separated by the same language. Now, please, can we talk about something else? Who fancies a curry next Thursday evening?"

I could sense Dino rolling his eyes and so continued looking down at my cigarette, wishing that time would pass more quickly.

"Rough trip huh, Joe?" I wasn't really used to hearing sympathy from Brad, he much preferred being combative. He continued, "I'm sorry. I know you and Ted were close pals. He was a good guy. We had a few drinks on the day of the funeral, kinda outta respect, ain't that so Dino?"

I looked up towards him and nodded, "It wasn't the best. Gail seems to hold me personally responsible for Ted topping himself." I held up my hand to stay their questions. "It doesn't matter now. She's all over the place at the moment. It'll probably blow over." My ears were straining for the school bell to bring a swift end to the conversation.

"How come she blames you?" Brad was indignant. "I mean the woman's an A1 bitch so it don't surprise me. But to sock you of all people when she knows darn well it was her behaviour that made his life a livin' hell...man, she's got a nerve."

"There's nothin' so wild as the temper of a hot blooded woman. Take it from one that knows!" Dino was grinning. "It's like if Maria even thinks I'm making eyes at another woman she goes crazy. Man, she's got a punch that could fell a buffalo."

We'd seen the evidence. He'd arrived in London three months earlier sporting a thick lip, where Maria had got him with a small can of tonic hurled across business class, for chatting up an attractive stewardess. Initially lodged in temporary accommodation, they had leapt at the chance of renting Ted's old house when, newly repaired and redecorated, it had come back onto the market.

"Oh you better believe it Dino." Brad was warming to his subject; never a fan of Gail's he was always keen to dish the dirt, no matter how often we had heard it before. "There ain't a bar or diner round here where she didn't let rip at Ted. Why once, right here, she darn near killed him with a wine bottle."

Dino whistled in spite of the exaggeration he knew the story had accrued and turned to me, "Sounds like you got off lightly, Joe. So, did you manage to tell Gail to get her mail redirection service sorted out, cos I've got a whole new bunch of stuff addressed to them?"

An odd queasy sensation shivered through me, scorching the back of my throat with bile. "Funnily enough Dino, it slipped my mind. You know, it might have been seen as a trifle tactless to raise the issue at the graveside."

"How were the kids?" Brad broke in. I could hear the same tone of concern in his voice that I felt when I thought of them.

"Coping," I replied, "Gail's got them in bereavement counselling."

"Gotta be better than her doing it herself. The only grief she knows is when her bonus is below six figures."

I shrugged, "Well I guess she's got her wish now, sole custody so she can screw them up completely."

The clouds were coming over and I took a long final drag on the roll-up and exhaled just as Dino muttered, "Oh Jeez, we're busted."

In a low voice Brad reeled off the register of yummy mummies who were eyeing us from the other side of the road with evident distaste.

"Oh well, break time's over," I sighed and we drank up in sombre silence.

My spirits were not lifted by the ensuing battle to get the girls to do homework and to practise their instruments. The low level headache that follows beer at lunch coincided with Nell finally agreeing to scrape her way through her violin pieces and my temper was further frayed by Jenny telling me that her P.E. kit simply had to be washed and dry by the following morning.

The relief I felt when finally I flopped down on the sofa at half past nine was destined to be short-lived. Having found an old episode of *The Sweeney* to watch, I had just spooned in the first mouthful of spiced couscous (empty packet contents into pan and add boiling water for the middle-class, middle-aged version of Pot Noodle) when the phone rang. Swallowing too quickly and trying to balance the pan on the overcrowded coffee table, I lunged for the phone in expectation of hearing Eithne's soothing lilt.

Miranda sounded weary, "Hi Joe, you busy?"

"Just having supper." I hoped she would take the hint, as I squinted at John Thaw laying into a moustachioed blagger.

"Ah great, you've got the kids to bed then." Even from the end of the phone I could hear a forced breeziness in her voice. "How's it going?"

"Oh, you know, struggling along. How can I do you, Miranda?" I didn't want to banter; I could smell my food cooling rapidly.

"Um, look, sorry I was so grotty yesterday morning, it's not a whole lot of fun living here at the moment."

I took a swig of red wine to stop myself from saying "I know, my whole bloody house has been reverberating to the sound of Hugo's hubris" and waited for her to continue.

"Anyway I've been thinking about what Gail said and something's been bothering me."

My heart sank and I zapped the TV off. "Go on," I sighed.

"Oh, I know, I'm sorry but look, you told me she said that TMB would sack anyone even suspected of insider trading, didn't you?" I grunted in confirmation. "And yet

69

that's exactly what she accused you of blackmailing Ted with. Well it doesn't make sense. If she was concocting a lie to get you out of her life she'd hardly put her career at risk in the process, would she? She and Ted must have believed that you were responsible."

That sliver of fear I had first felt at the cemetery chilled me anew. During my fruitless hours spent wandering the maze of possibilities, I had chosen not to dwell on this point. When it was articulated by someone else it sounded like evidence of my guilt. Another large glug of wine moistened my mouth sufficiently for me to speak.

"Kristina," my voice was toneless, "I need to talk to Kristina." Gail had accused me of getting the nanny to steal from her. There had to be more to it than the fury of a cheated woman.

Miranda caught her breath at my ear and I had a sudden yearning for her to be sitting snugly next to me. "You think this is revenge for being dumped when Ted went back to Gail?" Her excitement communicated her love of a juicy bit of gossip.

"Oh, I don't know. Ted told me that he and Kristina split up amicably; that she understood he needed to be with his family. They carried on seeing each other as friends right up until he went back – not that Gail knew. But maybe, after he'd gone, Kristina felt hard done by or needed money…"

"Of course, and Ted must have told her you were forwarding his post, in case she needed to get in touch with him. So she sends the blackmail letter to his old address and you dutifully pass it on with all the other letters. But why implicate you?" Miranda's rising glee was checked by this thought.

"If she really did…I suppose because I was so adamant that he should save his marriage. I told him that his first duty lay with the children's happiness and that he and Gail

70

owed it to them to try and patch things up. I can't say that I ever really considered Kristina's feelings in the equation."

"Mmm. Okay, so do you know where Kristina is now?"

"No, but Marta may. I was going to ask you yesterday, if I could have a word with her about it, but you…um…well the timing didn't seem right."

Miranda ignored this, instead asking crisply, "Why, were they friends?"

"I'm not sure, but they always seemed pretty chummy at the playground and Marta brought Chris round to play with Fisher a few times when I was there. Maybe they've stayed in touch or work for the same agency. You never know." I tailed off.

"Yes, maybe. Okay I'll talk to Marta tomorrow. Goodnight then."

"Is that it?" I felt cheated, my interest aroused then left unsatisfied.

"Yup, that's it, you can go back to your dinner for one." There was an edge to her coquettishness; she wanted me off the phone now.

"You made my salad go cold, ratbag."

"See you around Joe" and the line went dead.

The Sweeney was halfway through and I had seen the episode before anyway. I ate my tepid couscous with glugs of wine but without relish.

In the aftermath of his banishment to Belsize Park, I'd thought I'd been Ted's closest friend. He had bought himself a big TV and an ounce of grass. The two of us had then proceeded to lose a month of nights watching classic rock videos through a haze of beer and smoke.

71

Kristina had also been a regular visitor, though never when I was around. Gail had sacked her the same night as she'd thrown Ted out, waiting until the nanny had got in from her night off and gone to sleep, before dragging her screaming from her bed to the pavement—much to the annoyance of the neighbours.

After about ten weeks, when Gail felt that Ted had learned his lesson, she had sent through her terms. She would take him back on condition that they move to Houston, that he never have contact with Kristina again and that he confess his sin to the children and beg their forgiveness. There would be no negotiation, he could take it or leave it.

A month later they were gone. He left me the telly. Now every time I turned it on I felt bereft and guilty.

Chapter 6

Of late photopsia, the kaleidoscopic flashing lights I see, has even invaded my dreams. Only images drawn from the visual reference library of my youth remain uncorrupted, perhaps because they are so sharply etched upon my mental retina.

That night, the vivid longing I'd felt when talking to Miranda crept into my lonely bed, coupled with my sleeping thoughts and rolled me back twenty years to the outskirts of Cambridge and the party at which I'd hoped to meet her again.

Once again I was clutching the bottle of vodka that had cost me the last of my student grant, and being told that only those with vodka and a gilt-edged invitation were permitted entrance. The First XV, in morning coats, were tossing gatecrashers into the river as the gilded youth of the late eighties pretended they were Sebastian and Julia Flyte and I looked on from a distance, desperate for a glimpse of Miranda

Then I was running forward, shouting her name; through the hospital laundry where I'd worked all summer and out into a crisp October morning, running towards her in delight. The frames slowed as her face remoulded itself from consternation at being accosted so wildly, to gradual recognition and finally a small smile of amusement. Even in my sleep my heart sank as it became clear that, unlike me, she had not spent the vacation in fantastic reverie about us. My spur of the moment suggestion to spend the afternoon at the Arts Cinema received a polite shake of her Timoteied head. It was too late; she and Hugo were now sharing a flat.

A jump cut spared me both from reliving the moment I was told that my poor eyesight was degenerative and the maul of drink, drugs, depression and essay crises that followed, during which I hardly thought of her. And again my heart quickened to see her appear at my door on that rainy May afternoon, asking whether I wanted to go for a drink.

Most of the university were still stuffing themselves with final morsels of revision or regurgitating their intake under invigilation. Idly watching the swans and the tourists clamber out of the Cam in the drizzle, we chatted about the stresses of student life, the startling fact that we were two-thirds of the way through our time in this beautiful city and of our plans for life outside it.

Something was not being said and all the while I was hoping that she would tell me that she'd split up with Hugo. Maybe she was nervous, but I must be patient and let her raise the subject. Finally, as I returned with my fifth pint and her third cider she looked me directly in the eyes and said, "Has it really sunk in yet, your diagnosis, I mean?"

I was taken aback. I had made no secret of my RP but thus far its only outward manifestation was at night, when people assumed my difficulties were due to my being drunk or stoned—which was usually the case anyway. After a while most of my peers had forgotten to ask about it, or tired of my dismissive replies. There was going to be no great single event, no road to Damascus blinding, so they had moved on to more immediate problems such as those thrown up by the plot of *Neighbours*.

"You look like a mackerel," she giggled nervously as my face betrayed my thoughts. "Look, if you prefer not to talk about it, I understand. Just, I heard through friends of friends and thought that you might need a friend who's not such a close friend to talk to." She shifted awkwardly and turned her gaze to the bubbles in her cider.

74

I wanted to lean over the table and hug her and cry into her soft hair. Instead I took out my cigarettes and fiddled with the packet.

"I, um, try not to think about it too much. When I was first told it explained a lot of things; like why I can't see in the dark and spend my life getting concussed by lamp-posts and falling into Hobson's Aqueduct. I've had to stop riding a bike and playing rugby too. I never could drive, which I guess is a blessing. Oh I don't know Miranda, there just seems so much more to worry about in life. Like how the hell I'm going to pay off my overdraft, you know?"

She put her hand to my cheek and held my gaze. The sun was breaking through the clouds and it illuminated her irises for a couple of seconds so they glowed amber. "You are so brave, Joe. If it ever gets on top of you, I want you to know that you can always come to me. I've seen what depression can do to people; people I care about."

My heart was aflutter. She looked away, out over the Cam. I had to ask now.

"Miranda, I don't suppose you would like to go out with me, er please?"

She turned slowly back to me, a wisp of a smile playing at the edges of her crooked, unmade-up mouth. "Oh, Joe, you're so sweet. I'd love to continue seeing you as a friend but my heart belongs to Hugo and... and, well, we are very much together."

"Oh well, it was worth a try. I guess my girlfriend would be a bit put out too." I gabbled on, disguising my disappointment. "Well, in the immortal words of Benny and Bjorn 'if you change your mind, I'm the first in line', okay?"

She smiled, relieved that the awkwardness had passed. As we stood to leave she leant forward, gave me a sisterly hug and said, "Just remember, winter, spring, summer or fall, all you gotta do is call." We linked arms and set off back to college.

The drizzle had turned to fat summer drops that spattered heavily over us as we ambled along the Backs. Intermittent bright sunshine glinted off the wet sandstone of the older colleges and even the Cam seemed less murky. I felt light-headed and exhilarated. My thin white shirt was soon soaked and clung to me. Imagining myself the image of a sweat-drenched Robert Plant I was overwhelmed by the thought that "today, I too am a golden god!"

Miranda's small firm breast was pressed against my bicep, her hair mingling with my own, which was if anything longer. I reached down and tentatively took her hand, "My lady, would you care to dance?"

And there with King's College as our backdrop, I took her in my arms and we twirled in the giddy approximation of a waltz. In that moment, as I felt her heart beat next to mine, I found a beauty in the world, which I have spent two decades trying to recapture.

I broke the spell by leaning forward to kiss her. The look of dreamy transport left her beautiful hazel eyes and she turned her face away so that my lips planted themselves on her ear instead. Softly she put her hand on my chest and pushed me away. "Joe, that was lovely, but let's not spoil it, let's leave it there."

My embarrassment and rejection expressed itself in petulance and acrimony. I demanded to know why; accused her of leading me on. Even after twenty years the anguish I felt at recalling my outburst was painful enough to wake me.

As I contemplated another morning of sweeping up crushed Golden Nuggets and wiping congealed milk from the kitchen table, it seemed that my time at Cambridge had been the preparation for someone else's future. I consoled

76

myself with the knowledge that many of the gilded youth of yesteryear, Hugo included, had succumbed to the tarnish of middle-aged spread and that finally, in preparing futures for my own children, I was taking a course which suited me.

Autumn had arrived with a vengeance. The denuded trees rattled in the gusting wind and cold drizzle dripped from the sky. The girls ran into school, glad for the comfort of clanking dust-coated radiators. Setting forth to walk the mile back, I told myself that I must now look too soggy to be invited to sit on the leather upholstery of the parents driving home, but felt better as I strode past their stationary line of automotive hubris that stretched the length of the hill. At least I was getting the twenty minutes exercise recommended by the government. I just hoped that the tightness I felt in my chest was due to the traffic fumes trapped in the damp air and not all the cigarettes over the past week.

As I turned down a side road to avoid the bustle of the High Street, I could hear raised voices and the unmistakable klaxon of white vans at loggerheads. Sure enough, at the head of two lines of traffic a pair of builders' vans stood nose to nose, each refusing to back up. Their drivers were yelling insults at each other in different Eastern European tongues. Five minutes later, as I let myself into the house, I could still hear the blaring horns.

I spent the rest of the morning ironing (burning myself only once) and then tidying the house. The cacophony from Miranda's was so great that I had no compunction about turning my stereo right up. My life may have moved away from the late eighties but my musical tastes maintain strong links. I was halfway through my second Blue Aeroplanes album when I detected a different key warbling in the background. Pressing the phone to my ear, I recognised the way she caught her breath before she spoke.

77

The jangling guitars and the removal of a couple of chores from my list had cheered me up and I felt flippant. "Miranda! Now you can't be ringing to complain about the music. It only just covers the racket your miners are making."

She laughed that tinkling girlish chuckle of the garden party. "No, no you go for it, Joe—drown the bastards out! But listen, I need to show you something, are you busy?"

I guessed she was angling for an invitation to get out of her place. "Tell you what me old mucker, I was just about to make some lunch, why don't you leave your building site for a bit and join me. That is if you can navigate the minefield your husband's Eastern Bloc agents have laid between us."

She came bearing the first edition of *The Evening Standard*. Time was I would rush out from my own building site of a flat in Paddington to see whether one of my pieces had been printed in the Londoner's Diary column. Eighty words paid quarter of the monthly mortgage interest. More than eight pieces a month and I could afford to do some home improvements. It took five years but then I sold for double the purchase price. Christ, nowadays I'd be featured on *Property Ladder*!

The headline shouted "Top Banker's Tower Bridge Suicide." That's as far as I got; nowadays newsprint is too small for me to attempt, even with my strongest reading glasses.

"Bloody hell, it gets more like *The Sun* every day. I knew I was right to quit when I did." I tossed the paper back. Miranda huffed and started to read as if to a child; "Horrified onlookers watched helplessly as a man believed to be a leading City investment analyst leapt to his death from Tower Bridge at shortly after nine this morning. Sources within the Square Mile confirmed that the forty-one year old employee of failed bank Lachmann Brothers is rumoured to have been under investigation by the Financial Services Authority. The River Police later recovered a body near Deptford and are awaiting formal identification. Lachmann's, which went into receivership earlier this week has so far refused to comment."

"Tabloid sensationalism," I declared dismissively. "Anyway what's the big deal? Win big, lose big, I'm sorry for his family but don't ride the highs if you can't take the lows."

My house is very brightly lit, guests often compare it to an operating theatre with its rows of high voltage downlighters, so I could see Miranda's nose wrinkle in distaste at my pronouncements. I held my hands up, "I know, I know, the politics of the student bar. But come on Miranda, whether or not Hugo is in the City, you have to admit, they've had it good for a long time. They can't expect my sympathy when they get caught by their own Ponzi scheme."

"Perhaps you'll be a little more sympathetic if you listen and find out who this is," she said acidly. Then, after a short pause for effect, "It's Daniel Morgenstern." Her voice cracked as she spoke. I felt a corresponding lurch in my midriff. Rachel's pretty dark features, quirky upturned nose and the faces of their three children filled my thoughts. Noa, their eldest had been Jenny's best friend at nursery. "Oh shit, oh bloody hell."

Miranda and I stared at each other for a few seconds during which she slid her hand into mine and squeezed, the way Nell and Jenny do when they need reassurance. "Ruth just rang me. She told me why too."

Ruth Levy and Daniel's wife, Rachel had been best friends since they had started primary school together in

Manchester. They now lived on opposite sides of Belsize Square and regularly attempted to out-bake each other.

"Apparently, Daniel became really depressed after he found out that Rachel was having an affair. Not so much because she was being unfaithful, but because of who it was and the fact that she was paying him for it." Miranda paused for effect. "It seems she was giving the plumber overtime!"

Despite my shock, I couldn't resist a touch of levity. "Gosh, Daniel must have felt she was really plumbing the depths!" We shared a grim, short-lived giggle.

"Of course, we all knew she was seeing someone." She saw me shaking my head. "Well all the girls anyway. It's easy enough to spot; there's a certain look, a glow of…satisfaction."

"I'll keep my eyes peeled," I replied wryly "but I thought that's what you got when you were happily married."

Miranda sniffed and I wondered whether she ever dreamed of a handsome prince satisfying her. "Anyway," she continued, "that's not all. I've spoken with Marta. She was predictably vague. She *thinks* that Kristina has gone back to Prague." Both my head and my insides slumped; Miranda hurried on. "However, she was able to confirm that they both came through the same agency—Polish & Check. And that's what's really interesting, Joe, guess where Rachel's plumber came from."

"Let me guess; was he a Polish plumber? My mind strained to catch her train of thought. "So, what, two City families plus two suicides multiplied by one employment agency equals one huge conspiracy?"

"Precisely. A bit too much of a coincidence, don't you think?"

"Miranda, that's what I think every time I open my front door and see yours. But we live in a rarefied atmosphere up here and it breeds coincidences. I know you have the journalist's nose for a story, but I'm meant to be the paranoid conspiracy theorist." Under different circumstances I would have lapped up her latest gossip story, but not now. Half the nannies and even more of the builder's vans in the area appeared to belong to Polish & Check. Its unique idea to provide both high quality tradesmen and qualified nannies had garnered the agency a fine reputation amongst 'top people' and it had even been featured recently in a glossy magazine. "You'll be telling me they're digging your grave over there next," I nodded over her shoulder.

Miranda cocked her head to one side and the tresses of her hair fell away. For the first time, under the bright artificial light, I saw the traces of crows' feet. The blue tones of sleepless nights were still discernible beneath her beautiful hazel eyes, in defiance of her carefully applied foundation.

"I'm sorry, Miranda, I don't mean to make light of this. I'm just pissed off because now there's no chance of finding anything out from Kristina. And because this whole thing with Ted and then Gail has left me feeling emotionally drained. I guess there's only a finite amount of grief one can take."

Miranda shook her head. "Yeah, and maybe there is a finite amount of Polish workmen one can take too. You're right, I'm probably just being paranoid."

For lunch I made mushroom omelettes and we chatted about schools and the closure of yet another local shop in the High Street; anything that steered a path clear of that which preoccupied our thoughts. Then we shared a mango, which Miranda porcupined perfectly with a few deft movements of her long elegant hands. For once, she had joined me in a

81

bottle of white wine, the last of which we were sipping as her builders recommended their bone-rattling din.

Miranda grimaced and, rising, said, "That's my cue to get back to work."

"You just want to slip those silent headphones on again, don't you? I bet you look gorgeous in them." I felt a little frisky and it dawned on me that I had filled my own glass more frequently than hers.

She pouted and left me to clear up.

Alone with my thoughts swirling around like dregs, I was unable to find anything palatable to digest. I had lived amongst the bored housewives and testosterone driven men of affluent London for long enough to know that there was more copulation during daylight hours than at night, but this usually resulted in a costly divorce case rather than suicide. People were simply too selfish and arrogant to take the blame themselves. They preferred to take the money and the house, and sometimes even the kids.

If the muscular builders and toned young nannies *did* have a scam going, it would be for trinkets. Maybe Rachel's behaviour had helped push Daniel over the edge, but it wasn't the cause. Killing yourself to avoid the stigma of professional misconduct, now *that* made far more sense.

Chapter 7

I should have known that Miranda wouldn't let her suspicions lie there. Once she'd taken an interest in something she remained persistent to the point of being dogged. I guess that's why she never really gave up on me or let Hugo's boorishness drive her away.

The final year of my English degree had a compulsory paper in 'tragedy', a major part of which was Greek tragedy. My grammar school had preferred modern languages to classics and my knowledge of Oedipus was confined to Freud. I had to start going to lectures to make up the deficiency and it was in the queue for one on 'The Libation Bearers' that I had seen Miranda again. She had bobbed her hair and was wearing a baggy argyle jumper, which looked so public school I could only assume it was Hugo's. My joy at seeing her overcame the embarrassment I felt at remembering our previous parting. She frowned at me for a second and I bent my head in shame, making to walk past her. Then she touched my arm and smiled. The world flooded with colour and I felt a thrill run up my arm and down my spine. I looked deep into her autumnal eyes and said "Sorry". She gave me a gentle slap on the bicep and we entered the lecture hall together.

As the term progressed I felt less at odds with the university. Now that I could select the majority of the subjects I studied, I found I enjoyed the work. All of us in our final year saw we had an end to work towards and were drinking less and, in my case, had stopped smoking dope. People seemed to find me better company and my friendships, especially that with Miranda, burgeoned. And friendship was enough; having believed I'd lost it once, I was happy to have it back on any terms. Maybe too, my needs had changed. I felt part of a whole, no longer the outsider.

Then one night just before finals, Hugo burst into my room. He had been at some Old Etonian claret-swigging dinner and now he fancied a bit of sport with his wench. Miranda and I had had our heads stuck in Aeschylus and were sharing coffee and Rich Tea biscuits. Florid faced and clad in Georgian garb, he went to grab Miranda and knocked her coffee over my lap. I stood up to remonstrate and he spat out, "How dare you, pleb!" I might have ducked his clumsily swung fist had I been able to see it coming; as it was it broke my nose.

The chair I broke over his head returned the favour. Miranda, by now in tears, interposed herself between us. Every ounce of me burned with the resentment of the injured party. Yet as she led Hugo out of the room, it was his bruised knuckles that I noticed her raise to her lips.

The following day Miranda didn't attend the lecture. On my return I found a letter scrawled on Smythson stationery in my pigeonhole.

Wynde,

Our mutual friend informs me I owe you an apology, so here it is.

HFG Lethbridge.

P.S. Thanks to your tantrum I enjoyed the mother of all blowjobs last night!

I vowed my revenge.

After we left university Miranda and I had both been drawn by the legends of Fleet Street to the stark realities of Wapping. No more the dingy pubs of folklore, but the brash mechanisation of corporate journalism. For five years I stumbled round the West End from reception to party, grubbing up tittle-tattle for the various diary columns. Eventually I rose to the dizzy heights of 'Debutantes' Correspondent' for *The Mail*. Miranda meanwhile went from fashion to interiors and ended up with a by-line in one of *The Sunday Times'* colour supplements.

Though our paths rarely crossed, the journalistic world is so self-obsessed that we could easily keep tabs on each other and from time to time we would meet in Campden Hill to compare freebees. Her acquisition of goody bags was relentless, as was my steady decline into alcohol dependency. Our chosen profession suited us both well.

She and Hugo had moved to Kensington, occupying a grace and favour apartment provided by his parents. Each time I met up with Miranda I would try to chip away at their relationship. I questioned the wisdom of not playing the field, implying that I knew that Hugo had no such scruples. However, such was my naivety that I merely succeeded in pushing her closer to him and myself off the wedding guest list. The few mutual friends we had told me that it had been a lavish affair at the Lethbridge country seat in Shropshire. They also informed me that the newlyweds had announced that they were moving to Hong Kong at the end of that summer.

Ten days had passed since news of Daniel Morgenstern's death and other momentous events in world financial markets had somewhat eclipsed his small domestic tragedy. No doubt mindful of the whiff of scandal surrounding his passing, his family had requested a private ceremony, which was held at Golders Green Crematorium. There was chatter of course around the dinner tables but, in general, everyone was too worried about their own positions to pay much heed to another's perceived weakness.

Miranda had, herself, been keeping a low profile. The other residents of Fawkes Close and its environs had been laying siege to her in person and then by phone and email. A community spirit was being built in opposition to the constant noise and mess. Every morning, before the chequered vans of the builders arrived, Hugo strode blithely out to his chauffeur driven Lexus. He returned late into the evening and long after the workmen had left. On Saturday mornings he avoided their disruptive presence by abandoning his family in favour of his tennis club where, a friend who is also a member told me, Hugo pronounced his 'bloody neighbours' were being difficult merely out of jealousy for his continuing ability to spend in these straightened times.

At home I silently cursed him as I listened to Nell's laboured breathing. Her asthma had flared up with the increase in dust and it was this, rather than my fading bruises and hurt feelings, which rightly commanded Eithne's sympathy when she popped in for a few days between Spain and Canada. She clearly thought that I was exaggerating the ferocity of Gail's outburst, to give vent to the misery of living opposite a building site. Indeed, she gave a rare display of losing her own sang-froid when a skip lorry woke us at six on Saturday morning.

So the following Monday, having been woken at six again when Eithne's airport taxi driver rang the doorbell, I had assumed that the text from Miranda was the precursor to an apology. As usual we met at Café Noir. In spite of the grind and hiss of the coffee machine and the buzz of conversation it felt like an oasis of peace after Fawkes Close. We found ourselves whispering out of some kind of reverence.

Miranda sounded full of purpose as we rattled through the usual small talk while the coffee was being brewed. I

86

half suspected that she was going to tell me that she was pregnant.

She had deliberately chosen the table closest to the counter. It was the brightest and a natural choice as I am less likely to knock things over if I have a little light to fumble around in. Usually, however, Miranda and I sat in our dark corner where even with a tall candle we played a chess-like game in which she moved sugar, spoons and croissant around the table to provide my fingers with the next thing they were seeking. I found a certain comfort in putting myself into her hands like this, so was a little wrong-footed by the change in routine.

Miranda sensed my surprise, "I want you to have a look at something, if there's enough light." She bent towards me confidentially, "Here."

She passed me a small, smooth, oblong object. First I turned it over in my hands, feeling its aluminium and plastic casing, the compass point menu button, four different sized jack sockets and small microphone grills on each side. It felt like a cross between a mobile phone and a large MP3 player. I slipped my hand into my pocket and found the glasses I keep there, a pair of maximum strength ready readers from the chemist, utterly disposable, which they tend to be after I've sat on them.

Squinting through the gloom, I could see a red light glowing and a jumble of information on the small and insufficiently backlit LCD screen. "Very smart. Is Hugo recording your arguments for posterity now, or are you wired to try and get me to incriminate myself?"

An indulgent smile flickered across her un-glossed lips and she dipped her chin slightly. "It's for you—a gift," she said quietly.

I was taken aback and flustered. "A gift for me? Ah, I've got it, it has a built in clock, synced to continental time so that when I complain about skip lorries arriving too early and try to record them it will show that it's really seven o'clock not six." I sat back triumphantly. Miranda was still staring at me, looking less indulgent, more exasperated.

"I'm not sure you should have that coffee if you are this hyper already." Then, "Or is it because Eithne was home this weekend." Her tone was both coquettish and slightly sulky.

"Well we had to do something after the lorry woke us at such an ungodly hour. I suppose Hugo used the opportunity to read *The Economist*." I tried to sound blasé, but the thought of her looking at my closed curtains from a lonely bedroom made me feel as if I had air bubbles between my vertebrae.

"Such ingratitude!" Miranda pouted and tapped the machine in my left hand. "Well I suppose it is a kind of a bribe Joe. I have a proposition for you."

"After all these years, Miranda you are sweet, but I'm afraid it is my turn to say no. You see I am happily married and…"

"Joe, can you just shut up for a minute and listen!" The rebuke stung though I knew I deserved it and I grunted apologetically.

Miranda was businesslike, as if she had rehearsed this. "As you can see technology has moved on a bit since the days when we had to nip off to the loo to scribble down our quotes before they became clouded by interpolation." I smiled at her, I had done more than my fair share of extrapolating from the source material to jazz-up a story.

"Son of Dictaphone," I pronounced.

"Precisely. If you just press that button there," her cool, slim fingers found my chewed stubs and guided them to a small shiny button. I pressed. The light disappeared, "and then this one," my finger was led towards another button and gently encouraged to push it. I heard myself saying "Very smart, is Hugo recording your arguments for posterity now?" I fumbled for the stop button, embarrassed at what was coming next. Her index finger slid between my own digits and deftly did it for me. "Hugo did give me one of these, to record the children's first words and silly things they say, but I also use it for my interviews. Some of these creative gurus can get a bit overwhelmed with the exuberance of their own verbosity. This makes it easier to follow their train of thought."

Although I sensed the direction in which I was being steered, I felt that I should play the game, "And you're presenting me with this wonder because...?"

Again she dipped her chin slightly and looked up at me, in a very appealing fashion. "What I always admired about your skill as a journalist was your ability to chat to anybody and have them talking frankly within a matter of minutes. You inspire trust."

In the face of such praise, I could only beam, safe in the knowledge that I was being buttered up. "Shame that was the one trick this pony had." I wasn't bitter, just rueful.

"I've made a list of all the people I can think of who have used Polish & Check over the last year or so and I'm going to try and talk to as many as I can get hold of. If you want to help me, it would make things much quicker and easier."

I wondered whether she'd be fluttering her eyelashes if I could see.

"Bribery, flattery and the chance to be your sidekick; what more could a man want to sell his soul?" I teased. "Come on though, Miranda, do you really think there's a story here?"

I waited for an answer but received only an angry huff. She started to fiddle with her spoon, tapping it on her saucer impatiently; exactly as I do with my white stick when I get stuck behind someone dawdling along the pavement.

"Joe, look this is a gut feeling, one I've had for weeks now. And after what happened to Ted and then Daniel, well it all crystallised into something. I admit it sounds tenuous but... but, well it just ties in with, oh I don't know, all sorts of things that I've heard, you know. Things half-said over lunch or coffee and, and well, it just all fits together and makes sense of a lot of stuff." She paused to gauge my reaction.

"I can see why you didn't train as a barrister." My mirth was at risk of becoming visible again. "Seriously though Miranda, are you sure you're not just trying to find connections to relieve the torpor of writing endless features on home improvements and soft furnishing?"

She was immediately defensive, "Look, I've done my time as a researcher, unlike you. I'm not saying that makes me an expert, but I think I know enough to know when I have a story that will stand up. This is one, and you should want to help. After all it concerns people you profess to care about."

I shook my head doubtfully, there just didn't seem to be enough substance. But if she was right, and Kristina had used me to get to the Hansfords... My coffee began to repeat on me at the thought.

Miranda's tone was growing shaky as her emotion rose. "Look Joe, you're a man. You don't spend your time amidst groups of gossiping, insecure women, picking up on hints and nuances, on subtle changes in appearance or behaviour. You just don't notice the same things we do."

I pulled a face and she paused, "Oh, sorry Joe, but you know what I mean."

Oddly it was the reminder of my exclusion from the coffee mornings and ladies-who-lunch circuit that smarted, not the reference to my visual limitations. Although I have to live daily with both, the one is an accident of genetics, the other a lingering form of sexual discrimination. Cracked nipples and whether or not Ugg Boots were in this season are not my favoured topics of conversation, but it was galling to be the only parent not invited along, or to hear the lull in conversation when I appeared.

Miranda alone had always brought me to the mother and toddler mornings and made a point of including me in whatever was being discussed. In fact many of the mums had initially assumed that we were a couple. I smiled at the memory.

"Okay, if your intuition tells you that there's something rotten in the state of Poland, how do you propose we check it out?"

Her original excitement came gushing back and she clapped her hands. Ildiko thought she was being summoned and we ended up with two more coffees. As Miranda outlined her plan and I overcame the urge to go for a cigarette, I realised that I too was excited. My searching eyes finally found hers; they were chocolaty hazel in the dim light. Fixing on them my resolve was set too, "Okay Scoop, give me my first assignment."

It felt good to be working together again; it brought back happy memories of sitting in my room overlooking the college's beautifully tended Georgian courtyard. Maybe it just felt good to be working again on something other than 'homemaking'. After nine years of focussing on the microcosm of my family it was reassuring to find I could re-integrate myself with the wider world.

Depending on the levels of disturbance we alternated between my sitting room and the cramped, windowless basement room that acted as her office. We had started that

91

afternoon, pooling our joint knowledge to draw up a list of friends and acquaintances who may have used P&C. Before hiring Marta Hugo had insisted on a wealth of references, so we trawled through these too, although in the intervening five years the greater proportion of the people who had written these glowing letters of recommendation had moved.

Miranda had suggested we use the premise of writing a feature article on Eastern Europeans working in London to ask those we spoke to about their experiences, both of the individuals they had employed and the agency who had supplied them. We mined for quirky habits amongst the nannies; quality of workmanship provided by the tradesmen; their willingness to work overtime or meet deadlines and finally for an assessment of general all-round satisfaction. Where the latter was high we asked for details of anyone that the satisfied customer had subsequently recommended the agency to.

It proved very effective. Well-heeled North West London is an incestuous community and people thrive on their ability to show off their knowledge of superior products and services. The prospect of having their observations recorded in an interview destined to appear as a double page spread in a Sunday paper proved too great a temptation for most; it rapidly overtook their natural aversion to gossiping publicly. Each number we rang yielded a further two or three. Soon we were receiving calls.

The list grew rapidly. Within a week we had scores of new names and I was spending my evenings after putting the girls to bed catching up on neglected housework. Miranda joked that I should employ a housekeeper via P&C and see whether I got seduced and blackmailed.

As the second week progressed we split the work differently. I dealt with the locals who had used builders and tradesmen, Miranda the women who had employed nannies or au pairs. The hesitant and critical responses stood out in sharp contrast to the predominantly favourable ones. After a fortnight we had a short list of nearly a dozen who had not been happy with the service they had received. In most cases they had used the agency both for nannying and building services. In all but two the problem had been with the nanny.

Miranda had her hair done and donned her smartest trouser suit. She spent the third week interviewing as many of the disgruntled as would allow her to buy them lunch. Those she felt would respond better to a male approach she left to me.

At the end of that hectic week we flopped down together on my sofa. Our four children were playing noisily upstairs and to an outsider we presented a picture of the happy family at home. The old itch to put my arm around her shoulder and pull her close to me returned momentarily.

As if sensing this, she swung herself back and around to face me and said, "Oh, we are so close, Joe." I laughed nervously and she shot me a look. "You can't still have your doubts, not after everything we've found out?" My hesitation clearly irritated her. "Come on, Joe. You've listened to the interviews; you must see the pattern. All the women I've talked to either work in the City or are married to someone who does and they all maintain that the arrival of their nanny has led to otherwise inexplicable changes in their husbands' behaviour; "like she has some kind of hold over him" as one of them said. How else do you explain that trader who has emptied the joint account to cover so-called gambling debts or the Network Manager who has begun 'investing overseas' leaving his wife with barely enough money to fill the family Volvo? And what about those other two whose husbands have suddenly lost perfectly secure jobs in banks they've worked at for years. How else do you explain their refusal even to discuss the circumstances? It's not coincidence, Joe."

I thought of the people I had spoken to. The divorced lawyer who had found solace away from the stresses of work in the arms of a young Czech electrician, only to find him leafing through the filing cabinet in her spare room-cum-office. The father of twin girls who lived in daily terror of the postman after a brief fling with a muscular roofer had ended when pillow talk turned to demands for information about a takeover bid he was involved in. His refusal had resulted in threats that his wife would receive pictures of the two men cavorting in the marital bed.

I sighed heavily, "Miranda, first almost everyone who lives round here, including you, is connected to the City in some way. Second, the credit crunch has claimed a lot of careers over the last few months and caused a lot of stress and soul-searching. Third, a lot of these nannies are young and very pretty. Rich successful men are used to getting what they desire, just look at Hugo."

It was a throwaway remark but Miranda jolted away, leaving me blustering, "Um, sorry, I didn't mean to imply..."

"You couldn't see the expression in their eyes, Joe!" she snapped. "It's like seeing the aftermath of some horrible explosion in which everything they built their lives around has been destroyed; trust most of all. And the common factor is Polish & Check."

"Well, it would be wouldn't it? That's the link we're looking for. That's why we contacted all these people in the first place. Look, I can see that in a few cases there has been some funny business. And of course it's awful, they've taken these strangers into their trust, given them access to their most precious assets—their families and their homes. When that trust is abused, especially with their spouse, the very person they trusted most, it must be horrific. But it happens, all the time, Miranda. Not everyone is as loyal as you."

She gave me a long-suffering sideways glare. "Change the record, Joe. Anyway this is not about us; it's about other people, lots of them, families and children. Exactly what you and I value most. If someone is deliberately setting out to destroy that—well it's wrong, it's criminal. And it's our duty to expose it." She was flustered and close to tears. Hormones, I thought, but I kept that to myself.

"Distasteful, yes, but I doubt there is anything criminal about it," I said soothingly. "Even if the girls and boys get paid off, it's not blackmail."

"What about Ted Hansford? Someone was blackmailing him. You, supposedly." Whether or not it was calculated to, her comment struck at the root of my reticence to see things her way.

"Well since any chance of talking to Kristina has departed on the plane to Prague and as I don't fancy another tongue lashing from Gail, I can't see how we can do more than speculate about that."

"I don't get you, Joe. One minute you are committed to this, the next you start back-peddling." She sounded thoroughly deflated.

Now I did put my hand on her shoulder, though fraternally. "It's not that, Miranda. Look, like I said, I agree that, in some cases these kids, because that's what they are, do appear to have made clumsy attempts to take advantage of their trusted positions. But I don't see it as systemic, or company policy. If it were I'd be happy to expose it, but where's our proof? We have a handful of allegations and suspicions but that's all. No one wants to take their grumbles any further, or go to the police. Most of them only

95

talked to us anonymously. I don't know what more we can do."

Miranda shrugged off my arm and unfolded herself from the sofa. "It's still wrong and makes me want to sack Marta and get rid of those bloody builders."

"Oh, right. That's what this is all about, is it?" I smacked my palm to my forehead and feigned shock. "You've had me calling up half of North West London because you suspect Hugo of…erm, making eyes at the comely Marta?"

"Shut up!" she snapped back.

"You've got to admit, she is somewhat shapely," I teased, "and those boots and leggings, and her little gypsy tops."

"She dresses like a tart," Miranda hissed.

"Come on Miranda, you were young once." Maybe had I been able to see properly, I would have noticed her tears before I heard her sobs. She stood in front of me limp and quaking, splashing the wooden floor with heavy drops. I stood to hold her but she recoiled from me as if we were both positively charged magnets.

"Miranda, I'm sorry, I didn't mean to…"

She turned her back to me and hugged herself, rocking slightly. I heard her breathing calm and after a couple of minutes could see her wiping her eyes and cheeks on the forearms of her mauve cashmere sweater. As she turned her blotchy face to me she muttered, "Okay, Joe. Just bad timing."

I was out of words and resorted to the clichéd offer of a cup of tea. The tension in the room seemed to lift as we moved apart and I left for the kitchen.

When I returned, having raided Eithne's secret stash of chocolate biscuits, Miranda had her back to me again; shoulders slumped and staring out towards her occupied home. I felt a sudden urge to loop my arms around her waist, to volunteer words of comfort and reassurance. Instead I cleared my throat and said, "Hob Nob?"

The low autumn sun caught the gold in her hair, giving her a glowing halo as she turned to face me. Her relieved smile was also radiant, though I suspected, equally merely an illusion.

After her third chocolate biscuit she seemed resolved, though her approach was oblique. "Are you happy using the MP3 recorder I gave you? It does make things easier doesn't it?" I nodded enthusiastically, my mouth full. "You know, you are right, Joe, we do need something more attributable. I think it's time you had a chat with Rachel Morgenstern."

I didn't quite spit coffee and crumbs all over the floor, though it took a few seconds for me to clear my airway and gasp, "Why me?"

Miranda was business-like, "Two reasons; first, she and I disagree over parenting issues; she's far too lenient with her little bully of a son. Second, she's always rather fancied you."

"Another one of the things you talk about at girly coffee mornings, I suppose." Still, I felt oddly flattered.

"Don't get too big headed, you're not that hot a topic of conversation."

Chapter 8

The house on Belsize Square, was, like its neighbours, an imposing four-storey stucco fronted Victorian property. Its perfection was only slightly marred by the estate agent's sign in the ground-floor window; the very presence of which emphasised the need for a quick sale.

I hadn't wanted to come empty-handed, but thought that Rachel would have had enough flowers and biscuits of late. Eventually I'd settled on some good quality coffee beans.

She opened the door wordlessly and I had difficulty locating her in the dark hallway. Instinctively, I put out my hand to locate her shoulder and my fingers brushed her chest, making us both shudder. We exchanged an awkward embrace, the skin of her cheek felt loose next to mine.

The belief that I was intruding grew as I followed her silhouette towards the large south-facing window in the sitting room. Always tall and slim, the figure she cut was positively gaunt now. A long dark dress drooped over her once erect trunk and when she turned to face me, her cheeks were sallow beneath bruised-looking eyes. She reminded me of an exotic flower that had begun to lose its bloom. I felt I should tend to her but didn't know where to start.

The house had been her fourth and favourite child. Money and attention had been lavished upon it and it in turn had performed regularly to impress friends and colleagues with its polished perfection. Now it was more like a tousled teenager, with possessions scattered petulantly near, not in, its cupboards.

Two of Rachel's children were, like my own, at school but the little one, Leah, was crawling around amongst the packing cases, scrumpling tissue paper as she moved over it, slug-like in her baby grow. I knelt down beside her and said hello. She raised her arms to be picked up and as I did so she hugged me to her chubby frame squealing, "Daddy, daddy."

The innocence of the little girl's hope punched a hole in the dam holding back my emotions, through which poured the weight of grief and anger I felt when considering her family's plight, that of the Hansfords and all the hurt in life from which I would fail to protect my own children. Hot tears streaked down my cheeks as I returned the toddler's hug.

Rachel was also in tears when she came over to take Leah from me. Seeing her mother upset and the dawning realisation that I was not her daddy, she began to sob loudly, which at least removed the risk of another awkward exchange between Rachel and me.

Leah was eventually settled in front of Baby Mozart after which Rachel made coffee from the freshly opened packet I had brought and we sat down on the sofa. Normally so fluid and elegant she seemed angular and unable to settle comfortably. Her eyes remained resolutely on her steaming cup as if making contact with anything living would bring on her tears again.

"Thanks for the coffee, Joe. I have really missed a good cup. I just can't bring myself to go out; everyone seems to be looking at me with such pity. I can sense the kind words hovering on their lips, but I just need space and time to think."

It is an advantage of partial sight over other disabilities that I rarely see the pity in people's eyes, but I certainly sense it. I wanted to tell her that its presence is dulled with the passage of time, though it never passes completely. Instead I kept my counsel; people talk more when they feel you are listening and I had no idea how to phrase the questions I had agreed to ask.

Rachel glanced over at the child enthralled by the idiot lantern, then quickly back to her cup. "But you're not here to offer coffee and sympathy are you Joe?"

Feeling even more like the bailiff I shook my head and sipped my own steaming drink. "No I thought I'd see whether there was anything practical I could do, moving boxes, changing light bulbs, taking Leah to the swings, you know."

Rachel raised her sunken eyes for a moment, scrutinising my face. As she did, I felt strangely vulnerable. It only slightly prepared me for the blow that came.

"I'm not a very merry widow, if that's what you're here for."

I could only hope that my aghast expression was a true reflection of the shock that exploded inside me. I held her cold, passionless gaze for a time as I composed my reply. "I'm sorry, Rachel, but even in more carefree days I've always valued my marriage above my short-term desires. If I can help you as a friend, I will do all that I can."

"What a shame we can't all be as smug as you." She was unabashed; a bitter, brittle note foremost in her voice. "You're right though, that's how it starts; the satisfaction of short-term desires. A bit of practical help, someone to do the things that Daniel didn't get round to doing...or couldn't do," the glint of a tear running down her cheek caught the low October sun streaming through the window "will never do now..." she looked down and pulled a hanky from her sleeve before noiselessly blowing her nose.

I shifted uncomfortably. Much as I wished to protest my innocence, I needed to hear more and, if I'm honest, I recognised the tactic she described. I had changed a lot of light bulbs in Miranda's house.

"I guess Daniel was never around much, even at weekends." It sounded limp as I said it.

100

"Daniel only seemed to need me around when it suited him. I had become an expression of his domestic perfection; part of the reward for all his hard work; 'look at what my success has brought me, has paid for'. My lover was different, he noticed me, he knew me as a woman—a feeling, independent woman." The tang of her lingering passion lent piquancy to her words.

I looked over towards her daughter, who was still absorbed by the DVD, and wondered whether the same distraction had been used while her mother was Pole dancing. Turning back to Rachel I tried to sound neutral, "I'm not here to judge you, Rachel, god knows I've felt taken for granted and lonely and yes I have thought of taking solace elsewhere. Maybe in my case the proposition is easier to turn down because all the women I meet look after children themselves and so are part of the world I'd want to escape."

She sniffed, clearly nonplussed, "You have no idea do you; how much pressure there is simply being a woman and living around here? Do you think we can just roll out of bed and put on yesterday's T-shirt and jeans or leave our hair un-brushed? You probably believe that we get all dressed-up for your benefit, you and all the other men but you're so wrong. It's all for the other women. It's like a costume drama. We dress for each other every single day projecting the success of our *Stepford Wives* existence and terrified of the judgement of the pecking order. My clothes, my car, my sunglasses, how often I have my hair done and by whom; it's all part of some oppressive code. Daniel used to laugh and say that he worked to keep me in a position where I could spend enough to keep him hungry for the next promotion. It's a machine. A vicious, unforgiving machine!"

"Jesus, I never realised, um, you all look so..." natural would have been the natural word, but I knew how much

101

botox and collagen and nipping and tucking went on, so settled for "effortless."

Rachel snorted. "The worst thing is, you men take it all for granted. Then after your children have wrecked our figures, the little criticisms start getting dropped into conversation; the comparisons with your friends' perfect wives. I used to feel like screaming at Daniel 'you and your self-obsessed City chums have no idea what's going on while you are at work; how many of those wives you idolise are screwing their personal trainers; how many of us are on anti-depressants or in therapy; how truly bloody miserable we are because we have everything and are nothing.'"

She was staring at a point on the wall behind my head, as if all the men responsible for the golden cage were ranged there; she stood without it now, cast out by her husband's suicide, soiled goods. I cleared my throat awkwardly hoping the action would bring inspiration, "Er, did Daniel know about, erm, how you felt?"

Again a brittle laugh accompanied her answer, "He should have done, I dropped enough hints, but no when our relationship became sterile he assumed it was my problem; said he'd heard that anti-depressants can reduce sexual appetite. He bought me a vibrator, then a disgusting video and some costumes—all the things *he* really wanted. Finally he sent me to a sex therapist. He never once asked what I wanted. He never realised that I craved tenderness and understanding and time. Then he decided I needed a project, 'something to fulfil the artist in me' he said. So he suggested I remodel the house, 'express my inner self'. And boy did I find fulfilment in that!"

The bitter frustration of her tone had been replaced with a new cadence, one of husky excitement, one that did not brook interruption. I squeezed my now empty coffee cup.

"No doubt they're all painting him as just a pretty plumber but Zarek is so much more than that."

My hand, like the rest of me, felt momentarily numb as I absorbed the name and the shock that came with it. It was clear now why Miranda had sent me here. I forced my ears to tune back into what Rachel was saying.

"He has a degree in engineering and his English is excellent, with a gorgeous ponderous ring to it. At first I just flirted with him, I had no intention of doing anything more. But as the weeks passed and the work progressed, we found ourselves spending more and more time together. He noticed things that Daniel never did. He was more gentlemanly than Daniel has been for years. He left me in no doubt that he cared about my opinion." Her eyes shone with tears but she held them in check, "He began to stay behind after the others had left, to go through the plans, to fix the light in Noa's wardrobe and then, one evening, I went to give him a peck on the cheek to say thank you and we ended up screwing on the coffee table."

Her bluntness took me aback and seeing so, she laughed at me, "You're just like Daniel; it would never have entered his mind either. You should try it some time. You might even enjoy it."

I placed my cup on the coffee table in front of me.

"He was attentive and patient, so different to what I'd had to get used to. Have you ever lain there wondering whether you are just a spectator while your partner is trying for a personal best before they roll over and start snoring? But Zarek explored me; he listened for what gave me pleasure. I felt alive, tingly; someone was giving me what I wanted instead of it always being the other way round. God then it was like a drug. I needed him more and more; you'd be amazed how much noise the sound of drills will cover. It was my revenge on the whole bullshit system. Cake and consumption all in one."

"How did Daniel find out?" I asked, squirming awkwardly.

"I told him." She was matter of fact. "I had always given Zarek gifts, mostly financial, for the little extra jobs he did. That simply continued to apply for all his services. But then he got greedy. He felt I could afford to be more generous. I felt that he was exceeding the terms of his employment; was forgetting who was boss. He didn't like being put in his place and threatened to tell Daniel. I got there before he had the chance."

"Flipping hell, Rachel. You really think he would have gone to Daniel and told him?"

"Probably. Anyway I needed to regain control of the situation. I knew Daniel wouldn't want a divorce and neither did I. It had merely been a fling and it was over now. I knew that if I went to him and told him that I had seen the error of my ways, he would forgive me and who knows, maybe things would improve between us." The brittle laugh had returned. "What I didn't realise was that Daniel would try and buy Zarek off. Silly really, I should have known, in the City it always comes down to 'how much?'"

"Christ, Daniel had it out with him! Where?"

"Here. Daniel made me stay upstairs with the children. He said I had brought enough shame on the family and that it was his job as its head to sort this mess out. Zarek was to resign immediately; the agency would have to find a replacement. Daniel offered him two month's money in return for keeping his mouth shut. But there was an almighty row and Daniel ordered Zarek out of the house. He didn't come up to say goodnight to the children and when I finally came to look for him I found him in his study, staring at some figures on the computer screen with an open bottle of whisky beside him. He hardly spoke to me, just told me that I had screwed everything up and to leave his sight.

The next day he was calmer, but more worried than I had ever seen him. He apologised to me and explained that things were very bad at work. Well you know the rest, he was sent home that lunchtime. He said he had been asked to take unpaid leave because of some problem in his department. The following week, after the bank failed, he went in to see how he could help. They wouldn't even let him into the bloody building. The security guard rang upstairs and was told to inform him that the matter was now in the hands of the FSA; implying that Daniel was solely responsible for the collapse. So he walked to Tower Bridge and...and..."

Her fight with her tears was lost and they fell fast and heavily, spattering the recently upholstered sofa. She rocked back and forwards and gasped through her sobs, "It was where he proposed to me, after dinner at the Pont De La Tour." She hugged her knees and sobbed into her lap.

Disturbed by her mother's weeping, Leah crawled over to the sofa and tugged at Rachel's dress. I bent down and tried to pick her up, but she balled her fists and batted me away. So I lowered myself to the floor, shuffled over to sit by Rachel, then gently coaxed the little girl to pull herself up and nestle between us.

Rachel looked up, her face wretched, "They've made him their scapegoat, Joe. Isn't it bad enough that my children will grow up fatherless, without ruining his reputation? But no it all comes down to image. And to preserve their own they destroy someone else's and damn those who get crushed in the process." Again she hid her face as she attempted to cover her sharp, shallow sobs.

105

Increasingly unsettled by her mother's distress Leah began to cry too. With a deep, impatient sigh Rachel stood up, placed the toddler on her bony hip and began to pace around the sofa rocking slightly from side to side. "So now you know all the sordid details you can run back to your beloved Miranda and tell her just what she can look forward to from young Zarek. Let her know that he's gifted but greedy. Or maybe she already knows and wants to find out how to disentangle herself." She turned to face me, pity dripping from her voice, "She's using you, Joe. You're too much of a pushover for her ever to be interested."

I squirmed under her steady gaze. Miranda must have tried to speak to Rachel herself, before sending me. The quick spark of anger ignited in me at finding myself Miranda's patsy now flared as I realised that Rachel had been toying with me all along. Still, it made the next question easier to ask.

"So, I guess you already know that Miranda and I are working on a piece about Polish & Check having a sideline in blackmail." As I said them the words sounded melodramatic and ridiculous. "We want to use your story to illustrate what they are doing."

Rachel's furious disdain was like a hot gust of wind in my face and I shrank before it. "You aren't serious, are you? You want to use this *story* as entertainment! Are you and that gossip-mongering bitch so desensitised?" Still clutching Leah, who had gone strangely silent, she took a step towards me. The air seemed to flee the room and I braced myself. "These are real lives. My family's! You think I drove Daniel to do what he did, don't you? I wonder how you'll portray me—'the black widow' I suppose? Well think again, pal. If a word of this finds its way into print you'll find yourself trying to hold hands with Miranda in court."

"But you said yourself that Zarek was blackmailing you. He probably threatened Daniel too. Surely you must want to stop that happening to other people?"

Her sarcasm was biting, "Oh the self-justification of providing a public service, how very unoriginal! Forget it Joe. So I had an affair, big deal. At least I had the guts to own up to it unlike so many others," I felt her glaring defiantly at my half-turned face. "You know, it was fun until Zarek took a little too much for granted. Then it was over and Daniel and I would have sorted things out. That's what people do, if they're given the chance."

Leah was agitating for her mid-morning feed. Irritably Rachel plonked her into a highchair, uncapped a jar and began to spoon the contents into the toddler's open mouth. I drew a breath to make my excuses and leave, but before I could she rounded on me again.

"If you're so desperate to write a story about what drove my husband to his death go and ask those bastards at Lachmann Bros why they were so quick to blame Daniel for the collapse of their bank. He was a good, honest lovely man who gave the best years of our married life to that damned firm. He sacrificed so much, but that counted for nothing when those shits needed to protect themselves." Her shoulders hung limply now and her loose hair clung to her wet cheeks, "I can't allow my children to grow up with that hanging over them." She nodded at the packing cases, "We're going to stay with my family in Manchester. Then, when the house sells, maybe we'll find somewhere quiet near Tel Aviv and try to find a way forward."

She sounded so proud of Daniel and spoke with such conviction that, when I read the determined set of her mouth and chin under her pretty upturned nose, her resemblance to an old-time American pioneer was overwhelming. She too wore that mantle of fleeing oppression with all the pain it engendered and I knew that the long journey ahead of her

107

was a necessary part of her slow recovery. I held my hand out to her and said the only words that seemed appropriate, "Good luck, Rachel."

Chapter 9

Outside, the cloud seemed to have dropped a thousand feet. The coffee in my stomach felt like battery acid and was making my whole body quiver. I tapped my way angrily towards the bus stop. Miranda was at a Pilates class until midday, so I had to content myself by leaving a terse, cryptic message on her voicemail. Even the prospect of meeting Brad and Dino for a pub lunch had been soured. I needed to order my thoughts and feeling suddenly cold strode past the bus stop and up through Belsize Village towards Hampstead and The Duke of Wellington. As I walked past Starbucks, so long the haunt of Ladies Who Skinny Latte, I recognised the self-conscious chatter of a group of local fathers having their mid-morning power coffee.

In the wake of the credit crunch the preponderance of Eastern European au pairs at the school gates was being replaced by former City traders sporting ten day stubble like a badge of freedom. In pressed designer jeans they talked guardedly of headhunters and leads they were chasing up, comparing 'dedicated out-placement executives' as if they were personal trainers. If the 'flesh traders' had been rehabilitated in their eyes, I wondered, how long they would need to be unemployed before they recognised the significance of my job and became less condescending.

Dino and Brad were already at the pub. Judging by the volume of their greeting they probably had been since opening time. They had locked horns on their favourite battleground — global warming. Dino, the Democrat New Yorker with a soft spot for Hilary Clinton and Brad, Pacific North-West Republican to the core, seemed only to find common ground in criticising the arcane workings of British infrastructure. After the morning I had had I was happy to sit quietly with my pint and listen to them squabble.

Then Glenn arrived with the impact of an incendiary bomb, holding four pints in his hod-like hands and declaring, "I dunno what you blokes are getting so worked up about. It doesn't really matter whether the States does anything about climate change or not, either way you're fucked. The future's in the hands of the Chinese and the Indians. Within fifty years the US will just be a sideshow; if it hasn't collapsed into civil war."

The fulminating of the two proud Americans was only cut short twenty minutes later by the need to order food and more beer. Though we had called a halt to hostilities while we tucked into bangers and mash, Brad and Dino still had fight in them.

"Joe, man, what's with the frikkin' postmen over here?" Brad demanded. "Every letter I've got this week has been soakin' wet."

"Climate change," muttered Dino.

"No they've always had lousy stinking weather on Mud Island, mate," Glenn chimed in. "That's why the Poms are so hopeless at cricket; they only ever get to practise indoors."

Through his heavy cold, Dino sounded even more nasal than usual, "Yeah 'n' while we're on the subject, why the hell can't your stoopit limey Royal Mail operate a proper redirection service?" I braced myself for the inevitable, 'in the US…' but Dino instead dropped his voice. "I mean, I know the guy is dead and I don't mean to bring it up again but," he looked from Brad to me, "how long am I gonna be getting his mail? I gotta bag full of it and it just keeps on coming. It's morbid man."

"I had a mate back in Oz who got a tax demand addressed to his dad two years after the old fella had kicked the bucket," chortled Glenn, "Death and taxation eh?" The others must have shot him a look because he stopped

110

abruptly. "Oh, shit, sorry mate. Ah well, comes to us all sooner or later and at least it's quicker with a gun, eh?"

"Well I don't see how China's gonna stop from breaking up itself without Western co-operation. They need us." I could feel Dino's discomfort.

I tapped him on the arm, "Look, I'm going to send Ted's kids a scrapbook of stuff my girls have done for them. Why don't you drop all the post round to me, I'll go through it and forward anything that looks important. That's always assuming your notoriously efficient American postal system doesn't manage to lose it."

"Yeah, well the next lot goes in the trash," Dino growled, "I'll drop by tomorrow before my run."

With tremendous self-control I had managed to keep it to two and a half pints at lunch and had left the pub feeling like an air-sprung god. By the time I had walked back down to Fawkes Close though the euphoria had worn off and I felt like a bag of shite. I rang Miranda's doorbell and a dusty gnome of a man who reeked of stale sweat answered.

"Mrs Lethbridge in?" I was conscious of the beer and cigarettes on my breath but doubted that he'd notice.

"No Inglisch." His reply was as predictable as it was unhelpful. I pushed past him and headed to Miranda's gloomy study.

He trotted after me whinnying Zarek's name. I supposed he thought I had come to complain about the noise. Zarek appeared at the bottom of the stairs as my fingers located Miranda's door handle. I ignored him and entered without knocking.

I heard her start and the headphones clattered onto the desk. Then she sniffed and I knew that coffee would soon be at hand. There was a forced lightness to her tone that experience told me would be accompanied by the flicker of

111

a smile at the edge of her crooked mouth when she asked, "Goodness, did you have to get her drunk to talk?"

"Ha, ha. No there was a lunchtime meeting of the Hampstead Motherfuckers' Club." That would have removed her silly grin. I'd had enough of being toyed with.

She had her back to me and was busy with the espresso machine. "Oh, Joe, you are so…unspoiled."

A double macchiato later and I was flying again; I started to regale her with my reported speech but she cut me short. "You did remember to turn on the MP3 recorder didn't you?"

"Yes mum," I mugged at her then triumphantly pulled the machine out of the pocket of my fleece, where it had been all morning. I felt only slightly chastened when she noted that it was still recording, but hoped that we wouldn't have to sit through my tuneless and obscene rendition of 'Run to You' sung as I walked down the hill from the pub.

After I had wished Rachel 'good luck' Miranda, mercifully, turned the MP3 off. I'd been scrutinising her face by the light of the anglepoise on her desk. She was now midway between frowning and scowling, wordlessly tapping a biro on her mouse mat. Then she sighed in annoyance, "Oh well, you did your best."

Had I not been so pissed off I might have felt crushed; obviously my best was far from good enough. Colour rose in my cheeks, aided by the beer and caffeine. "Thanks a bunch, Miranda. Sounds like I got further with her than *you* did. And, under the circumstances, I don't see how I could have done any better. Anyway, she's adamant that you can't use any of this." I pulled myself up short; maybe there had been enough angry words already today.

Miranda tutted, "Maybe if I…"

That small, dismissive noise flicked the 'oh bugger it' switch in me. "Maybe if you had told me that you had already tried to talk to Rachel then things might have gone differently. How the hell do you think I felt when I realised, especially after what's happened with Gail? You could at least have told me she was shagging Zarek, for god's sake!"

Miranda remained silent; I ploughed on cruelly, "After all I understand you're a gossip-mongering bitch. But I'm a man so I suppose I only qualify to run errands for your club?"

She kicked my shin painfully.

"Oh come on Miranda, admit it, Zarek and Kristina are just after a bit of value added. You're right, they see us with all that we have and think 'I want a piece of that'. There are a lot of lonely thirty and forty-somethings out there whose spouses are wage slaves and who are up for a bit of comfort. So Zarek and Kristina make a bit on the side for being a bit on the side. So what? There's no law against it. Everyone pays for sex in one way or another."

"Go and make your cynical speech in the pub with your piss-head friends, Joe. I've got work to do." Her voice was tart, willing me out of the door.

"Oh well I do beg your pardon, Miranda. Maybe it's you who needs to get out more, so you can get a bit of perspective on this obsession of yours."

There was an icy silence between us, but then something in the air changed and she turned away to fiddle with the espresso machine.

"What is it Miranda, what aren't you telling me?" Somehow I knew the answer as I asked the question. Just as I knew instinctively that, though she had turned towards me, she was looking away from my face as she spoke.

"Promise me you'll actually listen to what I have to say before you dismiss it?"

I'd never heard her beg before, so I nodded.

113

She took a deep breath, "Okay, it's Marta. It's as if she's got some kind of hold over Hugo."

Tedium slouched across me, replacing interest with annoyance at not having left when I'd had the chance. I kept my jaw firmly clenched, knowing that there was more to come.

"You remember her jaunt over to Poland a couple of weeks ago? Even you said it was short notice. I'd have expected Hugo to go ballistic; he certainly wouldn't let anyone behave like that in his office. But in her case he simply waved his hand and said 'Oh, dear, just make sure she lets you know earlier next time'. Now she's informed me that she can't baby-sit tomorrow night. Well, it's part of her contract so I told her she had to; I've arranged to go out and that's that. Do you know what the impudent little madam said? "Hadn't you better check that with Mr Lethbridge?" So I *did* ring him, to let him know just how uppity she has become, but instead of backing me up my darling husband laughed at me and said I was being hard-hearted. He even said that if I wasn't happy for her to suggest a substitute babysitter I should consider rearranging *my* plans!"

For once, I was inclined to agree with Hugo. "You can't honestly reckon that Hugo's shagging Marta. No, no way!" Nothing would have given me greater pleasure than for Hugo to prove what a selfish bastard he was and, yes I could imagine him slavering over a hot secretary, but not Marta. He'd class her as 'trade'.

Miranda was waiting for me to say something. I cast around but could only manage, "Anyway, surely they're never in the house alone together, are they?"

She harrumphed. "See, I knew you'd think it was stupid. Argh, maybe I do too, but she's got so over-familiar and, well, superior. I can't stand it."

The echo of Rachel's complaint about Zarek was unmistakable. God I'd had enough of all this! Whatever the truth behind it, 'the story' had become too mired in marital disharmony for my taste. I wanted out and suspected Miranda would prefer me to go. She needed someone to support her theories, not question them. Besides, I needed to clean my teeth before pick-up.

I stood up and said simply, "Like I said, you should get out more. Drop the story and take me to an art exhibition or something."

"Okay, maybe. I'm sorry, Joe, I should have been straight with you and you did do a good job with Rachel. I think she needed someone to talk to anyway—a man."

"Yeah, I'm sorry too Miranda, I didn't mean to get shirty. I've really enjoyed doing all this—working together again. It's been fun."

She brightened a little. "How about coffee next Thursday? Usual place, my treat for your hard work?"

I nodded and left, striding past Zarek who I greeted with a cheery "afternoon" and following the trail of cigarette smoke upstairs to the open front door. There was half an hour to drink lots of water and get rid of the smell of beer from my breath before I was due at the school gates. My Gap jeans may not have been pressed but I still had standards.

Most people can, I think, imagine what they would dislike or miss most were they to lose their sight. Few ever ask whether it has its upsides. There is the obvious advantage of free public transport within London and reduced fares beyond. However, for me, the thing that makes my disability as much a privilege as a curse is the daily kindness I experience from others. In a world where we are bombarded with examples of man's inhumanity and

115

'stranger danger', it's easy to forget that the vast majority of people are decent and compassionate. Those who are not are, in my experience, usually ignorant rather than malicious. Of course, jealousy plays a large part in man's abuse of his fellows and very few people are jealous of the disabled, free travel passes notwithstanding.

The young hoodie helping me over the traffic-choked High Street had a proprietary grip on my arm. He was merrily ordering the ambling shoppers dazzled by early Christmas decorations 'owtdaway' as we pushed through the autumnal evening gloom.

Many years ago, I learned from the glinting scowl of a facially pierced QPR supporter who offered to help me over Shepherds Bush Green late one night, that I was displaying the same ignorance and prejudice I so loathe in others, by trying to ignore his kindness. As we wove through the drunks and junkies sprawled out on that triangular testament to the supremacy of the car, I had to admit that my independence had become strictly mental. In physical matters I was going to have to start asking for, and accepting, help, with good grace and from whoever was prepared to give it.

It was rather the same when I started using a white stick during daylight hours. I felt I was admitting defeat but after six or so years of, what Eithne assured me was perfectly avoidable cranial bruising, it was probably time to do so. Overnight, people stopped getting angry when they walked into me. Lampposts jumped out to head-butt me less frequently and offers of guidance over the road flooded in —often from total strangers. The human race has reached its dizzy evolutionary heights as much by problem solving and cooperation as by natural selection. My daily difficulties are easily solved but only if I cooperate.

Safely deposited at the correct bus stop my hooded guide patted me on the shoulder and asked "Ya wight fwo here bwo?" I nodded and patted his scrawny bicep, thanking him a little too much for his comfort. He turned away and shambled off.

Behind me a woman bathed in sickly Trésor perfume remarked loudly to her friend how uncouth and ill-attired the youth of today was; "Trying to look like hoodlums. That's what hoodie is short for you know?" A minute later the bus arrived and she tried to barge past me, so I whacked her ankle with my stick.

The bus dropped me in front of the girls' school. I stood in my usual spot by the gate straining through the excited babble to hear Jenny's distinctive tenor discussing the day's events with her little sister. By the time they ran up to hug me I already knew that the chicken sausages at lunch had been 'gopping', the new winter coat sported by Miss Davies 'supercoowell' and the mental maths test 'pipsy'. This makes it easier for me to navigate my exit without knocking into too many hyper members of the three-foot high club while appearing to give the girls the attention they crave at the end of a school day. Guided now by Nell's flashing trainers and the familiar calls of 'make way for The King' from the older kids we made it unscathed back to the bus stop.

I hadn't forgotten about the playdate, it had just slipped my mind. When I got back to the house Veronika was already there, trying hard to maintain an effortless calm while her two boys shrieked and play-fought with increasing ferocity amid the building materials.

Tall, Nordic and glamorous, Veronika had no doubt once been stunning. Now however, it took leather boots and camel-hoof leggings to attract the whistles and admiring glances—for the most part in appreciation of her audacity. Bathed in the bright light of the porch, the lithe figure clad in a tight cropped jacket and red suede thigh-highs momentarily had its desired effect on my soft-focus eyes

117

and vivid imagination. My reverie was swiftly broken by the equally desperate call of Nell's need to empty her bladder.

"Hallow daahling." There was a breathlessness to her rich silken voice. My unsuspecting lips received a collagen-plump kiss and I felt her uplifted breasts pressed to my chest. The keys fell from my fingers, jangling on the tiles. She drew away, rested a hand on my hip and sank to her knees in front of me, lingering there as she retrieved them.

Once inside, the children's thoughts turned immediately to food. They disappeared upstairs with a promise of pasta and pesto within ten minutes and I put the kettle on. Veronika stood close by, resting her heavy gaze upon me while I opened cupboards and rifled through the fridge. Cheddar and grater in hand I glanced at her as we sat down at the kitchen table. Her languid grey eyes sought to hold mine and convey the prospect of athletic afternoons together.

"Oh, how *wonderful*, it's Luca's favourite meal! You are *so* thoughtful," she purred. A mental bell rang and my defences shot up.

"So how is Eithne?" She asked with disinterest as she leant forward and slowly licked her index finger to pick up a stray ribbon of cheese. "Is she away, *again*?" I heard her tongue rasp gently against her long, straight digit.

"Erm, yes," my reply was cautious, "but only in the Manchester office, and she's back tomorrow."

"It is *so* difficult for you, she is *always* gone." The sympathy in her voice was cloying and the beautiful polished hand that now rested gently on my forearm somewhat disturbing. I stood up and nodded towards the cooker. She sighed slightly and stretched out her hand to be helped up. She rose effortlessly, a testament to three yoga classes a week, not needing my supporting arm which she nevertheless held for a few seconds too long.

I tried to busy myself, wiping the work surface and getting out plates and cartons of juice, glad to have my hands occupied. Veronika draped herself over the marble countertop and sighed as she told me how often her husband was away and how tired he always seemed to be; all the while I could feel her hungry eyes roving over me.

Then out of nowhere, "You look *so* sad and lonely, Joe."

Taken aback by her directness, I looked up from the cheese grater and into those beckoning blue-grey pools. Her cool hand rose to stroke my cheek and I heard the gentle brush of the Lycra on her thighs as she took half a step towards me, her lips slightly parted softening her taught face.

My heart quickened, my own mouth, firmly shut was dry and tasted stale. Her hand was behind my neck now, drawing me towards her. Her other hand had moved to rest on my belt buckle. I could hear the children playing happily upstairs. Her half-closed eyes never left mine. Nimble fingers unfastened my buckle before exploring below. The small of my back ached where it was pressed up against the work surface. As her lips brushed mine, her lower hand squeezed and she moaned suggestively.

A sudden bubbling hiss from behind me caused us both to flinch and allowed me gently to push her away. "Looks like supper's ready," I mumbled hoarsely as I watched the starchy mess gush from the pan of boiling pasta and spread over my polished hob. "Do you mind calling the children down, please."

She tossed her head and her hair arced round, brushing my face like a rebuke. As I listened to her provocative footfall cross the parquet floor of the sitting room, I had a strong mental image of her rotating buttocks in tight

119

trousers. I refastened my jeans with difficulty and, full of rueful relief, ladled out the pasta.

Chapter 10

I *had* forgotten the coffee Miranda and I had arranged for the following Thursday and knew that it showed in my voice when she called to ask where I was. Others have the luxury of checking the caller identity before picking up; I could do so but by the time I've found my glasses the voicemail has usually cut in, so I tend to answer regardless.

On that grim, misty November morning the prospect of Café Noir should have been a comforting one, but I'd been in a foul mood since Monday when Eithne had announced that she'd be working late the next two nights to clear her desk before flying to Montreal for a fortnight. The ensuing argument had left her furious and me resentful and guilty. After all, I knew that she wanted nothing more than to spend more time at home, something that our large mortgage and my minimal earning capacity hardly facilitated, and yet somehow I felt taken for granted.

My sulk and her absence made the children grouchy and difficult, so that both nights I had hardly been able to put them to bed quick enough. Left alone with my thoughts I had initially found another focus for my frustration in brooding over how best to approach Gail. Should I tell her what Miranda and I had discovered, such as it was; that it appeared she and Ted weren't the only ones being scammed? Even if I assured her that I'd check all the post before sending it on, I couldn't prevent Kristina from going direct to TMB. I could just hear Gail's scathing response and that, inevitably, had recalled her taunt about trust being the crutch of the ignorant.

Only the prospect of actually having to speak to my wife had stopped me from phoning to check that she really was at her desk and not out gallivanting with Jean-Pierre. After all, everyone else seemed to be at it, though I'd been the last to know.

She'd finally come home at 2 am on Wednesday morning and I'd pretended to be asleep as she scurried round the bedroom preparing for her imminent departure. At breakfast I had, for once, made no effort to deter the girls from giving their mum a guilt trip about going away and she had left without kissing any of us goodbye. On the way back from school I'd stopped at the off-licence and bought myself a bottle of whisky.

Consequently, I now had a thumping hangover, fuzzy brain and eyes more opaque than ever. Listening to Miranda gripe about her family's conspicuous consumption was not high on my list of preferred options; rather a couple of ibuprofen, a litre of water and a long shower. She had, however, sounded in need of a friend. So, always a sucker for a damsel in distress, I trudged mournfully up the hill.

Despite the gloom of a day that had, as yet, refused to throw off its covers, Hampstead was thronging with people sporting dark glasses, peering into bright boutique windows and hoping to be mistaken for somebody famous.

The steamy air of the café was in sharp contrast to the core-chilling mist outside. I heard a chair scrape as Miranda stood up and, unusually, came over to guide me to the table.

"Thanks for coming, Joe." She was husky and I guessed she too had had little sleep or had been crying. I was beginning to sweat and the prickliness left me wondering just how little whisky I would find in the bottle. As I peeled off my jacket and fleece, I hoped it was only my hypersensitive nose that registered the sour smell of my moist armpits.

I ordered a Coke, not wishing to risk the laxative properties of espresso, and downed half on its arrival. "You sounded upset my oldest friend. Trouble at mill?"

122

"Promise you won't give me a lecture if I share this with you, Joe," her voice was small and possessed none of its usual coquettishness. I nodded, which hurt the back of my neck. I was happy simply to listen.

"Well, apart from the fact that I feel disgusting because those Polish imbeciles have disconnected the boiler so there's no hot water in the house; only that things have gone from bad to worse with Marta. She's become even more bolshy and off-hand. On Monday, I asked her to tidy up the children's toys in the living room and she told me that I set them a poor example and should learn to tidy up after myself. Then there's the food that she takes from the fridge, it's as if she deliberately chooses the things that she knows I have bought for myself and eats them to annoy me. I sat down with her yesterday and, very calmly, made my points and gave her an opportunity to explain herself. Do you know what she said to me?"

I raised a questioning eyebrow and waited for her to continue, all the time dreaming of the soothing properties of a hot shower and maybe a little nap.

"She told me that Hugo and the children are perfectly happy with her services and that she believes that the problem lies in my attitude...which she puts down to jealousy." She rocked back in her chair radiating defiance and anger.

My brain was feeling claggy and slow, "Jealousy?"

"Of her! Of her relationship with the children! She practically told me that she's a better homemaker than me!"

"She does bake exceedingly good cakes," I mumbled, regretting it immediately. "Um, what does Hugo say about all this?"

I guessed she was scowling because her reply sounded as if it had been forced through a tight gap in her mouth. "My darling husband still thinks she's wonderful. He feels that it would be disruptive and upsetting to the children were we to let her go. He even said that he has been considering giving her a pay rise because he rates her so highly! Can you believe it?"

I remained silent, picturing the scene between husband and wife; dispassionate logic confronting wounded pride.

"Are you just going to sit there in silence, Joe? Usually you have so much to say." She was simply giving vent to her ire on the closest target. I stayed quiet, swirling the remaining half inch of coke around the bottom of the glass and wishing I'd learned how to say no to Miranda.

She harrumphed loudly, but was in full spate now so was not going to be put off. "Well, obviously I couldn't leave things like that, so this morning I had another meeting with her and read her the riot act. I told her that I would not accept such behaviour and that she owed me an apology. She laughed in my face! For once I found myself envying my mother. She would have put the puffed-up little brat over her knee and spanked her. I had to content myself with telling her that it was time for her to find another job. You know what she said? She told me that she thought I should check with Hugo before making such a big decision!"

I shook my head in what I hoped looked like disbelief, my interest just about still alive.

Miranda ploughed on. "So I dialled his number there and then, to show her just how wrong she was. He's in Glasgow this week at some investment conference. And as far as I'm concerned he can bloody well stay there. When I told him I was dismissing Marta on the spot he actually instructed me not to do anything rash. We could, he said, discuss it when he got back to London and I had calmed down. Then he told me that he was terribly busy and had to get on."

I felt a small inward glow of satisfaction; maybe finally Miranda was starting to see what a selfish git she had married.

"So I hung up on him," Miranda continued, "and Marta asked me in that ever-so-innocent voice she uses whether I had changed my mind. She had a sly grin plastered over her silly little face and I'm afraid I lost my temper. I demanded to know how long she'd been sleeping with my husband. When she denied it, I asked her how else she was blackmailing him. I said I knew all about Zarek extorting money from Rachel Morgenstern and that I'd talked to others who her agency had been blackmailing too. I even told her that I was writing a feature article exposing their whole sordid scheme in the national press. The little bitch just laughed in my face and told me I should see a doctor to get my medication changed!" Miranda was so pumped up that her breath was coming in short bursts.

"Christ Miranda," I shook my swimming head, unable to express what I thought of her precipitous outburst.

"Oh don't tell me! You agree with Hugo don't you? You think I'm being neurotic; go on say it!"

Though I couldn't see her in the gloom I raised my eyes to where I thought her face would be and licked my dry lips. "Miranda, I have never agreed with Hugo on anything apart from his taste in partner. I have no view on Marta other than that she is easy to talk to and easy on the eye. I would love to be able to afford some help about the house, however, I also recognise that the more gadgets you have in life the more there is to go wrong."

"Well thank you very much, Joe! So that's it then, I'm a spoilt cow with too much time on her hands and this is all my overwrought imagination? Is that what you think? Well, I'm sure Ted and Daniel are delighted to look down and see you sleepwalking through life."

The area between my shoulder blades felt clammy and my head was beginning to thud as the painkillers wore off. Miranda too was irritating me intensely.

"Oh just sit back and let it all flow by Joe, why don't you."

That was it. "Oh give it a rest Miranda!" I snapped at her. "Maybe Hugo and Marta are right; you're not exactly a bundle of fun to be around at the moment. I know the work and noise get you down. It's the same for everyone in the Close and none of the rest of us will get any benefit from your home cinema. You've become really prickly of late and now accusing Marta of shagging Hugo and blackmail! Well, yes I can see her getting a little defensive and asking for a second opinion. Hugo's selfishness verges on solipsism; I've been trying to tell you that for years but in your infinite wisdom, you made your bed with him—and I'm not into threesomes."

I forced my chair back so violently that it overbalanced and clattered to the tiled floor. The café went silent and I dropped to my hands and knees and began to grope for my jacket and stick.

"Sit down!" she hissed. I hesitated and pulled on my fleece as I waited to find out what was coming next. "It always comes back to this doesn't it, Joe? Well let's clear it up once and for all shall we and then maybe you can move on and become a fully paid up member of the adult human race."

Sorely tempted as I was to walk away, my curiosity rooted me there. I heard her suck in air to compose herself and when she spoke much of the vehemence had left her voice.

"Getting into Cambridge was my dream come true. A chance to experience a life I had only glimpsed on the telly or read about in my bedroom in Bognor. For you and Hugo

126

it was different. You both believed you had a right to be there and you both have chips on your shoulders about it; Hugo because the university let in the hoi polloi, like you; and you because they still admit the likes of Hugo. My dad was the same; 'hobnobbing with the nobs' he called it. He was proud of his clever daughter of course, but he thought I should go somewhere closer to home, with a radical campus, like Sussex. "Those toffs will chew you over then spit you back onto the floor," he told me. "Blooms that grow unexpectedly tall and lovely only get cut and dried." He was a clever, funny man who felt he never got the break that he deserved. So he spent his whole life trying to make ends meet; six months a year at Butlins, the other six chasing any odd job going. And every night he'd dull the pain of his broken dreams down at the pub—until he died there, aged forty-eight. Hugo offered me hope of getting away from all that, of writing my own future rather than always being at odds with the present and past; to show dad it could be done. You have always reminded me so much of my dad, Joe, and that's why I care for you. But I've only ever wanted to try and help light your way a bit; I could never be the light of your life. I tried to be that for dad, but he was too far down the well of his own despair. If you start drinking again, especially on top of all you smoke, your girls won't have a dad to see them graduate or walk up the aisle either. Just like you, dad was a lovely bloke, loads of his mates from the pub turned up to the funeral, but that's no substitute for an extra thirty years with your family, is it?"

She was sobbing softly to herself now and I felt the remorse of a boy watching a writhing butterfly after he's pulled its wings off.

In a choked voice I tried to make light of it, "I thought girls were meant to marry boys who reminded them of their fathers."

She shook her head, "Does Eithne remind you of your mum?"

I shivered, "No, I can't get her to beat me as regularly. I'm sorry, Miranda. And thanks, you *have* always been there and it *has* always helped and in my own warped way I have always been grateful for that. I'm truly sorry if I haven't done the same for you."

But this belied the hollow, dyspeptic ache I felt in the pit of my stomach. Something had just died and was starting to rot.

She was rustling about in her bag and pulled out a large tissue. Having blown her nose, she started to compose herself. "Look I've got to go now, I have a man to see about a boiler. What are you doing tonight?"

I hesitated. I had been planning on watching *Shaun of the Dead* for the fifth time, to concentrate on the action in the background that friends said was the funniest part, but which had so far eluded my narrow field of vision. "Oh just babysitting," I answered, contrition overpowering resolve.

"Good, Christian is at camp and Hope has got a sleepover so I'm going to try and crack a feature I'm working on, but I'd appreciate some company for an hour or so. Why don't you go home and straighten yourself out, have a shower and come round with your baby monitor at about eight, if that's okay? Oh and put your best thinking head on, I may want your undiluted opinion on something."

"Gosh Miranda, I'm flattered that you think my knowledge of anaglypta wallpaper is so invaluable!"

This time we split the bill. We left together and walked, slightly apart and in silence down the hill. We both, I think, felt drained. Outside my house she turned to me, raised her chin and sought my eyes. She looked vulnerable and small and for a fleeting second, old. "Wish me luck, eh?" She

128

smiled weakly and standing on tiptoe gave me a peck on the cheek. It was the first in seventeen years.

In many ways I have not changed much since being a student. One reason I frequent Café Noir is because it reminds me of a grotty dive in Cambridge called Los Bandidos where I lost more than a few afternoons. I am always tempted to ask Ildiko for a tequila slammer. So, fed up and nursing a hangover, and finding myself with seven hours until the girls were to be dropped home after playdates with classmates, my instinct was to call Dino, Brad and Glenn and see whether they were up for a pub lunch.

Instead, I decided to try and walk it off on Hampstead Heath. I rolled a large precautionary joint, found a hat and a warm leather jacket and set off in a dark frame of mind.

An hour later on Parliament Hill, I felt little better. I'd spread a Sainsbury's bag on a damp bench that commemorated some otherwise forgotten soul and sat down. My head buzzed partly from the previous nights' toxins, but more from the morning's exchange. I had known when, forsaking all others, I'd vowed to spend the rest of my days with Eithne that my friendship with Miranda would remain platonic. But to hear that I had merely sparked her sympathy was belittling.

My fingers closed on the joint in my pocket, confirming my intention all along. Lighting it and inhaling a long draught, I tried to push all the corrosive thoughts from my head. To send them scudding away with the low clouds crossing London. Today though, even the juxtaposition of my idleness with the millions of drones slaving in the city below me, failed to bring its usual glow of satisfaction. The balance within me had been altered; by Ted's death; by Rachel's wretchedness; by the descent of my oldest friend

129

into depression and paranoia; by receiving a few home truths from her.

I pulled hard on the sickly sweet reefer and churned her words over and over. With repetition, and THC, some of their sting was drawn. She *had* always stuck by me; always sent cards and letters when she was abroad; always forgiven me after I had repelled her. We acted like two magnets; each of us could turn and use our mutual attraction to push the other away, but never so far that we could not be drawn back together when one of us chose to turn the other cheek.

My mind drifted through its own clouds that parted to reveal a reception at a Mayfair art gallery some fifteen years ago. It was shortly before Miranda and Hugo had left for Hong Kong. I had been sent by the editor of *The Independent's* diary column to a private view of Koo Starks' breasts. Randy Prince Andy's former squeeze turned photographic artist had perfected a way of making 3D representations of her upfront assets through laborious superimposition of many layers of photomontage.

It was the third reception I had attended that evening and I was feeling somewhat jaded. The flesh chest and body piercing of the artist was far more alluring than its figurative representation. I had got my quotable one-liner from Miss Stark and noted that a couple of the seedier Tory frontbenchers had come along to ogle as well—story in the bag. I was about to leave when I heard Miranda's familiar tones cooing to Koo that her artworks were a must-have for the chic metropolitan home.

Though I kept an eye out for her pieces, I had rarely seen Miranda at work. I found a wall for support, lit a cigarette and watched the two women try to play each other to the maximum advantage. Miranda was far less direct than me, nurturing her interviewee rather than luring her. She gave the impression of being genuinely impressed by the artwork in front of her. As they laughed at some reference to personal shopping at Harvey Nicholls, I surreptitiously scribbled down Koo's quip about needing a Range Rover in Knightsbridge simply to accommodate her purchases.

When I sensed that they had got what they wanted from each other, I relieved a passing waiter of two glasses of Champagne and sauntered over.

"Hello again Ms Stark, hi Miranda, would you like a drink?" The former model was already turning away but Miranda took a glass. She smiled uncertainly, I assumed embarrassed by my non-invitation to the wedding. I decided to make her squirm a bit.

"Good nuptials were they? Honeymoon must've been exotic, judging by the tan."

"Nepal and Thailand, and yes it was lovely thanks." She laughed nervously, "I'm sorry we couldn't invite you to the wedding. Hugo has such a large family that we could only invite a few close, mutual friends."

I could feel my irritation bubbling up and swigged down the whole glass of Champagne. "You deserve better."

She grimaced, afraid I was going to make a scene, then hissed, "Not you Joe, never you. A friend yes, but not too close. I've never led you to believe otherwise. Can't you see that's why I couldn't invite you to the wedding? You and Hugo…it wouldn't have been…comfortable."

"Comfortable! What like one of your bloody perfect interiors?" My words came out far louder than intended and she winced. "They're temporary too, just like your marriage. A perfect blend of complimentary tones, everything arranged just so, the right match? It's all bollocks. You wait till Hugo tires of the décor Miranda, then you'll find you're just as replaceable as all the other soft furnishings." I knew I was ranting, that I should go but I needed to get her to agree to come to dinner with me; so I

131

could persuade her of the error of her ways, before it was too late, before she left for Hong Kong and maybe forever.

"You need to grow up, straighten out and find a purpose in life, Joe." A withering look, a dismissive toss of the head as she turned on her heel and was gone.

And that was that. As with so many things, when the object of desire is removed from the shop window, you move on; and so I did. My liver told me just before my page editor that it was time to leave. I found a job that involved less bodily abuse. As I felt less strung out so my self-confidence in social situations grew and I became less angry and defensive. I also stopped reading the papers – a little inside knowledge can spawn a great deal of contempt.

Three years later they were back. My girlfriend of the time and I received a gold-edged invitation to The Landmark Hotel in Marylebone for their welcome home party. Miranda must have considered that my time in exile was over and that I had grown up and moved on; I think I thought so too.

The two of them looked glossy and chic and I felt conspicuous in my off the peg M&S suit. Of course, I got pissed and went to kiss Miranda goodbye, awkwardly and with purpose. My girlfriend had seen both that and the obvious love Miranda radiated for her husband. Later in bed, after she'd shared her observations with me, I had my first bitter taste of impotence.

At the party, Miranda had told me that she and Hugo would be going to Glastonbury the following week courtesy of the BBC, where she was working as a researcher. They would be staying in a Winnebago, so there was no risk of Hugo getting mud in his coiffeured hair. I was too broke to afford a ticket and getting too visually impaired to gatecrash safely. Instead, I spent a green-eyed weekend watching

132

coverage from the confines of my sofa, ashtray resting on the cushion newly vacated by my now ex-girlfriend.

I saw them in the VIP tent, bouncing around to Radiohead and looking blissed-out. In my silent rage I cracked the glass of cheap vodka I was clutching. On the Monday, through a blinding hangover, I rang the Human Resources department of the American bank at which Hugo worked and, purporting to be a shocked client who had also been at the festival, lodged an anonymous complaint about drug-fuelled bad behaviour. The suggestion was enough. Hugo was sacked and I glowed with satisfaction at revenge served so cold that its origin was untraceable.

Shit however floats. Hugo merely set up a hedge fund, one of the first. Over the course of the next five years he proceeded to make a killing.

One morning, as I poured brandy into my coffee to steady my hands, I realised that I needed to move on.

Ireland, the home of so many legendary alcoholics, may have seemed an obtuse choice but, in truth, it was the best offer I got. In Leeson Street surrounded by serious drinkers, I felt self-indulgent and foolish. I eased up on myself, then met, then married, Eithne, relieved that her Dublin degree and upbringing were unlikely to bring us into contact with the demons of my past.

Amidst a euphoric crowd of twenty-somethings we surfed the wave as the city finally lived the American Dream on European money.

Just before the Millennium, Eithne landed the job she had always wanted and I was back in London. We rented a flat in Belsize Park—because Marillion had made it sound romantic in one of the songs we made love to.

Coincidence or predetermination led Eithne and Miranda to join the same NCT class, so once again Hugo and I had to shake hands. Before long our wives were inseparable,

133

comparing cravings and little kicks; although Miranda's attempts to lure Eithne back to the Catholic fold fell on deaf ears. Watching Hugo smarm Eithne had made my skin crawl, but it was on his advice that we approached Freddie with an offer on the only unsold house in Fawkes Close. With the money from my flat in Paddington and a small legacy from Eithne's spinster aunt we could just afford it— as long as the interest rates stayed low.

Miranda even helped choose the colour scheme and cot for Jenny's bedroom. Much as it galled me to feel indebted to Hugo, I told myself that without my intervention none of us would be in Hampstead anyway—the house was my commission.

It was only after Jenny's birth, when we briefly considered entrusting the care of our beautiful daughter to a complete stranger that a sense of my responsibilities dawned on me. Eithne's hard-won career was important both to her and to us as a family, but I merely had a not-so-well paid job that got harder to do as I lost my sight. In my ignorance I even believed I'd have time to write about my new life as a Hampstead househusband and so help with the mortgage.

On the other side of Fawkes Close, Miranda had reached much the same conclusion. Hugo was delighted that 'the little woman' was to follow his mother's fine example and devote her life to raising his son and heir – with help, of course.

So Miranda and I were thrust together again, into a world of smelly nappies and baby massage. If she had any reservations about our renewed proximity, she'd kept them as quiet as I had.

I finished the joint and after tossing the roach into a bin, ambled home for a shower and a snooze full of jumbled dreams. It took a few rings of the bell to get Miranda to the front door and when she opened it she sounded bleary-eyed and was yawning.

"Sorry, did I wake you up?" I asked rather too breezily, before compounding the insult in my muddled embarrassment. "Even to my eyes you look crap. Does morning sickness stretch to the evening?"

She sighed irritably, "Thanks, Joe. Make a girl feel good about herself, why don't you?"

"Er, sorry, I just meant…"

"Yes, okay Joe, when in a hole. Anyway, it wasn't you before, was it?"

"Eh?" a little fuzzy, still I wondered if I'd missed something.

"Oh, nothing. Probably just kids playing ring and run. And well, maybe I did doze off for a moment. It's so stuffy in my study, but I've got to have the boiler on full blast to heat the water up. At least I can look forward to having a nice long soak in the bath later—at last! Cor, it's bitter out here though, that's woken me up."

"Maybe you should ask the builders to put a window in the outside wall before they leave." I suggested unhelpfully.

Under the porch light I saw her pull a face, so changed the subject before she had a chance to start moaning about them again. "Anyway, I'm glad my imminent arrival inspired such anticipation in you or did the effort of concocting your latest riveting article on the character of chintz and the joy of Spode send you off to the land of nod?"

"Some people find my advice invaluable when refurbishing their homes. I get letters telling me I've helped change their lives."

We were still at her front door and I felt strangely exposed. Were my neighbours in the houses behind me

135

watching us? It was probably just dope-induced paranoia, but it struck me that there was something rather tawdry in negotiating my admission to the home of another man's wife. I lurched forward. "Come on then, take me into your beautiful boudoir, baby."

She didn't move but snapped, "Oh god, you're stoned aren't you?"

I felt about fifteen again, being interrogated by my mum after getting home from school; 'No mum, I haven't really been smoking. I had to sit in the smoking carriage because the train was so packed, honest.' I tried to meet Miranda's hard stare but couldn't. "Only a little," I mumbled.

"Just great," she exploded, "marvellous, you are sooo…flipping hopeless! Why can't you just grow up? All I asked you to do was to keep a clear head for one evening so we could talk about something really important, and you can't even manage that. Are you so badly addicted? Well, you're no use to me like this. You've let me and yourself down, Joe. Just go away and leave me alone."

She went to slam the door in my face. A summer holiday working as a double-glazing salesman had taught me how to prevent that, although then I hadn't been wearing canvas shoes. My toes crunched as Miranda pushed harder.

"Oh, come on, Miranda, I'm fine. It was only a little one; we can still talk. Tell me what's up. I'm sure I can help. Is it Hugo? Is he…is he, I don't know, have you found proof he's shagging Marta or is it something worse?"

"What are you blathering on about now?" she spat. "You can't even sort your own life out, so you have no business to pass comment on others'. Why can't you just act your age, we're not students anymore."

I suppose I should have been stung by this, but the truth is that I was comfortably numb from the small joint I'd had after tucking the girls into bed and telling them where I'd

136

be, so I assumed Miranda was just letting off some steam. "Look, Miranda, honestly if you want to talk, I'm here to listen. Now can I come in?"

I started to push past her, but she put her flat, cold palm to my chest and pushed me back. For a moment I thought I was going to lose my balance and I grabbed instinctively at her wrist to steady myself. She uttered a little shriek and I instantly let go, stumbled back over the threshold and into a squat bush. The paranoid sensation of being watched increased exponentially, firing icy shivers of self-consciousness down my spine as I scrambled to my feet.

"Miranda, I'm sorry. I didn't mean to…I was just off balance…I'm sorry."

She had moved forward and the beam from the security lamp above the porch fell obliquely across her face, making dark hollows of her eyes and mouth. In silhouette, the well-cut clothes that usually emphasised her trim figure appeared, like her, crumpled. When she spoke the quick fury had left her voice. Instead she sounded exhausted and put upon. "I know Joe, I know. But it's too late now; tonight's not the night okay. I've got a stinking headache. I've got work to finish and you are too wrecked to be of much help. So go home, sleep it off and call me when you're worth talking to. Okay?"

"Good night oldest friend," I said quietly after she had shut the door. Trudging back across Fawkes Close, I still couldn't shake the sensation of someone following me with their eyes and wondered what they would have made of the scene they had witnessed. Lovers tiff? In some ways it was, just without the fringe benefits. Once I'd shut and locked my own door, I made straight for the drinks cupboard and retrieved the remains of the whisky.

Twenty minutes later, I was back again and after a bit of rummaging, found an ancient bottle of Pernod, four inches of which I poured into a pint glass of water. Halfway down that bottle a certain degree of honesty allowed me to admit that what Miranda had said was pretty much true. That hurt in a different way; a deep metallic ache only quelled by a further well-packed joint. To the tortured lyrics of Nick Drake's 'Bryter Later' album, I finished the bottle and fell asleep with the delicious sensation of twisting the knife in my heart while under anaesthetic.

Later, much later... Memories of a stereo, in the corner by the bathroom, playing this song fourteen years earlier, raking like sharp nails over a healing scab, bringing renewed pain and a sense of relief.

My cracked tongue and throbbing head forced me to roll off the sofa and crawl to the sink for water. Sickness flooded my stomach with the sudden shock of chilly liquid on top of the disorientation of movement.

The song was ending. I walked with tangled feet to the stereo and waited for the final bar to fade. Stooping too low, I swayed dangerously as I switched the box off.

Light and heavy headed, I shambled up the stairs. I didn't check the girls for fear of waking them; instead I fell onto my bed, closed my eyes and implored the world to stop spinning.

Adrift in the doldrums before sleep, I pictured Miranda's hand on my chest, pushing me away and her saying, "But it's too late now."

Repelled; my misjudgement; my fault; again...

Chapter 11

In retrospect, it was unfortunate to answer the door the next morning in the way that I did; though feeling the way I did at barely 6.30 am, quite understandable.

I had tried to ignore the first ring, hoping it was just the postman letting me know he had left a parcel on the doorstep. The second ring, I assumed, meant that I had to sign for it. The thought that it might be a delivery from the Wine Society had me staggering out of bed and weaving my way around the bedroom in search of my jeans. I found them bundled round a smoke-perfumed T-shirt by the bathroom door and lurched down the stairs as the bell rang again. I paused a second to do up my zip. Wearing no boxer shorts it nicked my foreskin and I swore loudly.

As I reached the bottom of the stairs, smarting the bell clamoured yet again. This time a solid five second peel followed by a pounding knock. Head and penis pulsating I flung open the front door and snapped, "Okay, okay, keep your fucking hair on, it can hardly be a matter of life and death."

Automatically sticking my hand out to receive whatever it was I had to sign, I struggled to identify the two dark shapes until I heard the crackle and squawk of a police radio. "Oh, hi, er officers, erm can I help you?" My sluggish mind crawled around in an attempt to remember where I had left my dope the night before, but to no avail. With a mighty effort of concentration the shapes solidified out of the mist and I began to make out the features of the policeman and woman in front of me; enough to recognise them as local bobbies from Hampstead Police Station who had attended that summer's school fete. My heart began to slow a little; this probably wasn't a drugs bust then.

"Good morning, sir. It's Mr Wynde, isn't it?" The male PC had a lilting South Wales accent. "Sorry to disturb you so early. We're asking all the neighbours whether they saw or heard anything out of the ordinary last night."

"Er, no, I don't think so," I replied, my head swimming through the treacle of the previous night's disjointed memories. "Has someone been burgled?"

"No sir, nothing like that. How about your neighbour, Miranda Lethbridge, did you see or talk to her at all?"

"Oh, erm, yes, I popped round to see her yesterday evening, but she wasn't really up for company and I came home."

The woman police officer noted this, scratching onto a clipboard whose clip glinted in the low sun. "What time would that have been, sir?"

"Dunno, about quarter past eight. I'd just put my daughters to bed." I hoped it wasn't illegal to leave your kids in the house while you popped over the road; my mum used to do it all the time with us. "I had the baby monitor with me though," I added quickly. It's remarkable how easy it is to lie to the police when you are worried. I wondered whether I even still had a baby monitor. In fact, I'd given Jenny the cordless phone with my mobile number on redial and strict instructions not to worry, but to call if she or Nell needed me. I suspected the police would take an even dimmer view of this though.

Again the female officer scratched on her pad.

"Er, look do you want to come in. I need a coffee and you're welcome to join me."

"No, thank you sir." The Welshman sounded firm but disappointed, "we need to get on round all the neighbours. "So what did you do after that?"

"Er, well, I er..." another lie, I couldn't tell them I'd got stoned, "I er, came back here and er, had a couple of drinks, um, maybe one or two too many and then went to sleep until just now, er, yeah that's all." How convincing? "Er, what's all this about, if you don't mind me asking?"

The two constables exchanged a look and the woman nodded. "Mrs Lethbridge has had an accident," she replied crisply.

"Oh shit, erm is she alright, can I help in any way?" my heart, whose rate had calmed slightly, started hammering at my ribs again.

"I'm afraid not sir," the policeman said flatly, "she's dead."

If they were scouring my face for a reaction I would not have noticed. I felt like I'd been inverted and had to grip the doorframe so as not to fall. Lights of every hue and size exploded in front of my eyes and I began to shake all over. Then my stomach joined in on the act, acidic remnants of the previous night's Pernod shot up to my throat, rasping at it painfully. I remembered the lamb dhansak I'd reheated in the microwave, half a second before it reappeared on the doormat in front of me. My knees buckled and I pitched towards it.

Seconds roared past my ears, then a pair of heavy black shoes moved in front of my face, sidestepping the semi-digested mess. The male constable bent down and grabbed my biceps to lift me to my feet. Doubtless for him this was just a routine manoeuvre, performed most nights and more at weekends. For me, it compounded the misery and I began to sob.

Jenny appeared at my side, her small hand slipped into my shaking one. "Daddy, are you okay? Why are the police here? Are they going to arrest you?"

141

An involuntary laugh galvanised me. Wiping my eyes, I drew myself up and shook off the policeman's helping-hand, muttering, "Thanks." Then with a deep sigh I looked down at my puzzled daughter and tried to think of something to say.

"Hi, Jen, did you sleep well?" Under my hand I felt her head nod mutely; she was staring at the police. "Well grab yourself some breakfast and I'll explain in a minute."

I turned back to the two constables a little sheepishly and forced a smile. "Er, look, I need to get the girls ready for school. Can I do anything to help? Like, er give Miranda's children breakfast?" Resurgent comprehension of what I'd just been told bent me double again, "Oh Christ, I can't believe it." My words came in gasps as my throat seemed to tighten. "Are the children okay? How did, er, what happened to her? Have you got hold of Hugo, her husband?"

Jesus, poor Hugo! I could only imagine how much worse this would feel if they were bringing me news of Eithne's sudden death. "Tell him, if there's anything I can do to help...anything..." I trailed off.

"She was alone when she was discovered. Should her children have been there with her?" The policewoman had her pen poised with renewed interest.

"Daddy, Chris is at PGL this week, remember?" Jenny was still at my side, eager to help me where she could.

"Oh yeah," everything was swirling around and I desperately needed to sit down, or wake up or...anything but this. It all just hurt too much. "I think that Hope, her daughter, had a sleepover with a friend. Miranda, was glad because she needed to finish some article she was working on and then she was going to have a bath, I think that's what she said, I can't really remember. Marta, the nanny, will

142

know where Hope is; she keeps the diary. But what happened to Miranda?"

The female officer finished scribbling and there was an awkward silence before Jenny piped up, "Dad, that policewoman looked at me and shook her head. What did she mean?"

"One of my colleagues will be round later to ask your dad some more questions. But for now, Mr Wynde it's probably best that you concentrate on getting your daughter ready for school. What time are you planning on taking her there?"

I told them my routine and they left. Following them out into Fawkes Close, I peered around. A police car and an ambulance stood outside Miranda's house, which, judging by the unfamiliar fluttering sound, had been taped off. A police van was parked next to Robina and a pair of constables asking Lucia and Freddie questions. The pair who had just finished with me was now at No. 6. I supposed that those neighbours not talking to the police at the moment would be peering from behind curtains or wrapped up and standing in their doorways. I wondered whether any of them had seen me throw up and that made me feel nauseous again. Jenny's warning came too late, I stepped back to close the door and my bare foot squelched into something tepid and sticky.

I tried to lose myself in clearing up the mess and following the morning routine of getting two primary aged children ready for school. Being nine, Jenny is a self-starter and anyway likes to live her life by a schedule. Her six-year old sister is, however, more like me, a slow and sulky riser who needs a good dose of carbs and sugar to get her moving.

I battled to deny access to all thoughts of Miranda and what might have happened to her. When they threatened to

143

invade my mind I fought them off, directing the ire I felt at her loss against their unwanted presence. It took all my remaining energy to locate the girls' PE kit and fill their snack boxes and chivvy Nell along, whilst battling the lethargy caused by my heavy night. Still, though, salvos of questions burst over my head; 'How? Why? When? Was there some mistake?' Jenny too wanted to ask these questions, but sensitive to my shocked silence limited her interrogation to staring expectantly at me.

The phone had rung twice. It had made me flinch to hear it, but I felt too fragile to answer. In the void that followed its second clamour, I was suddenly sniped by the understanding of how abandoned Ted must have felt when I had failed to answer his calls. Robbed of what little fight I had left, I slumped down over the work-surface and held my pounding head.

Between mouthfuls of Crunchy Nut Cornflakes the girls were whispering about the police and the sick. The latter indicated that daddy was unwell and would be grumpy and unlikely to respond well to questioning. But Jenny had overheard much of what had been said and seen the emergency vehicles outside. Like me, my girls wanted and deserved to have answers and information to help guide them through this alien version of their morning routine. It was better that they heard about Miranda's death from me rather than in an embellished account in the playground. I picked up my coffee and took it over to the kitchen table.

Everything ached as I sat down opposite their small, worried faces. I breathed in deeply and spoke gently but clearly. "The police came here to tell me that Miranda has had an accident."

I heard Jenny open her mouth to interrupt, but held up my hand and continued. "I don't know exactly what happened, but they told me that it was serious and, I'm afraid, she has died." I struggled to force the final words out against the constriction I felt as the shock gripped me by the throat again.

Even if I couldn't see it etched on their faces, the anguish I had caused was overwhelming. Nell immediately burst into tears and shrank into her chair. I drew her closer to me and, quivering uncontrollably, she buried her face in my chest. Jenny had turned her face away from us and was hugging herself as she rocked back and forth. Though she'd known already, she had needed to hear it from my lips for it to be incontrovertible. Just as when I walk into a lamppost, injured, impotent, rage threatened to engulf me.

Removing her tear-streaked face from my T-shirt and between sobs Nell demanded answers. "But it's not...it's not fair when...when mummies and daddies get...get taken away! I don't understand daddy? Why...did she...have to...have to...die? She...is so...so...nice...I want her...b...back. I love you!" She squeezed me as hard as she could to her, defying any force that might try to take me away.

I felt Jenny's eyes on me as well; the limits of her sophistication had been exposed; she too needed answers. However I responded, I was not going to be able to remove their fear or prevent the nightmares. Death's random harvest had again been reaped close by, this time slashing and burning the adjacent meadow of their closest friends. My ignorance of the circumstances could only fuel their darkest imaginings.

Dismayed, I fell back on platitudes. "I'm afraid I really don't know anything else yet. But I'm sure it was just a horrid accident, like falling down the stairs, and that Miranda would not have suffered."

"Do you think that she has gone to heaven, daddy?" The hope in Nell's small voice and her need to find something

145

positive in this new world left no question in my mind about my answer.

"Of course she has Nell. Miranda was a wonderful, kind, loving person and God gathers all of those people close to Him so they can watch over us down here, on Earth."

"So, she's an angel now, daddy?"

The lump in my throat made it difficult to answer. I wanted to lie down on my bed with an arm round each of my girls and the duvet pulled over our heads, to shelter from all the shit that life could and would throw at us. "Oh Nell, yes, yes she is an angel now and she will always be there to protect all those she loves."

"Why didn't the angels protect *her* then?" Ever the budding rationalist, Jenny was angry and upset. "Don't Chris and Hope need her more down here?"

"I don't know Jen, like mummy says 'The Lord moves in mysterious ways'."

"But mummy and you don't believe in God, you said so."

My head was thumping sickeningly. I could see my own angry incomprehension reflected in Jenny's arguments. Had it not been for Nell and her sensitive, fairy-tale imagination, I might have avoided the whole Heaven issue, but we all need fairy stories in times of despair.

Nell was sucking her thumb and looking at her wiggling toes. I put my finger to my lips, knowing Jenny was still looking at me for an answer. I couldn't see but I bet she was frowning hard. She did however remain quiet.

The peel of the doorbell meant further discussion was postponed. My jangled nerves made me slop coffee over the table and Jenny tutted as I muttered "Shit, shit, shit!"

There were four silhouettes this time. The woman police officer and her Welsh colleague, radios still crackling and

146

two men who as I stared at them solidified into suits. This time they accepted my invitation to come in.

"It's okay, daddy tidied it all up," Jenny reassured whoever must have glanced down at the doormat as they entered.

The shorter of the two newcomers stepped forward and introduced himself as DI Sharratt, of Holborn CID before informing me that he had a few questions. Then, turning to the girls, he asked whether they would like a special treat.

Jenny shot back, "Daddy says we shouldn't accept treats from strangers."

I heard a stifled giggle from the policewoman and Sharratt sighing, irritated at being answered back. "Mr Wynde, with your permission I would like to offer your very clever daughter and her sister a lift to school in a police car while you and I have a talk." The girls could hardly contain their excitement and looked at me beseechingly. Relieved of the trauma of the school run with a hangover on this of all mornings, I nodded my assent.

Five minutes later with a whoop of a siren and flashing blue lights they were off. I turned to Sharratt and his colleague, who he introduced as DS Wragg, and joked, "Can you come round every morning? I've never seen them get ready so quickly."

Sharratt ignored this and said crisply, "Now Mr Wynde, shall we get on?"

Never at my best during the daylight hours of morning, I was also acutely aware of my breath, upon which I, and I was sure the two sharp-sensed men in the room, could smell last night's fug of spirits and grass. Worse, in the morning's chaos, I had forgotten to air the sitting room.

The cold realisation that tobacco, rizlas and weed lay waiting for us on the coffee table slapped me only after I had suggested we went through to be more comfortable. A

147

host of worries concerning the current penalty for possession and what Eithne would say whirled around my head, vying for my fractured attention with the need to know exactly what had happened to my oldest friend. I could still feel the sensation of her hand on my chest.

In the minutes that they had been in the house I had had time to stare at the detectives through the streaking comets of my wrecked vision. DS Wragg was young, lean and angular. He remained in the background picking things up off the work surface, examining them and then putting them back in the wrong places.

DI Sharratt was older and had the look of a man who had been up all night, every night for the last fifteen years. He was squat and muscular with a strangely long face and opaque, industrial grey-green eyes. He possessed the air of one used to landing both the first and last punch. He got in his first jab when I offered tea and biscuits.

"I don't do Hampstead niceties, Mr Wynde, so kindly sit down and answer my questions."

We were standing facing one another, so close that I could smell the bacon fat on his breath. My stomach squirmed and I was glad to slump down onto the smaller sofa. I tried casually to toss a magazine over my bag of grass and the torn pack of king-size rizlas. The attempt was too clumsy not to have been noticed by both policemen. They remained standing.

Annoying blue dots of light kept bursting and swirling in front of my eyes. It was overcast outside and I had been too flustered to turn up the dimmer switch when we'd entered the room, so I was having difficulty focusing on the men's expressions. However, I could hear Wragg sniffing conspicuously and sensed their irritation—though whether this was directed at me or against life in general, I couldn't tell.

DI Sharratt cleared his throat. "It would appear that you were the last person to see Mrs Lethbridge alive last night," he stated. I felt myself nod. "Did she seem unusually upset or depressed to you?"

"No, she was feeling headachy and a bit irritable. She had wanted to crack some article she was writing and she'd asked me over to keep her company and give my opinion on something or other, but...but, well when I got there she didn't feel up to it and I came home."

"And this was at what time, precisely?"

"About 8.15. Look, what's happened to her?"

I could feel Sharratt and his colleague scrutinising me, weighing up my level of ignorance. It was DS Wragg who replied, nasally and with relish, "Shut herself in the garage and turned the Merc's engine on. Not quick, but highly effective. The nanny, Miss Majewski, found her when she arrived for work this morning."

It felt as if he were sitting on my chest and telling me this. I could do nothing save for shake my head and fight for breath.

They left me to the howling silence for a few seconds before Sharratt added, "Do you have any idea why Mrs Lethbridge would want to take her own life, Mr Wynde?"

I blinked hard against the tears prickling the edges of my eyelids. "She wouldn't...I mean, I don't believe she would. Erm, she's a Catholic, it's a sin to..." My thoughts meandered, but all the time my fuzzy brain was screaming "No, no, it's wrong, it can't be," like some primal incantation.

I only half heard the next question and Sharratt's irritation bubbled to the surface when I asked him to repeat it, "Pay attention, Mr Wynde. We do understand from your neighbours that you and Mrs Lethbridge were rather close. Obviously you must be upset, but this appears to be a

149

straightforward case of suicide. Unless, of course you have any factual evidence to the contrary."

In the silence that followed Wragg picked one of my CDs from the shelf, glanced at it, gave a snort of derision and tossed it onto the coffee table.

Thoroughly unsettled now, I persevered, "She had a lot on her mind at the moment; the building works were getting her down and all the neighbours were giving her a hard time about it. Her son, Christian, is having a few problems at school and Hugo, her husband and she had had their ups and downs. But there was nothing really insuperable. No, all that was wrong with her last night was that she felt a bit fluey." A wave of nausea washed through me as I recalled, "I even teased her that it was morning sickness."

"She was a bit more than sick this morning." The more I was able to focus on DS Wragg the more his features resembled those of a lean weasel. "So she was pregnant then—were you the father?"

"No! We were always just good friends, we'd known each other since university. And I'm sure she was just under the weather. I was just winding her up, that's all." I fought to keep my voice calm, afraid my defensiveness would be interpreted as guilt or having something to hide.

"And now you live practically on top of each other, very cosy. I bet you've got pampas grass growing in the garden 'n all." Having grown up in the suburbs, his allusion to the signature plant of wife-swappers was not lost on me—I just chose to ignore it.

DI Sharratt seemed un-amused too. As his temper frayed his Mancunian accent came to the fore. "Mr Wynde, your full and truthful cooperation would be appreciated. We can always do this formally down at the station if you would prefer. Now, not only does it appear that you were the last person to see Miranda Lethbridge, but one of your

150

neighbours overheard you having an argument with her. Isn't that so?"

"We had a disagreement," I corrected him. The memory was sharp and it twisted in my chest.

"About?" Sharratt prompted, his eyes mining my face for information.

I fought to focus both mentally and physically. I could feel myself blinking and avoiding his gaze. "Like I said, she wanted my opinion on something but I'd had a couple of drinks and she felt it would cloud my judgement. She was angry and sent me packing."

"So she told you to piss off and you had a fight." Wragg's insinuation stung with its accuracy.

"Not quite," I replied, regulating my breath to keep calm.

"Lovers' tiff then, if you prefer. So you went round to give her one and she turned you down 'cos you was too pissed...or stoned was it? Yeah that's it. Cos you *were* giving her one, weren't you? " Wragg's weasel face twisted into a sneer.

That was it. All the anger and indignation that I felt at Miranda for betraying me, for leaving me to face this alone; all the irrational self-pity her death had given rise to, flared within my aching, befuddled head. "Look, people might fornicate like vermin in whichever sewer you crawled out from, but some of us can maintain friendships without resorting to copulation."

"Oh la di dah." His mockery had me clenching my jaw and fists.

Sharratt's lathe-like eyes were on me. He let a few tense seconds pass then his flat Mancunian vowels cut back into the exchange. "Don't push your luck pal. This place reeks of cannabis. How about I get a few snot-fingered PCSOs to turn your nice house upside down looking for your stash? DS Wragg here would love to start rifling through your wife's knicker drawer." His eyes were cold and dull and his long, hard face expressionless. A memory of the winter sea against the harbour wall in Morecambe Bay flitted across my mind's eye, sending an involuntary shiver through me.

He sensed his advantage and landed his knockout punch. "Then of course who would look after those two lovely girls of yours if I have to arrest you for further questioning. Maybe even a call to social services regarding your fitness to look after your kids at all..." He tailed off leaving my imagination to complete the sentence.

I was cornered. "Look, I admit I had a couple of spliffs last night, I don't think that's illegal. I went round because she'd said earlier she could do with a bit of company. I don't know what she wanted my opinion about—maybe she was still working on a story we'd researched together. What I do know is that when I got there, I got the distinct impression I'd woken her up and it had put her in a bad mood. She had a go at me because she'd asked me to bring my best thinking head over. I told her I was straight enough to discuss whatever it was, but she told me to go home and sleep it off. We exchanged a few words. I tried to push past her but she barred my way. So I came back here and well, had a couple of drinks..." I tailed off, feeling Sharratt's hard eyes on my guilty face.

"Really Mr Wynde, and then?"

"Well, I got pretty wasted and fell asleep on the sofa. I woke up some time in the night feeling like shit, had a glass of water and crawled up to bed. Next thing I know your lot woke me up this morning."

"Is that it?" Sharratt was unimpressed.

"Yes, that's it. But she was going to have a bath. And she told me to call her. I was going to do it today and

152

apologise to her. She can't have been planning to...to..."
The realisation I would never be able to call her again
prised open the wound inflicted by news of her death and
put cold metal to its persistent ache.

"Yeah, right. You just wanted to arrange another night of
kissing and making up on the couch while her hubby and
your missus are still away?" sneered Wragg. "Very, very
cosy."

This time I ignored him and kept looking in Sharratt's
direction. "That's all. Honestly."

"Honestly?" he intoned and I heard him stroking his
stubbly chin. "Honestly, this is just a waste of my precious
time. You know, Mr Wynde, if this kind of thing happens in
Somers Town, the local plod don't even bother calling us
out. But because Mrs Lethbridge was," he glanced over to
his colleague, "some la-di-dah Hampstead banker's wife,
we have to drop everything and come running out here to
listen to the likes of you. Real policing, Mr Wynde, is not
like Inspector Morse." So saying he flipped over the copy of
Uncut magazine on the table and picked up the bag of grass.
"Is this the lot?" I nodded meekly. "Consider yourself
cautioned," he growled. "DS Wragg."

He handed his subordinate the bag and Wragg left the
room. Sharratt stood and I sat in silence. I heard Wragg take
a long pee and then flush the toilet. My head ached, my
tongue felt furry, multi-coloured lights pulsated in front of
my eyes like an Ibiza club night. Most of all, I felt hollow,
down and defeated.

Wragg returned crumpling the little plastic bag. I heard it
land lightly on the magazines in front of me before
Sharratt's condescending indifference wrapped up our
'talk'. "In the unlikely event that you remember something
of actual interest to us, contact DS Wragg at Holborn CID."
He handed me a business card.

153

"Too flimsy for roach material," I muttered after I had closed the door firmly behind them. I flipped the card into the recycling bin.

It was barely 9.30 but it felt much later. I was still in the jeans and T-shirt I had flung on three hours previously. Alone finally, I was able to focus on the headline announced by that first shock visit. 'Miranda—Oldest Friend and Soul Mate—Dead!'

Fortunately, the pubs were closed, as were the off-licences. Instead, I rooted around at the back of the freezer for my spare bag of grass. Once it was in my hand though, the very thought made me feel ill, so I replaced it unopened.

I needed to think; a cigarette helped steady my stomach and breathing; a strong coffee sharpened my mind. After a quarter of an hour though, I gave up. Try as I might, there was no way I could make the words 'Miranda' and 'suicide' sit comfortably on the same page.

I dragged myself upstairs and back to bed but my thoughts wouldn't rest. Phantasmagorical visions of Miranda, Ted and Daniel flew in and out of view. The blood in my ears groaned with unintelligible messages.

Irritation drove me to shower and dress in clean clothes, though I found little comfort in either. I needed to leave Fawkes Close and walk and walk, away and fast. I hurried out of my front door and stopped dead; flabbergasted by the evidence of my unreliable eyes. I checked and rechecked. I had expected police cars and SOCO teams clad in white overalls but there was nothing to show that anything had happened at Miranda's house—even the police tape had vanished.

With the same disconnection as you feel when you see yourself in a dream, I floated over to Lucia's door and knocked. She wafted into view, looking relieved to see me and enfolded me into her doughty, perfumed bosom.

"So much bad news, Joe, so much. It's just too awful." She had obviously been weeping and as I released myself from her embrace she raised a well-used lacy handkerchief to her smudged eyes.

"Where have all the police gone?" My voice emerged hoarse and toneless.

"Oh, they left shortly after the ambulance took Miranda away." At this, new tears sprouted to be mopped away with the hankie.

"What, that's it?" I was incredulous "Surely they can't believe she killed herself? She's got two kids for Christ's sake!"

Lucia tutted her disapproval, "Joe, I know what a shock this must be, especially coming so soon after what happened to your friend Ted. I think we are all in shock, but really, as I told that nice Detective Inspector Sharratt, Miranda was very depressed—on the verge of a breakdown I'd say. Her moods were so erratic; it was difficult to know how she would be from day to day. Just look at how she was last night. She'd obviously asked you over and then she wouldn't even let you in. And shouting at you like that, and pushing you over! Well, that's hardly the behaviour of a woman in full control of herself, is it?"

Sudden hot claustrophobia enveloped me. I needed fresh air so excused myself abruptly, leaving Lucia mortified and explaining that she had merely been doing the washing-up when she had noticed us through her kitchen window.

I headed for the wildness of the Heath, stomping angrily up the hill, filled with a powerful sense of betrayal. Two of my friends were dead; I could do nothing to change that. Could I have done more to prevent it? I felt alone, abandoned, powerless; a minute, insignificant speck advancing by micrometres across the surface of a world I could not properly see, could never hope to experience fully and that I understood less and less with each passing friend.

A whoosh of silver flashed past my feet in the middle of the zebra crossing over the High Street. My rage burst forth in a string of expletives and I brought my white cane thwacking down on the boot of the speeding car. It screeched to a halt and I heard the driver open his door. Seething blood and adrenalin took over, blurring my vision even more than normal. I strode to the driver's side and kicked the door shut.

His leg must have already been half out because the door jammed and he screamed, "I'll have you for assault!"

"And I'll have you for attempted murder!" I hurled back. "Now fuck off before I ring the police."

A small crowd had gathered and, in true British tradition, sided with the underdog, berating the balding driver in his hairdresser-class Mercedes for not stopping when he should have. I eased the pressure on the door and he snatched his leg back into the car and sped off to an assortment of cheers and jeers from my newly-formed supporters club.

After profuse thanks and reassurances that I really was okay, I continued on my way, then changed my mind mid-step and turned off the main street and into Steele's Passage, one of the small, cobbled alleys that criss-cross Hampstead Village. I tapped warily down the steep, uneven Victorian steps, but still snagged the tip of my stick in a plastic bag of rotting rubbish. The street sweepers rarely came down here; there were no houses and none of the shops used their back doors, so no one complained about the mess.

I could smell that Dusty was in even before I heard the wheezed, "Hello brother!" from his den in the old air raid shelter.

156

Local legend had it that Dusty was an acid casualty from the late sixties, who had wound up sleeping rough in the World War Two relic one night and never left. Others suggested that he was an original member of the Sex Pistols, but had got too spannered one day and been kicked out. He certainly appeared to have misplaced an important part of his mind somewhere in the not-so-recent past.

Local teenagers relieved the boredom of their long summer holidays in baiting him and, over the years, had discovered that yelling, "This is the police! It's a bust!" could provoke him into comical violence.

I liked Dusty and dropped by most weeks, occasionally giving him things he needed or could swap or sell. In return he shared his unparalleled knowledge of late 60s psychedelic rock music. With his guidance and eBay's resources, I was slowly building an authoritative collection. He would marvel at my iPod and the small speakers I occasionally brought with me to play the music of his undamaged youth.

"You got the musical box today?" he asked hopefully.

I shook my head and felt his disappointment. To compensate I fished out a small pouch of tobacco from my pocket. "I've got some of this though, if you fancy." I smelt the crust of dirt in his hair crack and rise as he nodded vigorously. "Papers too," I added passing them to him. It wasn't much, but I knew he would make it last and I felt like making someone happy today; if only in the hope it may relieve some of the burden on my own heavy heart.

Dusty was already rolling up with practised expertise. "So how's it going?" I asked. "Winter's coming, you prepared?" He was humming and I detected a pair of affirmative notes in the tune.

"West Coast Pop Art Experimental Band" he blurted out. "Volume Three, 'A Child's View of Good and Evil'. Bob

157

Markley was at his craziest but Rod Morgan's guitar was on fire, man. Check it out." I made a mental note to do so and we chatted on about the LA garage band scene of the late 60s while he smoked slowly and with relish.

After forty minutes or so, my backside was numb from sitting on the rotting off-cut of carpet on the shelter's floor. I uncrossed my legs to let some blood flow to my feet and prepared to leave. Dusty looked agitated. I asked him whether there was anything he needed, wondering whether he had run out of batteries for the small transistor radio I had given him.

"The council, man, they haven't fixed the light. Kids man, at night, in the dark, Halloween. I need the light, it's the sun at night, no stars in the city, let the sunshine in."

It was a perennial problem. Either through faulty wiring or, more likely, adolescent vandalism, the street lamp at the top of the stairs leading out of Steele's Passage was more often than not broken. Never a popular cut-through, when it was pitch dark, the alley became a no-go area for all but gangs of pissed-up teenagers; the same ones who would then taunt Dusty with their cries of "It's a bust." Dusty knew that if I, a blind resident of the borough, reported the damage, Camden would make fixing the lantern a priority. Having no council tax book, he wasn't even on their radar. I promised I would do so.

Those few minutes in the company of someone content with so little had reminded me of quite how much I still had to be grateful for. The oppressive anger, and guilt, had lifted slightly allowing me to try and plan what I would tell Jenny and Nell when they got home from school.

Turning right out of the shelter, I followed the alleyway as it curved round the corner and past a urine-infused recessed rear doorway belonging to one of the shops. The top of the precipitous flight of steps leading down into New

158

End was marked, halfway across, by a four-foot high cast iron bollard. It was breaking a rib on this, one bright summer afternoon five years before that had finally persuaded me to start using my white stick during daylight hours.

Resting a hand on its pepper grinder top, I squinted up and saw that the glass of the Victorian lantern had indeed been smashed again and the bulb shattered.

Despondency flushed through me. All the delights of one of the world's richest cities around them and Hampstead's privileged teenagers were so bored they had to smash up streetlights. An assertion of individuality as selfish and pointless as that of their parents who, cocooned in their ubiquitous Teutonic cars, were unable to resist the urge to drive over busy zebra crossings.

Chapter 12

Miranda was buried a week later in the graveyard of Hampstead's Catholic Church. The Indian summer, such as it had been, was well and truly over and the drizzle incessant. Eithne and I agreed that it was important we attend as a family, so Jenny and Nell got the day off school. Then striking French airline pilots, determined to retain their right to the high-life until the age of 65, had left Eithne stranded in Montreal. Somehow, this was so inevitable that I couldn't even get angry about it.

Instead, Eithne had called while the girls and I were pushing cereal round our bowls hoping to stir up an appetite. None of us found any comfort in this reminder of her absence. Nell had burst into tears as she passed the phone to Jenny, whose tone made clear her bitter disappointment in her mother.

When it came to my turn Eithne's distraught voice sounded so distant that I barely registered what she was saying. "I feel like such a shite mother. It's my fault for cutting things too fine. I'm sorry Joe, I should've come home midweek. Will you be alright without me there?"

Her thoughts echoed my own. I had reluctantly accepted the necessity for her to remain in Canada; apparently Jean-Pierre was too junior to be let loose on negotiations without having his hand held. But when I thought of her, alone with her grief, waiting in an airport lounge with only muzak and angry passengers for company, my resentment softened.

I tried to sound upbeat, "At least I've got the girls for company, and Lucia is going to be with us. How about you? Are you bearing up?"

At my ear her breathing trembled and when she spoke her voice was choked with tears. "I love you Joe. Imagine

160

I'm beside you, holding your hand and say goodbye to Miranda from me."

The tiny church was crammed with sombre chic and smelt like the perfume department at John Lewis. The solemnity of the occasion was marred solely by the regular bleeps, clicks and glow of Blackberries stressing the truancy of their restless owners from work by means of constant emails and the latest on the FTSE 100. Only the handful of children present seemed struck by the gravity of the ceremony, remaining conspicuously subdued throughout the funeral mass.

Lucia had come to pick us up in good time and fussed over the children's unkempt hair and my ragged black tie, a remnant of my brief mod phase. Eventually, she had replaced it with a silk one from Freddie's wardrobe. He now stood impassively beside me, beyond range of physical contact with his wife who buttressed my other flank and led the professional mourners in loud sniffing and soft weeping. At regular intervals she rested her ringleted head on my shoulder and I made a mental note to ask Jenny to check my suit later for foundation.

I felt numb and separate from the proceedings. This was in part due to the Diazepam tablets I had been prescribed to help me sleep; when mixed with brandy they made the days seem easier too. Partly also, it was because the fact of Miranda's death had yet properly to sink in. I still found myself dialling her number for a chat or looking over to her house expecting to see her. One afternoon I'd even accosted a bewildered passer-by thinking it was her. Slowly the children's questions were beginning to cause the new reality to be built in my mind. Nothing, though, could make me accept that Miranda had taken her own life; so the groundworks lacked solidity.

No mention of her suicide was made during the service. I wondered whether the Catholic Church still preferred to

161

bury those it perceived as self-murderers in the un-consecrated ground outside the churchyard. If so, had Hugo donated heavily to the spire fund to get round the inconvenience? He himself stood erect and dignified in his Savile Row suit as he presented his eulogy. How touched the wonderful, generous woman with whom he had had the privilege to share so much of his life, would have been to see so many of the people she cared so deeply about in the church she loved so much. This service should be a celebration of her life and her spirit that would live on in our memories of her and in their two wonderful children.

Jenny and Nell were sitting with Christian and Hope on a pew at the front; Jenny clutching Christian's hand throughout. As the organ music stopped I heard Hope sobbing uncontrollably, then the soothing tones of Marta softly whispering that mummy had gone to a good place, where she could help look after all the angels.

Beside them sat an elderly woman who I assumed must be Miranda's mother. As I stared at her through the gloom, I saw that she wore a look of blank shock as if she had only just received the news. A couple of yards along from her, alone and at a safe distance from the children, was Hugo's equine-faced sister, Camilla. The Lethbridge parents had remained on an extended holiday in Barbados—London in early November apparently being a bit inclement for their aging bones.

After the organ had struck up the recessional, Lucia steered me out and towards the grave. Amidst the dozens of black umbrellas being raised, I had the sudden impression of being at the centre of a rising muster of crows. Heavy raindrops spattered down noisily upon them as if goading my dry eyes. The low keening of Lucia and the other emotionally repressed souls at the graveside, glad to find an acceptable outlet for their internalized grief, lent an otherworldly soundtrack to the slow-motion lowering of the

162

coffin. Except for the reassuring squeeze my hand was getting from Nell, I felt I could be watching this on television. The clatter of earth thrown down onto the coffin lid rang too vibrant in my ears and I had to turn away.

As the suited wage-slaves hailed taxis and muttered about falling markets, I asked Lucia to spot Hugo for me. She pointed him out and said she would keep an eye on the girls. Woozily I drifted over to him, bright firework flashes bursting before my eyes to fill the gaps in my view of the unfamiliar surroundings. Hugo's ramrod bearing contrasted sharply to the figure I cut, hunched over my stick and groping through a personal fog. I forced my shoulders back and tried to stand straight. Maybe he thought I was squaring up to him because he took a half step forward and drew himself up even taller.

Undeterred, I held out my hand for him to shake and mumbled, "Hugo, my condolences. Eithne sends her apologies, she's stuck in Montreal; plane strike. She's as devastated as I am. All of us will miss Miranda hugely. I'm so sorry. Um…you know where I am if I can be of any help." I couldn't meet his eye and for once I was glad of the excuse for it.

There was a slight whistling as he drew air up his long nostrils. I could visualise them flaring, as they had all those years before at the garden party, making his contempt for me apparent before he gave it voice. "The only way you can help is to stay out of my family's life. Had you any trace of gumption you would have made yourself scarce today."

"She was my friend too, Hugo." I fought to keep my voice steady.

"Oh, of course, your precious so-called friendship. A gentleman would have stood aside and conceded defeat graciously, instead of interposing himself between man and wife. Poor, sweet Miranda was a soft touch and you

163

exploited her pity, sowing your insinuations and steadily poisoning her delicate mind. Well, you've finally succeeded; you convinced her I was screwing the nanny and that lie took her from me! How does it feel, Wynde? Are you satisfied now you've finally separated us?" He gestured towards the grave and snarled, "She was being treated for clinical depression and you pushed her over the edge. Get out of my sight!"

Standing his ground, he glowered down at me. It's not good form to start a fight at a funeral, and I am sure that Miranda would have been mortified had I done so. Instead, I misquoted one of the few bits I remember of the Bible. To my fuzzy logic it seemed apposite.

"If I have a mote of responsibility for her death in my eye pal, you must have a whole plank."

His dumbfounded stare clung to my back as I slunk off for a cigarette.

The weight of truth in his outburst hung heavily on me too. I may not have believed that Hugo was shagging Marta, but I hadn't exactly leapt to defend his honour. Arguably my years of calling his fidelity into question, with few grounds for doing so, had left her more open to believing her suspicions. Although her treatment for depression was news to me, even Eithne had expressed little surprise at the prevailing belief that Miranda had taken her own life.

But try as I might, I could not see the Miranda I knew doing that. She didn't believe in punishing her children with anything more than a short spell on the naughty step—there was no way she would deliberately consign them to a lifetime of grieving.

Finding myself alone in this conviction, I had inevitably questioned whether it was not merely a self-defence mechanism. Just as the murderer is usually the last person to see the victim alive, so, surely the final one to have contact with a suicide must bear some responsibility for their subsequent actions. Hugo obviously thought so.

Jenny found me skulking behind a yew tree about two drags from the end of my crafty fag. She tutted and with the heartbreaking logic of the very young said accusingly, "Daddy, I don't want you to kill yourself as well. Please don't smoke."

Tossing the butt to one side guiltily, I bent forward to give her a hug, only to be pushed away with a, "Yuk, you smell horrid." I felt suitably rebuked as we held hands and walked back to rejoin the dwindling clutch of mourners.

Form dictated that there should be some kind of reception afterwards and so, although I suspected that Hugo would have preferred to have left the children with Marta and headed back to his share screens in Berkeley Square, he had had to get the caterers in. Nell had noticed them unloading their van in Fawkes Close while we were getting ready. I was determined to gain access, not only to Hugo's stock of fine brandy, but also to Miranda's office. Hugo's exhortation that I should stay away from him and his family simply made it necessary that I arrive with Lucia, Freddie and the girls, rendering it impossible for him to turn me away without creating a scene. His scowl amply reflected his displeasure at seeing me again.

Thirty or so guests and half a dozen circulating caterers already occupied the sitting and dining rooms. The buzz of conversation was muted and I assumed that most people felt it was too early to start drinking. Near the nibbles, I discerned a slender girl in a white blouse and black skirt who I assumed was a waitress, so I asked her whether she could secure me a brandy, for medicinal purposes. There was a rich Central European burr to her voice and I wondered whether Polish & Check had branched out into catering. She sounded less than hopeful when she said she would see whether she could find any. If she went to ask

Hugo, I thought, I'd have to check the glass for alien substances.

A few local mums were scattered about and, as I stood munching my way through a stack of finger food, they sidled up one by one to express their shock and sadness, and to offer or glean insights as to why she should have done it. A couple of them professed to have known that Miranda had been on anti-depressants since shortly after Hope's birth, but not to have guessed how low she must have been. I had had no idea but hearing it now declared it further evidence of Hugo's inability to be a supportive husband. The mums shook their styled heads and moved away. The hot canapés arrived and I positioned myself near the kitchen and grabbed Nell as she came past. Together, we spent twenty minutes ambushing the platters as they emerged. I didn't plan on cooking lunch at home.

I had given up hope of getting a brandy and resigned myself to having to drink the somewhat mediocre Soave (which had started to taste better by the third glass), when miraculously the waifen waitress found me. In her hand was a tumbler of amber liquid that I could smell from ten yards was a decent Armagnac. She passed it to me and apologised for the delay. I beamed at her; if Hugo had poisoned or spat in it, it made no difference to the taste, which I savoured.

I asked Nell if she could help me find "the old lady" who had been standing near her in the church. Her monosyllabic answer told me that Nell was finding all this as surreal as I was. It was the first funeral that either girl had been to; they had not had the blow softened already by the death of an ill or aged relative. I had been so bound up with my own shock and grief that I had barely taken the time to talk to the girls about theirs. I promised myself I would make the time to listen to them that evening, or tomorrow.

The elderly woman had been installed in a high backed chair in the sitting room and given a mum from Christian's

166

class to talk to. I waited for a break in the conversation before introducing Nell and myself. The mum from school seemed glad of the opportunity to get away and offered to take Nell to find the other children.

In a Liverpudlian accent that must once have been rasping, but was now dulled with time and weary sadness, Moira Blewitt told me to pull up a chair. I dimly remembered Miranda telling me that her mum had been some kind of children's entertainer at Butlins when she had met George Blewitt, who was working there as a clown. He had later been dismissed, for being drunk in charge of a squeaky horn, precipitating his downward spiral.

I guessed a lot of people had expressed sorrow for her loss already today so didn't. Up close, and even through my soft focus eyes, Mrs Blewitt looked careworn but redoubtable.

"Miranda talked about you a lot. With what she told me, I often wished she'd married you instead of that pompous gasbag." She nodded towards the dining room, where I could hear Hugo holding court.

"You and me both, Mrs Blewitt," I said sadly, "If only daughters always listened to the wise words of their parents."

"I can't make him see that she couldn't have killed herself. She'd never do anything to hurt her two kiddies. She'd never have abandoned them like that. But *he* won't listen to me. *He* says she was depressed and there are things I didn't know about her —my own daughter! I raised that girl. I know what she believed and I know how she felt about things. She was a good Catholic and she knew that self-murder is a sin. Miranda never stopped believing and she would have used her faith to work things through, just like she always did. It's what gave her the strength to stick by *him*!" Moira Blewitt spat out the word like a maggot she'd discovered in a mouthful of apple, "And now he should be sticking by her. You don't believe this nonsense either do you, Joe? I can see it in your face."

"That's what I told the police, but they weren't interested."

Her bony hand gripped my forearm and I struggled to find her eyes. They were the same beautiful hazel shade as Miranda's and my heart skipped as, for a moment, I thought she was back. I looked down, trying to catch the tears unnoticed.

Mrs Blewitt squeezed my arm. "Try again, Joe. For me and for her. Did she ever tell you how much you reminded her of her poor dad?"

I nodded, the rising bile I felt, elbowing my grief aside.

"She adored him. Real daddy's girl she was; she never really got over his death. That's why she chose Hugo, you know, because she reckoned he was a born survivor. She said you had your finger firmly on the self-destruct button. To lose her daddy again, now that would have killed her."

Moira's gaze seemed to X-ray me and she sensed my discomfort. She put her hand to my cheek, just as her daughter had so many years before and I raised my bowed head. "You were her closest friend, Joe. You're a parent, you know how we know these things instinctively about our children."

I nodded, unsure of what to say.

There was a wobble in her voice when she resumed, "It's eating away at me, not knowing the truth. I can feel her wandering in purgatory. Do this for her, Joe. Find out what really happened."

I put my arms around her shoulders and hugged her as if she were my own mum. In that moment, I promised her that

I would do everything I could and I felt her relax. Her cheek was wet as we separated.

"Thanks, Joe. Now go and find those lovely girls of yours and try not to get into a fight with my former son-in-law. At least not today."

Standing up confirmed that the brandy had mixed well with the Diazepam. After intercepting a tray of mini toad-in-the-holes, I felt suitably reckless to brave an attempt on Miranda's office. I slipped out of the dining room and down the stairs, as if I were going to the lavatory in the basement. To the left, behind hoardings, was the cavern that was to be Hugo's home cinema. A door to the right of this screened-off area led to the garage. Opposite, on my right, and at the back of the house, were three matching doors. Sandwiched between those of the boiler room and the toilet lay Miranda's office; in reality, a former utility room with a carpet.

I listened to see whether there was anyone else around then tried the door. It was locked. Running my fingers over the metal keyhole cover I reckoned it to be one of the original internal doors used throughout all the houses during the refurb. Reasoning that what worked in one house is usually true for all those built by the same developer, I reached into the bathroom and took the key from the lock. It turned in the office door and I was in.

The room was stuffy and dark; its air stale, as if no one had been in for days. The thick layer of builder's dust that met my fingertips when they found the edge of the desk confirmed this. I took a small Maglite torch from my pocket and let its beam pass slowly over the familiar jumble of paper and knick-knacks. Miranda's laptop lay on her desk and I flipped it open. Being a Mac user I had forgotten what a bloody awful racket Windows makes when it starts up and I froze, convinced that everyone above me in the dining room must have heard the terrible echo. All I could hear

169

though was the blood pulsing round my body and throbbing at my temples.

I breathed in through my nose and out through my mouth to steady my nerves, then sank into Miranda's swivel chair. In spite of having brought my best reading glasses, opening Miranda's documents file proved difficult. The cursor on my MacBook is a huge Day-Glo orange arrow with a tracker on it and I still lose it regularly. The tiny cocktail glass on Miranda's screen was impossible for me to track, even with the brightness and contrast turned right up. Racking my memory, I picked my way slowly through the Accessibility function and changed the settings to something more visible.

Time was passing rapidly and I began to sweat. People would wonder where I had got to. Lucia and the kids would suspect some accident had befallen me and mount a search party. Were I to be discovered, Hugo would banish me for life.

At last I was in. Miranda had a separate directory for her journalistic pieces that I knew was password protected. Was it only a fortnight since I had teased her about how obvious her choice of 'Christian' followed by his six-digit birthday was as a code?

"Okay you nerd, give me something unbreakable instead," she had challenged. I did and entered it now; it didn't work.

Time was ticking away, I felt damp all over. My scalp was itching. I typed in Christian's details, hoping I had the right date in February. My second attempt was successful.

I scrolled down the menu, looking for 'Checkitout.doc.' It wasn't there. I went into Windows Explorer—nothing. I went back into Word and looked under File to see the list of recently opened documents. I checked each one and found 'artical.doc' which could not be opened. My heart thumped as I checked for the file in Explorer and saw it had been modified and then deleted at 12.38 am on the morning of Miranda's death. She certainly had been burning the midnight oil. I checked the recycle bin; it had been emptied that night too.

Finally and with the foreknowledge of defeat, I went back to Explorer and searched the hard-drive for the words 'Polish, Check, Czech, blackmail, Morgenstern and Hansford'. My heart beat louder and harder with every failed attempt. I checked the clock on the laptop. I had been gone twenty-two minutes; a long time, even were I to plead constipation.

I was just changing the cursor back to normal when I heard the clatter of heels on the wooden stairs. I froze. My mouth was already dry from the brandipam cocktail and the dust, but now it felt full of cotton wool. I forced my fingers to complete their task. I made sure the mute button was on and hit 'shut down'. Windows announced it was still downloading number 5 of 13 updates. I cursed Microsoft silently and closed the lid. The laptop glowed and hummed to itself. The footsteps came past the door and then stopped. I held my breath, hoping it was someone inspecting Hugo's Imax. I heard the bathroom door open and close, and a muffled exclamation that I assumed had to do with the absence of a key.

As quietly as I could, I moved towards the door and slipped out of the room.

She must have changed her mind because we emerged at the same time, giving each other a shock. She uttered a short, shrill shriek and I dropped my white stick. Scrabbling around to find it, gave me a few vital seconds to compose myself and look less guilty. Though I had not been able to see her face, I knew by her angular stance and tweedy smell that it was Camilla. I could feel her watching me as I hunted for my stick and I was tempted to grab her well-turned ankle instead.

As I raised myself off the dusty floor she whinnied at me "I would have thought that you were on far too intimate terms with this house to get lost." There was the same nasal disdain in her voice as in her brother's.

"Too much of Hugo's VSOP, I'm afraid." The slight slur to my voice came naturally from the stickiness of my tongue. Beads of sweat trickled coldly down the small of my back.

"Make the most of it, this is the last invitation you will ever receive. Now, give me the bathroom key and I suggest you leave before Hugo throws you out."

"Oh don't mind me Camilla, you're hardly my type. Thoroughbreds are notoriously neurotic. I suppose that's why you can't shake the lettuce unless the door's locked?" With that I tossed the key in the direction of the hoardings and heard it tinkle to the ground somewhere behind them. Sensing her rage, I headed up the stairs brushing the dust off my suit as I went.

I had managed to grab another glass of wine to lubricate my tongue by the time Lucia found me. She tutted at my dusty and dishevelled appearance and she too suggested it was time for me to leave. It felt more like my own decision coming from her, so knocking back my wine and grabbing a final handful of spring rolls from the attentive waitress I made my way to the front door.

Camilla had already got to Hugo and their suspicious gaze harried me as I crossed the room. I tried to think of some parting shot but a vision of Miranda in purgatory floated past my mind's eye and prevented me from thinking of anything pithy.

172

Outside, in the bleak early afternoon, I felt suddenly tired and battered and old. With my defences down, cold realities loomed large. Miranda was gone, forever. I had witnessed her coffin being lowered into the ground; just as Ted's had been. But equally chilling and hard was my certainty that her laptop had been tampered with. In my time as a journalist, lowly as I was, I had learned one thing; you may abandon stories, but you never, never throw them away. Something felt very awry.

Lucia had said she would bring the girls back after they had had tea at her house. She had suggested I have a lie down. Staring at my reflection through my interference-dogged pupils, I had to admit that I looked very ropey. The dust on my hair, face and jacket made me look like a zombie extra from *Shaun of the Dead*. I got changed and went up onto the roof terrace to smoke a joint and put some distance between reality and me.

All it did was leave me feeling sick and disorientated. Fearing I was about to whitey, I took Lucia's advice and flopped out on the sofa but couldn't relax. As when I am overtired each movement I made, however slight, made the room spin rapidly away from me. Hoping that music may help sooth me, I wove my way over to the stereo. Fumbling with the CD felt like holding a discus in welding gloves, but eventually, I heard the familiar opening bars of 'Forever Changes'.

Forever young. Forever side by side, listening to this as we studied tragedy. Forever the playthings of the gods; flawed, vulnerable and mortal.

On the sofa I drew myself into a tight ball and allowed the bitter tears of my lonely misery to flow.

Jenny must have used Lucia's set of our keys to let herself and Nell in. They had probably been told to be quiet in case daddy was still sleeping. I was, though now I was being shaken awake and could hear crying. My fuzzy head took a few scared seconds to work out what was going on. I was stiff and sore and wedged between the sofa and the coffee table; it was dark outside the unclosed curtains; I felt crap. Nell was sobbing softly to herself and I detected relief and rebuke in Jenny's voice.

"Nell thought you were dead, daddy. I told her you had just had too much wine."

I wanted to cry, but was too dehydrated to do anything but gulp. Raising myself awkwardly to sit on the sofa I stretched out my arms and gathered the two girls to me. They felt so small and vulnerable and I felt not enough of a man to provide them adequate protection. I hugged them firmly and speaking into the crown of Nell's unruly hair promised, "I would never, ever leave you girls. There is nothing more important in my life than you two and your happiness." There was an awkward silence and to lighten the sombreness I joked, "Anyway you're my job."

"People leave their jobs all the time," protested Jenny.

Then Nell whispered, "Chris said his daddy said their mummy couldn't cope anymore and that's why she locked herself in the garage. Is that true?"

"Oh, Nell, I don't know. Miranda was obviously very unhappy and sometimes when people are that upset they get confused and desperate. I think perhaps that she simply had a horrid accident. That she was trying to ask for help from her friends, but it went horribly wrong."

Inside my head a voice demanded 'and if that's true where were *you*, so-called oldest friend?' leaving my heart feeling like it had been roughly shaved.

Jenny wriggled and I realised I was squeezing her for comfort. "Chris told me his mummy poisoned herself with the car. How did she do that?"

'Always the scientist', I thought and explained. After pondering the mechanics she continued, "I told Chris it would be okay, we never see our mum either."

I was shocked but I could see the child's logic behind her statement. "Jenny, mummy has to be away as much as she is because it's part of *her* job. That job pays for all the lovely things we have in our life and it also means that I can be at home to look after both of you. We should be grateful and proud of mummy, her work is very important; she's trying to save the planet."

"Like Superman," chimed in Nell.

"Honestly girls, mummy would love to be able to stay at home more." I hugged them both again. Thank goodness Eithne had not heard Jenny's rebuke. Always sensitive to the amount of time she spent away from the children, she lived up to her name when criticised over it.

Jenny was rooting about in the pocket of her fleece and handed me a piece of folded paper, explaining, "We had to go to Boots with Natania's mum and I saw this. Shall I read it for you, dad?"

It was a leaflet on giving up smoking. "I saw the message on your packet of smoking stuff, it says 'smoking kills'. Nell and me want you to stop."

"And it makes you smell like bonfires," Nell added.

"Do you promise, dad?" pressed Jenny.

My aching lungs heaved. As with so many hung-over mornings, the prospect of freeing myself from addiction shone brightly and blinded me to the rutted road that led there. Emboldened, I declared, "I promise."

Chapter 13

The other promise I meant to keep was the one to Moira Blewitt. All through the slow-burning hangover of the following day, the intuition that there was something very wrong about that missing computer file refused to leave me. On the contrary, it met and mated with my conviction that Miranda would not have taken her own life, then gave birth to a brood of little suspicions. Eventually, I peeled myself off the sofa and dug through the recycling for the card Sharratt had given me. The message I left on Wragg's voicemail stated that I had remembered something important.

Thirty-six hours later I had resigned myself to having to catch the bus down to Holborn. Procrastinating my way through a third cup of coffee and trying to summon the energy, I was going through the post. It was the usual collection of bills and invitations to take out seemingly cheap credit; the usual absence of premium bond wins and an inevitable 'To The Occupier—Demanding Your Immediate Attention'. Curious to see who wanted charity today I ripped it open. A heartrending picture of emaciated and haunted African youth stared out at me beseeching my generosity. I considered my own kids with their Nintendos and Mini Boden clothes then eased my conscience by resolving to write out a cheque later.

The reverie that had formed around my good intention was quickly shattered by a crash from outside. Peering through the window I saw a radiator, shiny in its polythene wrapper, upended in a half-full skip outside Miranda's house. I grabbed the chequebook and was stuffing my donation into the freepost envelope when I heard the gate creak open.

Only DI Sharratt entered the house this time, which was a relief. The lines on his long face seemed to have been scoured even deeper with the passage of the last ten days. Again he refused my offer of a cup of tea and got straight down to business.

"You said you had something important to tell me about Mrs Lethbridge. What is it?"

"Have you questioned her husband?"

"We have spoken with him, yes."

"So you know that Miranda believed he was having an affair with their nanny, Marta."

"We have been made aware of that." His flat Manchester accent made him sound profoundly bored. I hurried on.

"He's a bully and he took Miranda's acquiescence for granted. She knew that, but she stuck by him because she felt it was her duty as a mother and as a Catholic. She wouldn't have divorced him, however much he hurt her, so she certainly would never have killed herself over it. She would have considered it a sin; a betrayal of her beliefs and her family," and her friends, I might have added, but kept that to myself. "I spoke to her mother and she agrees." It was meant to be a statement of fact, but even to me, my voice sounded desperate.

"Well, that makes all the difference. Look Mr Wynde, grief makes people imagine all sorts of things. In my job you see it all the time, people trying to make sense of a sudden death. But, as an expert witness, I can assure you this is suicide, plain and simple. There is no evidence to indicate that it could be anything else."

I could tell by his tone that Sharratt had come here against his better judgement and was now regretting it so I took the plunge. "Do you know who Polish & Check are?" I assumed his grunt was affirmative. "Well, Miranda had this theory that they were blackmailing some of their clients.

177

She was working on an article, an exposé, about it and I'd been helping her with the research and interviews. We'd spoken to about a dozen people who had complaints about the honesty of the nannies or builders they'd employed through the agency. Ranging from catching them going through private papers to demanding money with menaces to keep quiet about extra-marital affairs. Miranda thought that was how Marta had got to Hugo. Judging by what Hugo said to me after the funeral she must have challenged him over it just before she died."

Despite having rehearsed this, as when Miranda had first delivered the theory, it struck a false, melodramatic note when I gave it voice. Sharratt remained silently unimpressed and I went for broke.

"You remember Daniel Morgenstern, the banker who threw himself off Tower Bridge last month? His wife, Rachel, told me that shortly before he killed himself she'd been forced to tell Daniel of her affair with a Polish & Check plumber who'd demanded large sums of money to keep his mouth shut. And my friend Ted Hansford also killed himself because he was being blackmailed by his nanny, after he slept with her…that was in Texas…" I trailed off, sensing deaf ears.

"Not really my patch, Texas," Sharratt said, dryly. "Seems you're a one man Bridgend to be around, Mr Wynde." The shadows lengthened in the deep creases that ran down his cheeks as he frowned. "And from what I know of the case, the authorities are more interested in the large sums going into Mr Morgenstern's account than anything leaving it. So unless you have any actual evidence or a victim who's willing or alive enough to give me a statement, this is all hot air. Perhaps I should have a closer look at you, Mr Wynde. A lot of your neighbours, including Mr Lethbridge, have been exercising their own vivid imaginations concerning your relationship with Mrs

178

Lethbridge during your wife's long absences. Then there's your visitor with the red kinky boots. My DS reckons Mrs Lethbridge got jealous about her and that's why she did herself in; either that or you and her had a suicide pact and you bottled it. So you see, there's no end of theories, just no evidence to back any of them up."

"We, we never had that kind of relationship, it was, it was well... er... deeper than that. That's how I know that she just couldn't have done it, no matter how bad things got."

"Her husband disagrees with you. He believes you pestered her to death."

"Since when did that self-centred prick know how she felt about anything? At least I cared!" I retorted indignantly. "I wouldn't put it past him to have locked her in the garage himself."

Sharratt smiled thinly, like an exasperated parent at a dull-witted child. When he spoke he sounded weary. "Mr Wynde, I deal in facts. Fact: she was found in her garage, the doors were closed and the car's engine was running— classic suicide. Fact: the hospital mortuary performed a blood test; they found high levels of the anti-depressant Citalopram in her blood stream, as well as alcohol and of course the presence of carboxyhaemoglobin, consistent with carbon monoxide poisoning. Fact: there were no signs of any struggle either on her body or in the house. Fact: Mr Lethbridge, was addressing a dinner in Edinburgh on the night in question. Fact: suicide is not a police matter. Conclusion: you are wasting my time, Mr Wynde."

I played my last card. "But I checked her laptop. The story she was writing was deleted after midnight on the night she died. That's suspicious isn't it?"

"Or maybe she finally realised it was a load of codswallop; more than likely to get her sued if it was ever printed." I heard Sharratt preparing to leave.

"Look, I was her friend, I knew her. She just wouldn't take her own life. She wouldn't abandon her children or her religion."

"Depression makes people behave out of character, Mr Wynde." His tone was softer and I felt something like compassion in his voice, just fleetingly. I stared hard at him; his face was still granite. "Your lot think you have it all, but it's all on the surface and when that surface cracks it's like pie-crust and it all collapses in on itself. Some take the easy way out, it's sad but true."

"So you're dropping the case," I felt hollow myself.

"There is no case, Mr Wynde. Like I said before, if this had been some Shazza in Somers Town, I would never have been called out. And you lot wonder why there's not more crime solved."

With that he strode towards the door. I remained where I was, looking at my feet, too deflated to move. The door handle squeaked under his grip and he let himself out. As he pulled it closed behind him he paused to growl, "Take my advice Mr Wynde, do me and your kids a favour and put this behind you."

The rain blew into my face with all the persistence of a nagging child as I trudged down the hill. God, the absentee father, never did the school run or he'd have had more compassion. With every cold, slippery step Sharratt's remarks resonated, leaving me feeling naïve and unsure of my judgement. Certainly, the rarefied atmosphere of leafy NW3 filtered the realities of poverty, murder and starving children. We, after all, could always salve our conscience by popping a cheque for a few quid in the post to Oxfam. But was I really so divorced from everyday life to believe Hugo capable of killing Miranda, or was I just lashing out, furious at my inability to save her?

180

Maybe Sharratt was right; I should move on, stop wallowing in corrosive waters. I had done my best to honour my promise to Moira.

My promise to the children was faring a little better. Though I had failed to give up completely, my intake had decreased dramatically and I hadn't smoked a single joint. I was trying to lay off the booze as well, something made easier by Eithne's return from Montreal – three days late and fuming.

Each night after Miranda's death had followed the same pattern – a sandwich, a bottle of red and a stack of music from the past. Each had ended with me, and the bottle, drunk. But a bottle shared is a bottle halved and with Eithne home each night for supper, cuisine and conversation had returned too.

She listened patiently as I poured out the bitter brew I had bottled up and fermented over the previous days and weeks. The nagging sense of responsibility I felt for Miranda's death; the pain at discovering myself so ignorant about the private lives of my friends; and my absolute conviction that, despite this, I knew that Miranda would never have deprived herself and her children of her life.

In all this, I was so desperate to be soothed by Eithne that I forgot that Miranda had been her friend too. I think it was the fourth night she'd been home, I was fidgeting with my tobacco tin, aching for a cigarette and conscious I was re-treading the same old ground when Eithne plucked the tin from my hand, placed it firmly on the coffee table and interrupted my maudlin monologue.

"Look, Joe you're not doing yourself any good with this. I know how much you adored Miranda. God, your puppy-dog eyes would've given you away even if she hadn't filled me in on your various attempts to seduce her!"

181

A jolt of fear shot through me and I opened my mouth to speak words that didn't arrive.

She continued. "It's alright Joe, you've nothing to be guilty about. It's only adultery if you act on your fantasies and I always knew I could trust you both."

"Is that how you justify spending so much time with Jean-Pierre?" The words were out of my open mouth before I had a chance to stop them.

Eithne bristled and there was a distinct edge to her reply. "Sure he's nice eye-candy and he's fun to be with, which is something I don't always get at home. But he's also my colleague. Anyway, I thought you wanted to talk about yourself. What do you think Miranda would say to seeing you like this?"

I knew exactly what she'd say, she'd told me on the day of her death. "But I feel responsible, Eithne. I should have…"

"What, Joe, what could you have done? Whatever led Miranda to that garage, she was an adult, not one of our children. After the pain of losing Ted, I can only imagine how awful this is for you; it must seem almost personal; that's survivor's guilt. Maybe we did all let her down, you me, Hugo, all her friends. But assuming all the blame yourself then grasping for other explanations just stops you starting to heal. It makes things worse…for all of us."

I mumbled an apology and shut up.

At the end of a week of recurrent rain and nicotine pangs, I was grateful for the regime change promised by half term. Eithne and I had vaguely discussed her trying to get some leave and us all going down to Sussex to stay with my sister. Dripping and grappling with P.E. bags and tired, hungry children, I was fumbling for the keys when the front door swung open and Eithne welcomed us home with a flurry of kisses. Skipping ahead she ushered us to the kitchen table for hot chocolate and cake.

"Watch out daddy minds that suitcase there," she warned as we filed into the hall.

"Ah, I wondered why you were home." I felt the heavy bag with my sodden foot and sensed our plans for the week were about to be torpedoed. "Where are they sending you this time...or are you leaving me for being a grumpy git?"

With a flourish she presented us each with an enormous chocolate sponge domino before gathering us all into her arms and lowering her voice to a conspiratorial whisper. "Your clever mummy here has not only wangled the week off work but has found us a little cottage by the sea where we can blow away the cobwebs together."

"Urgh, yuk, but I don't want to stay in a house with spiders mummy!" complained Nell.

Later, after she and Jenny had disappeared to pack buckets and spades, Eithne and I freed the laughter we had stifled and wept tears of mirth for the first time in weeks.

With less than two hours before we were due at Charing Cross, the practicalities of going away presented themselves with the arrival of Lucia in a perfumed cloud of excitement. She and Freddie were taking Natania to Capri for the week and she was checking I was still happy to keep an eye on their house. She looked crestfallen when I told her that we too would be away. I was immediately struck by how one-way the traffic of generosity between us had been during the last six weeks. She always went away at half term and I always minded her place. Had I not been so bound up with my own tortured thoughts, I would have considered this and warned her of our plan to get away too. She sounded a little huffy as she bustled off to ask Hugo or, more likely, Marta to do this small favour for her. I made a mental note to take Lucia out to dinner and apologise on our return.

Although I was sure that the set of keys I'd left with Miranda, in case I locked myself out, would still be in her drawer somewhere, I was reluctant to risk having to beg the same favour of Hugo. Instead, I double-dosed the houseplants with water and relied on their hardiness to survive a week's neglect.

We had been in Rye for three days before the black clouds that had been oppressing me were fully dissipated by windswept walks along Camber Sands and the sunshine of Eithne's love. The absence of tall buildings made the skies seem less bleak than at home, although they held as much wet weather. We were raked by it on the beaches, in the open-sided carriages of the Romney Hythe and Dymchurch Railway and atop the old lighthouse at Dungeness. But because we were all together and alone, we found a blitz spirit developed in the face of all adversity. Even when Eithne's Blackberry summoned her back a day early we laughed at the grim predictability of it. She was due to fly to New York on Saturday anyway so, determined to spend as much time together as possible, we packed up our soggy possessions and all traipsed back to the station.

The house was freezing when we got home; I had turned off the central heating to save money and gas. The chill made the place seem unnatural and Nell started to cry saying that she could feel ghosts. I knew what she meant, everything seemed disturbed; nothing obviously out of place just possessed of a different aura. I put it down to the cold, but still checked the desk for our passports and the cupboard where I had hidden the laptops. Everything was still there. Eithne made hot chocolate for all of us with the milk Jenny had reminded us to buy from the mini-market. Hugging the warm cups we curled up in a bundle on the sofa and watched *The Princess Bride*.

184

"Go well Joe, I love you." Eithne's soft kiss woke me at five the next morning. I grunted "You too, me too," before rolling into the cocoon she had just vacated and falling back to sleep, absorbing her lingering warmth.

Gazing at Miranda's porch later that morning, my hands mechanically cleaning the coffee pot, I replayed my final conversation with her for the umpteenth time. A week outside the enclave, without the bubble-wrap of drink and dope, had left me more clear-headed than I'd felt for weeks. The therapy of sharing my grief with Eithne and finding her sense of loss was as keen as mine, had helped objectify Miranda's death, making it less my responsibility. Scoured by rain and buffeted by wind the layers of shock and guilt and self-pity I had built around it had been eroded, leaving only the facts; Sharratt would have approved.

The visually impaired don't pick up on people dissembling in the same way as the sighted. Bill Clinton's inability to meet the eye of the camera when quizzed about Monica Lewinski passed me by. However, the awkward cadence of his voice didn't. The minute lacunae that crack the sentence structure; the stumbled-over words; the additional adverbs that really overstress the speaker's honesty; these are the aural giveaways I perceive.

That final night of her life Miranda, though she felt crap and exasperated, had still been full of fight and determination. She had gone back to continue work on her story, not given up because I couldn't be of help. She had told me to call round when I was straight. She did not kill herself; I knew it as certainly and instinctively as when Wragg had first told me.

Sharratt would argue that he too had a refined view and that he could detect no evidence to substantiate my intuition. He would, no doubt, tell me that I still lacked objectivity because I was part of the sequence of events and was emotionally involved. Sharratt was not, however,

185

looking for evidence to build a case. If anyone was going to do that, it was going to have to be me.

Equally clear to me was the conclusion that someone else must have put Miranda in that garage. Pursuing a killer, unless I trod very carefully, would put me, and possibly my family, at risk. My first duty was to protect them, but I couldn't let Miranda down, not again.

Somehow, I needed to find enough evidence to convince Sharratt and the only place I could think to look was on the hard-drive of Miranda's laptop. The file may have been deleted, but somewhere in my own memory-bank I had once stored the knowledge that it was unlikely to be irrecoverable. This however, marked the limits of my expertise with computers, especially those out of the Bill Gates stable. I needed a techie, someone who knew what they were doing. Taking a deep breath I did what I had resolved to do a few days earlier on Camber Sands and rang Dino.

Chapter 14

Before his wife's Wall Street bank had uprooted the family and deposited them in London, Dino had been a programmer and network designer for equity trading systems. Another dad on a spouse's visa, he made a bit of beer money now by fixing peoples' PCs, mostly unclogging them of porn-based viruses or baby rusk and posset.

"Hey, Joe," he must have read my caller identity on his iPhone, "Fancy a beer for lunch?"

"Funnily enough I was going to ask you the same, Dino. I want to pick your technical brains about something."

"For you my friend, I will charge my special rate. Two pints of Sussex and a burger and I guarantee to fix your problem with absolute discretion."

Though I had rehearsed my spiel scores of times, it still took ten minutes of idle banter about the half-term holidays and Brad's latest run-in with BT, before I could raise the topic comfortably. The arrival of our burgers broke the stream of preamble and I waited for Dino to take a large bite before starting my pitch.

"So Dino, say I have deleted a file in Word, put it in Trash and hit Empty Trash, is there any way of recovering the document?"

Dino ruminated over his burger before swallowing noisily and taking a glug of ale. "Yup."

"Is it easy to do?"

"What, can a technophobe like you manage it? With the right software and a bit of patience, which of course you lack, yeah. But I can do it for you and I have the necessary 'OnTrack Easy Recovery' file repair solution disk." I could feel the beam of technical self-satisfaction across the table.

"Oh...kay," I tried to sidestep his generous offer. "On-Track Easy Recovery, that sounds perfect. Thanks. Wow you really can't hide anything on a computer can you?" My mind strayed involuntarily to what I might find if I got access to Eithne's laptop before I wrenched it back to the task at hand. Hoping I'd be able to remember the product name I asked Dino my next question. "How about using the computer's memory to tell you when and who accessed which files on the hard drive? Is that easy to do?"

He paused, suspicious now, but his enthusiasm for the subject overcame his resistance. "Oh man! Now you're talking; forensic timeline viewing software. The cops use it all the time. 'EnCase Forensic v5', put in the disk and up pops a diary giving you a timeline view of all files and when they were created, accessed or deleted. I got that too. Not cheap but the mutt's nuts!"

"Cool, thanks Dino. For that invaluable seminar let me buy you another Sussex."

I'd hoped we could change the subject after I returned from the bar, but I had tickled Dino's curiosity and he was not to be put off so easily. "Okay Joe, now I've satisfied your thirst for knowledge, it's your turn. Usually, when you've got a problem with your Apple, you get straight on the phone and I come over and fix it for you. Correct me if I'm wrong, but I can't remember you ever volunteering to attempt home surgery. And the idea of you going out to buy any software yourself when you can scrounge it from me is unthinkable. I detect a hint of BS in the air, so how about you level with me, eh buddy?"

Underneath his mocking tone, I detected something between hurt and anger at being kept at arm's length. It was true; I did use his expertise regularly and mercilessly. As a foreigner in a new city, I knew he felt that it earned him a calling card and degree of respect amongst the indigenous population. I had just demonstrated the limits of that respect.

Steepling my fingers around my nose I pondered my next sentence with care. "I believe that someone I know was killed because of something they were writing. I've checked their laptop and that article has been erased and its former name changed to make it more difficult to trace. If I can recover it, it may provide enough evidence to force the police to take my suspicions seriously." There, I had said it! Would he laugh, or be as sceptical as Eithne and Sharratt.

Dino clapped his hands together and, following my lead, whispered, "You're talking about the late and lovely Miranda Lethbridge I take it?" I nodded, tingling with anticipation; might I have found an ally? He whistled. "Man, you oughta lay off the green weed, it's turning you delusional!"

I had been prepared for this, but it still hurt to be dismissed so lightly. "Thanks Dino. You carry on thinking that. I didn't want to get you involved anyway, because if I'm right, then doing what I want to do might mean I end up like her too."

I heard him wince. "So what are you planning? Just in case you don't come back, then I can at least tell Eithne and the kids about it."

His attempt at humour fell flat and I stared at my pint. "Don't joke about it, Dino. Believe you me, I'd prefer to leave the whole thing be, but I can't. Apart from having promised her mum that I'll do all I can to find the truth, the knowledge that I'm right is starting to haunt me. It's like one of those jobs you put off for so long that it screams at you every time you do anything else, until eventually it even invades your dreams. Miranda was my friend, I knew her for twenty years. She would never have killed herself

189

and left her kids in the care of a man for whom wealth, position and kudos are more important than family."

Dino was shaking his curly black locks from side to side, "And your well known fondness for Hugo doesn't cloud your judgement, maybe?"

"That has nothing to do with it!" I retorted angrily. "You're a Catholic, would you commit self-murder?"

Dino chewed on a chip and replied, "The two are not mutually exclusive, Joe."

"Look, Dino, I know I'm right on this one. Thanks for all your help with the software, but it's best I do this on my own." I drank up and made to leave, angry with myself for not handling things better.

I heard Dino rustling about in the pocket of the greatcoat he had recently adopted. "Hold your horses cowpoke," he commanded. There was the noise of a ballpoint being clicked and some scribbling. He handed me a wad of envelopes. "One good turn deserves another, I believe. Here's the latest bundle of Hansford mail for you to do with as you want. On the back of the green one from Chrysler you'll find the details of the software you will need. What kind of machine is her laptop?"

"How the hell should I know," I answered sulkily "But it's small and silver and I think it runs Windows Vista."

"How you gonna get hold of it, or don't I ask?"

"What you don't know can't hurt you. Suffice to say I hope to perform the operation on site when the patient's husband is away."

Dino was shaking his head again and sighed heavily. "I hate to piss on your parade, Joe, but even if you knew what you were doing, it's gonna take time. And you ain't got the expertise to even get started."

"Thanks for the vote of confidence," I muttered. "You offering to come along and hold my hand?"

"Hey man, shit no! You got the wrong kind of Italian. No way am I gonna get involved in breaking 'n' entering. If we got caught you'd get a slap on the wrist but I'd get deported. Bang! Advance straight to Heathrow; do not pass Go, do not collect 200 bucks. And that would be nuthin' compared to what Maria would do to me. She'd go apeshit; she'd have my balls for breakfast."

I laughed in spite of my glumness. Dino leant forward and clapped me on the shoulder. "However if you were to bring me a laptop on behalf of a friend and ask me to recover some information from it, well that would be a totally different matter."

Later, after pick up and supper, I suggested a game of Monopoly. Nell quickly tired of it when her infernally lucky elder sister bought Park Lane and Mayfair in consecutive rolls of the dice. So Nell and I paired up and my mind drifted to the problem of gaining access to Hugo's house.

Physically getting in should present no problem. I still had a set of keys; a relic of goldfish feeding duties covering the Lethbridge's many holidays. I also assumed that Hugo was possessed of the same inertia as the rest of the population and that the burglar alarm, if on at all in this crime-deprived area, would still be set to the date of the Popish Plot. No, the trouble would be finding a time when Hugo, Marta, the children and Hugo's newly-stabled sister would all be out of the house long enough for me to purloin and return the computer unnoticed.

We landed on Whitechapel, also owned by Jenny, who whooped gleefully. Nell threw all our pooled resources at her sister and stomped off muttering, "Stupid game!"

191

Jenny was triumphant and taunted, "I'm going to be a City fat cat when I'm older, loser!"

I told her I sincerely hoped that she would grow up to do something more socially useful and asked whether she really wanted to turn out like Hugo.

It was then that, quite unwittingly, Jenny presented me with the solution. "Dad, can Christian and Hope come round for a sleepover, to cheer them up?"

I passed her the phone and five minutes later it was all arranged.

Chapter 15

It was a surprise to open the door to Camilla. I'd assumed Marta would drop the children off before she finished for the day. Illuminated by the porch light Hugo's sister's chestnut mane, styled with a girlish flick fringe over one eye, gleamed unnaturally as it cascaded over her cashmere clad shoulders. Her nostrils flared when she addressed me.

"My brother seems to think you can be trusted with the children. He says even you can manage to remain sober for one night. Marta will pick them up at 9.30 sharp tomorrow. Make sure you have them ready." She thrust the children and their overnight bags at me and turned to leave.

"Have a good evening Camilla. I must say you look very smart. Are you and Hugo going anywhere special?"

"If you must know, it's my birthday on Sunday. We're going to a private view at Sotheby's after which Hugo's treating me to dinner at Le Caprice." Suspicion mingled with her smugness.

"Well, have a lovely time." I meant it. I didn't want them getting home too early. Relief at their plans meant however, that I had neglected to be my usual insulting self with her and I knew that somewhere under that fringe Camilla had arched an eyebrow. "It's good to see you both continuing the fine Salopian tradition of incest." Her horrified whinnying was muffled once I'd slammed the door shut.

"We're on," I announced to Dino as I walked back into the sitting room.

He was lounging on the sofa fiddling with my wireless router. "Not much love lost between you and Camilla, huh?"

I shook my head vigorously. "Well she's her brother's sister."

"I don't know, I think she's kinda cute."

"I suppose centuries of inbreeding has lent her a certain severe pedigree," I conceded, "but the spectre of Hugo would always be hovering over you when you were shagging her."

"You're a sick man, Joe," Dino proclaimed and turned his attention back to the router.

Five minutes later, Hugo and Camilla walked arm in arm out of Fawkes Close towards the High Street. I watched them as far as I could then waited twenty minutes, in case they had forgotten anything. The children were all in Jenny's room building a camp from duvets, pillows, mops and brooms. Dino promised to keep an eye on them and say that I had popped out to the mini-market to get milk and bread, in the unlikely event that they noticed my absence.

Lucia's curtains were drawn against the November chill as I groped my way, stickless, across the familiar Close. Miranda's keys still turned the two locks. The alarm started to bleep insistently as soon as the door opened. I fought desperately to see its glowing lights in the dark, using the very few rods that remain in the corner of my right eye. Having dimly discerned a greenish shimmer, I next located the small Braille dot on the 5 button and typed in 1-6-7-8. I'd double-checked the date but still held my breath. The bleeping continued. I typed it in again. Still the bleeping rang out insistently. My internal clock was counting 14, 15. 16. I closed my eyes, bracing myself for the klaxon that would drown out all other sound and once more typed in 1-6-7-8. 'Enter'—that's what I'd forgotten! I wrenched the torch from my pocket and shone it next to the 0 button. It was there and I stabbed it breathlessly. The silence brought such euphoria that I had to sit down.

194

Time was ticking by, still somewhat shaky, I rose to my feet and, arms outstretched at midriff height edged forward. Memorising the position of obstacles is part of everyday life for me, but a new woman in the house likes to stamp her mark on the place and this involves a certain amount of space planning. Only the low glass coffee table eluded me; the bruise it left on my shin a painful reminder of Camilla for days to come.

The basement still had a tang of dust, although Camilla had ensured that the builders finished the home cinema in record time. The scent of emulsion vied for supremacy with the grainy dryness and together they lent the space an unhealthy, oppressive atmosphere. Miranda's office door was again locked and I groped around for the bathroom key. It had gone.

I swore out loud and my voice echoed off the hard surfaces of the uncarpeted basement. Hurrying back up to and through the sitting room, I steered towards the bottom of the main staircase. At the return, on a landing there was another bathroom and that, I hoped, still retained its original door and key. It did. Remembering to skirt the sharp edged coffee table, I headed back down to the office. The key worked and, closing the door behind me, I risked turning on the light in the windowless room.

The naked bulb bleached my retinas for a full minute. As focus returned through blooms of random intense colour, I detected that the room had been stripped and newly repainted. The desk, the chair, the books and the shelves had all disappeared. Even the carpet had gone. I felt sick. It was as if Hugo had removed any trace of his dead wife; her sanctuary, somewhere that could have remained a shrine to her memory, was now a bare, whitewashed cupboard.

My shock passed slowly and I wandered in a daze back upstairs to replace the key in the bathroom. I would have to check the whole house for Miranda's laptop. Hugo's bedroom seemed a good place to start, so I headed for the second floor.

Relying on my sense of touch to identify objects is second nature; though after years of doing so the calluses on my fingertips are digital cataracts. It may appear like groping around in the dark clumsily (especially when I encounter an unexpected glass of liquid and inevitably knock it over), but it is remarkably effective.

The ability to look without needing to turn on lights becomes an advantage when you are in a house without the owner's permission. After five minutes of running my fingers over bedside tables, through the contents of drawers and around cupboards, I was sure the laptop wasn't there. I was also somewhat surprised to have learned that either Hugo or Miranda had a rubber fetish.

I couldn't face trying the two children's rooms and suspected it was unlikely that, even with Hugo's wealth and lack of empathy, he would give them an expensive laptop belonging to their dead mum. The whiff of Chanel No.5 told me that Camilla now occupied the spare bedroom and I set about looking in there. It was remarkably orderly and I perceived how a childhood incarcerated at Benenden had left its mark on her. That such sterile asceticism still dominated her outside its cloistered walls almost made me feel sorry for her. There wasn't even a novel by her bed.

Opening the door of the fitted wardrobe, I was assailed by the mingled scent of expensive wool and perfume. There was something else too, a faint odour of plaster dust. On my knees, I slid my hand between the cellophane sheathed dresses and skirts and at the back of the wardrobe found a large cardboard box, grainy with a fine coating of dust.

After dragging it into the room and with the little torch held in my mouth, I flipped open the box's lid. Miranda's Dilbert mouse mat lay at the top. My heart quickened and I

196

snatched out her thesaurus and OED. Next my hand closed around a familiar fluffy object. Since I had known her Miranda had treasured her leopard skin pencil case, a relic of her secondary school days. I held it to my nose and inhaled its scent, trying, without success, to feel Miranda's presence again. The pencil case felt hard and overstuffed; it was slightly unzipped at one end. I opened it up fully and recognised the smooth shape of the MP3 recorder. I hesitated then slipped it into my pocket; she had, after all, given it to me.

The rest of the contents of the box also came from her office. Files of cuttings, a couple of signed photographs and the various knick-knacks she'd accumulated in a decade or so of attending celebrity parties. There was no laptop.

Repacking and replacing the box, I began to feel desperate. Had Hugo given or thrown the laptop away? Unlikely. I had a cursory look round each child's room and found that Christian did have a laptop, though it was black and larger than Miranda's. Hope only had a toy pink one. Desperate for inspiration I clutched my head in my hands; it was hot and sweaty and thumping with the knowledge that time was ticking away.

Hugo's office was at the top of the house. Its iris recognition system and the elaborate lock set into armoured glass, made it impenetrable. I screwed my eyes shut and risked turning on the light for a few seconds. Having avoided the bleaching effect of the initial shock of light, I opened them again and what I managed to make out after a few seconds was enough to tell me that there was only one, rather large, PC on his mahogany statement desk. I flicked the light off, dialled Dino's number on my mobile and headed back downstairs.

He picked up immediately. "Hey Joe, I was getting worried. You got it?"

197

"Can't find the bloody thing anywhere. Got any ideas?"

"Well, where do you keep yours? Hang on; I can see it. Have you tried the coffee table?"

"I've tried every other sodding place, so I'll give it a go."

Lo and behold, under a copy of *Horse and Hound*, there it was. I snatched it up and left the house without resetting the alarm.

Dino didn't need to have the urgency of his task explained to him. If the laptop was in the sitting room it was being used and would be missed. A call to Le Caprice established that, including coffee and journey time, we probably had until about 11.15 pm. Would an hour and forty minutes be long enough? Worry tore at my nerves. This had to work, I couldn't think of any other way in.

Dino waved me away and I went to check on the children. They were fine and waved me away too. I needed to do something and remembered the stack of post that Dino had given me to forward to Gail. It was still on the work surface, so I gathered it up and started to sort through. Most of it was junk; an invitation to test drive the new Chrysler, a loyalty card for the local sushi restaurant, and money off your next Ocado delivery that I doubted would cover Texas. That pile went into the recycling, as did a collection of thick annual reports from various investment companies; neighbourliness only buys so much postage. This left another, much smaller pile of stuff that was probably also junk, but which I felt I should open to check. I was about to tackle it when Dino called me over.

"Okay, Joe. Looky here. This is a diary datasheet of all the activity on this baby for the week up to Miranda's death. Now what we are interested in is her documents and especially you said "Checkitout.doc". So, tum, tum, tum, she creates it on October 4th and plays around with it for a coupla weeks. See it gets bigger day by day, as more KB of memory is used. Now it's 362 KB on the day she dies, which is a pretty big doc. She first accesses it at 11.13 that morning, makes some changes that she saves, shuts down at 3 pm, presumably to pick up the kids. Now she's back in at 5.02 pm, then was back on at 7.50 pm. Then she had it open and it was backing up normally till, wow 11.54 pm. Now this is weird, the laptop hibernates 'cos there's no activity from then till 12.37 am, then the file is 'select all' deleted. Then she changes its name to 'artical.doc' then deletes it all over again before moving the blank doc to the trash and emptying trash. Then she shuts down at 12.39 am. Freaky, why spend all that time on a doc only to change its name and chuck it all in the trash?"

"My point exactly Sherlock. Can you make a copy of this for me?"

Still distracted Dino nodded, "It was only that file. Everything else is intact. I can give you a read-out of websites she visited too, if you want." Dino was in his element.

"Everything could be useful." I urged, "What about the document, do you reckon you can find that?"

"Hmmnh," there was a trace of doubt in his voice. "That is a bit more tricky, how long we got?"

I glanced up at the huge handed clock on the mantelpiece—then stared at it in disbelief. "An hour and five minutes! Oh shit, can you do it?"

Dino was not a naturally sceptical person. It gave him a funny aura that followed me as I escaped upstairs to put the kids to bed. I was glad to have the routine of teeth cleaning and verruca burning to occupy my racing mind for the next half hour.

Fear of being caught by Hugo while I replaced the laptop, already fluttered within me. Although we now had evidence of something fishy going on around the time she died, it was circumstantial and inconclusive. I wondered whether the police had established a time of death. They'd done a blood test so it was possible they could tell. Someone else must have destroyed that article—but who? Hugo had been in Scotland; presumably the police had checked his alibi. I looked at Christian and Hope in their winceyette pyjamas; would it make any difference to them to know that their mum had been murdered, rather than killed herself? When I believed that I was doing this for Miranda, or Moira, or even myself, it was easily justified. But exposing children so young to the sordid world of adult device was a far heavier responsibility.

The four kids were going to sleep in the same room and as I gave each a kiss goodnight, I tried to ignore the sickly sweet smell of marshmallows coming from under Nell's bed. Let them enjoy their innocence before it crash-lands, I thought. Oh to have it back myself!

Dino was still hunched over the laptop, muttering to himself. The CD drive was whirring loudly and his fingers were chattering on the keyboard. My "are we nearly there yet?" imitation of a nagging child elicited only a grunt in response. I nervously squinted at the mantelpiece clock again. "Less than half an hour to go, mate."

I was too keyed-up to relax and so paced between the kitchen and sitting room until Dino told me to get lost and stop distracting him. He sounded tense. I sat down with Ted and Gail's post and carefully prised open a Harrods-stamped envelope. It was a final demand for payment of a charge card bill, dated six weeks previously and for a ludicrous five figure sum. I let out a low incredulous whistle and Dino snapped, "Shut the fuck up man, I need to concentrate."

Calculating the accruing interest proved too complicated for me and only half my mind was on it anyway. I briefly wondered whether I should contact Harrods on Gail's behalf, but decided that she and they could afford the inconvenience so I resealed the envelope and put it in a Postpak for forwarding.

The whole process had only killed five minutes, there were still up to twenty-two to go. Dino was now singing to himself, urging the software to work with the expletive-laden lyrics of Notorious B.I.G.'s notorious big hit.

There was a shriek from upstairs followed by loud sobbing and Jenny imploring me to help. She was sitting on the put-me-up bed with her arm round Hope, trying to comfort the weeping little girl. I kissed Jenny on the crown of her head and then knelt down in front of Hope, took her hand into mine and gently asked what was wrong.

At first she ignored me, her hand rigid and face turned away as she tried to hold back her tears. After a couple of minutes my knees were aching so I sat down on the bed next to her and softly repeated my question. She began to shake uncontrollably before hiding her face in my armpit and sobbing, "I want mummy, I want mummy" again and again.

There are no words of comfort to relieve the burden of a child's grief at losing her parent. Mumbling, "I know, Hope, I want her back too" left me feeling utterly bereft. "But she is always nearby, in your memories and watching over you." My atheism had never seemed so cold and lumpen.

"Then why won't she come, if she is always so near? I need you now mummy! Mummy where are you?"

In spite of myself I shushed her, afraid she would wake the two sleeping children. She hid her face again and wept quietly. I held her, feeling empty and depressed.

Jenny crawled over to me and put her head on my shoulder, "Poor Hope. When I miss my mummy I cuddle the fluffy rhino that she bought me back from Africa.

201

Would that make things better Hope?" The little girl shook her head beneath my arm. Jenny persisted, "What about that lovely Victorian doll your mummy gave you, you know the one you got when you turned five. She's beautiful; she always reminds me of your mummy."

Hope looked up and rubbed her eyes with her small fists. She was wilting, exhausted by the release of so much emotion. "Melanie," she whispered, "I want Melanie."

"Where is she?" I asked softly, leaning down to grope for Hope's bag.

"In my room. At home."

My hand froze in mid-reach and my brain screamed "Jesusfuckingchristalmighty!" I'd completely lost track of time. "Okay Hope, I'll go and get her." I rushed from the room and downstairs.

Dino was still bent over the laptop and looked up in surprise as I hurtled into the sitting room and cannoned painfully into the arm of the sofa. "Hey man, I've found it, just trying to open it now. C'mon...nearly done, just a coupla minutes," he reassured.

"Dino! It's quarter past, they'll be home any minute!" My heart was racing making everything wavy. "Look, Hope wants her doll. I'll go and get that now, you bring the laptop over as soon as you're done, and be quick!"

Limping swiftly over the cobbles, I felt elation and panic; this better be worth all the theatrics. I wondered what I would find myself reading later. At Hugo's front door my left hand was shaking too much to put the key in the lock and I had to guide it in with the fingers of my right. I tore upstairs, more confident now all the obstacles were fresh in my memory, and into Hope's room. Short of time, I flicked on the light and peered desperately around. Melanie was on top of the bookcase and I offered silent thanks for her vibrant scarlet dress that drew even my faulty eyes.

202

Seizing her then clicking off the light, I hurried downstairs. Dino wasn't there. I called his mobile and heard it echo in the Close outside. Cutting the call short I hissed, "Don't worry, that was me."

As he handed me the laptop I heard a car slowing down on the main road to turn into Fawkes Close. "Shit! Dino, get round the back, it could be them." He disappeared between Hugo's and next door as the bright headlights of a chugging diesel rounded the corner into the cul-de-sac. Only a London taxi makes that loose tappet noise—nothing as proletarian as the Tube for Hugo. I edged back into the house, Melanie under one arm, the laptop gripped in both hands.

I slipped it back under the magazine, hoping it was exactly where I had found it. A heavy metal door slammed and I had only seconds to compose myself for the onslaught to come. We met in the hallway.

You don't have to see someone's face to know they are livid. Hugo's wine-infused breath was like the wind that precedes a brush fire, only with more spittle. He strode right up to my face and barked, "Had a good poke around my house while we were out, did you?" He seized my throat and pushed me back against the wall.

As I stumbled, Melanie slipped from under my arm. Conscious of her china head and value to Hope, I flailed my hand downwards and my fingers caught her thick hair. Holding her up, I croaked, "Hope's doll. She couldn't sleep."

Hugo's grip tightened. "Oh really? How convenient. Empty your pockets." I did as I was told and he snatched up his house keys. Any sorrow I felt at losing them was tempered with relief at having safely stowed the MP3 recorder back at home.

"What about the children? They're alone in your house, aren't they? I knew we couldn't trust you." Camilla's shrill voice was edged with excitement at seeing her brother as a man of action.

I had had enough of being strangled and knocked Hugo's arm aside. "My friend Dino is there. He's a good Catholic father of four, sober and thinks you're cute. Though that probably means he's deranged."

Turning to Hugo, I snarled, "Now if you don't mind, I would like to keep my promise to your daughter." I pushed past him but he seized my shoulder.

"I'm coming with you, Wynde. If you're lying and have left my children unattended in the house, I will ensure that everyone from social services upwards knows just how irresponsible and untrustworthy you really are."

"Oh fine, bring little sister too. She can get all juiced up meeting an admirer who isn't a blood relative."

Hugo steered me over to my house with Camilla clacking over the cobbles behind us. In times of great need even atheists pray, and I am no exception. It would have taken me a lot longer to get back round Fawkes Close than the two minutes that had just elapsed. My disability versus Dino's unfamiliarity with the layout, it was a close call.

"Hi honey, I'm home." A toilet flushed and Dino appeared at the top of the stairs, his newly washed face glistening under the harsh ceiling lights.

"Hi, Joe did you get it? She's still a bit upset." Then, as if just noticing Hugo and Camilla he trotted down the stairs and approached them with his hand outstretched. "Hugo, I am sorry for your loss, Miranda was a great gal. And you must be Camilla. Ciao bella! Joe has told me about you. Dino Cazale at your service." He stooped and kissed her hand.

"Satisfied?" I spat at the two Lethbridges, "Or do you want me to wake Christian so that you can remove your children for fear of neglect?"

"That won't be necessary." Hugo was unrepentant. "Make sure that they are ready for Marta at 9.30. Goodnight Mr Cazale."

I shut the door firmly behind them and hurried upstairs to give Melanie to Hope. She was already fast asleep and I tucked the doll in beside her. Back downstairs again I poured two enormous glasses of red wine and half listened to Dino waxing lyrical about Camilla's "cute aristocratic ass."

The two of us had flopped down onto the sofa with our glasses before he sighed, "Man that was close. A minute earlier and they'd have caught me creeping across the carport. You have no idea how near I came to pulling your door shut behind me when I came over with that laptop. Phewhee, Joe. Life with you is one long party, no wonder Eithne is away so much. I need a spell of R&R myself. Still I got me an introduction to the lovely Miss Lethbridge, so it ain't all bad."

"Knock it off Dino. She's a mare! Anymore of this simpering to the toffs and I'll donate your testicles to Maria myself. Anyway, what have we got?"

Dino made a drum roll sound with his forefingers on the coffee table and whipped a CD from his pocket. "Checkitout, and a log of all the activity for the last six weeks on that laptop. The lovely Camilla likes to surf websites featuring Argentine polo players, by the way. Do you reckon she'd stretch to an Italian stallion?" I hurled a cushion at him, it missed but the mantelpiece clock was left teetering.

Before he went home, Dino showed me how to access the files he had copied. I was profuse in my thanks and though he joked that this had been the best fun he could have had without going to jail, he sounded tired and there was a touch of remorse in his voice that I took to be guilt rather than the remnants of stress.

"Let's just hope it was worth it, huh Joe?" he sighed as he pulled on his greatcoat. "Next time, let's go to a gig instead."

I made myself a strong coffee and took it back to the sitting room, eager to look at the article. The computer's VoiceOver function could have read it to me but I needed to hear Miranda's voice in my head as I scanned her words; to pick up her nuances; to make her live again, if only in my imagination.

However, as hard as I tried, I could not ignore the triangular clusters of crimson lights that burst across my end-of-a-long-day sight. Even with the text adjusted to 18 point, white on black, bold and with the contrast altered to maximum, the words swam listlessly across the screen. The more I persisted the closer to the centre of my field of vision my ever-present arcs of interference exploded, rapidly rendering all efforts hopeless. I closed the Mac down, poured away the coffee and went to bed, trying to ignore the trickle of self-loathing that enters my heart when my eyes let me down so completely.

I dreamt in flickering Technicolor of Hugo atop a Camilla-faced steed in chequered livery. He was leading the hunt and pursuing me over fields and through bramble-filled woods. Melanie was cradled like a baby in my arms and as I stumbled onwards, I looked down to see her face was cracked and she was sobbing quietly to herself. I hugged her to me and told her I would get her home safely. She gripped me hard with her porcelain fists and pleaded, "No, no, please, no! Mummy's not there anymore! She's gone away forever. We have to hide round the back."

The bugle was sounded, wailing like an alarm, forcing us to run blindly on through the thorn-filled wood. Searchlights swept the area around us as Hugo's voice boomed, "Had a good poke around my wife did you?" Other huntsmen and women were closing in, murmuring, "He's untrustworthy, irresponsible, a drunk. Turn the hounds loose." The baying dogs moved closer and closer, then one brushed against my side.

I woke with a start; the sheet was clammy beneath me and the duvet clung to my sweat-damp chest. My lungs ached. Semi-conscious and clutching Melanie, Hope had curled up on the duvet next to me. I smoothed her matted hair and folded back the bottom half of the quilt to cover her. Cocooned in its warmth she started to breathe more calmly and regularly. I listened as she cast off and floated into sleep; her breaths deepened and seemed to draw away my own night terrors; so, eventually, I too slipped my moorings and drifted downstream on a pitch black river of dreamless sleep.

Chapter 16

The following morning Marta was, as ever, both prompt and eye-catching. Her long blonde hair gleamed in the weak morning sun, making the day seem brighter than it was. Her fine features broke into a perfect-toothed smile when I greeted her. As she entered the house to gather up the children, even my hazy vision could not fail to take in the length of the Lycra-clad legs being slipped out of her new and expensive Ugg boots. Miranda had never agreed with Hugo's premise that beautiful people should have beautiful staff. I caught myself staring and quickly looked away.

Hugo and Camilla were going to Bond Street to buy Camilla's birthday present, so Marta offered to have the girls over for lunch then take them to the soft play centre at Brent Cross; an offer too good for any of us to refuse. Half an hour later I was alone and flipping open my Mac, heart palpitating with the anticipation of being proved right.

The retrieved document was far from a finished article. For the most part it contained full transcripts of the interviews that she and I had carried out. Rachel's was there as was a pretty accurate summation of my exchange with Gail. Miranda had added a coda to this "*International element—blackmail follows family to Texas? How did they get new address? Arrival of demand kills hope of reconciliation. Amidst swirl of recriminations and bourbon TH quietly saves them all the trouble and expense of protracted legal battles and / or submitting to blackmail and swallows a bullet.*"

Put like that it made for a dramatic story.

There had already been a fair amount of speculation in the press about Daniel's death but, so far, no details of Rachel's affair. Miranda, it seemed, had been planning to allude to it, but without mentioning names. A tricky balancing act she hoped to carry off by referring to a *"top city banker who was driven past his limit after he discovered his wife was being blackmailed by a P&C project manager."*

In addition, Miranda had outlined the case of 'Samantha', the wife of a solicitor at a leading City law firm. Over lunch in her Finchley kitchen, she had admitted to having been reduced to secretly selling her jewellery to pay off the young electrician with whom she'd had a four month affair. And 'Sara', a middle-aged mother of three from Hampstead Garden Suburb who had dismissed their nanny whom she suspected of having an affair with her fifty-two year old stockbroker husband, only to discover the girl's replacement, also provided by P&C, going through his briefcase one evening.

I found my own interviews précised in the long, roughed-out paragraph that followed these more attention-grabbing cases. Included to lend weight to the allegations it contained tales of *"over-familiarity and flirtation"; "homemaker wives approaching forty and all too conscious of the attractions of their younger, firmer female employees to their glad-eyed husbands"; "fading roses flattered by the attentions of muscular young foreigners in close proximity to them during the torpid hours when the children are at school". "While many are too frightened or ashamed to speak even off-the-record it is clear that across London these liaisons come with a hefty price tag, sometimes in terms of marital trust and more often in sums of hard cash."* There was lots of smoke implying an underlying inferno of extortion.

Next came a download of Polish & Check (UK) Limited's accounts for 2007/2008. Registered in England since 2003, there were only two directors; Pavel Dabrowski and Milena Hlavacek; both at an address in Mill Hill; husband and wife maybe? On the list of shareholders were a

Zarek Grzegorczyk and a Marta Majewski. This second surname recalled Wragg's weasely intonation to my mind's ear and though I suspected that both were common enough Christian names in Eastern Europe, their appearance next to each other chimed discordantly. I toyed with calling Rachel to check Zarek's surname, but thought better of it, deciding instead to quiz Marta when she came back from Brent Cross.

Miranda's coup de grâce was to have been a showdown interview with Mr Dabrowski or Ms Hlavacek at their Mill Hill pile. She had got the address from the company register and had Google Earthed it. The picture showed a grand Edwardian house set in large, landscaped grounds. Business, it implied, was good; rather too good for a company with a stated turnover of merely £2.8 million for the previous tax year.

The final page contained the draft pitch she was preparing for the features editor. Under the title *"Do You Really Know Who's In Your Home?"* the main thrust highlighted the disparity between the care and precautions we take in selecting people to work in our houses and the unchecked access we then give them once they are there.

"Should we really be so surprised if unscrupulous workers from poorer countries find themselves sorely tempted to take advantage of our overweening appetites? After all they witness how incredibly wasteful we are on a daily basis. How ready we are to pay to get what we want as soon as we want.

Once they are employed we ask few questions for fear of causing offence. Often we leave them to work unsupervised for hours at a time with temptation staring them in the face. How carelessly we leave cash and cards lying around, or forget to tidy away important documents—something we'd never dream of allowing at the office.

210

And when we are around, how alluring it is to have the company of a young, fresh face in a world of stultifying routine.

We will ourselves to believe that they will act with the same integrity we feel we possess, at the same time as we are taking advantage of them. After all we only employed them because they were cheap.

So for the criminally minded amongst them it is a simple equation: 'if they are using us why shouldn't we use them? They have so much why shouldn't they be encouraged to share? Money can buy everything, why shouldn't it pay for a bit of silence?"

I sat back, my eyes aching and snow-blind from the bright screen. Rubbing them caused a shower of multi-coloured sparks to burst across the back of my eyelids. The perennial dull ache in my head was throbbing its way inexorably to the fore and as I trudged upstairs to rummage around the medicine cabinet for some Neurofen, it was joined by the painful acceptance that the article proved nothing. No one had gone on the record saying a crime had been committed; there was no new evidence for Sharratt. I'd have to look for another way in.

The children burst back into the house mid-afternoon. Some plan had been hatched between them, which involved a "secret meeting, and that means absolutely NO grown-ups" in Jenny's room so I made Marta a cup of coffee.

We chatted about how Christian and Hope were coping with the loss of their mother and I told her about Hope's upset the previous night. Ever practical, Marta declared her belief that children are resilient and able to find ways to cope with even the worst losses. She was, however, clearly dubious about Camilla's somewhat neurotic presence being of any help. I let her know that Hugo had warned me to

211

keep my distance but reiterated that, if there were any way in which I could help with the children, Marta should call me. She nodded her gleaming head curtly in recognition of the offer whilst signalling the unlikelihood of her needing to accept it.

"Oh, by the way can I check that I have your correct mobile number?" I added casually, "I've got a new phone and I'm updating all my details." She told me and I read it back from the screen, "And your surname? Only we know another Marta and Nanny Marta just sounds wrong."

"Majewski," she replied and started to spell it out for me. My heart skipped a beat and my finger was left hovering over the phone keys; I knew how to spell it already and, catching myself, quickly entered the letters.

Trying to sound calmer than I felt, I continued, "I guess Hugo has you doing a lot of extra hours at the moment." She nodded. "Only I really need a bit of babysitting myself. Are you still in touch with Ted and Gail's old nanny, Kristina? My kids loved her." The intensity of her gaze increased and I suspected she had narrowed her eyes. I hoped the default setting of vacuity in my own malfunctioning windows to the soul did not give too much of what I was feeling away.

"No, I am sorry, Kristina went back to Prague, her grandmother is sick. But I have another friend, Radka; she also is from Czech Republic and works as a nanny in Belsize Park. She is very nice, I will ask her if you like."

I nodded and thanked her. Then, since we were having that kind of conversation, continued as naturally as I could, "Incidentally, I also need a plumber. I heard that your boyfriend, um Zarek Grzegorczyk is it, comes highly recommended. Can I have his number too please?"

As soon as the words left my lips, I knew I had ridden my luck too far. Finally having managed to focus my hazy

212

eyes on her face, I could see that her lips were compressed and much of the softness of her youthful beauty had disappeared to be replaced by a determined set expression. "He is not here also," she replied irritably. "He has gone to Gdansk to work on the big ships. Now he is not my boyfriend. If you need a plumber, you must call the Agency, they have very many. Do you need their number as well?" Her normally bubbly voice was flat and imbued with an unfamiliar harshness.

"Oh I'm sorry Marta, I didn't mean to…Um, I'm sure I've got the number somewhere."

She stood up, her coffee only half drunk, and stalked towards the stairs. I reran what I had said through my mind, reassuring myself that it was innocuous enough—unless of course she did have something to hide. Certainly, her change in attitude had been abrupt enough to raise my suspicions further. I could hear her upstairs tersely ordering the children to do as she told them because it was time to leave, now. Hope was snivelling when she came down a minute later and, when she gave me a hug goodbye, her cheeks were wet.

I decided to pretend I had neither noticed the tears nor Marta's brusqueness. Instead, I thanked her generously for taking the children out for the day, only to be met by stony silence.

I called Dino after she had left and thanked him again for the previous night. Eager to hear about the fruits of his labour, his questions came tumbling forth, "So what did you find out? Were you right? Did someone rub her out? If so, whodunit shamus?"

"I wish it were that simple, Dino, but yes, I think it's given me another couple of pieces of the jigsaw. Not enough to go back to the police, but some interesting information and one or two things to follow up."

"Aw, c'mon man, you gotta share this with me. Call it my reward for helping you out."

I hesitated, unwilling to put him in potential harm's way, though equally conscious of his help thus far and the desirability of having another mind put to the problem. "Okay Dino, but remember I did warn you about the risks."

"What the hell, it can't be any worse than going to the pub and having you smoke all over me."

I told him what I had learnt from the roughed-out story and of my confirmation that Marta and Zarek were both shareholders in P&C. "I know it proves nothing, but her reaction to being asked about Zarek was weird. She was hiding something."

"Maybe she just thought you'd heard about them breaking up and were hitting on her, Joe. Hey, but the fact that she reacted like that does prove one of two things." I waited expectantly for something I had missed, "Either, that you're wrong about her being a honey trap – 'cause surely she'd've tried to protect herself in her default fashion. Or, that you're butt-ugly!" He guffawed down the other end of the line.

"Thank you for your startling insight, pal, it's invaluable! No it was a different type of defensiveness, more like self-preservation—'no comment'."

"So she's still raw about it. Some gals like to wallow a bit, not climb straight back into the saddle."

"And she was lying about Kristina, I could hear that in her voice. She used the same excuse about a sick grandmother on Miranda a few weeks ago, to get away for a long weekend.

"Hmm, well maybe. Hey, have you done with going through all that mail I gave you to forward on? There was a letter in there that sure looked like a billy-doo. I wouldn't've notice but I kinda thought it was from my niece

214

in Miami when it arrived. She writes in the same way; you know all round letters and circles over the 'I's. Anyhow it's from a gal and one who didn't know he'd died. Could be Kristina."

I walked over to the half sorted pile of letters and flicked through them, feeling for a smaller envelope. There were four. Cradling the phone between my ear and shoulder and giving Dino a running commentary, I cast around for a pair of reading glasses. Then I took the letters under the bright light of the extractor hood over the hob and peered at them. I put the typewritten one with Republicans Abroad stamped on it to one side, along with the two addressed to Kelvin that felt like birthday cards.

The remaining letter was in a cheap off-white envelope and franked in London SW1. It was addressed by hand with a distinctive feminine flourish. I hesitated. Sorting the post for junk mail was one thing, but it just didn't feel right to open someone else's personal correspondence. As my index finger hovered at an un-gummed corner, the image of Gail seething at me flitted across my mind. Having tried to convince her that I hadn't sent the first blackmail letter, I should damn well make sure I didn't act as postman for a second.

Youthfully cursive biro script on thin writing paper, covering just less than a page told me that I had made the right decision.

Dearest Ted,

I hope that you do not now hate me because of the pain that I have caused to you and the children. I know that what we did was wrong and I am sorry.

215

I have tried to call you but you must have changed your phone. Please will you call me? My number is the same one. 07877 643784.

I know I should not contact you but once when we were happy together you told me you would do anything for me.

I know our relationship caused you much trouble and you are probably still suffering because of us but I really need this one last thing.

I also am suffering and I must leave London and I need you to help me. I am prisoner here now, and I want so much to be with my family far away from this life but I need help to leave.

What we shared was special for me and for you I hope. I feel happy to remember our nights together when you held me to you so close. For those dearest memorys if you feel the same please call me. I need to explain to you.

Always your friend, Kristina.

Dino sighed at the other end of the phone, "Aw, man poor kid sounds desperate. And she doesn't even know Ted is dead."

"Yeah, very touching. I wonder how much she wants."

"You are so cynical Joe, where's your heart?"

"Safely incarcerated in lead," I mugged. "Right, I'll text her, pretending to be Ted, and arrange to meet up as soon as possible."

"Well, I'm okay for the rest of the week, so whenever suits you suits me." Dino sounded excited.

"No, mate. Sorry, but I'd better do this alone. If we go in mob-handed she'll get scared. It's going to be bad enough giving her the news about Ted. Christ knows how I'm going to get anything out of her if she's in floods of tears."

Dino sounded crestfallen, but had to agree. I promised I'd call to let him know what happened. I picked up my mobile and started to type.

Dearest Kristina, sorry 4 delay – was on hol. Wld luv 2 meet, 2moro? Send me address, will come 2 u, luv Ted.

I felt cold and numb as I pressed 'send'. Contacting Kristina shoved the pain of loss straight back into my face. We all dilute those memories that upset us, by visiting the well that contains them only once in a while and taking small draughts. In so doing, we gradually build our resistance to their corrosiveness. This letter and what I planned to do in visiting Kristina was a big slug all at once.

My phone signalled her reply within a couple of minutes.

So good 2 here from u. Come 2moro @ 2pm; 62B Lowndes St, SW1 luv K xxx.

What with picking the girls up, taking Nell to her violin lesson in West Hampstead, making dinner, ensuring homework was done and then supervising bath and bedtimes, I didn't think to check the MP3 recorder until gone 9.30. It had died too.

Minutes of fumbling for the battery cover revealed only that the machine needed a mains recharger that Miranda had forgotten to give me. I checked whether the one for my mobile would fit, which of course it didn't, then crept into Nell's room and unplugged the one from her DS, again without success. Next, I spent twenty minutes emptying out a box of redundant electrical paraphernalia in the basement, to no avail. Eventually, in desperation, I rang Dino. He was having a quiet night in with Maria and our conversation was brief; I should bring it round the following morning and he would see what he could do. Cursing my carelessness, I put the useless machine on the kitchen counter and grabbed a beer from the fridge—the first of too many that night.

I was staring vacantly at nothing on the ceiling and thinking how suicide remains one of the dwindling number of unmentionables in life, when the phone threw me hurtling back to earth.

"Hurroh," I slurred.

Eithne was still in New York and must have forgotten the time difference. "You sound happier," she said breezily.

"I'd be even happier if you were here on the sofa with me."

"Mmm, me too," she sighed, "But a week today and I'm yours to do with as you please."

"A week's a long time in chastity," I complained.

"Anticipation," she purred, "I should land at Gatwick at five and be home for dinner and a nice long bath and afterwards..."

"I'm counting the minutes. I've got the curry and champagne on ice for you."

"Mmnh, I'm not sure how appetising that sounds. Still it beats maple syrup on bacon."

"Yuk, that sounds disgusting!"

"It's breakfast-time adultery!" she giggled but the associations the word held triggered a spasm in me and I spilt beer down my front.

"Oh, bugger!"

"Uh oh! Guilty conscience. Have the hussies of Hampstead been hurling themselves at you again? Will they never learn?"

"No, er, well not recently. No it's not that, I just spilt my drink. Um, look, I'm afraid the kids are in bed, it's nearly ten."

"Good, as long as they're happy and healthy and you send them my love that's all I need to know. No, it's you I called to talk to, Joe. How are you, what have you been up to?"

My heart thumped happily. I wriggled myself up the sofa, brushed beer into my jumper, and put the bottle aside. "Yeah, fine, thank you my wonderful wife!"

She hadn't rung to hear further evidence of my inability to let my suspicions lie, and what could I really tell her anyway? So I changed the subject and we nattered happily for an hour.

Chapter 17

For me, South London starts at Hyde Park. I have never been comfortable in the large squares of Belgravia or the shabby gentility of the streets off the King's Road. The address that Kristina had texted was on one of the roads behind Harrods and I had been wandering around squinting at high-up street signs for several minutes before a friendly Bulgarian street-sweeper took me by the arm and led me to the front door of the house I was looking for.

Kristina answered the door immediately and I felt her cold gust of disappointment on seeing me. With her mouth and the door agape, I launched into my pre-prepared speech. "Hi Kristina, it's Joe. I know you were expecting Ted, but I have some bad news. Can I come in, please?"

Shorter than me, she had taken a step to her right and was peering past me, no doubt looking for Ted. Eventually, she cleared her throat, "Where is Ted, why is he not here?"

It was cold and I did not want to do this on the doorstep. I needed to talk to her; to be more difficult to get rid of than simply having a door slammed in my face once I'd delivered my news. "I have a message, but only if I can come in."

Her disappointment was masking something. It dawned on me that her reluctance to let me pass was born of fear. I tried to sound soothing, though god knows my insides were writhing themselves.

"Come on Kristina, it's me Joe, Ted's friend. I know you are frightened, but I am here to try and help you. I care for my friends and for their friends. Let me in and I can try to help."

Her suspicion was wavering and she stepped back from the threshold. I crossed it slowly, deliberately unthreatening. Inside it was dark and smelt heavily of beeswax polish; a

220

heady, sickly smell that reminded me of corporal punishment and detention. Kristina tutted as my white stick connected with a heavy piece of hallway furniture. She took my hand and placed it on her bony shoulder, as she had seen Ted do so often, then led me to a bright kitchen, where a baby sat in a large ball-pit, drooling and gurgling in a sea of primary colours. My heart was beating uncomfortably hard and I felt a tightness in my chest—I hate upsetting people.

At the breakfast bar, Kristina pulled out a stool and I settled into its suede-upholstered cushion, while she retrieved the baby and held it like a shield in front of her.

"Why is Ted not here instead?" She was trying to sound petulant and was pouting slightly; it didn't suit her.

I took a deep breath to steady my nerves and wished she were sitting down too, for the baby's sake. "Kristina, I'm afraid Ted is dead."

It was as if a vacuum had sucked the atmosphere from the room. I had fixed my gaze on the baby, terrified that in her shock, Kristina may let it slip from her arms. Above its pineapple hairdo she was shaking her head in silent disbelief. Eventually, with a gasp she groaned, "No, he contacted me yesterday. He is coming," desperate to convince herself.

"I'm sorry Kristina, the text messages were from me. I had to see you, to tell you myself. Ted moved back to America. When things didn't work out between him and Gail he, um... he, er... shot himself. I'm so sorry."

She began to sniff and I guessed she was weeping. Amidst the fluorescent ripples that distorted my view, I saw her shoulders slump and lunged towards her to save the gurgling child.

Kristina shrieked then backed away hissing, "Keep away from me!"

221

Backing off, I apologised, explaining I was merely worried she might drop the baby. When I was sitting down again she, at last, put the child back into the ball-pit.

She gulped down a couple of breaths and, her jaw jutting out, turned to face me. "Why do I believe you? What do you want?"

"When I went to the funeral Gail told me that someone had taken some documents from their house in Hampstead and used them to blackmail Ted. She thought that it was you."

Kristina bristled and shot back defiantly "She is lying. She hates me for my love-making with Ted."

I had to proceed carefully but there seemed no easy way to do so. "Kristina, I know how you felt about Ted, I read your letter to him. So I also know that you are frightened, of who or what I'm not sure, apart from that it's the same thing that forced Ted into a dark corner he couldn't escape from. I want to help you. Will you tell me?"

I studied her under the glare of the halogen downlighters. She was what, twenty-three? Twenty-four? Slim and supple with a bobbed bombshell. All the physical attributes of a honey trap, but none of the mental toughness. There was no calculation or cynicism there that I'd ever seen. Above all, she looked terrified and vulnerable.

She met my gaze, tears still glistening at the corners of her almond shaped eyes. "You think I have something to do with Ted's death, how can I trust you? You must go now. You must never come again."

I remained seated; it was now or never. "Right Kristina, how about I tell you what I know and will tell the police if you don't help me? Now sit down and listen." She gawped at me but obeyed.

"Polish & Check finds employment for good-looking young men and women in the homes of rich families. Many

222

of these families have bored housewives or undersexed husbands who are very happy to discover that a gorgeous young single person wants to sleep with them. No strings attached, just a bit of pocket money changing hands—at first. Then, however, the young person wants a little more, then more and more. If they don't get it they threaten to talk. How am I doing?" Kristina was looking at her hands. "What I want to know is who forces you to do it. You're too soft to be a prostitute and you're scared."

At the word 'prostitute' she jerked her head up and exploded, "Fuck you! Fuck you, fuck off!" The baby began to bawl and when she made no move to comfort it, I left my chair and picked it up. It was a little boy and his nappy was heavy. I looked around for a changing mat, but couldn't locate one.

"So Kristina, you tell me why I should believe that you weren't blackmailing Ted." I rocked the baby back and forth to calm him, feeling suddenly proprietary.

She turned the taps full on; tears came gushing out and her low moan rose steadily to a wail of pain and frustration. The baby was shocked into silence; I hoped there was no one else in the house.

The baby and I played peek-a-boo until she had finished. Sniffing hard, she ran herself a glass of water and swallowed in long slow gulps.

"I need money to leave here and go back to Czech Republic." Her voice was thick from sobbing, her face blotchy.

"Don't look at me love, I don't have to pay for my shags." It was cruel but I needed more from her, so wasn't inclined to remove my foot from the jugular quite yet.

"I didn't sleep with Ted for money. I liked him, his wife she is horrible woman and she treats him like shit. Ted was always so nice to me and so jolly. When we play together with the children it feels like we are a family. One day he returned from being at pub with you and I was babysitting and he was little drunk and kiss me on the cheek goodnight and so it started. It was good, for both of us."

"How much did he pay you?" I persisted.

Utterly affronted now she shrieked in my face, "No! No! I am not prostitute! He gave me little presents, yes, like lovers do for each other, but he never paid me! The money went to the agency." Again she looked down at her hands.

"I don't understand, Kristina, what do you mean 'the money went to the agency'?"

She sniffed loudly, "I tell only my friend Marta about Ted. But she tells her boyfriend Zarek who tells big boss of agency. One night Zarek drives me to boss's house. He tells me he knows I am being naughty girl. He says I must be paid for my extra time. He tells me Zarek will give me DVD for Ted. Ted must buy the DVD and give £2000 to agency." She was speaking into her lap, her shoulders rolled forward. She looked abject.

"The DVD was of you having sex with Ted?"

She nodded. "One day after I tell Marta, she and Zarek come to Ted's house with the Lethbridge children and we play in the garden. Zarek asks if he can store some things in my room. He says he wants to use Ted's broadband to make downloads of movies. I ask Ted and he says it is all right; he was lovely, kind man. We did not know Zarek had left tiny camera, like nanny cam, in my room. Every night it must come on. Next week Zarek returns to take away his things. Marta tells me this after Zarek gives me DVD. She says 'these rich Americans pay you too little, Kristina, you will get more now.' I was very upset, I cry and I ask Ted what we will do."

So Miranda had been right! The thrill of discovery also sent a chill through my blood. "Was Marta blackmailing

224

Hugo Lethbridge in the same way, Kristina? I already know that Zarek was using his relationship with Rachel Morgenstern to extort money from her."

Kristina shook her head, "I know nothing of this. I tell Ted that I think these people are my friends, but they are blackmailing me too. Ted said he believes me and so he will pay the money. After he does, we think it is over, we have the DVD. But the next month they ask for £2000 again, they have made copies. Then Ted says he must tell his wife about us and everything is finished."

She held her head in her hands and wept. "When Ted goes back to his wife it is for his children. He says he will always remember our time together but we must now stop meeting. I never see him again after. The agency finds me this job, far from Hampstead. The boss he laughs and tells me I am his good girl, I must try to sleep with husband of house, or wife, it matters not. He disgusts me but I need money to go home so I must take job. Now you must help me and give me money to escape. Please, I have told you everything."

She was desperate, but desperate enough to resort to blackmail? I doubted it—she was after hundreds not thousands. We were both flagging; I hurried onto my final questions.

"Kristina, did you know that Daniel Morgenstern also killed himself?"

She nodded, "I see his photo in evening paper."

"Like I said, Rachel was being blackmailed too. You really didn't know?"

Her head was bowed again and I missed her reaction, though I sensed it was a 'no'.

"My neighbour, my friend Miranda Lethbridge, you know Marta's employer, she was writing a newspaper article exposing your agency's nasty little scam. How they

225

extort money from people like Daniel and Rachel; how Zarek kept demanding more and more until he drove Daniel to his death. Rachel gave an interview, on tape, told Miranda all the sordid details." I paused for effect "And now Miranda is dead too."

Kristina uttered a sharp, involuntary cry. Her head snapped up and as she gawped at me the harsh, artificial light revealed that beneath the blotches her face was ashen. "I have said too much, you must leave now. Go please."

She all but bundled me out of the house. Her uncontrollable sobbing echoed in the hallway from the other side of the firmly closed door as I sat on the top step and rolled a cigarette. Already the adrenalin that had kept me focussed as I tried to scrutinise her reactions to my interrogation was evaporating and with it the clarity I had thought her revelations had provided. I felt suddenly deflated and confused; theories and faces jostled for centre stage in my head. The lights in front of my eyes were flashing and bursting rapidly in orange and mauve, like precursors to a migraine, indicating a growing intensity of pressure. The cigarette tasted of ash and the head-rush I'd got from it refused to go. Pulling myself giddily to my feet, I tried to work out which direction the Underground station lay in.

As I approached a zebra crossing, I heard a van rev its engine to my right. I glanced up automatically before stepping onto the first stripe, in time to see a flash of white as the Transit hurtled towards me. The engine noise was not slowing. With well-practised ease I stepped back onto the pavement and, raising my stick, swung it so that the hard acrylic ball at the tip caught the windscreen a glancing blow. I heard a satisfying 'crack' as the glass cobwebbed. "Arsehole!" I called after its receding padlocked doors.

A window cleaner came running over to check whether I was all right. I told him I was so used to it that it had barely registered, really. He laughed "They'll have to swing by Autoglass for a new windscreen though mate, good on'ya! Teach those Eastern European wankers to obey our Highway Code, won't it? Shame they didn't stop, I'd of given 'em what for. Introduced 'em to the old Millwall kiss." He made a gesture with his head that I didn't catch and chortled to himself.

Slowly my mind was processing the incident. "How do you know they were Eastern European?" I asked.

"It only bleeding said so on the side of the van didnit; Polish & Check. Those bloody jam rolls are everywhere, nicking our jobs. My bruvver-in-law's a plasterer and he ain't worked in monffs."

Keef, as he introduced himself, insisted on seeing me to the other side of the road and invited me to look him up if I found myself at the New Den on a match day, "I'll be there, never missed a game in furtee years," he assured me.

On the Tube I closed my eyes in a vain attempt to calm the pulsing lights. I really wanted to lie down in a quiet, dark room and sort through everything slowly and methodically. Instead, my mind was careening around and producing sparks as it hit brick walls.

Part of me was indignant. Why hadn't Ted told me that he was being blackmailed? He can't have been ashamed. When he'd told me about the affair, though inwardly I had disapproved, I had been there as his friend, just as he had been for me. And if he'd told me about the DVD? It would have inflamed my sense of justice and I would probably have advised him to tell P&C to wedge it and threaten them with the police. Maybe Ted had known that would be my reaction. Maybe the frisson of adventure and the novelty of it all had spurred him on. The money wasn't an issue; I had seen the number of zeros behind the Hansfords' current account. Perhaps, when the demand was repeated, he'd been

227

embarrassed to admit that he'd been so easily duped. But how could he have believed that I had been part of it? I puffed out my cheeks in despair; I was getting nowhere.

Marta and Zarek were the common links between the Hansfords, Morgensterns and Lethbridges. Is that what Miranda had found out too? Was that why she had been killed? Marta and Zarek, two shareholders, bringing in extra, untaxed revenue. Ground agents, passing on referrals to 'the big boss' in his big house. Company policy then—big business and worth protecting—but worth killing for?

Between throbbing temples my vision of Marta was reforming to something much more ugly. The Postpak for Ted would have been staring her in the face every time she came round with Chris and Hope, it would have been so easy for her to have slipped an extra envelope inside. It had been she who had found Miranda dead. Had she put her there, drugged and unconscious, to be gassed? She had keys to the house and every reason to be there. Seeing her coming and going was such a common sight, I wondered whether anyone would even have noticed her. Had Sharratt checked whether she had an alibi?

If I believed Kristina, and she was properly shit-scared, then she too was a victim of Marta's duplicity. And that led me to the bit I really didn't like. On any other day, I would put a near miss with a builder's van down as routine; to be expected of labourers brought up with different driving laws. However, a Polish & Check van outside Kristina's house and today? That was too much to be coincidence. I should ring Kristina and warn her, but I was underground. Shit, I was out of my depth; the clammy hand of fear pressed between my shoulder blades.

Inside me, the good citizen with faith in the justice system instructed that I go to the police. Even as the idea surfaced it was pushed back under by the weight of Sharratt's patronising scorn, "Where's your evidence Mr

228

Wynde? You're just wasting my time." I could almost smell the bacon grease. Why hadn't I checked the MP3 recorder earlier? Kristina was hardly likely to give him a statement, especially not now, and had she really said anything conclusive? What crime had been committed? A couple of grand allegedly paid in cash to a man whose name she hadn't told me; the potential plaintiffs now in Texas; one dead, the other keen to hush it up. "Nothing Mr Wynde, no evidence. There is no case."

Immediately I emerged into the November gloom overhanging Hampstead, I tried Kristina's mobile. It went straight to voicemail and I didn't leave a message.

Waiting for the green man at the pelican crossing, I felt suddenly unequal to the prospect of getting over the road alone. The urge to sink to my knees and howl threatened to overwhelm me and I peered around in desperation for support. Seeing a grainy human shape to my left, I called out, "Excuse me." My voice sounded reedy but it had summoned an elderly man with a walking stick. At once I felt guilty.

"Can I help you, dear boy?" It was a rich, fruity voice. His silk cravat and buttonhole suggested he was heading down the hill to The King Willy pub. As, arm in arm, we crossed the road, a cyclist ignored the lights, swerved and swore at us.

Once safely on the opposite pavement, I shook the old gent's cushion-soft hand and reflected that it never pays to be afraid to ask for help.

The following morning was one of those when the change in air pressure pushes your temples in and your eyeballs out. Flayed branches scratched at the miserable sky and my bones ached for warmth as the drizzle wormed its way through my skin. We had missed the bus by seconds and the girls had grumbled all the way to school. Nell had even managed to trail her gym bag through a saturated dog turd. As my sense of adequacy was leeched away, so frustration soured to impotent rage. Venting some of this on a parent whose urban tank was parked on the pavement in front of the school had eased the pressure briefly—until Jenny asked me what 'twat' meant.

My mind was still squirming beneath its accumulated burden as I pounded back up the hill. I had determined not to involve Dino further until I knew that Kristina was safe; so had yet to call him as promised. Instead, I had spent the evening brooding on what I had learnt and the night jolting awake just as a van ploughed into me. Whether it was Marta or Zarek or the 'big boss', I had obviously got someone at P&C worried. However, to get enough to persuade Sharratt, I was going to have to rattle more cages.

The opportunity presented itself before I had had time to consider my approach. Above the dull roar of traffic and the half conversations barked into mobiles, my ears picked out a familiar sound; the echo of heeled boots on paving slabs. The noise triggered a vision of my A level French teacher. Like her, the woman ahead had a long stride and knew how to make walking sound seductive. I peered through the gloom, pinpointing the heel-beat. After half a minute of casting about, my eyes were drawn to the familiar loose-hipped gait of a tall slim figure I recognised as Marta.

Quickening my own step, especially in dim light, takes all my concentration, lest I am to end up in A&E. So by the time I had caught her up, where the pavement narrowed and she had to slow down anyway, I had still given no thought to what I was going to say.

"Hi, Marta, how are you?" I was breathless, ruing every last cigarette.

"Oh, Joe! Yes, I am well. How are your girls?" She sounded aloof and unsmiling.

"Yeah, fine thanks. Lousy weather though isn't it? Is it snowing in Poland yet?"

"I don't know, but I think yes, probably." She had quickened her pace again, hurrying me along. Without holding on to her shoulder for guidance I was at risk of not being able to keep up. She was far from her normal affable self.

I put my hand onto her arm and she flinched. "Oh, I'd assumed your boyfriend would have told you what it's like over there in…Krakow, isn't it?" She remained silent so I continued. "Anyway Marta, I need to talk to you. It's important and I need to do it now."

"Leave me alone, I have nothing to say. Can you not see I am upset? All of this; the terrible thing that happened to Mrs Lethbridge, and then my boyfriend leaves me to go back to Poland; I want to be left alone." She sounded angry rather than sad.

"It's about Miranda, Marta. I need to know some things that I think you can tell me. I know it's upsetting for you and I am sorry. But I think that Miranda was murdered because of something she had found out. You can help me discover what that was. Please Marta."

We were still walking fast with me clinging onto her limp arm. She was staring resolutely ahead; as was I, in case she decided to walk me into a lamppost. "You are not police, Joe. I do not have to answer your questions."

"I've spoken to someone else who has told me how Polish & Check make their extra money, Marta. The blackmail scams, filming your employers in bed with the hired help. Now, I've got enough evidence to go to the police and I will, if you leave me no other choice. I know you are a shareholder in the agency and I'm sure you've done things that may not be strictly legal, but I can't see you as a murderer. So, tell me what you know, starting with who killed Miranda and when the police do get involved, I'll ensure they know you helped me."

"Miranda killed herself, Joe. She was not murdered. It is difficult for you, I know, because she was more than just your friend. But it is wrong to blame other people for her dying." Her voice was calm; I recalled her soothing Hope on the day of the funeral.

"Fine, Marta. Have it your own way. I have copies of the interviews and the article Miranda was writing; the ones you tried to destroy. I'll take them to the police. I just wanted to give you a chance, because they certainly won't." I let go of her arm and watched her long legs stride off up the hill. I could only hope that the fall-out from our exchange, when it came to me, would not be too bruising. My hand was trembling on the handle of my stick as I followed slowly in her wake.

At home, after strong coffee and a hot shower, I sent out an email to Dino, Brad and Glenn, inviting them round for a dinner of chilli and red wine. Despite my reluctance to put anyone else at risk, if my suspicions were well founded, I had set a dangerous process in train by confronting Marta, so it was only sensible to take a few precautions.

While I waited for their replies, I tried ringing Kristina yet again; again I hung up when I got her voicemail. Soon afterwards I received the first of three emails: Glenn would be late, as he was running a self-defence class in Camden Town. Next, Dino would have to leave early. Finally, Brad requested beer instead of wine.

I spent the remainder of the morning tidying the house and replaying everything to do with the case that the police didn't see as a case. Like the Mathematical Bridge in

232

Cambridge, it stood up but with no visible means of support. The trouble was, just like the bridge, as soon as you took it apart to see how it worked it proved impossible to put back together again.

The bare fact of the matter was there was no physical evidence that Miranda had been murdered. I hoped that by laying everything I knew out in front of a jury of my peers, one of them might spot something I had missed, or at least help me find a way forward. At the very least, I assured myself, telling others would provide me with a kind of insurance policy against the worst-case outcome. That was just enough to lift my anxiety at what I had done and allow me to breathe a little more easily

By the time I got round to making myself an omelette for lunch I was trying to second-guess Marta's reaction. She'd lied about Kristina's whereabouts and her assertion that Zarek was in Poland had rung false the first time and even more so when I had confronted her with it that morning. Besides, he was a shareholder and project manager with good English; he was too much of an asset to be allowed to nip off to Gdansk for a spot of moonlighting. Perhaps he too had been moved to Knightsbridge, from whence Marta could be summoning him to pay me a visit. I needed to know.

The last time I'd spoken to Rachel had been the morning in Belsize Square. She'd not attended Miranda's funeral and, having done two interments in as many months myself, I could more than understand why. Her mobile rang for a good thirty seconds before her weary voice crackled into it.

"Hi Rachel, it's Joe Wynde. How are you doing?"

She sounded surprised and wary, "Joe, um, hi. So-so, I guess. The exchange finally went through on the house and I'm up in Manchester now, looking at schools. Is it something quick, I'm about to meet the headmistress?"

This suited me, I didn't fancy long explanations, or chummy expressions of sympathies for losses sustained.

"I need a favour, please Rachel." I heard her sigh with irritation. "I need Zarek Grzegorczyk's number. It's for a friend who wants a project manager to oversee a refurb. The trouble is, after Zarek finished up in Fawkes Close he moved on and the agency can't or won't give me his contact details. You said he was good at his job and my friend's a bloke so there wouldn't be any risk of...um... complications."

Rachel snorted at my prissiness. "Yes, he was highly skilled professionally too, Joe. Okay, I don't remember deleting his number. I'll text it to you if I've still got it. Look I've got to go. Ciao for now."

"Right, thanks Rachel, you're a star. Oh, just one final thing."

"What?" Bored now she was eager to get rid of me.

"Did Zarek ever mention working in the Polish shipyards?"

"Of course not!" She scoffed. "That's hardly his area of expertise. Goodbye Joe."

By the time she texted, the following afternoon, it no longer mattered.

Chapter 18

Daily practice and Delia Smith have taught me to be, what my Irish grandmother called, 'a good plain cook.' That limbo afternoon, I welcomed the preparation of a meal as a creative distraction from my morbid thoughts. The CD of the West Coast Pop Art Experimental Band had plopped through my letterbox the day before and I hoped it would provide a suitable soundtrack.

Tears produced by the pungent Spanish onions trickled onto the chopping board as the space-rock, hippy-trippy weirdness of a bygone age filled the room. But this was different to all the usual pat Age of Aquarius dreaminess. These lyrics spoke of napalmed babies, child abuse, mental illness and the darkness of men's souls; all the grunge beneath the veneer. It's remarkable how viciously you can feed steak through a mouli when your head is full of black thoughts.

I've always found the chime of minor key melancholy irresistible, it harmonises with my own sense of loss. Thirstily drinking the Blues, getting wasted, chewing my ragged nails to the quick or provoking the occasional fight, all allow me to experience a vital pain. The sense of empowerment provided by chipping away at myself, on my own terms; then, later, of pride at being able to rise again to fight another day; conducts the rawness that enables me to reconnect with a world from which I all too often feel aloof.

If that sounds like flagellation, so be it. Maintaining a strong sense of self while living with a disability beats retreating into cloistered acceptance of being one of the wretched fallen. In my book, redemption is to be found not in the threats and promises of cold alabaster saints, but in the words and deeds of impassioned human beings.

No non-existent deity was going to mete out justice to those who had caused my friends to die. By recoiling from investigating Ted's death I had turned my face to the wall and allowed Miranda to be murdered. If I was to redeem myself it was now my duty to see this through, whatever the risks. The prospect left me feeling positively charged.

I left the chilli bubbling in the oven and strode out into the twilight to pick up the children. Fawkes Close was deserted. For once, there was not a single skip or builder's van about and it seemed eerily quiet, apart from the echoes of my tapping stick. As usual for the afternoon run I took the short cut that skirts the boundary fence of the sorting office. It avoided the traffic that would be clogging the misty air with fumes and left me alone with my thoughts. Once notorious for its flashers, it perversely made me feel safer. I was unlikely to walk into anything or anyone along its rarely used length. My stick and footfalls beat time, clicking and thudding, bouncing off the high brick walls and fencing on either side of me.

Steady, creaking footsteps started to follow me shortly after I entered the 300-yard long twitten. They were accompanied by heavy, measured breaths. I quickened my pace, so did whoever was following me. I stopped next to the lamppost that marked about halfway and fumbled about for a cigarette, turning the wheel on my lighter to full flame.

The footsteps behind me continued. I braced myself, unable to distinguish between shadow and form in the gloom. He was close now; sweaty, unperfumed save for the reek of damp cigarette smoke. Unfit sounding, bulky, I guessed he was older than me, say forty-five; older than Zarek anyway. He passed by, a dark shape in dark clothes, on a dreary evening, then stopped, turned and with slow, deliberate steps walked back towards me. I held my breath, expecting a fist to land on me at any moment. Instead, a flash of light erupted in front of my eyes, blinding me totally with its unexpectedness. I inhaled sharply and finding my cigarette lit started to cough.

The man gave a rasping laugh, then observed in a low guttural voice, "Surprises, Mr Vynde, can be pleasant or unpleasant. It is an unpleasant surprise to hear that you are making ah, false allegations against my company. Sometimes ve get surprises if ve go looking where ve should not, it can cause accidents. To awoid injuries it is best not to put yourself at risk, yes? I am sure this is vot you tell your children, yes, Mr Vynde?"

The threat was implicit. Eyes streaming and throat raw, my fear turned quickly to fury. "You fucking lay a finger on any member of my family and I will…"

"Vot!" His snort of derision cut me short. "You are no more than a fly on my vindscreen, Mr Vynde, I can have you squashed and viped away vithout getting my hands dirty. This is a friendly varning to you and your nice family. After all ve both vish only to protect vot matters to us. Good ewening Mr Vynde." He re-passed me and walked back the way he had come.

With trembling hands I finished my cigarette under the lamppost and tried to compose myself. The adrenalin was borne of fear certainly, but jubilation too. I had been right and they were rattled. Dabrowski may not have admitted anything in so many words, but the fact he'd warned me off in person had to indicate that he was behind Miranda's death. She had got too close to the truth, she must have confronted him on the day she died and that's what she'd wanted to talk to me about. But I'd been wasted and he had got to her before we'd had another chance.

The remainder of my walk to school felt spring-cushioned.

Brad was the first to arrive, with half a dozen large bottles of beer and a thirst. We bemoaned the imminent demise of the local butcher's shop and speculated over just how far the domino run of collapsing business caused by the credit crunch could spread. Twenty minutes or so later the doorbell rang again and I went expecting to greet Dino. Instead, a very sweaty, panting, Glenn tumbled in clutching a bottle of Aussie Merlot and apologising that "it might be a bit shaken up." He had run the three miles up the hill from the gym on St Pancras Road, stopping only briefly at the off-licence. I half-expected him to start ticking like a cooling engine.

Dino had still not turned up, or rung, but I put the rice on to boil anyway and began to explain why I had called everyone together. To say that they greeted my tale with scepticism would be korma to their vindaloo.

"Dude, like I've told you before, smoke too much of the ole Texas tea and you're gonna go paranoid. Huh?" Brad was speaking to me, but half-facing Glenn for backup.

"Possibly mate. I doubt it helps. But I reckon Joe's creation of this narrative is a manifestation of PTSD caused by Miranda and Ted's sudden deaths and his guilt and shame at not perceiving how isolated they had become."

"And I reckon you read too many self-help books for your own good!" I fired back irritably. "It's not me who's got post-traumatic stress disorder, mate; you're the one who's actually killed people!"

For a fraction of a second I sensed Glenn stiffen, then he quelled his rage and laughed. "Fair point, mate. But bear it in mind—okay?"

Embarrassed at my outburst, I nodded and excused myself on the pretext of checking the rice, leaving them to set the table and, no doubt, mock my delusions. Absently prodding the grains I called Dino but got his voicemail. I tried Kristina again, with the same result. I felt sick; everyone connected to the affair was being made unobtainable.

It doesn't take much distraction for me to misjudge removing things from the oven, but that night's searing burn and the long scar it left behind, bore testament to how preoccupied I was with worrying for Dino, and Kristina's, safety. I was smearing Flammazine (procured for me by a friend who works in A&E) onto my arm, when finally the doorbell clamoured and Brad let Dino in. In my relief I hugged him, his body was taut, I supposed with surprise.

"Crikey lads, is this the real reason you've got us here — to tell us you're coming out?" joked Glenn. The mood lightened and amid much backslapping and glass refilling, we settled down to supper.

Dino was still tense though, even after a couple of Brad's beers. I had hoped that his normally chirpy interjections would help lend credence to my retelling of events, but he remained stubbornly silent throughout my descriptions of obtaining the laptop and our subsequent discoveries both of Miranda's article and Kristina's letter. He showed more interest in my visit to Kristina, but returned to contemplating his half-eaten chilli as I described the incidents first with the van and then Dabrowski.

Brad and Glenn were much more voluble. "Fuckers!" exclaimed Glenn. "Sounds like you've really jerked their chain, mate. They'd better not try anything while I'm around. These hands are deadly weapons!"

"Yeah, I'm overdue kickin' some commie butt too!" Brad chimed in. "There's this one guy workin' on the house across the street from us keeps wolf-whistling at Kell', the bastard!"

"Well she's got a great bod, mate," quipped Glenn, dodging Brad's clumsy punch and laughing. Still Dino

239

remained silent and I wondered more and more whether I had done the right thing in bringing them all into this.

Glenn and Brad took coffee cups, chocolate and supplies of beer and wine into the sitting room and started to argue over which CD to put on the stereo. Dino quietly gathered up the plates and followed me into the kitchen. As he helped load the dishwasher he finally spoke.

"Where, exactly did you get the Digital Voice Recorder, Joe?" Shit, he sounded subdued.

"Miranda gave it to me for recording interviews. I'd left it at her place and picked it up when I was looking for her laptop. Thought it might come in useful."

He nodded and pulled it and a CD from his pocket. "You might say that," his voice was quiet, as if he had witnessed something disturbing and was still trying to make sense of it. "I took the liberty of uploading the files onto my PC and putting them onto a disk for you. Did she have one of these recorders too, maybe?"

I hesitated and tried to remember, "Er, yes I think so. Yeah, she said Hugo had given her one to record the kids with. Why, is that the wrong one?" My heart sank; fuck my luck if it was just a bunch of nursery rhymes and grade one piano practice.

"On the contrary, Joe. I think you lucked out." He handed me the CD "Track 8 makes for interesting listening."

Glenn had won the battle of the stereo and was playing air guitar to 'Highway to Hell' before I changed the disk. He protested bitterly about Poms having no respect for Aussie culture and took solace in a large glass of Merlot. I skipped to Track 8 and turned the volume up.

"I had to play round with the EQ to enhance the voice, and it's still a bit muffled, like the recorder was hidden under something, but you should be able to make out what

240

they're saying." Dino was becoming a little more animated now.

The speakers were hissing loudly and I recognised the pitter-patter of someone touch-typing, then a heavy sigh that made my pulse quicken. There was a knock at the door and we all instinctively looked up. Then we heard Miranda's muffled voice saying, "Come in."

Something made of plastic snapped shut, her laptop I guessed, and the door squeaked open then closed. A faintly familiar, rich Eastern European voice fully filled the speakers. "You wanted to see me Mrs Lethbridge? I understand there is a problem with the hot water."

In juxtaposition to his warm, rounded vowels, hers sounded sharp. "Ah, Zarek, finally. Last night there was hardly any hot water and there was none at all this morning. I believe you switched off the system yesterday while you fitted the new radiators, right? Well, you must have broken something. Where were you this morning? You should have been here to sort this out. It's completely unacceptable. I want it fixed immediately, understand?"

"I am very sorry Mrs Lethbridge. I will see to it straight away." His tone was placatory; presumably he was used to wealthy clients getting shirty.

He must have made to leave, but Miranda's icy rebuke made us all freeze. "I don't recall saying you could go, Zarek. There's another matter I need to discuss with you. Sit down."

We heard the second chair in the office creak as he obeyed. Miranda sighed again, then there was a soft smacking sound; her moistening her lips. She was nervous. My own heart was in my mouth, wondering what she would say and because, on these speakers, here, now she was alive again.

"Polish & Check are blackmailing their clients Mr Grzegorczyk. Knowing that you are a shareholder in the company, I would like to know your views on the matter." Her delivery was matter of fact, as if she were asking him whether he thought that beetroot tasted good in salad.

Zarek was silent. Miranda didn't press him. Finally, he cleared his throat and replied. "I know nothing about this. But if you have evidence, you must show me and then I will make my opinion."

Miranda laughed mirthlessly. "Oh very clever Mr Grzegorczyk. Why don't you go and look in a mirror. I know that you personally have seduced and blackmailed clients. I have spoken to some of them."

It was Zarek's turn to laugh now, "You women are such gossips, maybe because you lack other pleasures in life. I would not call a few baubles and a little pocket money blackmail, rather it is payment for good service...ha ha."

As he relaxed so, audibly, she became more tense, "People have killed themselves because of what you and your fellow blackmailers have done to them. Do you find that so funny?"

"There is much mental illness amongst you rich people who live here. You lead very stressful lives and you do not know how to relax properly. That is why you employ us from Poland and Czech Republic and other places. We are here to help make the solution to your problems. We are not ourselves the problem."

"Oh yes, that's how you sell yourselves, how you win peoples' trust. But you exploit and abuse that trust, don't you Zarek? You go through their drawers, take copies of confidential documents. You conduct cosy pillow talk with lonely wives or husbands and coax them into being professionally indiscreet. And if they won't give you what you want, money or inside information, you force it out of them, by threatening to wreck their lives. How many of you are involved in your grubby little scam? How many lives have you destroyed between you? Do you have no conscience?" she finished panting and shrill with emotion.

"I am sorry Mrs Lethbridge, I see now that all the disruption in your house has made things very difficult for you and caused you much stress. I assure you we are very nearly finished work. You will feel happier when we have gone and you have a nice new cinema for you and Mr Lethbridge."

"Don't you dare patronise me!" Her voice rattled the tweeters. "Let's see how insolent you are when I publish a detailed account of all your nasty little crimes."

"But you have nothing but a few old wives' tales." Zarek chuckled, "It will not be sufficient except to take you to court. Now if you are finished, I have work to do on your boiler."

I could feel the chill descend through the speakers. As a chair dragged, teeth gratingly, over the carpeted floor there was a sound like a baby sucking in breath for a monumental scream and then Miranda let rip, "This is my house and I give the instructions here! How dare you! Sit back down immediately!" The chair creaked again. "I don't know what you think you have on my husband, but whatever it is, even if he is screwing that little whore Marta, our marriage will survive it. You and she will leave our employment at the end of the week. And believe you me I have more than enough material," a fingernail double-tapped on hard plastic, "to make sure that neither of you ever work in this country again—unless it's from prison."

In the silence that followed there was a timid knock at the door and after a final, "Do I make myself clear?" Miranda barked, "Yes?"

"Excuse me, Miranda…"

"Ah, Marta, you are just in time to hear the news. You and your boyfriend will be leaving us at the end of the week." Miranda sounded victorious; it was unpleasant.

"I, I do not understand. Have I done something wrong?"

"Mr Grzegorczyk will explain as you both get back to work, goodbye. Oh, and remember you are employed to work until tomorrow afternoon—make damn sure you do so."

Marta's concerned voice was querulous, "Zarek, co sie dzieje?"

His reply urgent and commanding, "Zawolaj Pawal. Ja sie nia zajme powiedz mu ze musze sie z nim zobczyc po poludniu. On bedzie wiedzial co zrobic."

Marta sounded close to tears and pleaded, "Co to jest, nie strasz mnie!"

Zarek snapped back at her, "Idz! Szybko!"

Miranda cleared her throat impatiently. I heard Marta leave and then Zarek leaned closer to the microphone and whispered, "Mrs Lethbridge, I feel that you are making a mistake. Whatever your suspicions and the gossip, we are a reputable firm. We do not indulge in these games. We make good money by being professionals. I think you are mistaken. I think it is best you talk to Mr Lethbridge when you are more calm. It would be unfortunate if we fall out over a misunderstanding. And Marta, she is a good girl, a simple girl. She is my girlfriend and I do not hire her to the highest bidder."

"But you allowed yourself to be paid to have sex with Rachel Morgenstern. I suppose that was different was it?"

"Ah, so this is it!" Zarek chuckled indulgently. "'The woman scorned', I believe you say? Rachel is a most attractive woman and I was sorry for her; she is so lonely. She said I give her so much happiness that she must give me

244

something in return. She knows I want a new motorbike, so she helped me with money to buy one. It was what you call an arrangement between good friends. But then she tells me she loves me and I think this is not so good. I tell her she must stay with her family and this makes her upset. My work at her house was finished, so I insist we must finish too. Now I am afraid she is bitter and is telling these lies about me, saying I am a bad man."

There was more dead air, then Zarek cleared his throat and said gently, "I think maybe you are lonely too, Mrs Lethbridge. Perhaps I could help you to find happiness?"

Miranda's reply, when it finally came was virtually inaudible; a broken fragment of speech that was wrenched from somewhere far from her throat, "Please, leave, now."

Her office door clicked shut behind him and after a few seconds we heard sobbing. It continued for a full minute and a half throughout which Brad squirmed beside me. I was about to tell Glenn to put AC/DC back on when a low, disembodied voice groaned from the speakers, "I...I...just can't...do this...anymore...I can't stand...any of this...Enough...Enough...Enough!"

Her sobs continued. It was the lament of defeat, of exhaustion and temporary respite before the next retreat was sounded. Close by my heart, the lead ball where I store such feelings myself ached and released some of its toxins back into my blood stream.

"Christ!" exhaled Glenn.

"See why I was so late?" It was Dino. "And believe me, it ain't no easier the second time of listening."

"Jeez, she sounded really on the edge man. Nervous breakdown territory," this was Brad, "and I should know." Kelly had had her own whizz-bang following the premature birth of their third child, Ben, three years previously.

245

The shuddering breaths of my dead friend's misery continued. I closed my eyes and tried to focus my thoughts but lights of every hue exploded with random violence inside my head and I could feel no warmth, either within or on the surface of my body, just lifeless flesh.

Glenn stood up and turned the CD off, breaking the spell. "Bloody hell mate, remind me not to let you choose the music for my next party." It made Brad giggle.

Head in hands I willed the rising certainty, that I had been catastrophically wrong, to leave me. From what seemed like the other side of London I heard Glenn and Brad whispering to each other and Dino say, "No, it's okay, I'll stay awhile."

In a trance, I waved my friends goodbye from the sofa then heard myself tell Dino he could go too, if he wanted. He patted my shoulder and said to call him, at anytime, if I needed him. Then he too left.

Chapter 19

As on the night of Miranda's death, and countless others, I had taken my frustration out on my malfunctioning body, finishing first the beer and leftover wine, then smoking myself comatose. A cricked neck had woken me at some ungodly hour and I had smashed a bottle stumbling from the sofa. Bed had brought dreams of swimming backwards, away from Miranda's flailing arms as she drowned. Turning from her last rising air bubbles, I had collided with Ted. He had cleaved in two and I watched in horror as he disappeared beneath crimson stained waves. The morning made me wish that I had joined them.

How could I have been so certain, and so wrong? I could hardly deny the evidence of my own ears. Just like me, Miranda had chosen to believe in a conspiracy rather than face her sense of inadequacy. Being confronted with the truth had tipped her over the edge. I hadn't appreciated how ill she was; worse, Hugo was right, I had undermined her recovery by constantly questioning the health of her marriage. For Ted and Daniel too, the virus of infidelity had merely complicated other underlying issues and speeded their demise.

Self-esteem is difficult to rebuild when the foolish act that demolished it is performed in front of an audience; the more so if you have wrongfully accused some of its members of murder. The remainder of the week passed in a maudlin cloud. I did my best to be cheerful around the girls and we made a huge 'Welcome home Mummy' banner out of cut-up cereal packets and foil to celebrate Eithne's return. When they were at school, however, I mooched about the house, listlessly moving books or toys from one room to another, dogged by the sense of having let everybody down.

So it was that I found myself stripping our bed of smoky, sweat-stinking sheets at ten to twelve on the night before Eithne was due to get home. Along with the clean bedclothes, I had armed myself with a large vodka and tonic for my least favourite domestic chore. I attacked the easy bits first—pillowcases then sheet—leaving just the dreaded duvet cover.

Inside it, with my arms above me holding two corners of the 12-tog king-size quilt, I could feel my alcohol-filled sweat soaking into the clean fabric. Useless! I began to quiver uncontrollably and then the wave hit me. An amalgam of all the breakers that had bobbed me about or slapped into my face, this one broke over my head. Overwhelmed, I sank to my knees under a spume of eiderdown and let the strong undertow suck me down.

I don't know how long I lay curled up there, but at some point the swell receded. I wobbled to my feet and forced myself to complete my task. Eventually, I emerged sodden but successful and, after a long pause to gulp down lungfuls of unrestricted air, I directed my shaking fingers to the poppers at the foot of the cover. The seam was rough against my fingertips and I realised that it was inside out. The flow of inadequacy came buffeting over me again.

I cajoled myself back downstairs and made straight for the freezer—to numb the pain. I didn't linger, I needed to get outside, to be in the cool night air. Slumped on the roof terrace clutching at a well-packed spliff, the trauma of my worthlessness ebbed into a dark sea of anaesthesia and tears.

Adrift and careless of whether I bobbed or sank, the flotsam notion had bumped me twice before I took hold of it; I could bring Miranda back to life, pretend for a few minutes that everything was in place again. I could feel peace, however transitory.

The CD was still in the machine, I had felt too delicate over the previous days to risk reopening old wounds. I groped for the sticker marking the play button and the hiss resumed in the speakers. Track 1: her interview with the mother of three from The Suburb. I couldn't tell you what she sounded like, only that Miranda's gentle coaxing questions washed over my rucked-up feelings, smoothing them out. Next, I heard her gossiping over coffee with a group of other mums, many of whose voices were familiar. I also identified the sharp whoosh of a cappuccino machine, the clatter of durable coffee mugs in the background and the gurgle and suck of a breast-feeding baby. Slowly I drifted away into flickering sleep.

Hugo was barking at me, "Look, I know you're under a lot of stress but what you've done is quite frankly stupid!" I sat bolt upright, my head whirring like a gyroscope in honey.

"Are you listening to me?" Someone sniffled in the corner of the room. It was too dark, the anti-clockwise bursts of light around the edges of my vision were crashing into those heading clockwise; my chest hurt. "I said are you listening to me?" he barked again.

"Yes Hugo" Miranda and I answered in unison.

"Now go and tell them that you didn't mean it. Apologise to them and ask them to stay. I will sort this mess out when I get back on Saturday. As if I didn't have enough on my plate without your histrionics."

Miranda sniffled again. "But I know that I'm right, Hugo. I know what they're doing, it's wrong. It's destroying people's lives. I have a duty…"

"Your duty is to me and our children. The only person this nonsense is destroying is you!"

"They've got to you too, haven't they?" she wailed. "Oh, how, Hugo, how? Tell me, whatever it is I'll forgive you. I love you."

"Good God, listen to yourself woman, you're ill. Look I'll arrange another appointment with Dr Souzmann. Maybe she can give you something to make you less...overwrought."

"I need your support, Hugo, not drugs!" Her voice was full of bitterness but the fight had left it. "Are you screwing her?"

"Who, Dr Souzmann? Hardly, she's a bit old for my taste, darling." Hugo scoffed.

Miranda bristled, "Marta! Are you screwing our nanny? Is that why you can't bear to let her go? Do you let Zarek watch the two of you? Or is it you watching them?" Her voice rose to a hysterical crescendo that made the speakers buzz.

Hugo's laugh was cruel, "Why? Would that turn you on? Nothing else seems to nowadays. Or would you prefer it if it was that prick Wynde doing the business?" A vision of his smirking face invaded my furious mind's eye.

"Tosser!" we said in unison again.

Hugo's voice softened a touch, "Alright, look Miranda, I am rather preoccupied at the moment. You know how the markets are. There's an opportunity here in Edinburgh to set a paradigm, and earn us a fortune to boot. I simply need you to tell Marta and Zarek that you were a little hasty. I will square things with them on Monday morning. Now that's not too much to ask is it, darling?"

She was still sniffing, "I don't know what to think anymore," she moaned. "Do you promise you will talk this through with me, as soon as you get home? Properly?"

He sounded bored, he knew he'd won and wanted to move on to more pressing matters. "Yes Miranda, I will. Now, get a good night's sleep and I'm sure it will all seem much better in the morning. Why don't you go for a massage and facial at the club? That always perks you up. Now I must get on. Goodnight." The dialling tone purred over the speakerphone.

"Goodnight Hugo," she whispered and the sobbing returned to fill the dead air.

On the sofa, my head buzzing, churning over what I had just heard, I felt like a peeping tom. Nonetheless, I was fascinated and compelled to continue. Getting to my feet was an effort and I had to walk off pins and needles before hobbling to the mantelpiece to fumble for my glasses. From there I limped over to the stereo and squinted at the tiny blue display on the CD player. By not having turned on the lights, I had kept my retinas attuned to the darkness and it only took three or four minutes to see that track 8 still had eighteen minutes to run. In her distress, Miranda must have forgotten that she had left the MP3 recorder on after talking to Zarek.

At last Miranda blew her nose loudly and murmured, "C'mon M, it won't be so bad."

The swivel chair squeaked as she pushed it back and I listened to her leave the room. She shouted Zarek's name and a heavily accented voice replied, "Outside, phone." Her tread was weary as she mounted the stairs and then the speakers hummed with a blend of workmen's chatter, radio music and power tools for the next six or seven minutes.

The footfalls down the stairs were quick and light. The office door creaked open then closed and someone approached the desk. There was a click and the laptop whirred back to life. Shallow, rapid breaths accompanied the sound of computer keys being tapped. And then Marta's

251

voice muttered, "Check it out dot doc." A couple more keystrokes then the laptop was snapped shut. Her footsteps receded, the door creaked twice and she scampered back upstairs.

After another six or seven minutes I heard Miranda and Zarek thud downstairs and a neighbouring door creak open. Zarek said, "Okay…no not noisy…mmm twenty minutes maybe. Yes, yes." Then Miranda re-entered her office and slammed the door.

"Bloody humble bloody pie!" she erupted. "Smug little cow! 'Oh, that is alright Miranda, I understand it is a difficult job balancing home and career.' Well I'll show you, you little bitch. I'm going to dig and dig until I get enough to bury the whole bloody lot of you."

The laptop squealed as she wrenched it open and her fingers launched into a swift staccato on the keys. Sudden clanking close by stopped her dead. Another clank and she swore before wailing, "Will I ever get some bloody peace?!"

There was a noise like faraway wind whistling through a valley, followed by a deep exhalation repeated again and again. My mind scrambled for a distant memory: Eithne— antenatal class—circular breathing exercises to calm the nerves!

"Just twenty minutes, he said, just twenty, M. Make yourself a cup of tea, relax, breathe, M, breathe." She left the desk and the clanking continued. The CD finished before she returned.

It was past three in the morning, but I was too wired to go to sleep. I poured a large neat vodka and smoked a couple of cigarettes. Then I listened to the whole lot again. So she hadn't given up on the story and Marta had sneaked in to have a look at the article, making a note of its name. My mind whirled round, trying to make sense of what I had

252

heard, trying to identify every sound in a house I knew well, but not as my own. I put the recording on again, closed my eyes to concentrate and immersed myself in the world of that afternoon.

Nell and Jenny leapt on me in their excitement. Finding me on the sofa in the morning usually elicited a scolding from Jen, but today was "The Mummy Returns Day" and all else was superfluous.

I rose stiffly and my head started to pound. Clearing up the wreckage of another excessive night, my neck and armpits felt strangely stiff and swollen. My forehead was clammy and my vision even more opaque than usual. I tried to ignore it as I made breakfast; it being Saturday the girls wanted bacon and eggs, but nausea got the better of me and I had to leave Jenny in charge of the spatula. With my head over the bowl of the toilet I heard Nell chanting, "I'll get all his bacon!"

Jenny upbraided me for not eating the food she had put in front of me, but I felt too crap to see the irony. A shower and shave left me feeling cleaner but no better and halfway through supervising the preparation of a chocolate cake, I was told to go and put my feet up and stop getting in the way. The girls must have made their own lunch because they didn't wake me to be fed. Instead, they left a beautifully presented ham, honey, cucumber, cheese and marmite triple-decker that had me heading for the toilet bowl again.

By the time Eithne came in, to shrieks of joy and demands of, "Mummy, mummy what did you bring us?" I was barely lucid. Freeing herself from the clutches of little hands, Eithne strode into the sitting room, looked me over and pronounced, "You look shite, Joe. Be away to bed with you. I'll bring you a Lemsip."

253

Hand over hand I pulled myself along the banister for what seemed like a month before reaching the bedroom where I flopped down onto our nice fresh inside-out bed.

Chapter 20

I spent the next three days sweating it out under that duvet, drifting in the doldrums where confused memory mingles with vivid imagination, lost in recurring dreams with surprise endings. Eithne took some well-deserved leave to dabble in housewifery and allow me slowly to re-gather my physical and mental strength. When my fever passed she brought me soup and an audiobook.

As soon as I was strong enough I struggled downstairs, found my little bag of dope and remaining tobacco and emptied them down the waste disposal. The fool's gold had lost its lustre. When I felt like smoking again, I would switch to filtered cigarettes in the hope that I could break the association of rolling and smoking and so remove the temptation to use additives.

Rather than join the Yuletide lemmings who crowded the High Street eager to plunge into debt, I took to walking on the Heath each day, rebuilding my stamina and enjoying the fresh air in my lungs. During the evenings I plucked my Christmas gifts from the flea markets of eBay and Abebooks.

In the week before Christmas I visited Miranda's grave. Perched on a neighbouring sarcophagus and wiping away the odd cold tear, I chatted to her and willed myself to believe that I had closed a door on the previous three months and that Eithne had taken the key from me and put it somewhere safely out of reach. Whether or not I accepted her suicide, I had to accept Miranda's death. Her mind, I rationalised, must have been held hostage by some fanatic urge to impose order on her unhappy world. When thwarted, that urge had blown itself up, taking her with it. The toxic fallout had contaminated me too, but I'd been luckier than Miranda; my other half had come home in time to save me.

On an RNIB Christmas card I wrote to Gail, Kelvin and Fisher, wishing them 'hope at this difficult time of year'. Then I copied the benign phrase onto another card and sent that to Rachel's new address in Manchester.

On the other side of Fawkes Close, Miranda's demise did not deter Hugo from taking his annual jaunt to Courchevel. He simply booked the children into all-day ski lessons and enjoyed the pistes and après-ski with his sister instead of his wife.

The over-consumption embodied by a fat Santa toting a bulging bag of expensive gifts makes me queasy at the best of times. This year, however, I put my cynicism aside. So many fractured families would be struggling to find anything to celebrate with an empty chair at the Christmas table, it made me appreciate just how fortunate I was.

Eithne's parents' had invited us to their place in County Cork to see in the New Year and there the lack of artificial noise and the gusting fresh air further calmed my karma. On the final day of that turbulent year Eithne and I sat on a hillside overlooking the sea and watched the sun sink into the roiling waves.

"New year, new start," she murmured, echoing my silent hope.

When I said nothing she continued, "You know in an ideal world we'd have been able to share the burden of the last few months, talk things through night after night, instead of letting everything get bottled up."

My newly found calm fled in anticipation of the rebuke I knew I deserved. "I'm sorry Eithne, it all just got on top of me. I, I, it won't…"

She put her finger to my lips. "Look, Joe, I know that you know where the limit lies and I'm not looking to make

256

you feel any worse than I know you feel already. Christ, anyone would have struggled to cope with all you've been through recently. I just need to know that I've not to worry about your ability to care for our children when I'm away."

I flushed with resentment. How dare she? How could she possibly know how I felt? She hadn't been there! But even as I glared truculently ahead, I knew that she was right and that I had let her and the girls down as well.

An onshore gust bit through my tattered self-respect and chilled me to the core. Beside me Eithne's voice, buffeted by the roar of the sea and muted by my determination to block out any further criticism, became little more than a distant burble.

"Oi, buster, are you listening to me?" She prodded me in the ribs.

"What now?" I sighed. I wasn't going to win any arguments. Just like all the others, I'd had an affair with Polish & Check, cheated on my family, been caught and now had to pay the price, until Eithne decided otherwise.

"How about I try and go four days a week?" This was so unexpected that, when its significance did finally register, it immediately banished all other thoughts.

"Would they allow you?"

"Let them try and stop me. I'm a lawyer dontcha know? I know my rights," she giggled. "Besides Jean-Pierre's a big boy now. I think I can let him loose on the world stage. Sure, he's watched me in action often enough."

I pondered her plan. "We'd have to draw our belts in a bit, but I guess if interest rates stay low…"

"I hope you don't just love me for my money mister!" She prodded me in the ribs again. "There's more to life than providing for my family financially. I can help in other ways, if you're prepared to let me. We'll make it work, if you want it to."

I laughed nervously. "Of course I do. I spend my whole life wishing I could see more of you!"

Her arm slid round my shoulder and she drew me close. As she held me I felt our hearts beat in tandem again.

With the days beginning to lengthen and a sense that the worst was over, renewed hope took root. Others had obviously rediscovered their passion too, as Eithne observed the afternoon before the girls were due back at school.

"Come and see these two lesbians snogging each others' faces off!" she'd called from the kitchen. Not a natural voyeur, I nevertheless sauntered over to the window. Wrapping my arms around Eithne's waist and resting my chin on her bony shoulder, I squinted out into the watery January sunlight. Marta's tall, leggy figure and platinum hair were quickly recognisable, but the lanky dark haired one foxed me, as she was partly in the shadow of Lucia's house. As she turned to leave though, Eithne guffawed, "It's the bearded lady, Joe. She's a he!"

Zarek's handsome features swam into view amidst a mass of straggling, untied hair and I experienced a frisson of disappointment, as when you hear that the school bully has found someone to marry him; however that was all. The whole affair was now in the past; I'd put it from my mind determined to get on with my own family's life.

Further consideration of the matter was terminated when my wife took me by the hand and led me upstairs where our passion was drowned out by the soundtrack of the latest Harry Potter DVD keeping our children glued to the telly in the sitting room.

The following morning, as I watched Eithne tuck her wavy auburn hair into the new woollen hat I had given her for Christmas, I knew that what matters most is not what we have lost, but what we retain. I enfolded her in my arms and held her until the airport taxi gave a third long blast of its horn. We kissed and she turned to leave.

"Thank you," I called after her.

"Just doing my job," she replied. "Now don't you fall off that wagon, you hear."

The low sun shone through the denuded trees, further disrupting the light that reached my retinas, like an over-eager toddler's fist twisting a kaleidoscope this way and that. As she walked to the cab the lovage green, bobble-less hat danced amidst the pretty lights surrounded by a corona of beautiful russet and for a few fleeting moments, my vision felt perfect.

Unlike its artificial substitutes, that euphoria did not disappear in a puff of blue smoke or leave me feeling desiccated; its embers glowed for days to come, warming the hearth for Eithne's return.

Brad's house was freezing. Bits of boiler lay strewn across the small terracotta tiled utility room and his blue-tinged hands were smudged with grime.

"Happy frikkin New Year, Joe," he muttered as Kelly disappeared back into the kitchen to fetch more coffee and biscuits. The American School had yet to go back and the percussive din of some shoot-em-up kids' movie echoed through the house. "Hey, get the kids to shut that off and write some thank you letters, willya Kell?" Brad yelled after his wife, then shook his head despondently. "Man, this heap of crap belongs in a museum."

I peered into the dark boiler cupboard, but all I could make out was a red-jacketed hot water tank and a grey coloured box the size of a packing case. Everything radiated cold. "So, Kelly got bored of having you under her feet and set you some DIY homework then, did she?" I teased.

"Nope, I was reading online about some family who were staying in a holiday house with a faulty boiler, last fall. They all woke up dead; carbon monoxide poisoning." My stomach twisted uncomfortably at the words. He continued blithely unaware, "So I got to thinking, I wonder if that's why I'm always waking up with such a sore head, 'cos the boiler's screwed?"

I laughed, "Nah, that'll be all the crap American lager you drink, mate."

He ignored me. "So I call the landlord and say, 'Like when was that boiler last serviced, I wanna see the certificate?' And he like says it was done before we moved in, that was like over two years ago, man! But the frikkin asshole says, 'well it's Christmas time so I can't get a service engineer till the second week of January'. Well I said, 'Screw you. You take two grand a week and don't do squat to earn it. People don't take a Christmas holiday from dying!' So I went out and bought me a home-test kit and waddaya think it said?"

"That you're pregnant?" I suggested, patting his rounded tummy.

"That he's full of hot air!" Kelly guided my hand towards a steaming cup of coffee and grinned at me—all teeth and lipgloss.

"Have those kids started their letters yet, Kell?" Brad puffed, "And Joe, make sure you leave me some of those plain chocolate cookies. Man, it only says the goddamn boiler is chucking out 46% more carbon monoxide than is legally allowed!" There was triumph in his voice and he rewarded himself by cramming a whole cookie in his mouth with his grimy paw.

"So why are you, um mending it? Surely the landlord should send someone round on emergency call-out."

Kelly harrumphed and stalked out to start preparing lunch. Brad's reply was sheepish, "Er, kids were driving me nuts so I thought I'd have a go myself," he muttered. "Truth is, you don't get too many household boilers on planes."

"Meanwhile, we haven't had heating or hot water for two whole days!" Kelly growled from the kitchen, "And my hair feels like I got glue in it. But Captain Marvel says he'll have it fixed by this afternoon, don't you darlin'?"

We chatted for a bit, but I suspected I was distracting him, so joined Kelly next door and offered to chop the veg. I was telling her about Eithne's plan to go four days a week and how our family break had helped me put things into perspective, when a dull clanking noise from the utility room halted me mid-sentence.

Something akin to a neurological electric shock spasmed through me. As my realisation of its cause condensed, warm tears streaked down my cheeks. I laughed from mingled embarrassment and release, as if I had just broken wind loudly. But the hollow fear within me that accompanied the sudden revelation made that laughter joyless.

"Jeez Joe, you're trembling. Is everything okay?" Kelly's concerned voice was at my side, but I heard it as if she were on a different windy hilltop. I fought to control my breathing as my heart palpitated and my throat grew tight. Wordlessly, Kelly guided me to a chair. All my focus seemed drawn to one point; thoughts, mind's eye, flashes of white and colour, all sucked into one vortex of swirling, blue-green, pulsating light.

Brad's faraway voice was worried, "Jeez Joe, are you sick, man? How come he's gone so pale all of a sudden?"

I heard but could not answer. My mind was fully occupied, as if reciting Pi to infinite decimal places; the

261

same elements repeating again and again, but in a different, seemingly random order, all leading to the same end, endlessly.

"Hey, dude snap out of it! Do you wanna coffee, a Coke, a beer?" The last was accompanied by a wallop to my shoulder so jarring that it broke my trance.

"Flippin'ell, Brad," I wheezed, "I hope you're more gentle with the kids."

He looked at me quizzically as I rubbed my shoulder, more for the comfort of feeling my solidity than from his affable assault. "Whoa Joe, what's eatin' you? You've gone awful green. Did Kell get you to taste her cookin'?"

Regular, deep breaths, in—hold—out, and I felt grounded again, but my sense of revelation remained, undiminished. Distracted I croaked, "Look, just get me that coffee will you? I think I need to tell you something."

A pall of sadness was descending over me and I was beginning to tune out again as he turned away muttering, "Whatever, man."

'Leave it!' implored a voice inside my head. 'It'll pass, just like a nicotine pang.'

It didn't. With rising anxiety the voice admonished, 'If you give in you'll be letting Eithne and the kids down again.'

But all the while another voice, deep within me, kept up its steady counsel, 'Do that and your conscience will never give you peace.'

Desperate for distraction I strained to hear the real voices, the whispered words between Brad and Kelly as they busied themselves with the cafetière, "Hung over? Stoned? Breakdown? Ring Eithne?"

The kettle began to boil, drowning them out. For the most part, I had succeeded in bringing my heart rate and

262

breathing back to something approaching normal, but not so the maelstrom in my head. Everything shimmered, inextricably connected; as fragile as a frosted cobweb and as likely to turn to a sticky embroiling mess if I charged through it. But it was starting to solidify and as it did so, so did the knowledge that it wouldn't let me pass.

I all but seized the coffee from Brad when he and Kelly rejoined me. "Look, guys, I know that what I am going to say will sound preposterous and I know that I am meant to have moved on from all this, but just hear me out and then please tell me that I've lost the plot. Okay?"

The lines of uncertainty and concern etched on their faces defied even my soft focus filter.

"Right," I took an only-half-theatrical deep breath and set off on my vain quest to stuff the genie that had just been released back into its suddenly illuminated lamp.

"Brad, a boiler needs an exhaust pipe because it is a fuel engine and therefore gives off exhaust fumes in the form of carbon monoxide. Am I right?"

"So far so good, chief," though he sounded rather mystified.

"So if I disconnect the exhaust pipe and stand in the boiler cupboard with the boiler on…"

"Without ventilation, you'd die, sooner or later." It was a simple statement.

"Good," I replied, heart and mind racing ahead of my words.

"Good?" Disbelief and concern mingled in Kelly's tone.

"Yes, good. So if I fitted a new longer exhaust and had it leading into this room, I could kill us all, right?"

"Well, assuming that the windows and doors were sealed and we were dumb enough not to notice the pipe comin' into the room or wonder why we all felt like shit, yeah. It

263

could take a few hours, but eventually we'd all get overcome by carbon monoxide fumes and pass out."

"How about in a small basement office, say eight by ten feet?"

Realisation creased his brow, "Oh man, not this again! You can't still believe that Miranda was murdered? We all heard how she was that night."

"Oh Joe, and you were just sayin' how you'd got some perspective while you were away. You've gotta let it go." Kelly chided. "It's not healthy." She had adopted the voice of a disappointed mother who finds her seven year-old son still fiddling with himself in public.

I wasn't really listening. My heart and temples were thudding in unison now, spurring me on. "So it's possible, right?"

"In theory, yes." The reluctance in his voice amply reflected his doubts.

"Because that's what I heard in the background, on the CD Dino made for me, after you'd all left. That noise I just heard you making, with the boiler." Their attention had slipped away; I had lost them. Painstakingly, I explained how I had listened to the rest of the recording. That hearing the noises of Brad's struggle in the room next door had triggered my aural memory as surely as seeing a face they recognised would their visual one. "We know that Zarek was told to fix the boiler and I heard Marta have a look at the article Miranda was writing. They killed her because of it; I knew they did and now I know how."

Brad and Kelly's silence spoke volumes for how unconvinced they remained. But I was too keyed-up to be dissuaded. "Look, after I put the girls to bed, I went round to see Miranda, as arranged. It took ages for her to come to the door and she was woozy and complaining of a headache. That's consistent with carbon monoxide

264

poisoning isn't it? Like prolonged head-rush from your first cigarette of the day?"

"You're forgetting, those of us with sight would see a boiler exhaust pipe sticking in through the window." Brad reminded me gently.

I stuck my tongue out at him by way of response and ploughed on, "And you're forgetting that there's no window in her office just an air brick in the outside wall. The room next door to it houses the boiler. There's a small area for dustbins out back; it's covered, no one would have seen..." Tears pricked my eyes again, and a hard lump started to form by my vocal chords. I could visualise that bastard Zarek doing it. I puffed out my choked breath and continued. "That's the noise I heard. Oh my God!" A cold wave broke over me, "She said she'd dozed off and that I'd woken her. She said that she thought it was kids ringing her bell and running away." Had I saved her life, only to leave her to die a few minutes later?

I felt sick. The coffee repeated on me. Giddiness overcame me and I hung my head between my knees. Eventually, I sat back and Kelly handed me a tissue.

Brad leant forward and puffed out his round cheeks. "Ok Mr Joe, leaving aside my belief that you really should consult a therapist, let's just assume for a minute that there is a possibility that you could be right. Zarek feeds the exhaust into the airbrick and fills the room with CO. He hides round the back and comes out to ring the doorbell to check whether she's still conscious. When he gets no reply, he lets himself in. He finds Miranda out cold, picks her up and dumps her in the garage. Then he turns on the motor and leaves it running. One type of carbon monoxide is pretty much the same as another. Next, he destroys the article she's writing, lets hisself outta the house, disconnects the exhaust and puts it back to how it was. Any traces he leaves in the house are explained by him workin' there

265

anyway, so is his presence if he gets seen – overtime, emergency repairs, whatever. Okay, in theory it could work," Brad conceded. "But man, if he did, he woulda needed to have balls of steel!"

I left them to their now less-digestible lunch and kind of drifted down the hill towards the supermarket. The fridge and cupboards at home were bare and the girls had been clamouring for 'normal food' after all the festive feasting. The routine progression from fruit to freezer, plucking the items on my memorised list from their memorised positions in the aisles, left the majority of my brain free to test for flaws in my theory. By the time I had tracked down the relocated sponge scourers and was queuing to pay, I knew there were none.

I went straight to the drawer where I had put everything to do with the investigation and dragged out the MP3 recorder. I found the place I needed and hurried back to the kitchen to unpack the shopping. The sound quality was stodgy and though I could hear some light tapping, which I took to be Miranda typing, and the odd clunk, it was hopeless.

Maybe I still had a choice. Brad and Kelly could well yet write this off as another paranoid delusion of a troubled and obsessive mind. But I knew that I would never be able to dismiss it. I knew for certain now and that knowledge would never lie quietly buried within me. It impelled me to act.

With the phone clamped between my ear and shoulder while I continued to restock the kitchen, I called Dino. "Happy New Year mate, good Yuletide?"

His lethargy resonated down the line, "Yeah, hardly moved off the sofa, Joe. I'm detoxing for January though, and Maria musta shrunk all my clothes."

266

Small talk dispensed with I plunged in, "You know the CD you gave me of Miranda's interviews."

I heard him draw a sharp breath. His reply was world weary and cautious, "Oh, that again. Yeah."

"How much more of it was there on the MP3? I mean did it just cut out like that, because it ran out of space or batteries?"

He was defensive, "No, er let's see." I heard the creak of a leather sofa, a grunt and then the noise of him bringing a computer to life. "No, I put as much as would fit on the CD, about eighty minutes worth, but that recorder's got a one gig memory card. Battery life's about six hours new and fully charged. Looking at the MP3 file I've got here, I guess it musta run on for about another coupla hours. But I listened on a bit, it was just dead air, a few bumps and bangs but nothin' major."

"It's those bumps and bangs I'm interested in. Can you give them the same treatment as you did the rest? Bring them to the fore I mean?"

"Er yeah, but why? I thought that was all like ancient history."

"It was, but not anymore," I replied, "It's Brad's fault. I'll tell you later, can I come round on the way back from school?"

"Christ man, what's the hurry? I got a lot of sloth to catch up on."

"Believe me, Dino, it really is important, I promise I'll tell you later."

Next, I rang Brad back. I got Kelly and apologised for my odd behaviour that morning.

"That's okay, Joe, I understand," she replied soothingly "Bereavement and stress affect us all in very different ways." She fetched Brad who took the phone from her

267

gruffly. As I'd guessed, my suggestion and its proximity to Kelly's deadline met with his ready agreement. I texted him the number and told him to call me once it was done.

Finally, I called Eithne's office. Bloody Jean-Pierre rang me back with the extension number for a lovely Polish filing clerk called Ewa, who performed a rapid and revealing over-the-phone translation for me.

At pick-up the girls were overjoyed to find that we were going to Dino's for tea. As they constantly reminded me, Father Christmas was far more generous with his electronics for the Cazale children than for them. I told them this was because Father Christmas was Catholic by birth and part of the American corporate mafia by adoption. As soon as we were through the front door, Jen and Nell disappeared to inspect the latest haul of gadgetry. Dino led me through to his own techie paradise.

I paid my usual entrance fee— listening to five minutes about the latest technological wizardry— before he double-clicked the file icon and I heard the by now familiar low whirr of Miranda's laptop fan, the tap of her nails on the keys and her deep sighing breaths, interspersed with the odd sniff.

From the left hand speaker came more telltale metallic clanking, interrupted at one point by a louder clunk. After about five minutes it stopped and a door creaked open. Soft footsteps mounted the stairs and, after lots more typing, there was a low scraping sound from a new source. It reminded me of sandpaper on brick and lasted only about fifteen seconds; long enough for Miranda to groan in irritation, "Oh for goodness sake!" There followed an annoying, intermittent squeak, then we heard only typing, breathing and the computer's fan.

Zarek's feet made a jaunty descent of the stairs and I could hear whistling before the boiler room door creaked open again. A little more clanking before a further creak and bang, as the door was slammed shut. Next, there was a polite knock at the office door and Miranda's answering, "Come."

"The boiler is serviced now, Mrs Lethbridge, it will work properly. Maybe you will notice a difference in efficiency too. I will check your radiator for air before I go, okay?"

"If you must," Miranda sounded harassed. There was a rattling noise and a hiss. Then Zarek must have patted the radiator. "Okay, I am finished. Now I will go. Goodbye until tomorrow, Mrs Lethbridge."

She did not reply, but sighed heavily when the door slammed shut behind him. His boots ascended the stairs and faded into the distance. Miranda began to hum to herself. I recognised the melody of 'Andmoreagain' from Forever Changes.

The ringtone of my mobile broke the spell of that recreated evening. It was Brad, "Okay they're here and he said he thinks they need about an hour. When you coming over?"

"I'm at Dino's. About half an hour, okay?"

"Sure, and for what it's worth, I'm beginning to come round to your way of thinkin'. The frikkin' asshole told me I must've had a real cowboy trying to fix it before I called him in."

"He must have seen your spurs in the hallway, Brad. So long partner." I rang off and turned back to Dino. There was a familiar metallic ticking noise coming from the speakers now, that I couldn't quite place.

"So, how'd I do, Joe?" there was clear pride in Dino's voice.

"Crystal clear, mate, thanks, it's perfect. What you have just heard is how Zarek murdered Miranda."

His mouth hung open in amazement as I explained it all again. And whether through retelling or the acquisition of new aural evidence, the theory felt like it had gained substance. Dino's reaction was certainly less sceptical than Brad and Kelly's had been.

"Man, I'm sorry. I never thought to listen through the whole rest of the file. Like I said, there didn't seem to be anything much there. Jeez, to think that it's evidence of a murder and it's been sitting on my PC all through Christmas. I'm such a dumbass, Joe. Man, I'm so sorry. I was just so relieved to think I'd found proof that she had killed herself, to give you some sorta closure. I mean, she sounded so darn wretched."

"Dino, Dino, no one's blaming you. For goodness sake, if it weren't for all your hard work we would never have any of this in a state worth listening to. Anyway, Christ knows how I am going to prove it. I can hear DI Sharratt now, 'It's all circumstantial Mr Wynde, all a matter of interpretation'."

"I still feel awful, Joe. I mean me and the guys thought you were nuts, chasing after this. But it sure looks like you were right."

"Look, none of that matters. Now, I've got to get off to Brad's, but before I go can you do a couple of things for me?"

"Sure, whatever you want, Joe."

"First, is all this backed up and saved and safe, including all the interview files?"

"Yeah, of course."

"Okay, so can you clear a bit of space on this for me?" I handed him the MP3 recorder. "Say delete the first seven files, that should give me about forty minutes shouldn't it?" He nodded and did so. "Next, I need you to burn a CD of all of track 8. Finally, would you mind just listening to the remaining bit of the recording really hard and making a note of anything interesting? Doorbells especially." Dino nodded enthusiastically, keen to atone for what he perceived as a lapse.

The school run traffic had been replaced by that of the city's workers returning to their suburban homes. It would have been in full spate had it been going anywhere; instead it was nose to tail, belching fumes into the waterlogged air and creating small pungent pockets of pollution that smelt like burnt hair.

Bathed in the sickly light of the Victorian street lantern that stood outside Brad's house, the red and white logo made the van it adorned look like a bloodshot eyeball. A cloud of smoke streamed from the driver's open window. As I drew level I peered inside and found my stare met by a man with a flat iron-shaped face and a black beanie hat. He'd presumably been left on guard against Camden's guerrilla army of parking attendants.

"Good evening," I said brightly, "isn't the weather terrible?"

He grunted, exhaled high-tar smog and shook his head in incomprehension.

My eyes smarting slightly, I continued, "I just thought you'd like to know that there's a pair of traffic wardens round the corner." The dark brow of his beanie rose in consternation and as I walked to the front door I heard the transit's engine splutter into life and the taciturn man grinding it into reverse.

Once in the house, I followed Brad through to the kitchen and accepted a beer, if only to steady my nerves.

271

The sounds of whistling and metallic clanking emanating from the utility room forced their way into my consciousness in spite of my best efforts to subdue them with small talk. I had pretty much drained my beer when the door opened and Zarek's pony-tailed head appeared. "I am finished Mr Carmichael. It just needed some professional attention. Oh, hello Mr Wynde."

A violent urge to avenge Miranda surged through me. The bursts of light at the edges of my vision closed in across my entire field and flickered like strobes. I clenched my fists and jaw and waited for the ebb tide. Then, in as measured a voice as I could muster, I replied, "Zarek. I thought you'd gone back to Gdansk."

"Money in London is better," he stated flatly, "and it is cold in Gdansk in January. Also people like Mr Carmichael need me here to fix their central heating."

Under the kitchen's halogen spots I noted that he wore a broad, cocky grin.

"Yeah, you fixed it for Miranda too didn't you, Zarek?" I felt Kelly and Brad stiffen at the accusation, but if Zarek was caught off-guard he didn't reveal himself to me.

"It was a small job, just adjustment to make the system run more efficiently. Oh, and how are your girls Mr Wynde? They are so pretty and full of life."

The implicit threat caused hot and cold needles of sensation along the length of my spine. The strobe effect across my eyes intensified and it was only with supreme effort that I was able to control my reaction and utter a simple, "Fine."

Brad counted out four twenties and handed them to Zarek. The Pole thanked him and prepared to leave, but as he donned his donkey jacket I moved along the hallway and stood in front of the door, blocking his exit.

272

"I've got a present for you Zarek. A little something to listen to on these long, lonely winter evenings." I handed him the CD.

"What is this, some of your strange music?" He was puzzled and suspicious.

"It's the soundtrack to a murder story. I've written my number on the back of the CD case. After you've had a good listen give me a call and let me know what you think of it."

As instructed, Brad and Kelly had joined us in the narrow hall. I hoped they had a good view of Zarek's face, which to me was just a putty-coloured blur. His voice, however, had acquired a faint tremor, "Perhaps, if it is very interesting, I will visit your house to discuss it with you."

"Great, I'll be sure to invite some friends for company. See you soon, no doubt, Mr Grzegorczyk."

Outside, sleet fell through the inky black sky, glittering in the beam of the lantern and settling on Zarek's shoulders. The van had disappeared, doubtless attempting to stay one step ahead of the non-existent parking wardens. I closed the door firmly and turned to Brad and Kelly.

"Light blue touch-paper and retire to a safe distance." But the bravado stretched no further than my voice.

Chapter 21

I knew there was someone there as soon as I left the mini-market. The sensation of being under scrutiny was swiftly joined by deliberately soft footfalls almost in sync with my own. It was two days since I'd confronted Zarek and I had been expecting something like this ever since. However, all the rehearsals had included a bevy of appalled bystanders coming to the aid of a blind man. Suddenly, I was extremely glad that I had refused the glass of wine on offer at parents' evening.

Nell and Jen were at Lucia's, thank goodness, safe and awaiting my praise. In this dark, deserted street, it took an effort of will not to double my pace and try to hurry home to them. But my whirring mind told me my best bet was to let my pursuer believe I hadn't spotted him. At the junction I paused, as if unsure of my bearings; the footsteps paused too. Still nobody else within earshot. Ignoring the urge to glance behind me, I stepped off the kerb and continued, my back twitching.

Where was everybody? Just returned from their second homes and sheltering from the cold realities of this grim time of year in front of the telly, no doubt...apart from Dusty in his chilly shelter... I began to count my steps.

Still no one, no witnesses; my intestines writhed.

Time and my pace slowed. With my free hand I peeled the cellophane from the new pack of cigarettes, pushed one up and plucked it out with my lips. Slipping the packet into the breast pocket of my leather jacket, I pressed the 'record' button on the MP3. If I was going to take a pasting I would at least try and make it worthwhile.

Delving into my trouser pocket for my lighter I quickly located it and the menu button on my mobile. Three stabs and I knew I'd got to 'search phone book' before sliding my chewed index finger down past the Braille 5 to the 9 and pressing it four times. With my eyes screwed shut against its flare, I brought the lighter to my cigarette and lit up. A deep drag and I slid my hand back into the pocket, dropped the lighter and pressed 'dial'.

Another deep drag and...silence. The street was still deserted, apart from me and my shadow. Was I mistaken? Infused with adrenalin, I was quivering. Still silence.

A burst of techno about twenty feet behind me and a grunt of annoyance told me all I needed to know. Tossing the cigarette aside I darted round the corner and ducked down the tiny alley. My stick was too noisy to use so, relying on memory and the handrail, I hurtled down the slippery steps. Only on the penultimate one did I come a cropper, my foot snagging in an abandoned plastic bag. Pitching forward, I was unable to stifle a yelp as my elbow crunched into the brick wall.

The noise was enough to give me away. My pursuer's footfalls halted, changed direction and came thudding down the steps towards me. I hurried on towards the Anderson shelter, too nervous of colliding with one of the many obstacles in the dark to run. I didn't stand a chance of making it. There were heavy breaths right behind me now, then a hand grabbed my throbbing elbow. I yelped again and heard a faint shuffling sound echo in the shelter followed by a barely audible, "Bloody kids."

"Police, it's a bust. Come out with your hands up. It's a bust." I shrieked as loud as I could and felt the grip on my arm tighten and Zarek's voice at my ear.

"That is enough, Mr Wynde. There are no policemen here. No one is here except you and me."

"Oh, Zarek, it's you! Thank goodness, I thought you were a mugger." My heart beat heavily against my rib cage and I wondered whether the MP3 would pick that up too.

"You will wish I was a mugger, Mr Wynde. It is a shame you cannot mind your own business. But now at least you will see your friend Mrs Lethbridge again. I think it is your sadness at her death that has killed you. I think you will cut your wrists here and bleed to death." I heard a smooth metallic click behind me, then the point of a knife pressed through my jacket against my right kidney. Fear came in waves spreading from my chest, to my extremities. My bowels felt slack and my tongue leathery.

I tried to wriggle free, all the time listening for Dusty's wheezing breath. Zarek still had a firm grip on me and his right foot was pushing my own further away from my left, putting us both slightly off balance.

A sudden explosive peel echoed round the bomb shelter. It sounded like a rabid Doberman. Zarek raised the knife and loosened his grip momentarily. Still clutching my stick in both hands I drove the hard acrylic knob down onto Zarek's toes. He yelped and I spun away to the left yelling "Bust, bust, bust!" Zarek's knuckles cuffed my temple, but I was free and reeled away from him. Dusty whirled into action, hurling unintelligible expletives and dustbin lids before him.

With Zarek momentarily distracted I threw caution to the wind and ran for the first time in years. Following my nose, I headed for the urine-soaked doorway at the head of the steps down to New End. The lantern overhead was still broken and I groped the final few yards along the wall and round the corner, tucking myself out of sight from the alleyway. I heard a thump and a loud cry from Dusty then pounding boots coming towards me. When I judged them to be six feet away, I shot my stick out at ankle level wedging it in front of the cast iron bollard at the top of the steps.

The throbbing in my elbow faded to distant memory as my shoulder took the brunt of Zarek's muscular weight tripping over. He cried out and then there was a sound reminiscent of a melon being dropped onto a tiled floor.

He was groaning as I eased my way down the long flight of stone steps. Two from the bottom I slipped on something sticky and landed, knees first on his lower back and thigh. He protested groggily. I couldn't see a thing, but was too furious to care how badly he was hurt. I repositioned myself so that one knee was in the middle of his back and the other was pinning his right arm beneath him. Then I wrenched his left arm behind him so that his shoulder followed and his head lolled to one side. He was very woozy and rolled easily onto his back.

Sitting on his chest, I wedged my right knee into his free elbow, pushing it down onto the glinting cobbles. Flicking my white stick round in front of me, I laid it across his windpipe, flexed my shoulders and pushed down. He gasped and started to struggle. I pushed harder.

"Have I got your attention, Zarek?" I shouted. I felt him respond and pushed down harder still, arching my back. He was struggling to breathe now. "Your full attention?" I could feel his panic and eased off a little.

"I know you murdered Miranda Lethbridge, Zarek, to keep Polish & Check's blackmail business going. Tell Pavel Dabrowski to meet me tomorrow at The Duke of Wellington pub down there." I nodded towards New End. "Tell him he can buy my silence for fifty thousand pounds. Understand?" I pushed down as hard as I could and heard him splutter and gurgle. I took this for a yes, but as I rose I kicked him in the balls, just to make sure he didn't come back for clarification.

At the top of the steps again, I called out to Dusty. There was no answer and I could sense that he wasn't in the alleyway. My foot kicked something metallic and sent it skittering across the wet cobblestones. Swishing my stick across the area where the noise had ceased I found the flick-knife. It was still open but, thank goodness, clean.

Closing and pocketing the weapon, I called his name again. There was still no answer so, for the first time, I entered the shelter uninvited. I followed the flickering candlelight down and found him sitting cross-legged in the middle of the dim room; he was humming to himself.

"You okay, Dusty?" I whispered as if I were in a church. He seemed not to register my presence and I touched him lightly on the shoulder. He didn't react. I patted my pocket and took out the packet of cigarettes, placed them in front of him and left.

I took the long way home, unwilling to encounter Zarek again. The porch light to Lucia's house was on and she bustled out to meet me.

"Goodness me, you look terrible Joe. What has happened?"

I tried to shrug it off as she towed me into the hallway, "Oh I just slipped on the steps at the top of Steele's Passage. Caught my funny bone on the wall, it's nothing."

Lucia wasn't paying attention, however, and in retrospect, I understood that she must have been staring in horror at the bloody footprints I had just left across her hall carpet.

"You're bleeding," she screamed, grabbing the coat stand for support then crumpling to her knees.

Freddie emerged from wherever she stores him in the evenings, manhandled her to her feet and led her away. A couple of minutes later, he returned wearing yellow Marigold gloves and squirting a bottle of carpet cleaner.

Meanwhile, I had checked myself for previously unnoticed stab wounds and found none. My shoulder, elbow and temple all ached and I had blood on my shoes but otherwise I was intact. There were also dark sticky stains on the lower left leg of my light blue jeans and smears of bright blood on my white stick and my hands. Now holding my shoes, I asked Freddie whether there was anything practical I could do.

From his kneeling position where he was creating perfect circles of foam on the Axminster he replied calmly "Not really, Joe. Lucia's having a little lie down. Can't stand the sight of blood you know; won't go anywhere near uncooked steak, more's the pity. Kids are all in bed; quite happy for them to stay. You look peaky—early night would do you good I'd say."

"If you're sure, Freddie, that would be great. Um, apologies again about the carpet."

"Don't worry about it. Seen worse, at least it's fresh. Don't s'pose you know what type—beef, squirrel, dead fox?"

"Um, it was in the alleyway. It might just be human, maybe…"

"Bloody louts!" snapped Freddie. "Oh well, nighty night."

The house seemed eerily quiet when I let myself in. Still carrying my shoes, I walked into the sitting room and turned on the TV for company. Then, I stripped off my jeans and washed them and my shoes in the sink of the downstairs toilet, leaving the trouser-leg soaking in Vanish. After pulling on a pair of tracksuit bottoms, I made myself a sandwich and sent out a group text.

2moro nite. Duke of W. Celebr8n! beers on me! Meet my house 7pm, will xplain…Joe

I took a ginger beer from the fridge and retired to the sofa. *Crimewatch* had just started, which seemed appropriate. Once it had finished I went to bed and did not have nightmares.

279

Chapter 22

I awoke thinking of Harry Potter and, as consciousness slowly blew through the fog of sleep, recognised Jenny murmuring in her sister's room. Lucia must have dropped them off first thing. I tried to prop myself up on my elbow, winced and remembered why it hurt. The red LED numbers of the bedside clock radio refused to come into focus, but the light edging the askew curtains was watery and monochrome. Reluctantly, I hauled myself out of bed and padded over to my younger daughter's bedroom.

A two-headed form glowed on the bed and spoke in a voice muffled by the duvet. Harry was aloft above Hogwarts chasing down the snitch and dodging Malfoy's evil intent. I sat on the end of the bed and listened. My mother had read to me on such mornings when I was little; the pain at my inability to do so for my girls was lessened by my pride at Jenny's willingness to step in unbidden. I hugged them both and drifted downstairs to prepare breakfast.

A well-stacked plate of toast with Nutella greeted the two of them when they descended twenty minutes later, clad in school uniform and having plaited each other's hair. They demolished it and their orange juice, then demanded porridge too. I myself settled for a bacon sandwich and two cups of instant coffee. At just after eight the three of us, wrapped up like arctic explorers, quit the warmth of the house and braved the icy walk to school.

The weeping leaden sky hung around us, intermittently allowing glimpses of the moon, which appeared to be lingering while the weak sun made up its mind whether it could face its shift. The girls grumbled about not having access to flue powder to get them to school. My bacon sandwich was lodged halfway down my oesophagus.

On the approach road to school we passed the same stressed mothers as every morning; queued in their oversized wheelie toys, so tantalisingly close to being able to drop their progeny off and escape to their Pilates classes or a Starbucks cappuccino. They tested the claims of the botox peddlers as they frowned and scowled at each other's stationary Land Destroyers, nose to tail as far as the eye could see. The steady chugging of scores of four-litre engines provided a rhythm section to the freeform jazz of whining infants and exasperated adults.

The school was abuzz with that Friday fizz, familiar to generations of children ticking off the lessons before the onset of the weekend. I hugged and kissed both girls for longer than usual, and as they strained to get away, extracted solemn promises that they would remember to clean their teeth. At the gates I handed their bulging overnight bags to the mum who was bravely hosting the 'mega-sleepover' that the girls and a dozen of their friends had organised, and ignored the muffled crinkle of multiple crisp packets that escaped from Nell's pink rucksack.

I hadn't been back to the Café Noir since that last time with Miranda. In the meantime, Ildiko had returned to Szeged. Her replacement, a morose and lead-footed local girl who had been sacked from The Duke for nicking alcopops, took my order in silence and shuffled away on squeaky trainers.

There were very few customers in the café and I wondered whether it was the harsh meteorological or economic conditions keeping people away. How soon before some niche chain store owned by a firm of faceless venture capitalists obliterated this remaining corner of independence too? I downed my strong coffee and sopped up its bitterness with a plump croissant. Unable to face introducing the new waitress to my bowel-driven bolero, I hobbled out and tapped briskly back home.

281

After a shower and shave I loaded the washing machine and made a half-arsed attempt at tidying the house. Weather permitting, Eithne was flying back from Copenhagen that night and I had hoped we could enjoy the luxury of a lie-in the following morning. How likely was that now?

Taking a rarely-used box of writing paper to the kitchen table I sat down and tried to compose a letter to Eithne, in case she came home to find me in a police cell, or a hospital ward or a mortuary fridge.

Spooked by the task ahead, my mind kept drifting. How electronic our lives had become—was this really the first time I had expressed my feelings in ink since the love-letters of my late teens? How infrequently today's post contains anything handwritten other than the occasional card.

Tears spattered the page as I struggled to find words to corral my teeming emotions. How could I explain that what I was preparing to do was worth risking our family happiness for? That I wasn't merely proving a point, or exacting revenge on someone else's behalf? That since discovering the truth I had felt compelled to establish it, beyond doubt, for others to see and had consequently put us all in danger. Better to face Zarek and Dabrowski on my own terms than get knifed in some dark alley one night—or worse, have them carry out their threats to Nell and Jenny. Amidst looming dread, that thought alone bolstered my resolve.

I finished the letter and rang Brad. We arranged to meet for lunch at The Duke and I busied myself until then in opening the week's pile of windowed envelopes, paying bills, filing bank statements and shredding documents. The impression of putting my affairs in order was not lost on me.

282

Brad arrived in the middle of one of Pete the landlord's diatribes about the increased duty on alcohol. I ordered two pints of lemonade. The pub was nearly empty and Pete's girlfriend, Trisha, was up a ladder hanging a banner that feted the local rugby club's run of twenty-three wins in a row. As yesterday's *Ham and High* newspaper had trumpeted on its front page, this was a regional record and worth celebrating. With the following day's game already declared a walkover because the opposition had flu, a big knees-up was planned that night at The Duke—the club's spiritual home.

"It's gonna be one helluva night!" Brad enthused over his steak sandwich. "I can hardly wait."

I was sorry to wreck his plans, "Um, I need you to do me a favour tonight actually mate." I explained and, reluctantly, he agreed. It cost me lunch.

In the drizzle, outside the mini-market, Brad smothered me in a bear hug and, clapping his palms on my back, growled, "Take care of yasself, okay buddy?" I waved him goodbye and felt giddy as I headed up the hill with my clunking blue plastic bag.

There was a small discoloured patch across a pair of York Stone slabs at the foot of the steps leading into Steele's Passage, but otherwise no evidence of the previous night's events. I could assume that Zarek had passed on the message.

Dusty was inside, sheltering from the drizzle. A vanilla scented candle gave off a sweet smell, worse than his natural odour. I handed him the bag. He pulled out the four pack of Kronenburg 1664 with glee, "Numbers! That's groovy! You want one?" I shook my head.

"A present to say thank you for saving my life last night, Dusty. Are you okay?"

By the light of the candle I thought I saw shadows furrow his brow, "Last night I met with evil, man. A demon came here with a sword. I only had a battered shield to defend myself with, but the power of peace is stronger than the will of the warmongers and the demon is no more."

Fear oozed through me, "What, he's dead? Did you see a body? Where, at the foot of the stairs?"

Dusty cackled at me, phlegm bursting like bubblegum in his throat. "No man, he ran away from me, cowardly custard!"

My relief was only partial and though we chatted for a few minutes about the 13th Floor Elevators, it failed to soothe me as my visits usually did. Promising to return after the weekend, I said goodbye and left.

The reek of synthetic vanilla dogged me for the rest of the day, giving me a low-level headache to accompany my rising apprehension. I had to force down a ham and cheese sandwich to quell my fluttering stomach and had just gone to the toilet for the fourth time in an hour when the doorbell rang. My jangling nerves stayed my hand at the latch and I called out, "Who is it?" My voice sounded high and frightened.

"It's us, you pillock!" Glenn shouted through the letterbox. "Remember, you summoned us here?" His bonhomie cheered me a little and I let them in.

Twenty minutes later they were heading up to the pub, leaving me smoking yet another cigarette and contemplating yet another trip to the toilet. After waiting a further five minutes I took a deep, trembling, inward breath, checked my pockets, picked up my white stick and left the house, not knowing when I might be coming back.

The Duke of Wellington was packed, but as promised Pete had stuck a reserved sign on the table in the back corner.

My appearance with a pint at first failed to shift the couple sitting there, however my white stick rendered their argument of not having seen the sign hollow.

The clock on my mobile said ten to eight; I tried not to gulp my beer down and entertained myself by using my foot to check that there was a stool opposite the banquette I occupied—there was.

By ten past my beer had evaporated and my bladder was protesting. Doubts erupted within me like lightning sprites; bright flashes of electrical clarity that, for a second, seemed substantial, before they disappeared completely.

My bladder was really giving me gyp now and reluctantly I had to leave the table and head to the toilet, which is in an outhouse behind the pub. I crammed the pockets of my fleece with my belongings and left just my jacket to save my place before clattering my way through the crowd and out of the back of the pub.

Someone caught the door to the gents as it swung closed behind me, pushing it open again. I had been heading for the urinals, but the blow that landed between my shoulder blades propelled me across the slippery floor and into the stalls. With his other arm he knocked my stick from my hand then landed a punch to my kidneys that sent me crashing into the toilet pan. Slumped over it, I gasped in agony as my arm was yanked up into a half nelson. He kicked the stall door closed, forced me to my knees and then pushed my head down over the filthy smelling bowl.

Using one strong hand he prevented me from moving while he frisked me with the other, quickly finding the MP3 recorder. I tried to protest, but he pushed me down closer to the discoloured water and hissed, "Shut the fuck up." It was Zarek.

The outside door squealed open in the background and I heard an unfamiliar voice exclaim as they tripped on my stick. I made another attempt to call out, but Zarek pulled the chain to cover the noise, dousing my head in the process.

I was fighting for air when he finally allowed me to surface, but doubted my panting would be cause for alarm; the sound of two men wrestling in a gent's toilet seldom raises eyebrows in Hampstead. Besides, the hand-dryer was howling and then a blast of cold air that chilled my wet head indicated that Zarek and I were alone again.

He dragged me to the dryer and held me under it until I could smell my hair burning. Laughing cruelly he yanked my head back and made me look in the mirror. One side of his face was an unnatural shade of pink and I realised that there was a large plaster stretched from his eyebrow to his chin. Its light hue was accentuated by the discolouration around it and as my focus sharpened, I could see that most of the left side of his face was an artist's palette of dark mixes. The object I was meant to be focussing on though was a glinting silver block in his hand. Cheese and ham coagulated in my gut as it dawned on me that it was probably loaded.

"Now we go outside to the car," he commanded, waggling the gun menacingly.

I needed to play for time, "I've got to go for a slash first," I demanded, "unless you want me to pee all over the back seat." I could see Zarek frowning, but he didn't stop me as I unbuttoned my jeans. I took my time, forcing my bladder to squeeze out every drop. At last, I heard voices in the corridor and Glenn's distinctive chuckle.

The door was flung open but as I turned to wash my hands, I found Zarek blocking my way. I couldn't locate the gun. "We go now," he hissed.

As arranged, Dino was at the urinal but Glenn was lingering by the door, trying to light a cigarette. "Piece of shit!" He hurled the lighter to the ground, sending it skittering across the tiled floor. "Either of you blokes got a light? Mine's buggered."

Before Zarek could react I'd pulled out my lighter and was proffering it. Glenn sparked up gratefully then said, "Thanks mate. Here, do you want one?"

I accepted and turning to the Pole, said, "Tell Dabrowski I'll be in the bar when he wants to talk." Then to Glenn, "Do I detect an Australian accent? Bloody shame about the cricket. Still, I don't reckon your lot stand a chance next year when they come over for the Ashes."

Furious, Zarek left, as did a lot of the tension in the small toilet block. Dino, Glenn and I stood silently in the vacuum for a few seconds. I exhaled the cigarette smoke I had gobbled down and said in a rather small voice, "He's got a fucking gun, guys. If you want to pull out now we can. What do you reckon?"

Dino's fear mirrored my own, but Glenn's bluff reply cut off anything he'd been about to say.

"Well he better not try to use it or I'll stick it up his arse." He handed me my stick, "Come on Joe, I'll take you back to your table, mate."

My jacket was still on the bench, my empty pint occupying the space in front of it. I shuffled round the small oak table, pushing it out slightly so that I could sit down. It scraped heavily over the floorboards. I flopped down and having folded my stick in half, placed it under the table. The cushioned seat was lumpy and I wished I had a drink to sip as I waited. Dino and Glenn had returned to the bar, but it would draw suspicion to ask them to get me a pint.

A cold draught blew into the pub as three darkly clad figures marched through the entrance. I peered at Glenn who was standing beneath a downlighter; he nodded. My heart rate quickened and I tried to eke out a few drops from the bottom of the glass to moisten my mouth.

A stocky man with cropped salt and pepper hair approached. I recognised the smell of stale sweat and cheap, high tar cigarettes from our first encounter in the alleyway by the sorting office. Remaining seated, I struggled to focus on his face. This was the least gloomy corner of the pub and with effort, I began to pick out his features. "Mr Dabrowski, why don't you sit down?"

He perched uncomfortably on the stool and swivelled round to motion to Zarek, jabbing his finger at the unsatisfactory seat. Then he placed the MP3 player between us. "So Mr Vynde you planned to record our conversation too. Did you think I vould reweal myself to you?" He laughed without mirth.

"Actually, though that would have been a good idea, I brought the machine to prove that I am not bullshitting you." I lied. "If you listen to it you will hear that not only do I have a recording of Zarek fixing the boiler to murder Miranda Lethbridge, but I also made one last night when the silly boy admitted it and threatened to kill me. Go on, have a listen."

A scowl twisted the man's heavy-set face. "If you have this ewidence vy do you not go to the police?" His voice was laden with suspicion.

"Miranda was my friend, but she was an idealist. I'm a realist. Going to the police will not bring her back and I need money. You can have the original recordings and the disk with her interviews and article on it. Your boy Zarek failed to destroy those too. You also have my assurance that I will keep my mouth shut. In return, you pay fifty thousand into an offshore bank account and guarantee to leave me, and my family, alone. Oh, and that includes any freelance revenge work that Zarek might wish to undertake. I take it he was using his own initiative last night. You strike me as being a bit more professional than that."

The man nodded. "You are a greedy man, Mr Vynde. But I do not believe you have this ewidence."

I reached into my jacket and threw him a printout of Miranda's article. He scanned it quickly and looked up at me. "This is nothing."

I pointed at the MP3 recorder, "But that is. Did Zarek play it to you?" Dabrowski was silent. "And as I said, your man also admitted to murder and tried to kill me last night. I've got the knife, covered in his fingerprints, Mr Dabrowski." I smiled with more mirth than I felt. "Even if the police can pin nothing on you personally, the investigation will damage your business beyond repair. A firm like yours trades on its reputation, doesn't it? I can't see the nice, discerning people of the well-heeled areas you like to work in, employing nannies from a company that has the stench of scandal hanging over it, can you Mr Dabrowski?"

He was worrying at the nail on his index finger and I could feel his temper rising; no doubt he was unused to insubordination. I suspected I would be getting a kicking were we not in a crowded pub. "How do I know that you vill keep your side of the agreement ven you have the money?" It was like listening to ice splintering.

"You mean, will I behave more honourably than you did with the Hansfords and the Morgensterns and whoever else you've swindled?" I scoffed, "You'll just have to trust me! But rest assured Mr Dabrowski, if anything happens to my family or me, my solicitor has been instructed to send a file with Miranda's story and copies of all the recordings to the police. So, please feel free to take out your own insurance policy." My heart was thudding against my ribs; I cursed the smoking ban; I cursed the empty pint glass in front of me; I cursed Dabrowski; I wanted this over with.

He laughed, a throaty, grating splutter. "Wery good Mr Vynde, maybe you should come and vork for me." I glared at him. "But," he continued, "in a vay you do already." He pushed over a slip of paper and seeing my awkwardness, laughed again, cruelly. "Of course you are cripple and cannot read this. It is a bank account, in your name vith thirty thousand pounds sterling. Ve opened it for you ven you started making nuisance. It makes you a complicit vith us." By the overhead light I could see his bared yellow teeth as he grinned at his skill with technical English.

I needed time I didn't have to think, to work out whether this was a bluff. I blurted out the first question that struck me as a sensible response. "How did you manage that Dabrowski? You can't just set up an account in someone's name, you need all sorts of proof of identity."

"It is so easy. Ve vait until you go avay on holiday, then Zarek enters your house. He makes copies of your passport and some bills to send to bank and he opens Internet account using your computer. At end of veek, Zarek goes back to your house and destroys letter from the bank—so simple! They vill only send one statement at end of year, maybe you vill see it but it matters not. This is service ve prowide to many of our clients. It gives incentive to keep our secret." He laughed again, so hard he started to wheeze.

I thought of Rachel finding Daniel Morgenstern "in his study, staring at some figures on the computer screen with an open bottle of whisky beside him." Jesus, no wonder Sharratt had thought that the authorities were more interested in the sums entering Daniel's account than those leaving it.

"This thirty grand is mine then, if I agree to keep quiet?"

290

His unblinking yellowy eyes met and held my stare and I registered a curt nod. I pondered for a moment or two, folding the slip of paper he had given me into four, scoring it along the edges. I tapped it twice on the oak table then slipped it into the breast pocket of my leather jacket. "Okay. I will accept your low offer, but on one condition. You dispose of Zarek. I don't want him hanging around North West London anymore."

This time Dabrowski exploded with a kind of asthmatic bubbling that spattered my face with sticky gobbets. "You vant me to get rid of one of my men? Wery good Mr Vynde, ha, ha. You are funny man, but I think no."

"Oh come on Dabrowski, the lad's a liability; a murderer who's now waving a gun around. I wouldn't want to carry that kind of risk in my organisation. You can't even trust him to silence a blind man – he's hopeless." I sat back on the banquette and took a deep breath.

"Perhaps you are right," conceded Dabrowski, though without conviction. "There is a project in Chisvick I vill send him to. So, ve have a deal, Mr Vynde?"

I nodded and we shook hands.

My heart rate was that of a terrified rabbit as I stooped down to pick up my folded white stick. I could smell Dabrowski's sweaty trainers under the table and the huge gulp of air I took in was foetid. I jammed my shoulder against the underside of the heavy piece of oak furniture and sprang upwards. The table tipped away and began to topple. Dabrowski was still seated on his backless stool and was easily knocked off balance. My empty pint glass slid to the floor and smashed loudly. I hurled my full weight at the falling edge of the table and heard a brittle crack as its opposite edge and I landed heavily on the Pole's ribs. His reaction was lost in a rising crescendo of screams and exclamations round the pub.

291

Thundering footfalls came galloping in my direction and then stopped dead with a loud thwack and grunt. Something heavy hit the floorboards a couple of feet away and I guessed Glenn had put his self-defence skills to good use in felling Zarek. A battle cry rose from the other side of the bar and the pissed-up rugby boys got in on the action. Pandemonium ensued. Dabrowski was pushing back on the table causing my own bruised ribs to feel as if they were griddling my lungs. His face was convulsed with rage and pain; the table began to lift.

I tried to roll away as I felt him free himself, but the edge of the table caught my hip and then he was on top of me. His breathing was heavy and irregular and right in my face. "You told Zarek to kill her didn't you, you bastard?" I screamed at him.

He spat at me and I felt his balance shift as he pulled back his right fist. I continued struggling, trying to roll away. "Why kill her, why?"

He sneered, "I vas simply protecting my inwestment." The kaleidoscope of flashing lights in front of my eyes disappeared as if all the bulbs had gone off in the pub. The blackness of my impotent rage was all consuming. I lashed out blindly, connecting with nothing. Then stronger, unseen hands took control of my body and dragged me away.

Chapter 23

Holborn Police Station was very much more alive than I felt. My earlier adrenalin high had long since worn off and been replaced by a corresponding energy trough that remained untouched by the lukewarm watery coffee I had been given.

Sharratt and a DCI Weston were sitting opposite me in an interview room that contained no fewer than four 'No Smoking' signs so large that even I could not fail to see them; each time I did, it sparked another pang. My eyes were aching from the harsh white glare of the striplights that now glinted off the stubble surrounding Sharratt's grimly set mouth. His boss remained inscrutable and had said little.

"Took your time didn't you?" my rebuke was tempered by relief that I was merely bruised and exhausted.

Sharratt nodded. "Shooting in Kentish Town. Still your American pal was very patient." Poor Brad had spent the entire afternoon with his well-upholstered backside planted on a functional plastic chair, waiting for Sharratt. It was probably the first time he had been in a police station. "All the same, we got there before you could cause too much damage."

He and Wragg had arrived at The Duke in time to witness the end of my struggle with Dabrowski. It had been Glenn who had dragged me off and Wragg who had received the black eye intended for me; that had been enough to get Dabrowski arrested on the spot. Zarek had still been out cold, the gun tucked into his waistband. The iron-faced builder, I had misled over parking wardens, had been rescued, trouserless, from the clutches of the First XV. A fourth man, their driver, had also been detained, initially for parking on a double yellow line outside the pub. Wragg was currently off presenting a search warrant to

293

Dabrowski's wife at their home in Mill Hill. He was probably slavering at the prospect of rifling through her knicker drawer.

However, for now, it was Marta who was providing all the evidence. Sharratt had picked her up at Hugo's house, on his way to The Duke. She had hardly been put in the back of the police car before she'd started talking. Through sobs of anguish, she admitted that she had been dreading this moment for weeks. Too scared to do anything up till then, she had kept quiet and done her penance by caring for Miranda's motherless children. Now, though, she felt that the police had released her and she would answer all their questions.

According to Marta, Zarek had told her that it had all been a terrible accident. He had only meant to leave Miranda unconscious for long enough to allow him to erase all traces of the story from her computer. Dabrowski had been sure that Miranda would have to back off once it was demonstrated to her that she was not safe in her own home. The plan had been for Zarek to ring the doorbell every twenty minutes, hide until he got no answer, then let himself in and switch off the boiler. After wiping the file, he would air the basement by leaving a window in the cinema open, allowing Miranda to come round slowly with no more than a stinking headache.

Unfortunately, I had turned up and Zarek had panicked. Assuming that I would stay, he had left Fawkes Close to ring Dabrowski for instructions. It had taken ages to get hold of his boss and by the time he returned and rang the bell, Miranda was dead and I was gone.

Marta was beside herself as she recalled how Zarek had said that he had had no choice but to try to make it look like suicide. He had found my MP3 recorder on Miranda's desk and, checking it, had heard part of the interview with Rachel. To find out how much I knew and in case the police

294

did get involved he had taken the machine. Dabrowski had moved him onto a job in South London a few days later to get him out of the way while things settled down. However, it was felt that Marta had to stay on to avoid raising suspicion. She was so blonde that she had believed them and did as she was told.

"So it's my fault after all then." I felt glum. There was no satisfaction in being proved right, or even in knowing that justice would be seen to be done; too many lives had been irreparably vandalised for that.

Sharratt knew that too, "I wouldn't take anything that Barbie doll has been fed too seriously. Let's see what happens when I tell young Mr Grzegorczyk that his squeeze has dropped him in it. It won't be long before he tells us he was acting under orders; they always do sooner or later. Honour amongst thieves doesn't exist, Mr Wynde, no matter where they hail from."

His phone began to sing in his pocket—the theme from *The Sweeney*. It was the first laugh I'd had all day and I heard the DCI stifle a chuckle too. After a succession of "Right", "OK" and "good", Sharratt slipped the phone back into his pocket and his craggy face broke into a series of crevasses that approximated to a smile. "Dabrowski's screwed now! That was DS Wragg; he's found Kristina. Poor kid was shackled and being kept as their slave. She's all right though and very keen to make a full statement."

A man of action, he was on a roll now. "Gary wants the computer forensics boys up there. He reckons there's a load of stuff to keep them busy. Is that okay by you Chief? He's also nicked Milena Hlavacek for possession with intent to supply; says there's at least half a kilo of uncut Charlie in her dressing room. Apparently she's not happy and he reckons a few hours without her favourite nose candy and she'll be ready to tell him her most intimate secrets." He rubbed his hands together vigorously and continued, "I

295

think I'll go and give Mr Dabrowski the good news in person, if that's okay boss?" DCI Weston nodded and we were left alone.

I'd been staring at the man opposite me. Even through my soft focus eyes he looked like a relic of a bygone age. He and his crumpled grey suit were both nearing retirement. When he spoke, his voice was measured and world-weary. "He's a good man, Sharratt; prickly and hard to fathom at times but an honest, hard-working copper."

"So I shouldn't be expecting an apology or a thank you card from him in the near future, then?"

DCI Weston cleared his throat and I felt his tired grey eyes on my tired grey face. "I wouldn't hold your breath."

"It would have saved a lot of trouble if he'd given me a fair hearing though," I countered irritably.

"From what I hear, Mr Wynde, you didn't exactly present yourself as a reliable witness."

If this was meant to make me feel contrite it failed. I pulled out my cigarettes and opened the packet. "Are you going to nick me if I spark up? It's been a long day."

He smiled in an avuncular fashion and said softly, "Only if you fail to offer me one."

Sharratt coughed and I think grimaced when he came back into the room; the smoke laden air made my vision of him mistier than ever. He nodded at his superior, "Dabrowski wants a lawyer; he's clammed up. Gary's on his way back with Kristina and Ms Hlavacek. I think Mr Wynde can go home now. We know where he lives when we need to talk to him again."

Relief suffused my tired and aching body. Along with half the pub, Glenn and Dino had simply had to give their names and addresses, but I had been bundled into the back of a jam sandwich and brought down to the station to give a

296

statement. Five hours had passed since then and I longed for my bed.

DCI Weston agreed, "Get uniform to take Mr Wynde up to Hampstead."

It was past three in the morning when the well-tuned police car pulled into Fawkes Close. Our journey up the hill had been rapid and for the most part conducted wordlessly. Only in Camden Town, where a group of revellers weaving down the middle of the road had received a blast of siren, did I speak. "Blimey, I thought being seen with a white stick got people out of the way." The driver grunted and we lapsed back into silence. The woman police officer in the passenger seat escorted me to my door and watched me let myself in. I wished her a safe night and lifted a weary hand to wave in the general direction of the police car. It revved throatily and was gone by the time I'd shut the door.

Having propped my stick up in its usual place, in the corner by the front door, I shuffled into the kitchen for a glass of water. The answerphone light was flashing and I was going to check the message when I thought I heard movement upstairs. I groped around the work surface for the letter I'd left for Eithne; it had gone. The prospect of curling up next to her and putting the last couple of days out of my mind filled me with elation. I left the phone and softly climbed the stairs.

A burst of pain and stars brought me to my knees as soon as I reached the landing. The centre of my face felt like someone had pressed a hot iron to it. Before I could work out what I had walked into, the back of my neck exploded in a welt of agony and I fell into a boggy pool of semi-consciousness.

I dimly felt my spongy skull thump, thump, thump on each stair; like Pooh trailing behind Christopher Robin. Where were we going, trespassers will be...

We were nearing the top of the house and I was worried that we might wake Eithne; I must have moaned her name because Hugo's chubby schoolboy face swam into view. He wore a cruel, lop-sided grin, "Not here, more's the pity; her plane's delayed by snow, she did leave a message. Lovely letter you wrote by the way, very touching, especially the tearstains." Derision dripped from his words.

Somewhere a spark of anger fired within my groggy body. I forced myself to stay conscious. Hugo was panting with the effort of dragging me behind him and stopped for a rest. "You never did know when to give up did you? Anyway, what were you doing in the back of a police car and where's Dabrowski?"

My girls pinch themselves when they need to distinguish between dream and reality. Surely this was just concussion on top of exhaustion. I must have slipped on the stairs and cracked my head. I closed my eyes.

Hugo cuffed me so hard, I felt my lip split. My eyes filled with tears of pain and incomprehension. "Don't snivel, Wynde, I never did, and you've cost me a pretty packet."

"Just protecting your investment." I moaned; Dabrowski's words finally made sense.

Hugo gave a callous laugh, "Come on, wakey, wakey. Where's the smart-arse remark? Aren't you going to tell me I should be grieving the loss of my wife, not of my money? Now tell me, where's Dabrowski?"

My mouth had filled with blood and I had to spit it out onto the carpet. "There was a fight in the pub. Rugby boys got a bit leery and Zarek pulled a gun. Someone called the police and Zarek and Dabrowski scarpered, I dunno where they are now. The police took ages getting witness statements from everyone, so they gave me a lift home. But I don't understand", I moaned, "They were blackmailing you too weren't they?" I gave up trying to focus on anything as I struggled to keep the pulsating multi-coloured flashes of pain and tiredness from making me vomit.

Hugo's hand smacked theatrically on his forehead, "I always knew they only let you into Cambridge to fill the pleb school quota. Good God, you're dense! Of course Marta tried to bed me, but if I want a bit of trade I don't shit on my own doorstep. She's so thick that it was bloody obvious what the scam was, so I met with Dabrowski and made him a proposition. I'd recommend his agency to potentially lucrative clients, for a fee. Any extras, I'd get a cut. I told him what his people should look out for; anything with 'confidential' written on it; memos to grandly titled twats, asset write downs, mergers, ratings, profit and loss accounts, credit assessments—anything that looked serious. On that point at least my darling wife was correct; it's remarkable how trusting and careless people can be with their staff. That jubb Morgenstern proved especially profitable."

By now, Hugo had lugged me to the top of the stairs and dropped me face-down on the carpet. My split lip stuck to the fibres as the blood coagulated and it hurt to make myself audible. "So you destroyed whole families to make a few measly quid in some grubby little blackmail scam. What a fine businessman you are. Your kids will be so proud."

Hugo exploded at me. "You have no appreciation of the money to be made from knowledge! Others lost hundreds of millions in the post-Lachmann collapse. But by having Zarek install a pair of strategically placed microphones in Morgenstern's house I was able to discover weeks in advance just how far up shit creek Lachmann's was. I was always one step ahead. I began to discreetly short anything to do with them so, when the stampede got going, I really cleaned up. Then, just when one or two rumours started circulating about my activities, I had Zarek tell Morgenstern

299

how helpful he'd been in providing insider information and show him how well he'd been financially rewarded for it. It was pure genius! Morgenstern carried the can all the way into the Thames and Lachmann was delighted to have found its scapegoat."

"But his family?" I protested

"Collateral damage." His tone was dismissive. "There's no money in being sentimental, no gain in supporting lame ducks, or cripples." He kicked my ribs for emphasis.

"What about Ted Hansford? Was he collateral damage too?" This was a land of alien morality where my friends and acquaintances were merely tokens on a life-sized Monopoly board.

"What, your fat friend from the home of sub-prime? He and his vulgar wife were ripe for the picking. People like that don't deserve wealth; they don't know how to wear it. I enjoyed dismantling their tacky nouveau world. It's all a matter of knowing how people will react. I've never known a Yank refuse a free lunch, and he just ate and ate. But his guilt money was nothing compared to what we got from his loudmouth wife. All those shouted phone-calls with colleagues; lots of lovely sensitive documents strewn about the house —it was a jackpot waiting to be scooped! Tell me, does Mrs Blobby still think that it was you who was blackmailing them? Sending fat boy that note to implicate you was the icing on the finger bun for me."

He rolled me onto my back and forced my jaws open as if worming a cat. My face hurt too much for me to resist. I thought I tasted paper, but then he pushed a bottleneck between my teeth and I felt a scorch against my cut lip. Whisky fumes filled my nose and mouth. The sour liquid made me gag, but Hugo clamped a gloved hand over my stinging mouth and broken nose. Forcing my head back to open my throat he murmured, "Down the hatch, there's a good chap," as if addressing a favourite hound. I swallowed automatically.

As the smarting round my mouth subsided the throbbing at the back of my skull increased. Under my blood-matted hair my cranium was bulging outwards. It felt cracked in several places, ready to be peeled off in bits and the yoke exposed. The whisky made me feel faint.

"Dabrowski and Zarek murdered Miranda," I croaked "But I suppose you class that as a friendly fire incident."

"Regrettable, but cheaper than a divorce. Dabrowski was at pains to explain it was an accident, but I told him the greater shame of it was that you hadn't been there with her. Then I could have had both my haemorrhoids lanced at a single stroke. Even you must admit she was becoming tiresome and increasingly unstable. Inferior blood will out I suppose, still you'd know all about that."

I ignored his riling as revulsion and incredulity spread through me like a virus. "You allowed your own wife to be killed to protect a business venture?"

He pulled out his mobile and speed-dialled a number; I heard the answering service pick the call up. "I'm at our mutual friend's house," he barked, "clearing up the mess you should have attended to. Call me." He turned back to me, forced the whisky bottle into my mouth again and held it vertical until I choked, spluttering snotty burning jets from my nose. "What was the alternative? I could hardly go whinging to the wooden tops could I?"

"You supercilious tit." The words slipped out unbidden, "I'm sure your children will think the world of their father when they know you stood by and let their mother be murdered."

"Camilla will raise them properly," the subject clearly bored him. "Meanwhile, I've taken the book down and will have a well-deserved sabbatical. Who knows, I might

301

arrange to bump into Eithne on some lonely shore, show her what she's been missing." He sneered and tipped the bottle up again. The whisky going down met a bolus of the previous lot re-surfacing. Hugo tutted and sat me up against the wall; the world around me bulged and contracted crazily.

He forced my jaws apart yet again and emptied more whisky into me. It no longer burned; my whole face was numb. This time he held my nose and mouth closed while he stroked my throat, almost tenderly, until I had to swallow.

"However, before I leave on my travels, you need to *depart on a trip* yourself." He gave a nasty, knowing laugh and comprehension dawned on me. "You've tried to interfere with my pension plan, you little shit, but you're about to find out just how dangerous it is to stumble blindly about in the dark." His jeering bully's face, though featureless to my eyes, bulged across my entire field of vision.

"You never left the student bar did you?" he continued. "Still getting wasted and playing with toys; pretending it's work when all you do is piss about at home with children and brain-dead women—you're a joke! Well it's about to kick you in the arse, just like your pathetic attempt to wreck my career. Remember Glastonbury do you? Tonight it's your turn to discover what a dangerous mix whisky and LSD and dancing can be. Poor Joe Wynde, they'll say, he always did have problems with addiction and the dark."

Rising fury at what he had done was doing battle with increasing wooziness caused by the whisky, the pain and the acid. I needed to concentrate, to try and work out a way to stop him pushing me over the balcony.

Maybe he heard the whirring of my brain because he leaned close to my ear and whispered, "It won't work.

302

You've been thoroughly outclassed! Face the facts; you're one of life's losers. How you could have thought you held the least attraction for Miranda, escapes me! Or were you simply blind to her pity?" His patronising chuckle echoed round my jump-cutting brain.

He slid open the patio door and shoved me out. I skidded on the cold wet tiles and lost my balance. My forehead smacked down and I think I blacked out.

Whether it was the chill night air, my throbbing head or the sensation of being in motion that brought me round I can't say, but I gradually regained painful awareness of my body's prone position; somewhere frosty; something wrong; someone tugging at me. I tried to speak, but my jaw appeared to be locked in place and only grunts emerged. I wanted to tell them to "let me go back to sleep, just for a few minutes, it's still dark."

Images danced randomly across my gluey eyelids; Miranda's face rotating on her laptop; Zarek firing a knife from a gun; Hugo pouring blood from a bottle; children on smiley acid-house faced space-hoppers. 'Stitched up by the acid man, he'll kill ya mate...he'll kill ya mate...he'll kill ya mate...'—percussive beats throbbing in my temples, drumming the message out in time to my still fighting heart.

The acid had really taken hold now, there was no point fighting it, I just needed to focus on one thing, then use that concentration as a rendezvous where I could muster my tattered mental powers...or something like that...ebb and flow...concentrate...ebb and flow...concentrate. I tried to use my breathing to find a rhythm to work to.

Then, in the slack water between breaths, I registered the familiar creak of the gate; too quiet for Hugo to have heard surely. Do the blind have aural hallucinations? No, I could hear the key in the door, I began to moan and writhe on the cold tiles. The phone rang shrilly; four rings, then it

303

stopped. Not the answer phone then—that needs six. My heart raced, making breathing through my shattered nose even more difficult. I groaned again, more loudly, desperate to distract Hugo's attention.

A penalty taken to my ribs forced the air from my lungs. "Stop whining! No one can hear you, or see you. That's what happens if you let your wisteria run rampant."

I cast wildly about for the source of his disembodied voice; out here in the dark night he was barely even a shadow to me. Dimly, very dimly I thought I could hear footfalls on the stairs. I redoubled my moaning and, having located my limbs, crawled stiffly across the slick tiles towards the chest-high parapet. *Please, please don't turn on the lights,* I begged silently.

Hugo grabbed hold of my collar and yanked me up to standing. I tried to push him away, but lost my footing and fell to one knee.

"It's no good, you might as well submit to the inevitable," he chided. Still gripping my collar and with an arm under my chest he half carried, half threw me into the wisteria. I was reeling dizzily, the naturally flashing lights of my kaleidoscope vision interwoven with a Paisley pattern of swirling shapes that moved out of sync with the roar of blood rushing in my ears.

Hugo's grip loosened slightly as he propped me against the parapet wall. Now! I had to make my move now! I dropped my head and charged. He must have sidestepped me because I only caught his hip; a glancing blow that cannoned me onto the floor.

Face-down I felt his knees dig heavily into my back. "Good God, you're pathetic, how can you bear to live with yourself? You're nothing but a burden."

So saying he clamped a gloved hand over my mouth. I tried to bite but my face wouldn't obey. I felt dizzy and sick

304

and yet divorced from my body as he dragged me up the wall and then hung my head over the side. The pavement below swam in and out of Technicolor focus. Fuck, it was a long way down. As if reading my thoughts Hugo panted "About fifty feet I'd say."

I heard the door slide, almost silently, open and so did Hugo. He spun round and was halfway through saying "What on Earth?" when there was a blinding flash as the outside lights were switched on; then the crack of shattering glass and Hugo staggering back into me, crushing my chest against the wall. The blood, whisky, pain and drugs fairly shot out of my mouth and hurtled towards the pavement below.

Pushing myself back, away from the edge, and wrenching round to face the light, I had a moment of clarity. Eithne was standing in front of Hugo pointing a smashed bottle at his face, which was pouring blood from a gash across his forehead.

Hugo let go of me and I slumped into the cushioning wisteria. He was advancing on Eithne in slow motion saying, "Now, now my dear, just a little misunderstanding between friends. There's really nothing for you to worry about." I sensed her hesitate and knew Hugo was about to launch himself at her.

Like some waking Leviathan, I inched forward and extended my hand painfully slowly to grab at him. There was a ripping noise and a shower of metallic objects tumbled to the ground. His trouser pocket hung limply in my hand. He batted me aside and continued his advance. Eithne jabbed the sharp shards at his hand causing a dark rose to spread between his gloved fingers. He was swearing loudly at her now. I had finally found my voice and was screaming incoherently. Eithne was looking wild-eyed from one to the other of us, trying to comprehend what was going on.

I tried to rise again but my body wouldn't respond. My cheek was resting on something sharp and cold and it was all I could do to push it away. As my fingers brushed it I recognised the shape of a key, something familiar, comforting; it felt good. I closed my fingers around it and held on tight.

Hugo lunged at Eithne and knocked her to the ground. The remains of the bottle shattered around her limp body. He wheeled round and grabbing my neck in one hand and my arm in the other jerked me to my feet. My whole body shook as he propelled me back towards the parapet. Back and back through the snapping wisteria and over the top of the wall. I felt my balance shift from the terrace to the street side. My feet were lifted off the tiles.

Against the dull orange light of the London night sky Hugo's livid eyes held mine. I fought for breath but his grip was tight around my windpipe.

"Goodbye oik, this will be the only pleasure I've had in knowing you." His left eye glinted unnaturally and his hand left my neck and shot up to his shrieking face.

As my knees gave way I saw Eithne, ashen and clutching the stumpy neck of the bottle. Then I heard sirens and The Close was filled with the most beautiful flashing lights I have ever seen.

Chapter 24

My first psychedelic experience occurred when I was about five years old. I had spent the morning at the hospital having my lazy eye pored over by the first of many so-called experts who were to miss the blindingly obvious retinal discolouration of my RP over the next decade and a half.

As part of their examination process it was, and still is, necessary to put dilating drops into my eyes. Apart from stinging like hell, this makes the pupils larger and allows a better view of the inner eye, retina included, when they shine their white lights so painfully in.

In spite of the discomfort and boredom I had experienced, I was in a pretty good mood when I climbed into the passenger seat of our silver Mk 1 Ford Escort. As a reward for not screaming and fighting in the hospital, mum had promised, and just given, me a medium-sized bag of sweets. Through my belladonna-misted eyes I made out blackjacks, penny chews, rhubarb and custards, aniseed balls, shrimps and, best of all, flying saucers.

The sherbet inside the shiny blue hull fizzled on my tongue and I began to notice the warped and swirling colours that smeared past the car windows as we trundled through the Sussex countryside. My jaded and dilated eyes were sending confused signals to my young brain but instead of feeling disconcerted or queasy, I sank back into the vinyl of the seat, popped another saucer and let the wash of distorted shapes and colours carry me away on their blissful waves.

Back at home, I spent a good hour lost in the minutiae of our small garden; scrutinising the strangely shaped bugs with their waggling legs and lying on my back watching the pretty dappled lights dancing through the leaves of the rhododendron bush.

But even as I was relishing all this I could feel that it had lost some of its original intensity. My trip round the garden was also a search to recapture that first rush of discovery and perfect contentment.

After the final effects had worn off, my disappointment was so palpable that my mum, assuming I'd been brought down by a long morning of being treated like a lab rat, rummaged around her handbag and produced that rarest of treats, a walnut whip. I realise now that it had been her treat to perk herself up at the end of a stressful day; back then though, I simply scoffed it down. Even it, however, failed to assuage my hunger for a return to altered reality—I was hooked.

It's been a long journey of diminishing returns, as any addict will tell you, whether their poison is smack, sex or Special Brew. Only your first experience of something has the novelty-value that makes it exquisite. Maybe it's their very mortality that lends those fleeting moments their frisson. Some squander a lifetime trying to recapture that feeling. Only the very lonely limit the radiation of their doomed quest to themselves. The fallout of people's shattered dreams destroys the love in those around them first.

The realisation came last week; as I launched Nell on her first solo bike ride without stabilisers. Her whoops of joy rekindled the exultation of the instant my dad launched me down a bumpy track in Sussex. Our mayfly moments of transcendence are meant to be snapshots in an album, looked upon fondly for their residual warmth. By seeking to conjure them again I risked being too addled to appreciate the heat of joyous discovery glowing from my children.

At the very least I don't think I'll be dabbling in whisky or mind-altering substances again. The risk of flashbacks is just too great and I still get nightmares about the stomach pump I was given by the ambulance crew who arrived with Sharratt and Wragg.

Someone at Holborn nick had finally got round to checking Dabrowski's mobile and picked up Hugo's message. Wragg had rung to check I was okay and got Eithne instead. He had told her to wait for his arrival and under no circumstances to go looking for me herself, which guaranteed that she would follow the trail of blood up to the roof terrace. At least it had also led her to arm herself with the empty whisky bottle.

Hugo spent six weeks in a prison hospital, but still lost his right eye. He will just have to get used to living with imperfection like the rest of us. A local plastic surgeon has offered to repair the damage to his face before the trial, free of charge! According to the press, the oleaginous little quack has even approached Channel 4 to make a documentary of the operation, in a bid to raise the profile of his ailing private practice. It turns out it was his hairdresser-class Mercedes that I whacked all those months ago on the zebra crossing. Maybe he can give a family discount and reduce the flare on all the Lethbridge nostrils.

Hugo, Zarek and Dabrowski have all been charged with conspiracy to commit murder. The trial is scheduled for next March—at the Old Bailey no less. In addition, Hugo has been charged with attempted murder, Zarek with possession of a firearm with intent to endanger life and with involuntary manslaughter and Dabrowski with false imprisonment. Even with the ten years Sharratt expects Hugo to get, he could be out within five.

The good news is that the Polish authorities want Dabrowski for fraud, so will extradite him at the end of his sentence. Also, the tougher gun laws and my recording of

Zarek threatening to reunite me with Miranda, should ensure he gets life and is classified as a Category A prisoner.

Similarly, Hugo's central role in the conspiracy and attempt to pervert the course of justice are unlikely to count in his favour. I'll make sure to bring my best white stick and most downtrodden expression to the witness box.

Milena is charged with false imprisonment and possession with intent to supply a Class A drug. She and Dabrowski are being linked to a people-trafficking and prostitution racket, though God knows how long that will take to come to trial. Both Kristina and Marta have provided statements incriminating the pair and Kristina has been flown back to Poland to spend some time with her parents until she is needed to give evidence in court.

Christian and Hope are down in Bognor with Miranda's mum, Moira, who seems to have found previously untapped reserves of energy, even dusting off her old entertainer's act for them. We've been down a couple of times and, though it's obviously confusing and hard for them, the two children appear at least to be getting the love they need to help them to heal.

The FSA has exonerated Daniel Morgenstern and various others under investigation, from any wrong-doing after the police computer forensics people found a wealth of evidence to show that the inside information had been purloined rather than given freely. Doubtless the FSA is, even now, preparing some meaningless statement concerning 'care of sensitive data'.

Gail is still unwilling to talk to me, though I suspect that has more to do with her inability to admit that she was wrong, than any residual belief in my guilt. In fact, when Sharratt contacted her, she denied that there had been any blackmail attempt and maintained that the only money she paid P&C was in legitimate agency fees; obviously her job still comes first. Still, at least she now allows Kelvin and me to chat whenever we want. So, last Thursday, it was a positive pleasure to be woken at one in the morning and hear him gleefully describe Karl the pool-boy's dismissal for smacking Fisher.

The following morning I received a visit from Sharratt. Wragg stayed in the car, with the engine running for the whole time. Sharratt smelt of sausage and brown sauce and for once accepted the cuppa I offered him. He instructed me to leave the teabag in and said 'stop' only after I had spooned a third sugar into the mug.

"One thing I'll say for Hampstead is you get a better class of biscuit up here," he said, cramming another chocolate ginger thin into his mouth. "Now Mr Wynde, I need to talk to you about the money you say Dabrowski paid into your account."

I sighed wearily, "I didn't think it could possibly be a social visit. We've been through this; he and Hugo were setting me up, just as they did with the letter they sent to Ted. Come to think of it, some of it's probably Gail's money."

"Well now, it's a strange thing, but not everyone who paid money to Polish & Check is in a hurry to come forward and reclaim it. I imagine they have their reasons. That gives me a headache. It would appear that Lethbridge and Dabrowski opened several accounts for holding cash before transferring it overseas or investing it. There's nearly a hundred grand kicking around for anyone who wishes to make a late claim. The thirty grand in your account is an anomaly. There's no record of where it came from or who it should be returned to. I spent three years training as an accountant before I joined the Met, Mr Wynde, and I don't like anomalies." He took a noisy sip of steaming tea before continuing.

311

"The paperwork for seizing criminal assets is a pain in the backside. And now that the Vice Squad and the Human Trafficking Team are involved that can only get worse. Somehow, I doubt that the defendants are going to advertise the fact that they broke into your house and fraudulently opened a bank account in your name. So that leaves you with a couple of choices. You can come down to Holborn with me, waste hours of all our time complaining that you have inherited thirty grand from somewhere and risk implicating yourself further. You can leave it untouched; but as a taxpayer and one of the poor sods who'll be paying for the incompetence of the banks for the rest of my days, I find the thought of giving them yet more free cash rather depressing, don't you? Or..." He paused, then the corner of his mouth twitched slightly.

"Do you have another suggestion?" I was puzzled and a little wary. Somehow I didn't feel quite off the hook yet.

"Well, Widows and Orphans can always use a large donation. That's where I'll tell DCI Weston the money has gone." He ran his fingers across his high forehead. "I've met a fair few City types in the course of my work, most are greedy bastards with little mind for anyone else. I'd like to think that money could go to people who would feel its worth, rather than being some fat cat's bonus. The account is in your name, Mr Wynde—perhaps you could find a way of investing it conscientiously." His cool grey-green eyes penetrated the mist of my vision until I blinked. He pushed his chair back abruptly, stood and took my hand in his calloused paw, "Discreetly of course, Mr Wynde."

It is never as easy to withdraw money from a bank as it is to deposit it; even less so when it is a large sum and you want to give it away anonymously. My online attempts proved fruitless and the man in the Indian call centre intransigent. Eventually, after I had threatened to close the account entirely, a supervisor was summoned. With evident

312

pain, he agreed to make the two BACS transfers I had requested.

Thus, I hope that the finance director at the Metropolitan and City Police Orphanage received a pleasant surprise when he saw that several thousand pounds had appeared overnight in the fund, with the reference, "In recognition of selfless sacrifice."

The recipients of the second, equal amount, are, I know, "overwhelmed and delighted". This week's headline on the *Hampstead & Highgate Express* reads "Mystery Donor Plugs Funding Gap for Local Playground." The paper details the long standoff between the Corporation of London (which owns the area where Ted and I met in the sandpit) and HPAG (the Heath Playground Action Group), an organisation of local parents and users of the Heath.

The Corporation's generous refurbishment plan has been on hold for months, and the playground closed, as the two sides argued over who should pay for exacting and expensive additions demanded by HPAG. Also quoted is the anonymous caller who told the *Ham & High* that, "the donor felt it was a shame that children were being denied the benefit of a refurbished playground whilst a few nimby adults put their efforts into legal wrangling rather than fund-raising."

Who knows, perhaps a fair proportion of the money I deposited in the Corporation's coffers was originally in the personal accounts of some of HPAG's members. This time the reference read, "To get the job done! Plus a little extra to decorate the Wendy house with bears and balloons and call it 'Ted's Place'".

After further negotiations with the call centre, I transferred the remaining money into my own current account. It took an insultingly long time to clear, but when it finally did I withdrew five hundred pounds from a cashpoint and went straight to the pub.

Pete was polishing glasses behind the bar. "Ah ha, bad penny, I wondered when you were going to turn up. You're barred!"

I looked at my feet, "Was there a lot of damage?"

He began to count off on his fingers. "Three broken chairs, a small table and a broken mirror."

"And the carpet had to be cleaned—professionally," shouted Trisha from the back of the bar.

"Will three hundred cover it?"

Pete opened his mouth to speak but Trisha cut across him. "Three fifty and give him a pint on the house."

I counted out the money and handed it over. He grinned and passed me the foaming pint. "Clean slate. Anyway, ta, the publicity's been great. And Paul the Prat got his jaw broken. I've had three whole months without his moaning voice in my lughole every night."

I knew what he meant about the publicity. Ever since the story broke there's been a steady stream of news tourists coming to Fawkes Close and posing for photos. I think I preferred the builders. Dear, kind-hearted Lucia lets them use her downstairs loo if they are caught short and distributes tea and anecdotes on wet days. I'm beginning to pity the celebrities I've always scorned. My white stick negates any anonymity my ordinary looks may have given me; I can't leave my house without being snapped or bombarded with questions and I can't even run or drive away.

Yesterday I went back to the cashpoint and withdrew the last two hundred pounds before gratefully closing the Internet account. To celebrate, and ring the changes a little, I'd arranged to meet Brad, Dino and Glenn at a gastro pub in Primrose Hill where I bought them lunch and thanked them all profusely again. It was Eithne's day off and she was picking the girls up from school so I could savour my three courses and the burgundy I'd selected; Brad drank Belgian beer.

It was, however, a subdued gathering. Kelly has just been recalled to Chicago, as her firm is pulling all its ex-pats out of Europe. Brad was putting a brave face on it, telling us that they had to be grateful that she had a job in the present climate and looking forward to his first Thanksgiving with his folks in five years. But underneath we all sensed how upset he is to be leaving and how slim his prospects of finding work at home are. Dino fears that Maria could be next and Glenn revealed he is thinking of volunteering as a P.T. instructor for the Territorial Army in a bid to boost his family's credentials to stay on.

After we had finished and gone our separate ways, I headed up to Steele's Passage and found Dusty sitting on the roof of the Anderson shelter, basking in the first rays of spring sun. "Makes you glad to be alive don't it man?" he grinned. I had never noticed quite how crooked his teeth were before, or how few he had left.

I smiled, struck again by how big the little things are to those with next to nothing, then I handed him a small white box. He opened it painstakingly so as not to tear the cardboard, though his blackened fingers left smudges all over it. His face broke into the most enormous childlike smile when he saw what it contained.

"For me?" he was incredulous. I nodded. Jumping down off the shelter, he executed a little jig around me. "Groovy man!" he exclaimed. Then hugged me and planted a sticky kiss on my forehead.

I explained how the MP3 player worked and how to scroll through the hundred or so albums I had loaded; all his

315

recommendations or things I had found by association. He was fascinated by the sound quality of the earphones and kept shouting to tell me how the music was in his head. When I left him he was loudly accompanying The Electric Prunes singing 'I Had Too Much to Dream Last Night.'

That left about fifty quid. I caught the bus down to Belsize Village and filled my shopping bag then meandered back up the hill on foot, through streets strangely devoid of skips and past parking bays which, a few weeks earlier, had been clogged with white vans. Stopping at the stall outside the Community Market, I spent the remaining money on a bunch of bright spring flowers.

The churchyard was empty and the mound of earth over Miranda's grave still fresh from her re-interment following the post-mortem. I sat down on a neighbouring grave and tried to arrange the bouquet tastefully. I couldn't find words to express my feelings, but reached into my jacket pocket and removed the key ring which she had used to hold her set of my keys and which Zarek and Hugo had used to gain access to the house. The little plastic tag had a window with a piece of paper slid behind it. I read it one final time "_The Backs_" then pushed it beneath the soil and smoothed the ground over.

I lugged the heavy turkey home, dressed it and put it in the oven, before setting about the vegetables. Eithne, Jenny and Nell were giggling as they played Pictionary in the sitting room. Tonight the four of us would enjoy a family dinner; a belated thanksgiving for all that we have.

* * *

316

There are in our existence spots of time,
That with distinct pre-eminence retain
A renovating virtue, whence–depressed
By false opinion and contentious thought,
Or aught of heavier or more deadly weight,
In trivial occupations, and the round
Of ordinary intercourse–our minds
Are nourished and invisibly repaired.

William Wordsworth, *The Prelude*